Alan —

Enjoy the adventure!

Mike Mullane
Astronaut
STS 41D, 27, 36
2/15/96

P.S. Read with Willa —
it's Hot !!

DEDICATION

To my wife, Donna, who never stopped believing in my dreams.

ACKNOWLEDGMENTS

This book would not have been possible without the love, support and friendship of many people.

I thank my mother and father, who lovingly nurtured my passion for the sky. Little did they realize that it would ultimately blossom in the fire and smoke of three space shuttle lift-offs. (Dad... I know you were there for the last two missions.)

I thank my children — Pat, Amy, and Laura — for their courage on the LCC roof. You will forever be my ultimate joy.

I flew with the best of the "brotherhood": STS-41D crewmembers Hank Hartsfield, Michael Coats, Steve Hawley, and Judy Resnik; STS-27 crewmembers Robert (Hoot) Gibson, Guy Gardner, Jerry Ross, and Bill Shepherd; and STS-36 crewmembers John Creighton, John Casper, Dave Hilmers, and Pierre Thuot. Their skill, humor, and love of flight are in these pages.

I was blessed with relatives — uncles and cousins — who were generous with their praises, honest in their criticisms, and unflagging in their support. Thank you, Uncle Bud, Hal, Mary, and Barry. But most of all, thank you, Peggy. You were my very first fan and I could never have finished without you.

I thank my Uncle Richard — a World War II marine aviator and a second father to me. (I know you're reading these words.)

A special thanks goes to two wonderful women, themselves authors, who were always there to encourage me — Mary Lynn Baxter and national best seller, Sandra Brown.

My brothers and sister — Tim, Pat, Hugh, Kathy, and Mark — were always pushing me with, "When can I read your book?" Thanks for the faith.

I was most fortunate to have these wonderful friends to call upon for their technical expertise, editorial review and support: Dr. Terry McGuire, Barbara Armond, Rebecca Sallee, John Wisotzkey, Judge Ed Taylor, Cindy Barth, Dr. Joe & Terri Boyce, Nate Lindsay, Bob "Mc", Doris Chasey, Patricia Kelliher-Puckett, Dan Schneider, Deborah Peacock, and my incredibly patient typesetter – Clarence Bowman.

Finally, I would like to graciously thank my publisher, Jim Van Treese, for his faith in me and in Red Sky.

Ye shall know the truth and the truth shall set ye free.
— John 8:32

viii

CHAPTER 1

Saturday, 27 August
Earth Orbit

A human eye would surely have been held captive by the sight. Until seconds ago, all had been pre-Genesis black. But now, on the southeastern horizon, a thin, graceful arc of the deepest purple — so close to black as to be almost indiscernible from it — divided the void. The color spread outward, racing south and north from its point of birth to further define the disk. Layers of rich blues and greens quickly followed, pushing the indigo away from the earth's limb. Yellow, orange, and red sequentially took their place in the blossoming kaleidoscope.

By now, a human observer would have made a vain cry to freeze the scene so its magnificence could be fully comprehended. Like sky-bursting fireworks, the beauty was too transient. The pure, white light of the sun was being split by the earth's prism — the atmosphere — to yield a spectrum with the intensity of a million rainbows.

Dawn exploded into the vacuum eighty-one miles above the arctic wastes. But no mortal was present to be awed by the scene, and the robot was disinterested. She cared nothing for the visual grandeur that now melted into the quickly rising star. Instead, she obediently executed the bidding of her earthbound masters. South and eastward lay the enemy, always vigilant, always hiding. Only his sky was vulnerable, and the robot prepared to exploit that weakness and steal the secrets he labored to protect.

Millisecond flashes of flame blinked from jets as she twisted her twenty ton bulk and brought her long axis earthward. Wings of solar cells responded with vernier adjustments to stay bathed in the life-giving photons of the sun. Film-drive motors switched on to begin their warm-up. Dish-shaped antennas took new orientations. Gyros measured attitude. Bright-object sensors sampled the electromagnetic spectrum for the blinding threats of enemy lasers. Satisfied that she was in position and all was safe, the robot opened her eye. The plate rotated quickly, soundlessly, to reveal a nation's treasure of optical technology — an immense mirror as flawless as a Royal gem. Sight was life in this Cold War, and clever men had extended their vision beyond continents with the billion-dollar Cyclops.

Beneath the behemoth, great islands of arctic ice sped past at five miles per second. Hundred-mile-long fractures, like black veins, began to intrude into the white. In the warmer latitudes, the cracks grew more numerous. The ice islands were halved, then halved again, and again, until a flotilla of dots — icebergs — appeared on the blue-black purity of the Barents Sea.

The robot stared blankly at these wonders of nature. Her computer told her they were of no interest. It was the work of man she was to record. And, in that mission, she hurled farther into the late-morning sun, into the enemy's sky.

The ocean shallowed. Its color lightened. A craggy coastline appeared. To the navigator subfunction of her brain, the landfall was seen only as an array of electronic bits, a unique pattern of ones and zeros. But to the machine, it was a screaming voice of execution, *Now*!

Light! It flooded the Soviet heartland, reflecting from every object: harbors, airfields, missile installations, factories. Light! The enemy was powerless to contain it. It scattered and bounced, each wave a record of the object illuminated. In a useless chaos it rose into the abyss and poured through the machine's aperture to be finally captured by the mirror. The optics ordered it. Rays were bent, chopped, tuned, amplified, focused. Images reappeared behind lenses. Film was pulled into place. A shutter blinked open, and the enemy was stripped of another secret.

❖

Red Sky Control Room
36 kilometers northwest of Moscow

"It looks good, Comrade Minister. Very good. We will get another kill." General Pavlovich Chernavin reassured his superior, Minister of

Defense Zhilin, of the progress of the operation. The two men stood alone on the most elevated dais watching the hive of activity on the four tiers below. There, two hundred officers and technicians of the PKO — the Soviet space defense forces — manned concentric arcs of computer stations. Most were married to their keyboards and screens, only briefly removing their faces from the monitors to refer to sheaves of technical documents or to the large-screen Mercator projection of the world that dominated the front of the cavern. Sinusoidal curves of an orbit inclined to the equator by eighty-seven degrees waved across it.

"For both of our sakes, it must be a kill."

The chill of the reply evaporated the confident smile from the general's face. He had made the statement because his minions had earlier made it to him, not because he could infer it from any of the data on the multitude of screens. That had to be left to a small army of young men that excelled with computers and celestial mechanics and superconductivity and a hundred other scientific and engineering disciplines. He only understood on the simplest of terms how it was possible to successfully attack an object that was hundreds of kilometers in the sky and traveling at tens of thousands of kilometers per hour. But they had done it eight of ten times in the past, and now, he silently asked the stars to make it nine of eleven.

These were hazardous times. The Party secretary was dying, or so it was rumored. He had not been seen in public for over two months, or so it was rumored. A power struggle, more hotly contested than in recent successions, was splitting the Politburo, or so it was rumored. Even at his lofty level, *Glavnyi Marshal Aviatsii*, General of the Air Force, real information on these matters was sparse. But thirty-seven years in a uniform had made him wise enough to not ask questions.

"I share your passion for a kill, General. I do not want to return to Moscow and have to explain another failure." *Particularly to that mad man, Kobozev*, was an unspoken thought. "But of paramount importance is that we make no mistakes that might compromise the existence of Red Sky."

"There will be no mistakes, Comrade Minister." Of *that* the general was certain. There were only two possible outcomes: a miss, which would go unnoticed by the Americans, or a fatal hit that would leave nothing to inspect.

"There! There it is! The Pechora radar has acquired the craft." The officer pointed to a flashing message on the large screen. Other digitized information was immediately deposited on the same projection by a rapidly moving cursor. A small representation of an American flag appeared over Spitsbergen and began a creeping blink along one of the sinusoids. Like traders reading a stock market ticker tape, men raised their heads from their desks and stared intently at the screen. A cheer rose from the floor. The minister turned to the general for an explanation.

"They celebrate because the radar data shows the Americans have not commanded the spy craft into a different orbit, an unlikely event given the perfect weather conditions for overhead photography. The orbit still has a perigee — a low point — of one hundred and thirty kilometers. We can continue the attack."

The minister allowed himself a smile at the news. The Americans thought themselves clever to temporarily drop their machine so low over the motherland, no doubt to achieve better detail in their photos. But, in so doing, they unwittingly exposed their handiwork to a quick death.

"And what is the orbit life at that altitude?"

"Two days, Comrade Minister. Three at the very most."

Three days, he considered. Far too brief a time for astronauts to get to the machine and see the evidence of attack. No... Red Sky would disable the spy craft and prevent its reboost to a safe altitude. The enemy would assume a technical malfunction, and the laws of nature would do the rest. Atmospheric drag would pull it to a meteoric death. *If*, he reminded himself, *all went well*. A month ago, it had not. The same spy satellite had escaped destruction when Red Sky had malfunctioned. Blissfully ignorant of their close call, the Americans had rebooted the craft and had since returned one of its three film pods. That thought piqued a question. "Will the attack be made before any more film is returned?"

"The film drops are very predictable, Comrade Minister. The next is not scheduled for eight days."

"Excellent." He watched the flashing tri-colored flag inch across the Novaya Zemlya nuclear testing facilities and imagined the machine's eye blinking in the images. In three days the film would be so much cosmic dust. It would be a bit of additional good news to take to the viper.

❖

Earth Orbit

The robot sailed through the darkness, her eye now shuttered closed. An imperceptible wind of atomic oxygen beat against her skin and enveloped the machine in a ghostly fog of St. Elmo–like, white fire. Occasional flashes of tropical lightning erupting from the nearby planet, overpowered the glow, and illuminated the red, white, and blue banner emblazoned on her skin.

Like a great beast back from the hunt, she groomed herself. She switched on heaters to guard her body from the abysmal cold. Star trackers watched the night sky for the two points of light out of the millions that would tell her of her attitude. Gyro-stabilized accelerometers whispered her velocity. Current sensors spoke of the reserves in her batteries. She had survived the hunt without injury and now searched her silicon brain for her next duty.

It was to eject the number-two film bucket — an unexpected command. The film drop was not to have been for another eight days. The take-up spool in the return pod was only partially full. Why should it be dropped? For all her power, she was incapable of knowing. Reason was not a faculty. Her creators had endowed her only with the power of blind obedience. She would never understand that, two days ago in a California factory test, a thermocouple had failed prematurely, that the film in her number-two pod was temperature-protected with thermocouples of the same questionable lineage, and that it would be best to send back the film now and not risk an intelligence loss due to a five-dollar component failure.

A vibrating crystal gave her a heartbeat of time, and she sampled it to find the drop was less than fifteen minutes away. Immediately, she ordered a drum roll of jet firings to begin the three-axis maneuver that would aim the pod at the precise angle to bring it safely through the intense heat of reentry and into the middle of an invisible oval in the Pacific sky. There, air force aircraft would snag it from midair as it descended by parachute.

She armed the explosive charges that would shatter steel and release the courier and then silently counted to the fire command.

...four...three...

A hail of steel hit her. A battery was penetrated and disemboweled, an inertial measurement unit destroyed, a fuel tank holed. Four objects shredded the robot's skin at the point where her masters had emblazoned their flag, then thudded into the pristine surface of the mirror. The impact converted the perfect parabola of quartz silica into a useless cloud of dust. But, still, she maintained life enough to count.

...two...one...fire!

The number-two film pod, bearing an eighteen inch scar from the attack, separated from the dying hulk and began its forty-minute reentry fall.

The machine died.

❖

Monday, 29 August
Ellington Field, Houston, Texas

Even though the sun had just risen, Judy O'Malley was already drenched in sweat. In the Venusian furnace of a Houston summer, respiration alone was enough exercise to bring a second skin of wet. It limped her hair, soaked her blouse, bubbled on her lip, and ran in rivulets from her armpits. It was the type of sweat that made a joke of antiperspirants and dark blouses, the type of heat that made women avoid using the bathroom because of the difficulty of rolling up sodden pantyhose.

She stared across the tarmac and watched the yellow ball hover on the horizon. Only in Houston did it do that, she thought — *hover*. In the rest of the world it rose in a steady movement across the sky, but in the dog days of a Houston summer it stalled on the horizon. It stopped until the air was liquid and stagnant with heat, until shade was made meaningless. Then, it would crawl across the sky in a seemingly quarter-time movement that would send people fleeing into homes and cars and offices to the safety of their life-support systems — their air conditioners. And before dropping below the western horizon, it would stall again and superheat the air to ensure the irrelevancy of night.

Judy pulled her saturated blouse from her belly and waved it in an attempt to fan some cooling air across her skin. It was as ridiculous an effort as a rain forest explorer fanning himself. At its release, the fabric caved back onto her flesh.

She turned and had made one step of her escape to the lounge air conditioning when she was suddenly stopped by the strangeness of the moment. She was alone. It seemed to her that in the past, at this moment, she had never been alone. Someone had always been with her — another wife, the NASA family escort, somebody. But the news reporter had finished his questions and left her standing alone on the aircraft parking ramp. There were others nearby — astronauts and their families — but they were oblivious to her, too engrossed in their own departure preparations.

Those proceeded with characteristic NASA efficiency. Bags were being hurried onto the business jet that would transport the wives. Maintenance personnel connected starting units to the T-38 jets that the husbands would fly. In a protocol, long ago perfected by the NASA PR bureaucracy, the women would precede their men to the Cape. The press contingent waiting there was eager for the popular shots — gleaming white, blue-streaked T-38's rolling to a stop; gallant, smiling astronauts vaulting from their cockpits; wives racing to embrace their soon-to-be heroes. It was the stuff of *Life Magazine*.

Judy surveyed the scene from which she suddenly seemed so detached, so invisible. Excitement, as real and pervasive as the heat and humidity, gripped the players. They were high on the anticipation of the adventure and chattered and laughed and joked too loudly. Sweating news cameramen orbited the knots of families, their boom microphones lapping up the conversations. They focused on the mothers, who were always emitting the brightest human-interest glow. One had her three-year-old dressed in a miniature blue flight suit, complete with an American flag, a NASA patch, and his daddy's wings. That novelty had made her the center of media attention.

Older children agitated impatiently on the ends of mothers' arms, excited at the oft-repeated promises of fun on the beach and visits to Disney World.

The husbands and fathers — the astronauts — stood nearby. Judy watched them act their part — casual, confident, cocky. Their ocean-blue flight suits were festooned with patches which exaggerated their masculinity, like chaps and spurs did for cowboys. Accouterments of big, multifunctional wrist watches and gold-framed aviator sunglasses further distinguished them. Some wore baseball caps with gold-trimmed "scrambled eggs" on the bill and their mission patch silk-screened on the front. At this moment, they were gladiators preparing to enter the arena, knights bidding their maidens farewell.

Other parts of the play caught her eye. Near the visitor lounge, one of the wives restrained her young son from running to his father. The child could not understand the word the mother was speaking — *quarantine*. There would be no good-bye kiss from daddy. To minimize the possibility of infectious disease jeopardizing an orbiting crew, NASA had quarantined them for a week from their children. The isolation extended to even this moment. In a mimic of his mother, the boy blew a kiss toward his champion.

Standing away from the others was Bob Pettigrew — the pilot for this mission and the rookie of the crew. He was a bachelor marine aviator, renowned among the astronauts for his seemingly inexhaustible stable of beautiful young women. One of these, wielding mountainous, unhaltered breasts, clung to his arm and laughed mindlessly at something he had just whispered in her ear. His hand delivered a discreet squeeze to her tight, jean-clad ass.

In spite of his flippant use of the female sex, Judy greatly respected the man. He was brutally honest, wearing no airs, making no pretenses, as quick to laugh at himself as others. She and her husband, Mark, had long enjoyed his friendship, but, in the past eighteen months — in the closeness of being on the same crew — Pettigrew had become family.

Like her, he was in his early forties — old for a shuttle rookie. A two-year incarceration in Hanoi as a prisoner of war had delayed his career ascent of the astronaut pinnacle. Besides his age, he was also unique in size. At six feet, four inches and a muscled, two hundred and five pounds, he was the ninety-nine-percentile astronaut.

With a practiced flick of her head, his companion rearranged her mane of severely bleached hair, then stood on her toes to deliver a familiar kiss to his lips. Judy could easily appreciate what she saw in him. Pettigrew could turn any woman's thighs to jelly. He had the chiseled features common to Hollywood leading men, but his boyish smile and space-black eyes that hinted of speed-of-light adventure made any celluloid heartthrob look ordinary.

Judy continued to watch their antics and wondered how much longer the relationship would last. The marine changed women like most men changed shirts. But she forgave his philandering. If women gave of themselves too freely and got burned, they certainly couldn't claim fraud. With Pettigrew, one got what one saw, no apologies offered. It was all on display, except — she was sure of it — his loneliness.

She had once suggested that observation to Mark — that Pettigrew was an extremely lonely man. He had laughed, "Why is it that married women refuse to believe a man like Pettigrew isn't happy having a different beautiful woman every couple of months? He can't be lonely!"

Judy had dropped the conversation. As with most military pilots, Mark's ability to understand the subtleties of human behavior was deficient. She knew he was wrong. Pettigrew wasn't the happy man that most people saw and she frequently wondered why.

Her attention was next drawn to Senator Vernon Rush, NASA's latest VIP shuttle passenger. Even though he was dressed as the other astronauts, right down to the aviator glasses and obnoxious wrist watch, the most casual observer could have easily picked him out as a fraud. The magical aura of "astronaut" did not surround him — that glow of cocky self-confidence, of fearlessness, of an inflated ego wrapped in an "aw shucks, ma'am" veneer. But he tried to possess it. They all did, Judy thought, every last one of them. Brilliant scientists, important politicians, foreign princes — they had all marched through the portals of the Johnson Space Center for their passenger training, had seen the aura, and had immediately craved it. But none had gained it. It didn't come with the coveralls or the watch or the aviator glasses or even with a single space flight. It came from a lifetime in the air, of making war in the sky, of making love to the machines of flight, of a hundred brushes with death — the aura that said, "I've been there."

Judy watched as one of Rush's aides documented the senator's adventure with copious photographs. It was obvious that the session was killing Rush. He knew that the aura abhorred cameras. But, as a career politician, he could not refuse. These pictures were needed for his reelection campaign. So, he hid on the far side of a T-38 while the staffer directed him into the classic fighter pilot pose — a casual lean against the wing, helmet tucked in the crook of an arm, and a bright, confident smile. He was a water boy dressed in football pads, a laughing stock to those who really played the game.

"He looks like a real warrior, doesn't he?"

Judy had missed Mark's approach and answered him over her shoulder. "More like a little kid being prepared for a portrait. I feel sorry for him." The staffer was now having him comb his hair.

Judy finally turned to her husband. "What's the latest? Is the countdown still on schedule?" In these final forty-eight hours before a launch, it was the most asked question of a husband by a wife. Their lives would be ruled by the progress of the countdown. Bags would be packed by it, meals eaten by it, sleep arranged around it, travel dictated by it, sex ruled by it. If there was a hold in the countdown, there would be a hold in their lives.

"Yea. They're looking at a problem in one of the LCC computers, but it's minor — nothing that's going to hold us here. They should have it fixed in the next couple hours."

Judy understood the abbreviation — Launch Control Center. Every astronaut's wife quickly acquired a fluency in NASAese. They had to if they wanted to carry on a conversation with their husbands. After twelve years, Judy was an expert. She could easily translate or construct a sentence laced with terms like ET, SRB, MCC, and SLF.

"I've heard that before. If the launch slips more than a day, I'm going to have another fight on my hands. That condo manager said he could only guarantee my room for three nights."

"We won't slip."

It was said with the confidence of a man who had no worries if there was a delay. It had always amazed Judy how little regard NASA paid to the needs of the astronauts' wives. Their men were treated as national treasures, coddled and pampered at every turn. But the VIP status did not extend to spouses. Only their transportation to and from the Cape was provided by the agency. Finding a place to stay was a wife's problem, and invariably a big one, since an exact launch date was impossible to predict and tourists kept the "No Vacancy" signs out. There had been several times in Mark's previous three launches where weather delays had sent her to motel and condo managers pleading, like a destitute widow, not to be evicted.

A shout from the family escort interrupted them. The wives were being called to board their aircraft. Simultaneously, a jet starter unit was switched on, flooding the ramp with a deafening screech. Wailing protests came from two of the youngest children as their mothers handed them over to friends and grandparents. NASA officialdom had ruled that children could not be flown at government expense to their fathers' launch. They would have to fly commercial airlines — another worry heaped on women that were already buried in it.

Mark walked Judy to the stairway of the Gulfstream and they made their good-bye. This one was casual and easy, a sunshine-warm farewell made by a woman with the absolute certainty she would again hold her man. But soon, another good-bye would have to be made, this one in the frigid shadow of great uncertainty.

Judy climbed aboard the plane and walked to the rear. On this special day she wanted solitude, and she found it in a lone seat in back. The plane taxied, and she watched from the window and through the rippling waves of August heat and jet exhaust. Like a graduating college senior making a last walk of the campus, she drank in sights she would never again see — the neat rows of pin-striped T-38's, husbands hoisting parachutes into cockpits and balancing helmets on wind-screen edges, aircraft mainte-nance workers muscling fire bottles and starter units into place, the waving crowd of well-wishers, grandparents holding crying babies, the news cameramen filming their plane. She watched it all — every person, every movement, every object. But unlike the graduate who might be touched with a nostalgic sadness on his last school day, Judy was joyous. She would miss none of it. For twenty-three years, she had lived with the fear of losing Mark to a violent death. He had successively carried the titles of fighter pilot, combat pilot, test pilot, and now, space shuttle commander.

For twenty-three years! Twenty-three! And the worst have been here — these years at NASA! These space missions! But it's almost over! Just one more time! Oh, God, thank you, thank you, thank you! Thank you for bringing it to an end!

❖

Volokolamsk Forest
173 kilometers east of Moscow

"You will note from the CAT scan that the cancer has spread. It now encompasses eighty percent of the liver and has attacked the bladder and the lower right lung." Four men at a rustic wooden table intently followed the doctor's presentation. He held the heavy plastic film of an X-ray so it was backlit by a wheezing, gas-powered table lamp and used a ball-point pen to trace the irregular white area that defined the limits of the malignancy. At the head of the table, a fifth man appeared less interested. He casually handled a hunting rifle, stroking its twin blue-steel barrels with an oiled cloth. The others were familiar with the weapon fetish of

Sergey Kobozev, Party Secretary for Ideology and Propaganda, and were careful to ignore it.

"And what is the prognosis for our beloved Party chairman?" Kobozev asked the insincere question without interrupting his caress of the gun. The hand motions, slow and loving, reminded Musa Zhilin, minister of defense, of his long-dead grandmother stroking her cat. The analogy extended no further, however. His grandmother had been a saintly old widow. Kobozev was a poisonous snake. Some believed he was worse — that he was Stalin reincarnate. But Zhilin scoffed at such nonsense. There were no such things as ghosts or reincarnation. He could appreciate what had started the fearful rumors, though. There were great similarities in appearance between the two men. Kobozev had the same large, square head and the almost oriental squint to his eyes. His were gray, though, not the satanic black of Stalin's. A thick stand of white-streaked hair and prominent eyebrows gave the ghost believers some-thing else to hold onto, but unlike Stalin, Kobozev was clean-shaven and kept his body in athletic trim.

No, Zhilin thought, the man at the end of the table was no more of a ghost than he was. Kobozev was merely a man insane for power, willing to do anything to get it, anything to keep it. Every generation had them fresh born. They did not come from beyond the grave.

The opinion made Zhilin question himself for the hundredth time. Why was he allying himself with a madman? What was he doing in Kobozev's hunting lodge in the dark of night, amid the trophy heads and hides and western-decadent gun collection, listening to the chairman's private physician explain a cancer? Why was he gathered with other Politburo conspirators?

For the hundredth time, he came to the same answer. There was no alternative. Party Chairman Belidov was dying. Mikhail Sorokin held an eight-to-five majority control of the Politburo that guaranteed he would be the next chairman. And Mikhail Sorokin also held dangerous, liberal, reformist ideas on how the motherland would achieve that most sought-after prize, that salvation, that salve for a restless population — economic parity with the West. Sorokin's plan would reduce the armies, end support of client states, expose their borders to the fascist Germans, and promote a free-market system, free press, and free elections.

Sorokin had pleaded and won his case with seven others — that the ways of Marx were flawed. The Soviet Union was falling farther and farther behind the West. Only nuclear weapons and a massive army distinguished the USSR from a beggar nation. Consumer goods were shoddy or nonexistent, food supplies unreliable, the currency worthless. How long would it be before the population rose up, perhaps violently, and demanded a change? Soon, was Sorokin's prediction. It was best, he had said, to begin the change now.

But Kobozev was correct. Sorokin was a lunatic, a reactionary. His ideas were fearful, dangerous, even treasonous. Carried to fruition, they would lead to the destruction of the Party, to *their* destruction. And months ago, when the biopsy had proved malignant, when it had become obvious that a change of leadership was imminent, Kobozev had privately approached Zhilin to suggest another way to achieve equality with the West, a way that would maintain the status quo, maintain the preeminence of the Party, and maintain each of their lofty states in that Party. That's why he was here, he reminded himself, why they were all here — to avoid the deadly dangers of Sorokin's dream, the dangers of power returned to the people.

The doctor answered Kobozev's question. "Death will occur before the end of the year, perhaps in early December."

"Is it not possible to operate, Doctor? A transplant maybe?" The question held the plea of Andrey Yazov, minister of economics, a man who very much wished that he was elsewhere.

At the question, Kobozev's stroking hand abruptly stopped. He peered venomously at Yazov. No one at the table missed the silent message — an extension of the chairman's life did not fit into the plan.

The doctor continued, "I'm afraid not, Comrade Minister Yazov. For many years, Chairman Belidov has been taking blood thinners to reduce the dangers of a stroke. These drugs greatly increase the possibility of a hemorrhage in any operation.

"The situation is not uncommon in a man of his age. If you stop the blood thinning to operate, the patient strokes from a blood clot. If you operate while keeping the blood thin, the patient bleeds to death.

"No, I'm afraid all we can do is continue the chemotherapy, but at this stage that will hardly be more than a placebo. The chairman is terminally ill. Nothing will change that. His liver will fail and the toxins in his own body will kill him."

Kobozev liked the words. The barest hint of a smile said so.

"And his mental state, Comrade Doctor. In these final months will it be affected?" It was the question of Dmitriy Skripko, minister of foreign affairs.

"In the very last days, yes. The chairman will be in increasing pain and will, no doubt, request pain-killing medication. Those will incapacitate him. But I expect that he will remain lucid until very late in his illness."

"Lucid enough to conduct the affairs of state? Lucid enough, Doctor, so that a change of leadership will not be necessitated for three months?" Kobozev was asking.

"I'm confident that will be the case. Comrade Belidov is a very strong man."

"Yes, he is…a model for us all." Kobozev mouthed the sarcasm while carefully placing the gun on the table. "Are there any other questions for the doctor?"

Yazov started to open his mouth but saw Kobozev's scowl and thought better of it.

"No more questions. Well, Doctor, thank you for your time. You are dismissed."

The man opened his briefcase, stowed the X-rays, and stepped to the door.

"Oh… one last thing, Comrade Doctor." The man stopped with his hand on the door handle and turned to Kobozev. "It would probably be best for your own health if you forgot this meeting."

Kobozev's warning was hardly necessary. When he had first arrived and noted the KGB-uniformed guards outside and the minister for state security, Anatoliy Ryabinin, at the table inside, the doctor had felt a case of selective amnesia coming on.

"Of course, Comrade Kobozev." He made a slight bow and left the room.

Kobozev turned to address his guests but was preempted by Yazov. "We cannot continue in this! It is treason!" The man hopped his chair forward on the pine floor and threw his chest into the table. His arms reached forward in a hysterical supplication. "Treason! Belidov and Sorokin and the others will uncover the plan! We will all be executed!"

"Comrade Yazov…" Kobozev's voice was precisely in control. He

appeared as a parent calming a child. The age difference in the men —
Kobozev being twelve years older but looking twenty years senior —
added to the effect. He picked up the rifle and resumed the lazy strokes
of its steel tubes with the cloth. "The others will know nothing. Red Sky
has been and remains a 'most secret, eyes only' project. The others have
no access."

"The stars above! Chairman Belidov has access!" Yazov's right eye
began a nervous, blinking tic.

"And he is told only what *we* … what Defense Minister Zhilin tells
him!" Kobozev's minuscule patience was gone. He detested the weak,
wishing the conventions of man allowed for their easy elimination as in
the animal world. "He is told that Red Sky is still in the infancy of its
check-out! That it is suffering from design and construction flaws! That
it will not be operational for at least a year! He knows nothing of its true
status! None of the others know! None of the others *will* know!"
Kobozev's voice dropped to a near whisper. "Unless, of course, we are
betrayed." The word generated a Last Supper silence. Only the sputtering
of the gas lantern invaded. Yazov could feel all eyes on him. Even the
glass eyes of the wall-mounted animals seemed to him to swivel in their
sockets to warn against betrayal. He wanted to run screaming from the
room. His entire life, he had been a loyal Party member. How did he get
here?

His wife. She had made him vulnerable to the blackmail. For years
she had been abusing his position of minister of economics. For years she
had been embezzling, or, rather, forcing him to embezzle. How many
rubles? The numbers had become so vast as to lose meaning. Through the
black market she had converted them to the real things of value — to
gems, gold, furs, art, perfume, Parisian fashions. His house was stuffed
with the booty. He was here because of the greed of his wife.

How did Kobozev find out? Probably from the KGB. He had
Ryabinin in his pocket.

And he was here because the others needed him. Red Sky consumed
huge amounts of state resources. As minister of economics, he controlled
those resources. He was a key player in the Red Sky project. That is why
the other four needed him in their treachery.

And when he had emphatically refused Kobozev's initial recruit-
ment, the viper had calmly set on his desk a complete dossier of his sins.

"Comrade Yazov," he had said, "at his ascendancy, Mikhail Sorokin would be most interested in this information. One of his revolutionary ideas is to punish those who abuse their Party privileges, who bleed the motherland, to let the people adjudicate punishment. It would perhaps be in your very best interests to do what is necessary to ensure Comrade Sorokin does not replace Belidov."

That is why Andrey Yazov, minister of economics, loyal Party member, could not run from the room.

"So, comrades, we understand each other. We cannot turn back." The others had long ago passed the point of no return. The comment was for Yazov. "We must continue with our plan. As the doctor has shown, we have only three more months to succeed. Comrade Zhilin, please tell us of Red Sky's status."

The defense minister sat forward in his chair. "Red Sky's attack on the American reconnaissance satellite was a complete success. They were unable to reboost it to a safe altitude and earlier today it reentered the earth's atmosphere over the South Atlantic and burned up."

"Then Red Sky is ready?" KGB Chief Anatoliy Ryabinin was asking.

"I regret, no. The machine is still beset by pointing problems. It is taking multiple firings to ensure a high probability of kill. For a demonstration firing against a hundred spacecraft, we need to be certain that each shot counts. Additional tests are still necessary."

"More tests? We won't have to wait for Sorokin to uncover us. The Americans will do it for him." Yazov resumed his doom-saying.

"Andrey does have a valid point. We flirt with disaster by continuing to test Red Sky against American assets." Yazov had a momentary ally in the foreign minister.

"The Americans will never know of the attacks… not until we want them to know. We will continue to be very selective in our targeting to ensure they are unable to trace Red Sky." From the very beginning, Kobozev had insisted on such testing. He feared that engineers might *solve* problems by making Soviet targets *cooperative* — akin to shooting tethered animals, he thought. If he was going to bet his life on Red Sky, he wanted proof that the machine could kill an unhobbled, vigilant enemy, not some engineer's promise that it could. And how frightened would the president of the United States be if he was confronted with a list of destroyed *Soviet* assets? What proof would that be of Red Sky's lethality? No, the *fait accompli* of a Soviet anti-missile system would come in the form of a list of destroyed American satellites. That, and a live demonstration, would effectively amputate the land and sea based ballistic missile legs of the American nuclear triad. No sane president would contemplate war with the survivability of his missiles in question. He would fold in the face of Soviet demands and a new world order would be introduced, one that would see the Soviet Union as the preeminent power and Kobozev at her helm.

Kobozev looked at Zhilin. "Hurry your preparations."

"General Chernavin is already greatly concerned at the limited time to prepare for a one-hundred-satellite kill. He will need significantly greater allocations."

"One hundred?" Yazov snorted derisively. "Oh, *that* will really frighten the Americans. They only have *thousands* of warheads. They will laugh the Iranian Initiative back in our faces."

"My dear Comrade Yazov, you demonstrate an abysmal ignorance of man's fear of the unknown." Kobozev seemed to dismiss him further by seizing his rifle and rising from the table.

Yazov wanted to shout, *Stop! You cannot talk to me like that! My ministry is more important than yours! I control the lifeblood of the nation!* But the speech died in his throat. Kobozev turned suddenly and assumed a too-threatening posture — feet spread, rifle held diagonally across his chest. Without comment, he broke the breech of the weapon, pinched out two cartridges, and tossed them on the table. Yazov was not the only one to startle at the fact that the weapon had been loaded.

"Now, it's empty." That fact was obvious. What wasn't obvious was the purpose of the show. The four at the table exchanged confused glances at their leader's behavior, but before anyone could question him, Kobozev eased the breech closed, raised the weapon to his shoulder, and sighted along the barrel — first at the head of a bear on the wall behind Yazov. Wrinkles appeared in his index finger as it slowly took up the slack in the trigger. One hammer fell, giving a sharp, unproductive *click*. Then, he sighted lower — past the boar's head, past the wolf's head, and finally straight at Yazov's forehead. The minister of economics resolved to show no fear. He steeled his back, set his jaw, and stared into the gaping black holes. The last twist of lands and grooves was his focus point. The others watched the confrontation in shocked silence. Kobozev's finger drew slowly tighter on the crescent of the second trigger. Tighter…tighter…*Click.* In the deep silence, the sound seemed as loud as a shot. Yazov felt a flash of long quiescent manhood stir in his blood. He had not flinched in the face of the provocation.

As if the moment had never occurred, Kobozev stepped to the gun cabinet. "A beautiful weapon, isn't it? A custom made Holland and Holland, three-seven-five H&H magnum. You know, Comrade Yazov, it has a muzzle velocity of almost nine hundred meters per second. I felled many of these magnificent animals with this weapon." He replaced the rifle in the cabinet and pulled out another. "But this weapon… ahhhhh… *This* is my favorite, hand made by my great-grandfather." The rifle was obviously an antique. It had a very long, large-diameter barrel and a short, plain, dark-wood stock. The curved and twisted mechanical complications of an ancient hammer-and-trigger assembly projected above and below the grip. "My father gave me this weapon when I was just a child, and I used it to kill my first predator…" He paused, letting his eyes touch on each of his audience, "…a man." The others drew upright at the revelation and shared shocked glances.

"I was eleven years old and had gone into the forest with my father to hunt for deer." He spoke with his head down, his attention on the weapon. His hands never stopped fondling the perfect harmony of metal and wood. "It was during one of Stalin's genocidal purges, when starvation had driven many rural families to hunting. But, of course, hunting was forbidden. Guns were forbidden. My father, with seven children to feed, ignored the rules, and so we hunted.

"One day, as I came back to our camp, I found three militiamen arresting my father. They had bound his hands and were beating him. His screams covered my approach and I hid in some brush, not twenty yards away." His guests were stone silent, hanging on every word. "It never occurred to me to do anything else. I cocked the weapon." With the heel of his hand he pushed the heavy lever of the hammer into a cocked position. "Took aim." He brought the butt of the rifle into the crotch of his shoulder, then leveled the barrel at Yazov.

This time, there was no steel in the minister of economic's backbone. The others were similarly terrified. Had Kobozev gone totally mad? They leaned away from his target. Yazov's eyes grew as enormous as the black hole that was the end of the cannon. The aperture was less than a yard from his head. His throat bobbed in a dry swallow. A dew of sweat came to his forehead. "And squeezed." Kobozev's finger curled around the trigger, but he exerted no force. For long seconds he held the weapon on the trembling Yazov. Finally, just as it appeared that the man would fly from the chair, he lowered the rifle and calmly continued his story.

"The bullet hit the man's temple and exploded his brain over the other two. They started for their weapons, but I screamed for them to stop. They did, freezing in a helpless panic, the pink tissue of their companion's brain dripping from their faces. I ordered them to untie my father. They did. And he cut their throats." The others were aghast at the story.

"Now, what is the lesson of this, Comrade Yazov?"

Yazov had seen no lesson — only death at the hands of a psychopath. He was pale and nauseous, unable to answer.

"I will tell you. You had no fear of the first weapon because you knew it was unloaded — completely harmless. However, you were terrified of this rifle because you were uncertain of its lethality and my intentions. So it was with Stalin's militiamen. The two men lost their lives because they feared the unknown. They had no knowledge of how many weapons were aimed at them from the brush or how many bullets each weapon held. They did as I ordered out of that fear, just as I could have ordered you.

"But, in reality, they could have laughed in my face and seized their own weapons and killed me. Why? Because this rifle is a single-shot, muzzle-loading weapon. I had shot my wad, and it would have taken me over a minute to reload and fire again.

"And you, Comrade Yazov, could have similarly laughed in my face." With one outstretched arm, like he was pointing a pistol, he again raised the weapon into the weakling's face. Still not recovered from the just past terror, Yazov startled with a grunt and jerked backward with a violence that almost threw him from the chair. Kobozev squeezed the trigger. The hammer fell with another deafening click. The weapon was not loaded.

"So, Comrade Yazov, the fact that Red Sky has a limited capability is of no consequence. The American president will not know that. He will only know that his satellite fleet has been decimated. How? From where? How many machines is he facing? What can they do to his missile fleet? Answers to these questions will be unknown, and he will fear that unknown as certainly as those two militiamen had. And, in that fear, he will follow my orders as certainly as those dead men."

Kobozev stepped back to the gun cabinet, replaced the weapon, and retook his seat. "Now, Comrade Zhilin was saying he would need the assistance of your ministry to ensure the readiness of Red Sky. Can he count on that?"

Yazov had withdrawn a handkerchief and was patting the perspiration from his face. A weak nod was all he could manage for an answer.

"Good. Comrade Ryabinin, do you have anything to report?"

The others collectively sagged in relief that the lesson on strategic missile defense was over. The KGB minister shifted in his chair. "The Iranian plans go well. Agents are being moved into Teheran. We are in the process of finding a suicidal terrorist and locating an American target. I think one of their facilities in England would be most easily accessible."

"Those are all things we can control. What of Ayatollah Hashemi? He has promised us much, but will he deliver? The Iranian Initiative hinges on him."

Ryabinin took a deep pull on his cigarette and held the nicotine in his lungs as he composed his answer. He had struggled with that question ever since Hashemi's chief of staff had first approached a Soviet agent two months earlier. His message had been astounding. There was a power struggle in progress in Teheran, one that Hashemi was in danger of losing. That would be a shame, the messenger had hinted, since, in a Hashemi-ruled Iran, a Soviet naval presence would be welcome in Iranian harbors.

It had been a message from the gods! The Persian Gulf! Ryabinin still salivated at the thought. It would become a Russian lake! Soviet control would propel oil prices to unimaginable heights and plunge the Western economies into depression. The NATO alliance would collapse. Like a litter of pigs at a sow's belly, the capitalists would have only one objective — to find a teat, an oil teat. Those countries that cooperated would be given their suck. Those that did not would have to bear the wrath of their cold, jobless populations.

There was but one difficulty — actually, two. Hashemi was number three in the line to Iranian power. Two lives would have to be removed. "Could that be arranged?" the messenger had asked.

Ryabinin had lobbied the Politburo to approve the assassinations, but

Sorokin had bent Belidov's ear and marshaled the power to veto the idea. "Too dangerous," Sorokin had said. "It will further divert us from fixing the economy. Another state security intrigue that will do nothing to ensure the security of the state," he had ridiculed. The words had still been stinging when Ryabinin had made up his mind to side with Kobozev.

Quietly, Hashemi's messenger had been approached. Yes, he was told, something could be done to ensure Hashemi's ascension. And Red Sky would guarantee that the Americans would not interfere in the operation. The Iranian Initiative had been born.

But — would Hashemi deliver? Or would he double-cross them after he was in power?

Ryabinin released the smoke from his nose and voiced his thoughts. "It is most difficult to judge Hashemi's sincerity. We obviously cannot contact him directly. However, our profile of the man reveals him to be excessively mad for power."

Another Kobozev, was Yazov's immediate thought. His hands were still in a palsy.

"I have ordered our agents to overtly photograph and record all meetings with his couriers, and copies of those are being sent to Hashemi. The message should be crystal clear to him. We have documented your treason. I find it difficult to believe a man would betray us, knowing that we can immediately reveal him to his population as a traitor. So, in answer to the question, I believe he will most definitely deliver on his promises."

Kobozev nodded his head in agreement. Hashemi would deliver. Red Sky would hold the Americans at bay. He would be swept into the Party chairmanship, and Sorokin — Sorokin would be lucky to retire with a sub-minister's pension.

"Comrade Skripko? Is all in order to support the diplomatic aspects of the initiative?"

The foreign minister removed his glasses and rubbed the bridge of his nose. "Yes. I will personally deliver the Red Sky ultimatum to the president. All I need is the date so I can make the appropriate diplomatic arrangements, and a subject for the visit... I was thinking of an anti-missile treaty."

All but Yazov laughed at the foreign minister's joke. The image was just too vivid — the president of the United States expecting a discussion on limiting anti-missile weapons and, instead, being given an ultimatum whose very teeth was an anti-missile weapon.

Minister Skripko continued. "No, I think the subject should definitely not call attention to anti-missile defenses. I will ask for an audience to discuss the same general issues of nuclear disarmament that have been on our agendas for many years. There should be nothing suspicious about the request, either with the president or Belidov. In fact, I already have a trip to Canada planned for late November, so requesting a quick visit with the president before returning home should not raise questions."

"Excellent. Then, we need only to select a date for the Iranian Initiative. From what the doctor has told us, it must be in late November."

"I have a suggested date." The other four turned to the foreign minister, who was busy searching through a pocket calendar. "November twenty-fourth."

Yazov questioned for all of them. "Why the twenty-fourth?"

"It is a great holiday in America… Thanksgiving Day."

CHAPTER 2

Tuesday, 30 August
Kennedy Space Center, Florida

"This was a great idea, Mark! A great way to relax before the mission. And the view… I can even see our bird."

"Jeeeeesssssus." Pettigrew's sotto voce groan of disgust was camouflaged by the opening hiss of his fifth beer. The "our bird" comment was too much for him. In fact, virtually anything that Senator Rush said was too much for him. The marine had lived his life in single-seat fighter aircraft and considered those who had not done likewise as lesser beings. In his book, politicians were particularly dismal excuses for humanity — soft, pompous, egotistical, always ready to speak with authority on things they knew nothing about. Rush was whale shit, as low as you could get on the planet.

The senator, looking at "our bird," stood at the railing of the second-story patio with his back turned to the men. If he had heard Pettigrew's slur, he said nothing. Mark was glad. He knew the marine, uninhibited when sober, was out of control when drunk. He suspected he was probably itching for a chance to put the senator in his place — on the sea floor. He signaled his pilot with a two-fingered cut across his throat to knock it off.

"Yea, beer and burgers and sun and surf are hard to beat." Mark referred to the traditional mission-eve beach house picnic they were enjoying. It was the perfect way to recover from the exhaustion of the final days of the Johnson Space Center training marathon. A few unclaimed hamburger patties sizzled on a barbecue pit, while silver bullets of Coors beer chilled in a nearby ice chest. The men lounged in chairs sipping at their drinks. The wives were inside changing for the beach.

The gathering was at the astronaut beach house. Originally built as a private retirement home, Uncle Sam had acquired it during the mid-sixties moon race expansion of the space center. Its interior had been modified to serve as a small conference facility, and the upper echelon of Kennedy Space Center management employed it as such. But they had extended an open invitation to the astronauts to use it for the purpose for which it had originally been intended — isolated relaxation. And that isolation was now absolute. The only neighboring structures were situated slightly inland — the gray, steel skeletons of the Titan launch towers. Pads 39A and B, the space shuttle launch facilities, were visible two miles to the north. Otherwise, the house commanded a spectacular view of uninhabited and undeveloped beach and sand dunes.

Pettigrew pulled a cigar from his shirt pocket, expertly popped the head of a match with his thumbnail, and sucked the weed into an odious ignition. A blue pall waft over Rush and he turned to the source.

"Bob, I'm surprised you smoke."

"Why's that, *Senator?*" Since the politician had first joined the crew, the marine had refused to address him by his first name.

"Well, it does cause cancer."

"You worry about your health?"

Mark tried to telepathically order his friend to shut the fuck up. But the alcohol had put Pettigrew's brain on a different wavelength. The marine not-too-discreetly moved his hand to ensure the obnoxious curls of tobacco smoke would find the senator's nostrils.

"I'm not a physical fitness fanatic, but yes, I do try to watch my health."

"Then why are you flying on the shuttle?"

"I beg your pardon?" Pettigrew's question seemed totally irrelevant to the past minute of conversation.

"If you worry about your health, why are you flying on the shuttle? It may not be too good for it."

Mark rolled his eyes in hopeless resignation. Though he agreed with Pettigrew's point — that flying a rocket was hazardous — this was not the time to discuss it. When Rush had first been assigned to the mission,

Mark had tried to point out the dangers inherent with space flight. As the commander, he considered it his moral obligation to do so. NASA headquarters should have been the voice of caution, but for political reasons, they were loathe to wave a red danger flag. Instead, they described the shuttle program in PR-polished terms that projected an image of absolute reliability — a space truck, a space airliner. So the task of telling shuttle passengers that riding a rocket was considerably more dangerous than anything they might have done in the past, and giving them an opportunity to change their minds, fell to the commanders. But none had ever backed out. Death in the sky was impossible for them to imagine. They hadn't been there. They had never had friends reduced to cinders. They had never delicately stepped around shredded flesh at a crash site.

Rush laughed, a nervous giggle that showed his intimidation by the marine. "Well, we sort of have some control over the risks of space flight, but you can't make a cigar risk-free."

"Yea, Bob. Maybe you ought to *quit.*" Mark prayed that his pilot would correctly translate the message, which had nothing to do with smoking and everything to do with his mouth — *shut it*! On the eve of a launch, there was enough pressure. Nobody needed more.

The marine winked at Mark's discomfort. "Okay, Senator. You talked me into it. I'll quit." He immediately ridiculed his seemingly miraculous conversion with his deepest drag yet. "Right after my last shuttle mission. Then I'll know it'll count."

Rush grimaced. Pettigrew's sarcasm emphasized his status as an outsider, how far he was from possessing the aura. He tried to hide his disappointment by stepping upwind of the marine's vice and changing the subject. "The last time I was at a beach house this remote was on a fact-finding trip to Nam."

"Jeeeeesssssus." Pettigrew's second groan was no closer to a prayer than his first. Even the "our bird" comment couldn't compare with the sacrilege of a noncombatant — a fucking politician — referring to Vietnam as Nam. Mark wanted to kill the marine and put on a face to show it.

Pettigrew made a feeble effort at repentance with a laughable cover. "Jeeeeesssssus, it's hot... just like Nam."

"When were you in Vietnam, Vern?" Paul Persley, one of the mission specialist astronauts of the crew, made the inquiry.

"In nineteen seventy-one. I was with the Vietnamese minister of defense. He took us to his private beach in a helicopter."

"Where was it?" Larry Austin, another mission specialist, asked the question.

"Let's see. It's been so long, and all those oriental names run together. It was Vinh something. Vinh... Vinh... Vinh Thuy. That's it. That was the place. Did you ever fly over it, Mark?"

"Not that I know of."

"How about you, Bob?"

The marine pulled a beer away from his face to reveal a spreading grin. Mark noticed and despaired. It was going to be one of those days. Pettigrew had short-circuited. Anything was possible. He wished the women would hurry with their preparations. The return of his girlfriend might divert the pilot from further antagonizing the politician.

"Vinh Thuy? Yea, I remember. Right next to Poon Tang." His blue word play skipped by everybody but Mark. "Used to fly over it all the time on the way to my targets."

"Really? What did you fly in Nam?" Rush fell blindly into the trap.

"I flew a bomber... a candy bomber."

"A candy bomber? You're kidding? I never heard of such a thing." Rush wasn't alone in his ignorance. The three civilian mission specialists looked quizzically to the marine for an explanation. Mark knew what was coming but was powerless to do anything about it. Pettigrew had hooked four fish.

"Candy bombers were probably the most effective aircraft we ever had in Vietnam."

"How so?"

"Well, you see, whenever the Vietnamese women and children heard jets overhead, they would hide in their trenches and spider holes, thinking they were about to be bombed. So I would dive down on their villages and drop canisters of Hershey Bars on 'em. That would bring 'em running out."

"I'll be damned. Now that's an aspect of psychological warfare that I never heard about... winning the hearts and minds of the people with air drops of candy. Amazing."

"Hearts and minds? Shit! It didn't win any hearts and minds."

"It didn't? I thought you said it was a very effective tactic."

"Oh, it was, it was. You see, you could never kill those little bastards when they were hiding in their holes. But the candy would get 'em into the open, and my wingman would be thirty seconds behind me and lay nape all over 'em."

While an amazed eight eyes bulged and four jaws slacked, the pilot sucked vigorously on his cigar until he had a tip of white ash, then swept it, airplane-like, across the floor at his feet. His target was a circle of ants that had found a dropped morsel of hamburger. He made a whooshing noise while sprinkling hot ash over the unfortunate creatures.

"The most fun was to circle back and gun the ones running around with their hair on fire." He repeated the cigar dive on three of the insects, which now ran in panicked, blind circles, their antennae blackened and shriveled by the rain of cinders. To the accompaniment of his best rendition of cannon fire, he lifted his foot and crushed the poor formicidae into three smears. "God, I miss the war." Mission completed, he landed his cigar in his mouth and grabbed for another beer.

The moment of shocked silence lengthened as the audience tried to cope with the horrific vision of women and children with Hershey Bars in their hands and flaming, jellied gasoline on their heads. Finally, the light came on in Larry Austin's brain. They had been had. He began a tentative laugh. "It's a joke, isn't it? Yea… it's bullshit!" The fog slowly lifted for the other MS's, and they joined in the laughter. It grew to a riot, with Rush laughing the hardest. To be included in the joke was to momentarily be one of the boys.

To Mark's great relief, the swimsuited women finally appeared from the house and ended Pettigrew's torture of Senator Rush.

"Surf's up!" He grabbed his giggling and jiggling date and ran towards the beach on a mission of lechery. In suitable intervals, the other couples followed — all seeking privacy for a final good-bye. Mark led Judy northward, regaling her with Pettigrew's candy-bomber story.

"Bob certainly can never be accused of putting on airs." She bent to splash some water on her chest. The day was a furnace. "I don't think he would act any differently if he was with the pope or the queen or the president."

"Being a POW probably did that to him… made him see life a lot differently than the rest of us. But I wish he'd cut Rush just a little slack.

The guy is okay. He really is sincere in wanting to help NASA. He sure doesn't need Pettigrew's bullshit right before the mission."

They continued their stroll, and Rush quickly faded from their conversation. Far more important concerns weighed them.

Mark made a disinterested, barefoot kick at a broken sand dollar. "I called Ty again last night."

The comment put Judy's gut on a falling elevator and interrupted her gait. She knew the purpose of the call.

Three months earlier, Ty Healy, a longtime friend, had come to Houston for a NASA meeting. He was a general now, occupying an important position at the Air Force Space Division in Los Angeles. It had been almost a year since they had last seen him, and she and Mark had invited him to supper. Over cocktails, he had delivered the thunderbolt.

"Mark, I know you don't want to hear this, but I want you on my staff. Space is becoming more and more critical to this nation's defense, and I need someone with your background.

"I've already got this approved through the appropriate channels. After this next flight, it's time to hang up your spurs. You can't fly forever. I wanted to and couldn't. You can't either. I need your expertise. The country needs it. You'll be getting orders shortly."

Orders! To leave NASA! A desk job! Judy had been delirious. She had thought the moment would never come. Her sentence was being commuted to time served — or almost. Finally, it was enough. Two tours in Vietnam had been enough. Years of test piloting at Edwards Air Force Base had been enough. Three space flights had been enough. Twenty-three years of watching Mark wrap himself in thundering, winged machines was enough. How many of their friends had not survived those same years, those same machines? Too, too many. *It was enough*!

On that evening, and in numerous phone calls that had followed, Mark had tried to change Ty's mind, begging for a reprieve like an alcoholic begging for a drink.

"Give me three more years, Ty. Two more. One more flight after this. Then I'll give it up. I'll come out there and do the work of ten men. Just give me a shot at a fifth flight."

The general had refused.

"What did he say this time?" Judy held her breath, fearing somehow, in his latest phone call, Mark had won his extension, that Ty had been hammered down.

"He wished me good luck… said my desk is already piled with work and to get my ass to Los Angeles."

Judy uncoiled. Her salvation was still intact. She loved Mark too deeply to not feel the pain he was suffering, but she would not lie to him. She would not pretend grief. She would not cry and damn Ty and the air force for doing this to him.

She was not guiltless in her feelings. Mark's love of flying had been with him long before she had come into his life. And that was exactly how it had been — she had intruded into his life. If she had been too love struck or too young or too stupid to see where that intrusion would lead, wasn't that her problem? He hadn't changed since their vows. She had. What right did she now have to rejoice in the end of his dream, to pray for its demise? It was a difficult question to answer, but she could almost convince herself she had earned the promise of peace of mind with her faithful and, for the most part, silent acceptance of two decades of a way of life that would have sent many wives to divorce lawyers — that *did* send many to the courts.

They said nothing more. In the most relaxed of moments, it wasn't Mark's manner to be talkative. In the agony of trying to come to grips with the end of his life in the air, he was a stone. For as long as she had known him, he had been this way — unable to share his heaviest burdens with her, to reveal whatever extremes of pain or joy surged through his soul. She had never seen him cry. Even while standing over the fresh graves of men who had been his best friends, he had not cried. He had always retreated into himself in his moments of anguish.

The silent stroll continued, and Judy reminisced on the childhood events that had brought her to this beach. She had been sixteen when she had discovered what God had intended — that a young girl's body commanded boys. In her case, exceptional beauty had allowed her to command any she had wanted. She had been blessed with perfect hourglass symmetry on a slight, five-foot, two-inch frame. Puberty had ripened her breasts to high, firm mounds and pointed them with sharp, pink-hued nipples. She had learned very quickly the power that they possessed. With the right blouse on, no boy could pass her without feeling a stir in his crotch. She had worn her hair at shoulder length — auburn tresses that had framed a face of large gray eyes, a wide, carnal mouth, a deep dimpled smile, and a peaches-and-cream complexion. Judy had been a much-wanted girl.

Before Mark, two boys had found an early nirvana in her body. Physically, the experiences had been less than fulfilling for her, but the back-seat, drive-in-theater passion had given her what she had needed to make the transition from girl to woman — the knowledge of how men were to be touched and kissed and stroked and teased; how her fingers, nipples, thighs, and tongue were to be employed.

It was in her high school sophomore year that she had become enamored with Mark. He was a senior. At the time, her girlfriends had laughed at her pursuit of a guy who was a nerd. He was an attractive boy, but a nerd all the same. He wasn't a jock, he was shy, he never dated, and he was continually occupied with various home-built rocket projects. Once a year, his name would be mentioned over the school PA system, to announce that he had won yet another state science fair prize. But in spite of this dismal teenage sex appeal, and for reasons lost in the hormonal ash pile of adolescence, Judy — the school beauty, the head cheerleader, the homecoming queen, the girl that could have any boy — chose Mark O'Malley.

Mark stopped their walk and glanced westward. "We better turn back. We're getting too close to the pad. The security people patrol this area." He shielded his eyes against the salt-air glare to view the launch site. A narrow ridge line of dunes and a mile of thickly vegetated lowland separated them from the massive steel and concrete edifice. *Discovery's* belly-mounted fuel tank covered most of her from view. Only the underside of her black-tiled wing tips could be seen extending beyond the edges of the solid rocket boosters.

"Okay. But let's go for a swim first. It's an oven out here."

"Not here, it's too close." He was left talking to himself. She sprinted into the surf, flattened into a freestyle, and pulled herself into neck-deep water.

"Let's go back closer to the house!" He cupped his hands and yelled, but the wind and surf swallowed it. Judy shook her head she did not understand.

"This way! This way!" He pointed south.

She ignored him, jackknifed into a dive, was under for a moment, then surfaced with something in her hand. Her motions indicated the object was heavy — too heavy to lift. Her arm could barely hold it near the surface.

"What the hell did she find?" Mark mumbled to himself while straining to see. "What is it? A shell?" She seemed to struggle more, as if the object was trying to get away. Finally overcome with curiosity, he dropped his towel, sunglasses, and shirt and followed after her.

"What did you find?" Ten feet from her, he raised up from his stroke and yelled the question.

"Here. What do you make of this?" With a spastic, girlish effort, she threw the mystery toward him. It landed near his head with a loud *splat,* and he grabbed for it.

"Whaaaa…? Judy! What are you doing? This is your swimsuit!"

She laughed at how ridiculous he looked in his close examination of the garment, as if there were hundreds of white, one-piece, size-four swimsuits floating around him and he might have been mistaken in his initial identification.

"I'm skinny-dipping, that's what I'm doing!" To punctuate the obvious, she allowed herself to sink a foot, then pushed herself straight up, arms extended over her head. The thrust carried the upper half of her body out of the water. Like car headlights, the untanned mounds of breast blinded him.

She swam forward, clasping one arm around his neck and grabbing for her suit. "Let me have that." But instead of dressing in it, she reached behind him and stowed the garment under the waistband of his own suit. "Now you can use your hands." Her eyes twinkled with evil intent.

It wasn't the first time he had been shocked by her uninhibited sexual play. In earlier years, she had entrapped him in other outdoor situations that had held the potential for excruciating embarrassment, if not a jail sentence.

She wrapped her legs around his waist and pushed up on his shoulders so that her nipples came level with his face. The chill of the sea had shriveled them into jutting promontories. Symmetrical threads of water ran from her hair, across her collarbone, and onto the slopes of white. Crystal beads of the fluid jeweled the very tips of the pink.

"Jesus, Judy!" Mark stole nervous glances in both directions. "NASA security might come by."

She laughed.

"I'm not kidding! When there's a bird on the pad, they really do sweep this area for terrorists."

She ignored him and steered a summit to his face, grinding her pubic bone into him in the process. The dual temptations, sharpened by his week of celibacy in the Johnson Space Center crew quarters, was enough to make him reconsider the risks. The fresh jeep tracks in the sand indicated that security had recently made their rounds. He wondered if maybe their privacy wasn't certain after all. She leaned to the right to bring the very point of her left nipple into contact with his lips. "No guts, no glory, Mark. Or, in this case, no fun."

The tease was too much. His head whipped around in another furtive survey. The coast was still clear. In a second, he had the softness in his mouth, sucking greedily. His teeth lightly nibbled the tip, and his hands came under her thighs to begin their probing fondle. The play brought her hips into the inviting rhythm of sex, and he was soon being tortured by a caged erection.

"I've got to set you down for a second. This bathing suit is gonna explode if I don't get it off." She released her leg lock and helped him to undress. For a moment, he considered throwing the suits to the beach but then thought better of it. Even Judy wasn't so uninhibited that she would like to confront the others as a real-life Eve — exactly what they would have to do if the tide stole their garments.

He used his free hand to stroke across her back and ass and fondle her breasts, while her neck became the focus of his mouth. It was a familiar but immensely satisfying foreplay.

Judy's hands covered his body. It was teenage hard — the shoulders, chest, belly, penis, ass, everywhere — and she envied its durability. Her flesh had not survived the twins and forty-two years with near the grace. Breasts and buttocks, though still firm, were definitely beginning their earthward fall. Stretch marks etched her belly, and gray was replacing the amber in her hair. Food seemed to go straight to her thighs, and she had to exercise like an Olympian to keep her weight at a girlish one hundred and ten pounds.

Mark, on the other hand, had only the salt in his hair, the lines around his eyes, and a barely perceptible bulge to his waist to identify him as middle-aged. His muscled shoulders, latticed stomach, and granitic legs and ass could have been the model for a Greek sculptor.

Their play intensified. Tongues traded wet dances. Mark's fingers twirled and pulled at her nipples. She moved behind him, biting the circumference of his neck. The action tightened his skin into goose flesh, and her hands reached around his sides to play with his own hardened disks. She felt lower, encircling his erection with one hand and gently massaging the twin masses beneath with the other. Mark groaned at the tease. His ten-day fullness, combined with the arousing novelty of outdoor sex, had rammed — he was certain — an extra quart of blood into his flesh. Judy tormented it masterfully, pulling its skin to snare-drum tightness on her downward strokes, relaxing her fist to merely a gliding caress on the upward cycle.

His free hand came behind his back and crawled between their bodies and into the curls of her pubic hair. Fingers quickly found the tiny knot, high in her crease, she had long ago identified to him as "the spot." He tried to play her game — a tease — but failed. She had always been explosively orgasmic, and after just a minute of slow finger pirouettes on the magic stone, another animal call joined the cry of the gulls. "I'm coming, Mark, I'm coming, I'm coming, I'm coming!"

As the eruption faded, he turned into her. "Now, is it my turn?"

She smiled. "Don't be in such a hurry. *Anticipation* is most of the fun."

"Yea, well right now I'm *anticipating* a jeep load of sky-cops coming down the beach."

She laughed away his worry. She had no intention of satisfying him quickly. When he was this way, when his sex was stretched and swollen and begging for gratification, then Mark O'Malley needed her and her alone. In these moments, no aircraft, no spaceship challenged her for possession. His passion for the sky, for space, for *flight* was nowhere in evidence.

They were now standing in waist-deep water — the surf had carried them shoreward during their preamble — and her gaze fell to his erection. Its slit was yawned open by the tightness of the dome. But the eroticism of the sight vanished, as she was also struck by the humor of it. She began to laugh.

"What the hell is so funny?" Mark was bewildered by the sudden mood change.

"As the waves pass, it looks like you have a periscope that's being raised and lowered."

Even as she spoke, the surf crawled seaward to expose the top half of the ruddy spike. She clutched her hands to her mouth in mock horror.

"Terrorists! It's the periscope of a Libyan submarine! Quick, run for your life!"

Before he could grab her, she had bolted toward the beach, screaming like a teenager. Except for a pause to grab the towel, she remained in flight until she reached the base of the dunes. There, in one flowing motion, she shook out the towel, laid it on the sand, and knelt to face him.

"What are you waiting for? I see a shark cruising behind you! You better get out of the water!" She cupped her hands in a yell.

He hesitated at the thought of traversing ten yards of open ground in broad daylight with a very prominent pink and polished seven inches of his body leading the way. "I thought we were going to finish this in the water."

Sensing his embarrassing position, she continued the harassment. "Are you kidding? Don't you know what the Red Cross says about strenuous water activities right after a meal? We could drown!"

"Damnit!" He slapped at the water. "Judy, somebody could see us up there! Come back in the water!"

Her answer was to recline on her side and present him with a full frontal view of her body. She began a scissors-style leg lift.

"Shit!" He threw his arms skyward in frustration.

After another minute of fruitless begging, boiling testosterone finally pushed him over the edge. If he passed up this opportunity for sex, the next would not occur until after the mission — another week away. He intensely studied both horizons. They remained empty. Then, stooping in a crouch, as if it would somehow hide his nakedness, he ran from the surf.

At the sight, Judy writhed in laughter. She had never seen a naked man running, much less a naked man with an erection, and the sight struck her as uproariously funny. With each stride, his penis flexed downward, then rebounded upward, giving the impression that it was the source of his locomotion.

Mark came to her side, made another darting scan of the beach, then dropped to his knees on the towel. He was glad to find the sand dunes provided more seclusion than he had originally suspected.

"Sure doesn't do much for a man's ego to have a woman laughing herself speechless every time she looks at his prick." He feigned a wound to his masculinity.

Judy raised herself to her knees. "I think that was the funniest thing I've ever seen."

"Well, the floor show is over. I hope it's time to do something about this." He nodded downward. "And, not to rush you, but I'm now *anticipating* a very embarrassing sunburn if we play Adam and Eve for too long."

"In that case…" Without any additional preliminaries, she leaned to his crotch and took the engorged flesh in her mouth. Mark's eyes rotated back in their sockets as if her suction had pulled them there. Her tongue began to alternately trace the hypersensitive crown and then probe its tiny slit. She enjoyed a new sensation — the different elemental salt tastes of sea and sex. Full mouth strokes along the length of the shaft vaporized his worries about NASA security patrols. He could have been on the fifty-yard line of the Super Bowl and wouldn't have noticed the crowd. She pushed him to his back and assumed a kneeling position between his legs. During the rearrangement, his steel never left her mouth.

For an interminable time, she pleasured him in this manner, always stopping whenever she sensed his climax was near. These moments were sacred to her, the last she would share with him before the mission, and she was intent on prolonging them. It was the only good-bye she was capable of. In three previous launches she had found words awkward and inadequate. She had tried to make them memorable — everlasting even. But they had never come out that way. Only Hollywood had memorable parting lines.

Finally, though, her own body demanded an end, demanded the intimacy of his flesh inside hers. She raised up and moved forward to straddle his hips, her hand taking hold of him and supervising the joining. She slowly sank onto the shaft, then began a measured, rhythmic undulation in time with the surf — to and fro, in and out, alternately flexing low over him, pausing, then arching straight upright. It was no matter that the man beneath her, filling her, was as familiar as the sun and wind, that the sensations of the coupling had been duplicated a thousand times before. She had always rejoiced in capturing him with her sex, and she did so now.

She watched him. His eyes were closed, his body lost in hers. She tried to will herself the same childlike serenity, but it would not come. Not on this day. Not on L minus one — launch minus one day. On this day, the question was always there to haunt her. *Will this be the last time?*

Unwelcomed, the words once spoken by a wife who had been turned brutally frank by drink, came to her. "Any astronaut's widow will be a national monument, a goddamn shrine. We'd better be prepared to go it alone if we lose our husbands. Men are so insecure. There isn't one of them out there who'll want to fill the shoes of a dead astronaut."

Go it alone. She couldn't imagine it. Financially, Mark's insurance would take care of her, but she could never live without him. The thought was as alien as living under the sea. It was simply not possible. She would die.

Who would need me? The children? She knew it was a joke to believe so. They were twenty-two-year-old adults. The son was a clone of Mark, already training for a life in the sky as an air force fighter pilot. Kathy was just as intense in her quest to become an architect. They didn't need her. They needed nothing more than their dreams. They were so different from her, so identical to Mark. Sometimes she wondered if she had really contributed anything to their creation. Had there been a fluke of nature at the union of egg and sperm that had erased her identity from her progeny? Had her children grown from a molecular helix that bore only Mark's fingerprints? She could believe it.

Alone.

She had visions of being a solitary person for the rest of her life. Even without the stigma of astronaut widow she could see no hope. Her long-time forte, her sex appeal — the single thing that had always made Judy O'Malley unique and desirable and needed — was fading. A glance downward provided ample evidence of that — skin indelibly marked by the stretch of twins, breasts sagging lower.

Please, dearest God in heaven, protect him. Bring him back safely. Make him need me. Make me the most important thing in his life. Make him need me, like he needs the sky, like he needs flight. Make him need me!

As if the prayer was instantly answered, his moaning chant rose to her ears. "Oh, Judy, Judy, Judy, Oh God, don't stop."

She knew it was his climax speaking, but that did not lessen the thrill of the words.

Over and over she stroked him with the wave.

Need me, Mark!

"Please… God." His eyes were closed. The moans rose in his throat and joined the wind.

Need me!

"Judy, I love you."

I have him now!

She stared, defiantly. There, in the distance, stood *Discovery*, shimmering in the heat, a siren ready to beckon.

He's mine. In these moments he's mine and mine alone! You can't have him!

But she knew she was wrong. Deep down, she knew her hold was momentary. Her own body could feel the end nearing, and she shouted to herself to stop. *Keep him forever in this trance! Keep him needing me!*

He gasped and thrust his hips off the towel, and she could feel the contractions of his body gunning the liquid silk into her.

Oh Mark, stay mine!

Her wave ebbed. The moment was over. Her so very brief moment was gone. She knew he would soon fall prey to the seductions of his other, more durable mistress waiting and whispering in the distance.

❖

Tuesday, 30 August
Pentagon

"Can you believe this? There's fifty!" Second Lieutenant Blaine Haswell whispered the number in his friend's ear.

"Fifty what?" Mike Mason, another second lieutenant and NORAD space surveillance analyst, whispered back.

"There're fifty stars in this room! And a coop of chickens."

Mason made a quick count. His friend was right. A constellation of general officers and a crowd of colonels were arrayed around a large oaken table where they awaited the arrival of their boss, Secretary of the Air Force George Casey. The men talked among themselves in low tones, occasionally referring to top-secret documents and a stack of photos. A gallery of their staff officers, of which Haswell and Mason were a part, crowded the back of the room.

"The next time it'll be the Milky Way in here."

Mason wondered if there would be a next time. This was the third meeting on the same subject — military satellite failures. The first had been convened over two months ago at the air force's space division in Los Angeles after three satellites had mysteriously failed within a two-week period. He had been a part of the NORAD contingent — North American Air Defense Command — flown in from Colorado Springs to support the meeting. Then, the conclave had been chaired by a two-star. The fourth, fifth, and sixth failures had gotten the attention of the heavies at the Pentagon and moved the burgeoning council to a three-star's office in that building. Now they were back in the Pentagon, this time in its stratosphere, the secretary's office — floor four, ring E, room 871 by Pentagon cartographers — among more glitter than Mason had seen on his prom night. Haswell was right, he thought. If there was a next time, they'd have a galaxy of stars.

The door opened and Secretary Casey stepped briskly to the front of the room. "Please, gentlemen, take your seats." Though the words were civil, the voice was ice cold. Mason had a feeling he was about to see a demonstration of the old military axiom, *shit flows downhill.*

"Now, what the hell is going on up there!" The shout brought Adam's apples into deep bobs and sweat to palms. "A recce bird... a goddamn, billion-dollar recce bird plays comet on us! This can't continue people, I'm telling you! It can't keep up this way! Nine! The number is *Nine* now! Three nav birds, a weather bird, one early-warning, three communication, and now a recce bird!" He paced behind his chair and ticked off the losses on his fingers. "What the hell is going on? Can somebody please tell me that?"

The question was addressed to no one in particular and no one in particular was eager to field it. The answer had eluded everybody in C Springs, everybody in Los Angeles, and everybody in Washington.

After an uncomfortable silence, the chief of staff of the air force — the senior military officer present — cleared his throat and looked to one of his underlings, Lieutenant General Eckart, commander of Space Division. The man was on the hottest seat, because it was his organization that oversaw the construction of the satellites. "Roger, why don't you fill us in on what you've found."

Mason chuckled to himself. The shit had already rolled down two steps. He wondered how long it would take before the turds fell into the lieutenants' laps.

General Eckart leaned forward to refer to his notes, not because he needed to, but rather to avoid the secretary's glare. "Sir, we have looked at these failures from every possible angle and can find no commonality between them. The affected spacecraft represent the work of five different contractors. The failures occurred in different systems and at different times in the lives of the birds. There were no common lots of microchips or other hardware. There is nothing we can identify that would suggest we have a generic problem in our designs or manufacturing process. Absolutely nothing. All I can say is, it looks as if statistics are playing catch-up with us. We've just run into a streak of bad luck."

"*Luck?!*" Casey struck like lightning at the choice of words. "Last summer I went to the wall with Congress to secure twenty-five billion dollars for your programs! I would have hoped that type of money would buy better *luck*!"

The general cringed at the diatribe. Casey started with another bellow but stopped in midsyllable. He collapsed into his chair, pulled his glasses off, rubbed his eyes, then continued in a strained but controlled voice. "Okay, okay. I'm sorry for that outburst, Roger. I know that your people have been busting their asses looking for an explanation. It's just that Senator Hoffman had *my* ass an hour ago because of this latest loss. Yelling at each other isn't going to fix a goddamn thing. We need to put our heads together on this."

The conciliatory tone relaxed everybody. A few cigarettes appeared, and calming nicotine was hastily inhaled. Casey picked up one of the photos. It was of the reconnaissance satellite film pod. "At least we know this baby didn't die from some defective microchip. What could have done this? What?" His voice trailed off into a whisper as he ran his finger along the blistered scar. Metallurgists had been unable to ID the composition of the impacting particle. The heat of reentry had eradicated the evidence. All they could say was it was not a laser cut or any other form of directed energy wound. The pod had definitely suffered a kinetic impact. He flipped the photo away. "Any ideas, Bill?" He addressed General Bill Griffing, NORAD commander. "Whatever hit the pod almost certainly killed the bird. Could it have been a Soviet attack? Could all of these losses that we've been chasing our tails on be the result of deliberate attacks? Did NORAD see anything out of the ordinary?"

Griffing shook his head. "No, sir. As with all the others, we saw nothing unusual at the time of the recce bird loss. There's nothing to point to the Soviets. Not a thing."

"They couldn't have snuck something in on us?"

"Sir, their anti-satellite capability is extremely crude. They use a large booster that we can detect at lift-off with our early-warning birds. Then, it takes them several orbits to maneuver close enough to a target to kill it. You can't hide that type of activity."

"A ground-based attack?"

"Negative. The bird was over the South Atlantic... near Antarctica when it was hit. In fact, none of the losses have occurred over the Soviet land mass."

"What about a space mine? Suppose the Soviets orbited something earlier and have just been waiting to nail our birds when they pass close by?"

Mason had been working fifteen-hour days to answer the question of object proximity, and he was glad to see that his efforts were not wasted. General Griffing referred to charts he had prepared.

"At the time of the recce-bird failure, the closest object was two hundred and sixty-seven nautical miles away. That was a wrench lost by a shuttle astronaut during a space walk several months back. The nearest Soviet object was the carcass of one of their boosters. It was seven hundred and thirty-two nautical miles distant, nowhere near close enough to be a threat. The nearest *operational* Soviet spacecraft was over two thousand miles away."

"So the Soviets look clean on this?"

"Yes, sir. And on the other failures also. We've done a similar proximity analysis on all of them and haven't found a single threatening conjunction."

"What direction did the object come from?"

General Eckart took the question. "We're still looking into that, but I don't think we'll learn anything. The gouge could have been caused by a ricochet from any direction."

Casey retrieved the photo and studied it again. "Could it have been hit by a meteor?"

The ball was back in Griffing's court. "All of our losses couldn't have been from meteors. But for this particular one, yes, it's a possibility.

Statistically, the chances are remote, but they're not nil. We did check with some astronomers to see if there was any unusual meteor activity in the area. There wasn't. But that doesn't rule out a natural phenomenon as the cause of this loss.

"And there's always the possibility — again, remote — that the hit was from a piece of man-made debris; nut, bolt, washer, wire. There's a lot of junk up there that we can't see with our sensors that could cause this type of damage. So, it could have been natural. It could have been man-made. The only thing I can say with certainty is that the Soviets weren't anywhere near it."

Secretary Casey didn't answer immediately. He was digesting what he had just heard, trying to find a stone unturned. There were none. "Okay. To review the bidding... The Soviets aren't the problem. We may be looking at multiple causes. We could have lost this last bird by an act of God. But the other eight?" He drummed his fingers on the table. "Shit. What about the other eight? God can't be that mad at us." He turned to General Eckart. "Roger, it keeps coming back to the contractors. With the exception of this" — he tapped on the photo — "the finger of blame is pointing directly at contractor error. I want you to go back and hammer on the builders. Get them to go through their drawings with a magnifying glass. And then tell them to do it again. Look at their quality-control programs and see if somebody has dropped the ball there."

"I'll talk with them." General Eckart's shoulders were slumped. He knew that Casey had pulled a punch. Contractor errors were his errors. If there were any, they would end up as logs around a stake, and his career would be tied to the post.

Casey next turned to General Griffing. "Bill, I want you to get your people to double-check those conjunctions. Triple-check them. Be absolutely certain we aren't missing something."

At the comment, Haswell groaned in Mason's ear. "Shit, man. There go our nights and weekends on another fuckin' wild-goose chase."

Mason was unperturbed by the turd that had finally found them. He thrived on challenges. But he agreed with Haswell's lament. In the end, it would be a waste of time. He had helped with the first analysis and would certify it as flawless. There hadn't been anything near any of the dead birds.

Secretary Casey was continuing with his orders. "And also, Bill, see what it would take to get sensors that could see the smaller stuff that's up there. Congress is going to ask that question and I want to be armed with an answer."

"Yes, sir."

The meeting shifted to a discussion of how the remaining spacecraft could be used to cover the gaps created by the losses. Mason paid no attention, instead focusing on the column of words he had jotted on his note pad — *luck, design, construction, microchips, soviets, mines, lasers, ground attack, space attack, meteors, God, junk.* All the words had been scratched through.

Something was wrong. Space had suddenly become very hazardous for American military satellites. Why? What were they missing? His brain climbed aboard the sled of logic and began its flight.

CHAPTER 3

Wednesday, 31 August
Kennedy Space Center, Florida

Judy O'Malley stood in another oven — this one, the roof of the Launch Control Center. It was the focal point of a fierce tropical sun. Rays blazed from a cloudless sky into her face, bounced from the five hundred foot high walls of the Vertical Assembly Building onto her back, and reflected from the white foam roof to broil her from all directions. She was certain they would have all suffocated if it had not been for the moderating effect of the sea breeze.

She and the other wives and their children waited on top of the five story building for *Discovery's* launch. The view was excellent, but that was not the reason NASA had put them there. Rather, it was the isolation the vantage point provided. Here they could be protected from the press — a press they all knew would turn rabid to get the story of the decade, a press that would jump any fence and brush past any guards to record their horror if the most unspeakably hideous things befell their husbands. The five floors of concrete under their feet protected them from the ghouls.

Judy stood alone to one side of the group, prayers flying from her soul — begging, pleading prayers that Mark be protected on this last ride, that *she* be protected. As impossible as it seemed, it was worse this time than in the past. In the Hollywood scripts, didn't the hero always die on his last flight before retirement, on his last combat mission before coming home? Had that happened to some of Mark's friends in Vietnam? Had it happened at Edwards Air Force Base? She couldn't recall any such real-life, last-flight stories, but her brain still would not release the image. It was an incapacitating horror, the cruelest of outcomes — that she could have gotten this close to salvation and have it snatched from her grasp. She begged God for a different script.

In her prayer, she squinted behind sunglasses into the east Florida lowlands. Swamp water glittered among a weave of palmetto, pine, and vine. It was a homogeneous green that made the works of man starkly foreign. Twin tan tracks of gravel, reaching to the limit of Judy's view, bisected the earth with a linearity that nature abhorred. It was the pathway used by the nine million pound land crawler that carried the assembled shuttles to their launch pads. The machine itself was parked a mile distant, appearing as some gargantuan, gray beetle.

Two miles farther to the east was the terminus of the track — pad 39A. Its gray steel scaffolding projected from the sea of green like the upturned bow of a sinking battleship. The prow was streamlined into the air by the rise of a massive white lightning rod whose three hundred foot summit dominated the countryside.

But Judy's focus was on none of this. *Discovery* dazzled and captured. The miles had turned her into something the eye could comprehend. Always, when she had seen the machine close up, it had looked incapable of flight. Nothing so titanic that men working on her appeared as insects, that automobiles and trucks and cranes and water towers were reduced in her shadow to H.O. scale models — nothing so massive could possibly rise from the planet. But, at this distance, she seemed a machine of flight. Her body was sleek, her lines pure, her wings as curved and graceful as those of the gulls soaring overhead. Even her color — sugar-white with spots of black and gray on her nose and wings — seemed an imitation of the creatures of the air. She looked beautiful, benign. But Judy knew otherwise.

"T-minus four minutes and counting. The main engine final purge sequence is underway, and the orbiter flight control surfaces are being moved through a…" The announcer accelerated his dialogue to explain each of the now rapidly passing countdown milestones. The PA system echoed from the VAB walls and blurred the words.

Judy glanced to her right to see how the rest of the wives were bearing up. It was all she could do to keep herself composed, and she had no desire to worry about the others. Still, as the commander's wife, she felt a responsibility. Jackson, Rush, and Pettigrew were the rookies, and her eyes went to their people. If Mary Jackson was feeling the stress, Judy couldn't tell. The woman was too busy trying to explain to her fussy three-year-old daughter and toy-wielding son what was happening with their father. Rush's spouse stood with her adult daughters and the senator's campaign manager. They looked as composed as if their man was going to step forward and deliver an acceptance speech. Pettigrew's friend also looked completely at ease. She had worn shorts and a halter top that had gained her the company of several NASA public relations personnel.

Judy watched her with intense envy. To be sure, her beauty and youth were the dream of most women, but it was not these she coveted. Rather, she longed for her childlike ignorance of the events that were only moments away. She had not the slightest perception of the danger her man was in. Laughing and chattering, she acted as if Pettigrew were pitching in a World Series ball game, instead of being perched atop four million pounds of explosives.

Then, Judy saw *him*. Alone, in the far corner of the viewing area, was Bill Gavin, the astronaut assigned to assist the wives during their stay at the Cape. She noticed he was not smiling. No, he understood what forces were soon to be unleashed. In NASA's jargon, he was designated the Family Escort. But she knew he was more than that. In the event of catastrophe, his title would change to Casualty Assistance Officer. He would be the man who would whisk them from this place to the seclusion of the crew quarters, where they would await word of their husbands' fate. Judy had selected Gavin for this flight and the family escorts for the two missions Mark had previously commanded. Three times she had to do it — pick the men who would escort her into widowhood. She hated it.

"T-minus one minute and counting. The sound-suppression water system has been armed. The hydrogen burn igniters have been armed."

Judy tried to swallow but had no saliva. Her heart shuddered her body, like the deep pounding of some leviathan's machinery. She heard it in her ears and felt it in her neck and chest.

"T-minus thirty seconds. Go for auto sequence start. *Discovery's* computers are now controlling the launch."

"T-minus ten seconds. We have a Go for main engine start."

The hydrogen burn system at the base of the orbiter erupted in a shower of sparks. It was the first visible indication the machine was anything but a granite monument. Judy stopped breathing.

"Nine."

"Eight."

"Seven."

She bit her lip. Eyes glistened.

"Six. We have main engine start."

Clouds of steam rose to hide *Discovery* from view.

"Three, two, one, lift-off! We have a lift-off and *Discovery* has cleared the tower!"

Her brain blocked out the enthusiastic voice that came from the speakers. She needed no translator for the spectacle before her. Her eyes would tell her the truth.

Twin flames, a thousand feet long, rivaling the sun in brilliance, stabbed into her and announced the rise of the colossus. Perfectly cut gems of blue-white shock diamonds formed in the exhaust of the liquid engines and competed for the attention of the eye.

Now, the wave of thunder from the main engines, delayed for fifteen seconds by the distance, finally reached her ears and ripped apart the morning tranquillity.

Screaming, growling, tearing at the sky, as if noise alone was its propelling force, the machine sought the east. Birds took flight in squawking terror, and the sound loosed tongues that had been held mute by the majesty of the moment. Shouts and cheers and applause joined the deafening clamor. The Jackson boy dropped his toy shuttle, held his hands over his ears, and cried. His mother stood fixated on the ascending comet, oblivious to his fear.

Then, just as ears had adjusted to the delayed shriek of the main engines, a second blitzkrieg of shock waves, born of the solid rocket boosters, exploded upon them. The roof heaved. Air was shaken from lungs.

❖

"Roll program, Houston." Mark made the call to Mission Control.

Beautifully poised on a torrent of blue-white fire, the machine executed a perfect pirouette and began a graceful arc to the east.

"Throttle down."

Pettigrew's voice was distorted by the hammering to his body. *Discovery* was accelerating too fast through the thick part of the atmosphere, and her computers commanded a reduction in power to keep her from being torn apart.

"Max q!"

Passing the sound barrier, shock waves danced across the external surfaces and intensified the shaking. The howl of air gripping at the machine permeated the cockpit walls and added to the thunderous din.

"Throttle up."

Full power was again being commanded.

"Eighty thousand feet, two and a half g's."

Mark's call of the g-forces was redundant. Each man felt the increasing heaviness on his chest and labored to inhale against it.

"P-C less than fifty."

A brilliant whip of yellow fire lashed the cockpit windows as the spent solid rockets were pyrotechnically separated. With them went all noise and vibration. They were enveloped in absolute silence. Only the chest-squeezing g-forces hinted at motion.

Mark began to relax. After the chaotic rush of events in the first two minutes, *Discovery* was now in steady-state operation, slowly flattening her trajectory. For the next six minutes, she would run to the east with her liquid engines set at full throttle. It was a comfortable feeling, and he allowed himself a glance away from the instruments. Their pitch attitude was still too high to see any of the Earth, but the sky alone was enough to steal his breath.

Space.

Black.

Total absence of light.

Even though sunlight deluged the cockpit, the sky was darker than any night sky he had ever seen on Earth. *Discovery* had entered her element and taken him to his. He was the addict, and the needle was slipping into his vein. Higher and faster, always higher and faster. *This* was life to Mark O'Malley.

Discovery was gone from sight. A ribbon of white smoke, erratically twisted by the upper-level winds, was all that remained of her passage. At the lower levels, the rocket exhaust had seeded the air with enough particulate to condense a cloud, and a tenuous acid rain fell on the pad. Several of the other spouses lifted sunglasses and brushed away tears. The novices prattled excitedly about the wonder just beheld. A mother attended to her wailing child. The PA speakers echoed word of *Discovery's* sprint.

Judy began to unwind. The noise and fire were gone, and the voice from the speaker was almost sonorous in its numerical cadence. The calls between *Discovery* and Mission Control were equally routine. Wives smelled the scent of success, and their talk resumed an air of casualness. Smiles and laughter reappeared.

It was the wail of a child that interrupted them. Mary Jackson's son had tripped, and now his toy lay in three pieces. The group moved to him, and several of the wives helped in an attempt at consolation. Purses were rifled for gum and candy and the treats offered. But the pacification failed and the crying intensified. In the commotion, Judy found she was the only one of the wives who heard the word.

Her head snapped back and she stared into the black horn of the speaker. *No! Please God, no! I didn't hear it! I didn't! Please! He didn't say it!*

But even as she was making the denials, she could see others — the family escort, the NASA guards, Rush's campaign manager — turning their heads to the speaker. They had heard the word, too.

Malfunction… Malfunction… Malfunction… Malfunction!

God had not spared her.

"…a major malfunction. Booster is looking closely at the status of the other engines."

"We've lost one!" Pettigrew's shout was simultaneous with a warbling alarm and the eye-stabbing, red glare of the main propulsion system warning light.

"Houston, *Discovery!* The left engine has failed!" Mark knew his call would only be confirmation of what the engineers in Mission Control were already seeing. Something terrible had happened in the guts of his machine, and she was now running wounded.

"*Discovery*, Houston! Abort RTLS! Abort RTLS!"

"Roger, Houston! Aborting RTLS!"

"Goddamnit!" It was Mark's blasphemy. The engine failure had occurred too early for them to make an emergency landing in Africa. Instead, they would have to return to Florida — an RTLS, a Return To Launch Site abort. It was a significantly more dangerous procedure than a straight-ahead flight across the Atlantic.

He reached to the right-center of his instrument panel and dialed RTLS on the abort mode switch. Computers ordered an immediate pitch around, an outside loop that pointed them toward Florida and put them in a heads-up attitude. For the next two minutes, *Discovery* would fly backward over the Atlantic, canceling her previously acquired thousands of miles per hour of velocity to the east.

Mark and Pettigrew hurried through the checklist procedures to reconfigure the machine for the flight home. Their eyes were never long from the engine displays. Another failure would be certain death.

"*Discovery*, we see a leak in the center-engine helium system. Switch to the B regulator."

Pettigrew made the change. There was no cockpit discussion on the seriousness of the call. All but Rush knew. The engine propellant pumps required a continuous purge of helium to prevent the formation of an explosive mixture of hydrogen and oxygen. If the purge ceased, *Discovery's* computers would automatically shut down the engine, ending any hope of making a Florida landing. They would be forced to ditch at sea. At the very high glide speeds of the shuttle, a ditch would be a crash.

"Shit!" The marine motioned toward one of the computer displays. "The B reg didn't stop it. We're bleeding helium."

Mark studied the numbers. Pettigrew was right. The helium supply for the center engine would be exhausted well before they were within range of landing.

"Interconnect the center engine to what remains of the left engine supply. After that we can use the pneumatic tanks."

"Yea, we can do that. But that's a big leak. I'm not sure even the extra will last long enough."

As if concurring with the pilot, *Discovery's* computers detected the near depletion of the center-engine helium and flashed a message of the danger. The pilot immediately turned to his right console and activated the switches needed to continue the supply.

"Okay, listen up, everybody. There's a damn good chance we'll have to ditch this thing. I want everybody to be thinking about their emergency escape procedures."

The word *emergency* grabbed Senator Rush like the results of a Gallup poll. The change in the g-forces at pitch-around had terrified him, but he had since taken false comfort in the fact that the tone of the radio conversations between O'Malley and Mission Control gave no hint of any life threatening danger — just a bunch of technical mumbo jumbo. But the word *emergency* liquified his bowels.

Another message from the computers announced that the left engine helium supply was now exhausted. Pettigrew switched to the last remaining source, the pneumatic supply. There was just over a minute remaining to MECO — main engine cutoff.

"We aren't gonna make it!" Pettigrew's eyes were riveted on the numbers. The helium pressure had fallen to fourteen hundred psi. At eleven hundred, the engine would fail.

"Come on, honey… just have a little ways to go." Pettigrew's voice caressed *Discovery* as if she were a woman and would respond favorably to his entreaties. "Only twenty seconds, baby. Just eighteen more. Fifteen seconds and eleven-fifty psi! Hang in there, baby! Twelve seconds and eleven-twenty!"

A warning tone knelled the death of the power plant. Only the right engine remained to push them toward land. Sensing the loss of thrust, *Discovery's* computers calculated the increased time it would now take to get within gliding range of Florida.

"Twenty-one seconds to MECO and only two percent fuel left!"

Again, the pilot tried to verbally entice the dying beast into giving more than the green numbers said was possible. "Hold on, sweetheart. Fourteen seconds, one percent. A little longer… eleven seconds, one percent. Come on, goddamnit, come on! …MECO!"

Fuel exhaustion ended powered flight. They were now riding a quarter million pound glider three hundred miles from the nearest runway.

"Nine seconds short! Put on your swimsuit!"

A loud thump sounded through the cockpit as the massive fuel tank was explosively separated. At last, free of all the encumbrances of her propellant system, *Discovery* soared gracefully clean on the fringes of space, fifty-seven miles over the Atlantic.

The absolute silence and weightlessness that came with engine shutdown was a new terror to Rush. He had the sensation that they were falling — which they were. The change jerked a short, involuntary scream from his throat.

Mark winced at the sound. It was primordial. "Hang on, Vern. We'll get you back." He did his best to calm the politician but suspected that his own voice revealed a personal his gut-level terror. "Just stay quiet down there and think about your egress procedures."

"Sure glad I didn't quit smoking," Pettigrew amended the comment.

Mark glared at his pilot. There was not a trace of fear on the man's face. He wondered if staring at death for two years in a Vietnam prison had done that to him — inoculated him against fear.

He returned to his instruments. The last race of the day had begun — distance versus altitude. Mark wondered which he would run out of first.

The need to see for themselves was so overpowering that none of the wives made a move to the television-equipped offices below. The runway was only a mile to the west — behind them, hidden by the VAB walls. But to reach it, *Discovery* would have to fly out of the east and through their view. They had to see that. No other eyes could be trusted to tell them, no television camera. They had to see. If their husbands ultimately lived, it would only be because the machine was able to fly past them to that cement. It was an oasis of life. Any other scenario was death.

The fact the broadcasts between Mark and Mission Control had become emotionless did nothing to reassure Judy. On so many occasions she had overheard astronaut conversations on the dangers of any aborted launch. When beer had brought out the bravado, they had laughingly joked at their simulation training on abort flying, bastardizing the official NASA lesson plan title of *Ascent Skills* to *Ascent Kills*. Those recollections, and now words that were unknown to past missions — *off nominal, low on energy, negative margin* — combined to terrify her.

Oh, Jesus! Her eyes had inadvertently touched on the small knot of men. Bill Gavin was no longer the only astronaut on the roof. She recognized two others in his company. Like evil specters, they hung in the background. She attempted to deceive herself that they were only there to watch the landing, but she knew otherwise. They were reinforcements, brought from downstairs to help console five new widows. She tried to turn away from them but could not. Their arms were folded across their blue flight coveralls, the sun flashing from their aviator glasses. They looked out of place, embarrassed, staring at their feet, at the sky — *anywhere* — but at Judy and the other wives.

Then, two nearly simultaneous explosions ripped through the gathering. The sound echoed off the VAB wall and hammered them a second time in undiminished fury.

"Oh, God, no! Jesus, God, no! It can't be!" Beth Persley's shout mixed with similar exclamations from other wives. Judy wanted to scream, but air would not leave her lungs. Her head snapped to the astronauts. Staring upward to the east, they appeared unaffected by the noise and made no move to gather the families.

"The sounds of *Discovery's* sonic booms have just been heard at the Kennedy Space Center." The announcer continued with an update of the shuttle's flight conditions.

It was finally too much. Judy lost control and broke into a childlike cry.

❖

Discovery passed twenty-five miles altitude, slowly leveling her nose to the horizon, slowly changing from a spaceship to an aircraft. In the denser atmosphere, the wind noise permeated the cabin in an imitation of a speeding subway. The braking effect of the aerodynamic friction squeezed the crew into their seats. Sweat, which had been trapped under his helmet in the zero gravity fall from MECO, now found its way over Mark's face. He gloved it off.

The nose dropped enough to allow a view from the forward windows and Mark studied it. The ocean dominated the colors. A swath of deep-water blue marked the Gulf Stream, and a filigree of turquoise defined the shallows. Between these, a mid-depth green covered the continental shelf. The curve of the earth was still very much in evidence, and above it, a hazy blue horizon was thickening and pushing the black of space toward zenith.

He could see across the Florida peninsula and into the Gulf of Mexico. The only clouds were well inland — a scattering of popcorn cumulus. Not much had gone right for the day, but at least God had blessed them with perfect landing weather.

"Seventy thousand feet. Thirty-two miles. At ten thousand feet, if it appears we can't make the runway, I'm gonna turn back to the southeast and ditch into the wind. Bob, you blow the overhead hatch just before we hit the water."

"Roger."

"JJ, as soon as motion stops, help Vern."

"Roger that."

"And vice versa for you, Vern… help JJ if he needs it."

"Rog… Roger." The politician's reply was fear-stuttered.

"That goes for all of you. Help each other to the extent at which your own lives are threatened, then get out." It was the most useless order he had ever given. When the motion stopped, they'd all be dead.

"Thirty-five thousand feet. Seventeen miles. We've gained a little, Mark."

"Yea. Probably from the tail wind." But it wouldn't be enough, was his next thought. From a thousand landings in the shuttle training aircraft, he knew that at this altitude they should be within eight or nine miles of the runway, not seventeen.

Mission Control transmitted a last *good luck*.

"I'm gonna be a real critic on this landing, Mark. Just remember, better dead than look bad."

The comment brought a smile to Mark's lips. The world was watching, and the fighter pilot's ego demanded that when there was an audience, it would be better to die than fuck up.

"Seven miles, seventeen thousand feet." Pettigrew began the last countdown.

The cockpit turned pungent with the scents of four sweating men. Adrenaline choked Mark's arteries and made his eyes and hands electrically quick.

"Thirteen thousand feet at six miles."

"Eleven thousand feet, five miles, two hundred knots."

Mark considered his options. The decision had to be made now. Either abandon the approach, circle into the wind, and ditch, or attempt to stretch the glide to the runway. If the stretch failed, a crash on the land would certainly tear the vehicle apart and probably be explosive. There were thousands of pounds of propellant still remaining in *Discovery's* internal tanks and tons of solid rocket fuel in the payload booster that was locked in the cargo bay. His eyes darted from the instruments to the swath of concrete. Like a mirage, it seemed to stay just out of reach. The sea tempted him with its glassy smoothness.

"I'm pressing for the runway." The decision was irreversible. "Bob, I'm gonna stay at two hundred. Hold off on the gear 'till I call for it. If it looks like we're gonna crash short, blow the hatch."

"Copy. Five thousand feet. Radar altimeter is in. Three miles, one-ninety-seven knots."

Flying the shortest distance to the field had kept them on a forty-degree angle to the runway. Mark intended to intercept the imaginary extension of the strip only a half mile from the threshold. It would mean a steep right turn only seconds before the touchdown flare. In the turn, the descent rate would increase further.

"Three thousand feet, two miles, two hundred knots."

Helicopters hovered on the far side of the runway, and fire trucks idled near the approach end.

"A thousand feet, one mile, one-ninety-eight."

"Arm the gear."

Pettigrew reached to his instrument panel and depressed the first of two push buttons that were required to lower the wheels.

They were twenty seconds from landing. Mark started his right turn and allowed the nose to drop to maintain airspeed.

"Seven hundred feet, two-o-three."

"Six hundred, airspeed's good."

In his peripheral vision, Pettigrew saw the ground reaching for their right wing.

"Five hundred, two-o-five."

"Four hundred, two-o-five."

Mark translated the information into ever finer stick inputs. He gulped air like a marathoner.

"Three hundred feet, two hundred knots."

He rolled the wings level and panicked. Forward, a swamp stretched to the ten foot rise of a dike. Beyond that was a grass surface leading to a concrete underrun, chevroned in yellow — a warning to pilots that it was not stressed for landing. Its rough surface covered the last thousand feet before abutting the usable runway.

"Two hundred feet, two-o-five."

Pettigrew's left index finger hovered over the remaining landing gear button. Mark held his call. Yards were going to matter, and once the wheels were deployed, the increased drag would reduce their gliding range.

"It's gonna be close, Mark!"

Not yet! Not yet! Not yet! Wait! Wait!

"Gear!"

Instantly, Pettigrew depressed the button that released the gear doors. The wheels folded downward, the cockpit indicators changing from "UP" to a barber-poled transition state.

"One hundred feet, one-ninety-eight knots."

"Come on, gear! Goddamnit, come on!" There were no supplications this time — Pettigrew ordered the machine. But the indicators seemed to have frozen in transition, while the altitude tape rapidly approached the color division that marked "Ground."

"Thirty feet."

"Twenty feet, two hundred knots."

The dike shot past. Grass replaced swamp. Mark braced for a wheels-up landing. There was nothing he could do to keep *Discovery* airborne.

"Gear's down!"

At the first syllable of the shout, the wheels touched. Landing was on the grass, sixty-two feet short of the cement underrun. There was still sufficient lift on the wings to keep the tires from sinking more than six inches into the earth. But the depression was deep enough to turn the lip of approaching concrete into a small cliff. The wheels hit it with a loud thump, and the vehicle wallowed sickeningly as the port-side tires exploded in the abuse.

An alarm tone warbled. Pettigrew read the message and shouted the warning. "Hydraulic system one is gone! You don't have any nose-wheel steering!"

There was another lurch as the wounded beast finally bumped onto the main runway. Mark was amazed that the gear had not collapsed. The drag on the port side blowouts was rapidly turning the starboard wing forward. Two hundred and thirty-thousand pounds of machine was headed off the concrete at one hundred and thirty knots. He jammed down on the right wheel brake. Another loud thud in the cockpit signaled the explosive destruction of the two right tires. *Discovery* vibrated heavily as the wheel rims were consumed in friction with the cement. He ignored the metallic groaning. Whatever happened on the runway had to be preferable to a departure from it.

"You've got it, Mark!" There were other cheers and screams from Persley and Austin. The nose was yawing straight. Their speed was slowing rapidly, and miraculously they were still supported on landing gear. With all the grace of a crashing skier, *Discovery* shuddered to a smoking stop.

"Houston, *Discovery*. Wheel stop." The standard call of mission end seemed ludicrous, but habit brought it from Mark's mouth.

He looked at the clock — twenty-four minutes since launch. In less time than it took most people to commute to work, they had flown five hundred miles to the east, attained an altitude of fifty-seven miles, landed a wounded monster on a patch of grass, and most remarkably, had lived to talk about it.

❖

Wednesday, 31 August
Cheyenne Mountain, Colorado

Lieutenant Haswell fell into line with the other military and civilian employees who were shuffling forward to present credentials to flak-vested, armed guards and then be passed beyond the chain link, concertina-topped fence. Conversations were loud and excited, unusual for 6:45 A.M. on a Hump Day. But the amazing flight of *Discovery* was on everybody's lips. The morning news shows had broken in on their regular broadcasts to cover the drama, and most of the country had watched it with shaving cream drying on their faces or coffee growing cold on the table.

The workers climbed aboard a relic of an air force bus, and it wheezed past a set of massive, one hundred ton, reinforced concrete blast doors and into the cavern aperture. Except for the paved roadway and steel netting hammered into the ceiling to catch falling rocks, the tunnel was an unfinished archway of ragged chunks of black, Colorado granite. In some places the stone glistened with the seepage of ground water. As always, Haswell felt a little claustrophobic at the thought that eighteen hundred feet of rock towered over his head and there was no apparent reason why it shouldn't come crashing down.

Several hundred yards inside the mountain, the bus squealed to a stop, and the forty passengers filed from it. The lieutenant suffered the transitional shiver of entering sixty-degree air and anticipated a cup of warming coffee. The office wouldn't warm him. That was kept cooler yet for the computers.

The group dispersed among the three high rise buildings that filled the central cavity. Haswell strode toward his building with the same indifference that a veteran coal miner might show to his familiar surroundings. But it had been much different on his first day. Then, he had almost walked into walls, his head had been on such a swivel. High rise buildings underground! And not only that, they were supported on barrel-sized steel coils designed to absorb the tremors from Soviet hydrogen bombs. There had been other wonders, like an underground lake of diesel fuel for the backup generators. Maintenance men actually navigated that in rowboats, giving rise to the claim that the air force had the highest navy in the world. Throughout his first day on the job, he had shaken his head in disbelief and muttered at least a hundred times, "Amazing! Simply, fucking amazing."

Now, it was just a job — just a seven-to-four job, like any other. He corrected himself in that thought. After yesterday's Pentagon meeting, it would probably be a seven-to-eleven job — eleven at night. The secretary wanted answers fast. The generals wanted them faster. The colonels wanted them fastest. And the majors wanted them yesterday.

He walked the stairs to the third floor office, opened the door, and squinted his dark-adapted eyes against the glare of the fluorescent lighting. It didn't surprise him to find Mason hacking away at a computer terminal. The man was always in the office early, typically doing something illegal with a couple billion dollars of Uncle Sam's equipment. If he didn't go to prison first, Haswell was certain that Mason would end up being the CEO of IBM or some other computer giant. Nobody understood hardware and software better than Mike Mason — nobody.

Haswell poured himself a cup of coffee, then walked to his friend. "Did you see that space shuttle launch, Mike?"

"Didn't see it but heard it on the radio driving up." Mason replied without stopping his work on the keyboard. "Wonder what happened to their engines?"

"Maybe a meteor hit them." Haswell laughed at his own joke. "Whatever happened, at least we won't have to worry about *that* failure.

Nothing orbits at forty miles, so nobody will be asking us to run a conjunction analysis. Jesus, those guys were lucky. When they were turning for landing, I thought the wing tip was going to hit the ground. It was that close." Haswell peered over Mason's shoulder at the computer screen. "What are you doing, now? Stealing ones and zeros from some bank?"

"Not hardly." A last keystroke filled the screen with text, and Mason slid back in his chair to give Haswell a better view. "There. Take a look."

The new arrival accepted the invitation, his eyes growing enormous with each sentence. "What the fu——?" It was a page of want ads — very special want ads.

Heterosexual couple enjoys watching other heteros. No swapping, just watching. Reply AZ4489.

Twenty-eight-year-old homo twins would like to see you COMING AND GOING. Reply NY6934.

Thirty-two-year-old, white, female trisexual seeks other trisexuals for a long-term, meaningful relationship. Reply MI1048.

Eighteen-year-old, white female with Rin-Tin-Tin fetish will give your German Shepherd a very nice home. Only BIG, well-behaved males need apply. Reply FL7520.

"What the fuck is this?"

"An electronic sex bulletin board. See anything you like?"

Haswell continued to stare in open-mouthed wonder. "How did you do this?"

"Easy. All it takes is a modem and a long distance access. Another hacker had the number on a game bulletin board. I was looking for a quick chess match and saw this instead."

Haswell still could not pull his eyes from the smorgasbord of kinky sex.

"Mike, when that phone bill comes up on your line, Major Jake is gonna shit! You'll never be able to explain it. You'd better terminate right now."

"It won't come up against my phone."

"It won't? Why not?"

"It's charged to Major Jake's office."

"Major Jake's! Jesus Christ, Mike! Are you fuckin' nuts?"

"Hey, not to worry. That was the fun part of this thing... breaking into the file of long distance access codes, using my modem and his number. There's no way anybody will ever be able to trace the call to this office."

Major Jacobson had yet to learn that one of his workers was an intractable hacker, a genius — a man in overdrive, born into a world in low gear. There were few challenges equal to Mason's talents — certainly not his current job, which was to oversee the use of satellite tracking computer programs written by slothful contractor personnel. His constant, illegal tampering was an escape from the boredom. If the air force couldn't give him a challenge, he would create his own, just as he had done at MIT. There, he had breezed through the computer science courses on his way to a summa cum laude graduation. His professors had been joyous to see him go. It had been like having Isaac Newton as a calculus student.

Haswell now relaxed in a perusal of the bulletin board. If Mason said there was no way to trace the call, then there wasn't.

"What the fuck's a trisexual?"

"I don't have a clue. Want me to call her?" Mason scooted back to the keyboard as if he was going to pull the freak right out of the machine.

"No! Fuck no! Don't get in a goddamn conversation with those weirdos. That's all we need… have one of them calling Jake's office asking to speak to the trisexual." Both men enjoyed the vision. "Would you look at that one… *a Rin-Tin-Tin fetish!* I'll bet she's a real dog." Haswell cracked himself up. "Can you get pictures on this screen?"

"You want to see a German Shepherd?" Now it was Mason's turn to laugh at his own wit.

"No, not the fuckin' dog! The woman."

"The technology isn't there yet. Give it another couple years, then we can see what a trisexual and a woofer fetish look like." A chirp from the computer turned Mason serious again, and he went head down to play the keyboard. The adult entertainment was purged from the screen.

"Hey! I wasn't finished reading."

"Sorry. That was just a little time killer I was playing with. I've got something serious cooking on the main frame."

"Like what?"

"Like trying to figure out what's happening to our military satellite fleet."

"You checking those conjunctions?"

"No. I'm looking at things from a different angle." The screen filled with prompts from the main NORAD computer, and Mason sorted through them.

Haswell noticed "Priority Access" flashing on the top line. "Who gave you that?"

Mason's only answer was a conspiratorial smile.

"Never mind. I don't want to know. That way I can't be called to testify against you at your court-martial."

"Not to worry, Blaine. Not to worry. The priority access was authorized by Major Jake. He just doesn't know that he authorized it."

"Wonderful. So what's this new angle?"

"The only thing that we know for certain is that the recce bird took a kinetic hit."

"Roger on that."

"Well, let's assume that all the others were similarly hit."

"A very big assumption."

"Yea, but for argument's sake, let's just believe it."

"Okay, Sherlock. I'm believing it. What's the new angle?"

"Suppose the Soviets are shooting at us?"

"Shit, Mike. Were you asleep yesterday? That death-ray angle was beaten into the dirt."

"Yea, but the assumption was that the threat had to be on the ground or in a relatively close orbit. What if it's a long-range, space-based threat?"

"Come on. That's bullshit. Our sensors could see something like that."

"I agree. If it's there, we're tracking it. It's that we just don't *know* we're tracking it."

"Man, you need some sleep."

"No, listen, Blaine. Suppose whatever it is rides piggyback on one of their other satellites or is disguised as a piece of junk. Shit… They've got, what? Two hundred functioning military birds, a couple hundred more supposedly dead ones, plus a hundred civilian types, plus a couple hundred or so wasted boosters tumbling around up there."

"Yea, that's about right."

"Okay. Any one of those could be the death ray, as you call it."

"Yea, you just said it. *Any one* could be… *any one* of a thousand objects. How do you intend to find *the* one? You don't know if it can shoot from a thousand miles away or has to be within five miles."

"I don't have to know that. Let's assume if it's there, it has to be within line of sight of the target."

"So?"

"So, if we look at the instantaneous position of each Soviet satellite at the time of each of our failures *and* find there was *one* satellite that was within line of sight on every occasion of a failure, what does that tell you?" Mason answered his own question. "It tells you that either there was one hell of a coincidence out there *or*... a death ray."

The computer demanded attention with another chirp, and Mason typed more instructions.

Haswell continued his challenge. "Mike, do you realize how long it'll take that machine to test your theory against every Soviet spacecraft? I'll bet at least a couple hours. There's no way you can hide that much CPU time. Major Jacobson will crucify you."

"It's only going to take about ten minutes. I'm not looking at every Red bird. I'm assuming the same bird killed all nine of ours, so there's obviously no reason to consider any spacecraft launched after our first loss. And if there *is* something threatening, it would have to be fairly large, so I didn't look at anything under ten thousand pounds. Those criteria cut the list way down."

The computer called again, and Mason ordered a hard-copy output. A high-speed printer began to screech out the data — for each American satellite loss, a list of line-of-sight threats.

"There... look! *KOSMOS* 1995, 2034, and 2041 all repeat for the first three failures!"

Haswell's skepticism began to soften, and he leaned closer to watch subsequent listings. There were seven candidates for the fourth American loss and ten for the fifth.

"2034 is still common!" Mason's excitement was growing.

"So is 1995. 2041 isn't listed for either."

The data for the sixth American casualty appeared.

"Shit! 1995 didn't come up." Forgetting the enormous threat a repeating number could represent, Haswell cursed as if he had just missed a bingo.

"There!" The exclamation, in duet, signaled the repeat of *KOSMOS*

2034 for the seventh loss.

"You may have really found something, Mike! I wonder what the hell 2034 is?"

More hard copy on losses eight and nine scrolled off the machine and ended the excitement. *KOSMOS* 2034 was not on either list. The computer had answered Mason's question. No single Soviet asset had been in direct line of sight of every failed American satellite at the time of each failure. The exercise had been the proverbial wild-goose chase.

"Nice try, Mike. Thought you really had something there." Haswell stretched in an expansive yawn, then turned for his own desk. "Call me if you bring up that bulletin board again."

Mason did not hear his friend's request. He remained at the printer, staring at the data. Where had he erred? Maybe the assumption that the same satellite killed everything was wrong. Maybe there were multiple threats. Maybe there was a combination of ground and space based threats. How could he ever sort through that? Maybe there was no threat at all.

Then what is happening up there?

CHAPTER 4

Thursday, 1 September
Houston, Texas

Sitting alone at the breakfast table, Judy sipped at a cup of coffee and watched the dawn. *September*, she thought. In Albuquerque, the morning air would already be cool and crisp with the hint of fall. People would be searching their closets for sweaters. The sun would appear blindingly stellar in an azure sky. But in a Houston September, the only hint in the air was of more tropical humidity and Saharan heat. Sweaters were months from being functional, and the low sun was so muted by the water vapor that it could be watched without so much as a squint. Judy fixated on it. In a hollow-eyed stare, she watched the dirty yellow disk rise above the backyard trees.

The coffee was slowly helping her recovery. She couldn't remember ever having been more wasted. Even the labor of the twins had not punished her as yesterday had. Nerve endings had been so scorched by the high tension and sustained fear that even speech and walking had been difficult. Like a mother who had just witnessed a car narrowly miss her child, she could not celebrate Mark's safety. Death's close approach had left her too weak.

And the short night had offered no relief. Every time she had closed her eyes, the final minute of *Discovery's* landing had played in her mind — the gasps from the astronauts as the spacecraft had first appeared over the beach, their disbelief at its low altitude, the prayers and curses screamed as the machine seemed to almost brush their heads, the shrieks from the wives as Mark had made his final turn and the wing had appeared certain to hit the trees, the panicked stampede to the roof edge to see the touchdown, and the agony of that view being blocked by the VAB wall. She could still hear the tortured wail of confused children abandoned by mothers mad with fear, the chaos of shouted demands for silence so the final outcome could be heard from the PA speakers, the announcer's jumbled words that hinted at disaster — *Landing short! Debris! Hydraulic failure! Flames! Smoke!* — and the distant sirens and the urgent rush of fire trucks and rescue helicopters. Whenever her eyes had closed, the insanity of the roof had immediately come to torture her.

She returned her attention to the morning paper and its front page photo of Mark and Pettigrew. *Astronaut Heroes!* proclaimed the caption. The men had their arms around each others' shoulders, like running mates for some political office, and each was giving an exuberant thumbs up. The picture had been taken at Ellington Field, where they had arrived to a tumultuous welcome by several thousand Space Center employees and friends. Judy suspected their embracing pose was not so much an exhibition of professional camaraderie as an attempt by each to keep from falling drunk on their faces. They, and the rest of the crew, had returned to Houston with their spouses in the Gulfstream jets which, thanks to a flight surgeon's prescription for tranquilizing beverages, had been stocked with beer. Mark and Pettigrew had almost single-handedly emptied the cooler on their aircraft.

She had been astounded by their celebration, expecting instead to see them ashen-sober, as she and the other women had been. But, in the reunion with the men at the crew quarters, only Rush and Persley had seemed to appreciate they had escaped death by the slimmest of margins. Those two had been bloodless white and shaking. Rush had even needed assistance in walking. Mark and Pettigrew, on the other hand, had entered screaming with excitement, spraying each other with cans of beer that someone had already passed to them. They had looked like ball players in a locker room celebrating a Super Bowl win, not men who had just felt the breeze from death's scythe.

She stared at the newspaper photo and saw herself — or, rather, only her left shoulder. The rest of her body had been cropped out of the picture. The exclusion piqued her, not because she craved a spotlight, but because she was struck by the metaphor of the editor's work. *Cropped out. You don't count — to anybody. Not really. Not with Mark, not with the children, and not even with the* Post *editor.*

She dwelled on that thought, spiraling deeper into an exhausted self-pity.

What am I doing? It's over. Mark survived. I survived. I should be screaming my joy. Never, never again will I have to stand on the LCC roof! It's through! Done! This is the first dawn of a new life!

The irony struck her — that Mark's astronaut career had even reached from beyond its end to steal the moment she had long anticipated would be one of the happiest of her life. She turned back to the sun and tried to slap herself into celebration by imagining what a sunrise in Los Angeles would look like, what the September air would feel like. But the diversion was unsuccessful. Her brush with widowhood, with terminal loneliness, with the living form of death had just been too close.

Finally, her eye caught sight of two mockingbirds that had found the remnants of a cheese ball on the patio table and were greedily attacking it. Their scavenging awoke her to the outdoor mess.

Yesterday, when they had returned to the house, neighbors and friends had followed to toast Mark's heroics. They had done so in grand style, and the homecoming had stretched into the early morning hours. She had been surprised by the abandon of the revelry. The media had rightfully branded the mission an expensive failure and was already searching for responsible parties. The shuttle would be grounded while the cause of the engine failures was investigated. She would have expected any gathering of NASA employees would have been subdued by that fact. But, as one friend had explained to her, Johnson Space Center had reason to celebrate. They had developed and validated the RTLS procedures and had trained the crew and mission controllers to fly it. While there might be a lengthy delay to shuttle operations, most of JSC could pride itself in having saved the crew and, in all likelihood, the entire shuttle program. It was cause for congratulations, and those had been exchanged throughout the night. The last of the self-invited guests had departed only three hours earlier.

She finished her coffee, poured a fresh cup into an insulated mug, then grabbed a garbage sack and headed for the yard. A litter of beer cans and paper plates was awaiting the first breeze to fly into the pool. She began the pickup, thinking that at least the house was sold so the disorder inside could wait. She included Mark among that wreckage. He was asleep, or, more descriptively, passed out. It was definitely not a morning she would have liked to have prepared for a troop of prospective home buyers.

The cleanup was done in ten minutes, but that was more than enough time for her to sweat through her robe. The pool glimmered a cooling invitation, and she was tempted to accept. The fenced backyard had ample privacy, and the gate was locked. The neighbors worked, and their children were in school. The only sound was the hum of a subdivision of air conditioners.

What the hell! If I can chance NASA security patrols, I can chance a meter reader.

Placing her coffee at the pool edge, she dropped her robe and dived, nude, into the water. It was hardly cooler than the air, but the difference was enough to refresh her. She glided through several easy laps. She often swam naked at night, but this daylight session was a first. Contrary to what Mark thought, she had a strong sense of modesty. She had enjoyed the rare thrill of trapping him in outdoor sex, but she knew she would have died of embarrassment had she ever been observed.

She stopped the laps and reconfirmed her privacy. The two mockingbirds had taken opposing positions on the fence line and were trading songs — a guarantee no servicemen were preparing to vault onto her isolated beach. She pulled herself into a floating chaise, grabbed her coffee, and paddled into the shade. The swim had been a superb idea. She felt more alive than she had anytime in the past twenty-four hours. At least she had escaped the whirlpool of depression that had been sucking at her twenty minutes ago. Even a glance at her body buoyed her spirits. Her weight was down, probably below one hundred and five pounds. Waiting for Mark to be exploded into space had not been conducive to a hearty appetite.

She dallied until the coffee was gone, then pushed off the chair and swam to her robe. The cool wet had uncoiled her enough that a restful nap now seemed possible, and she returned to the bedroom. Mark was in the same repose in which she had left him nearly an hour ago — sprawled on his back on top of the sheets. She doubted he would move for many hours, his alcohol-induced slumber was that deep.

Coming to the bed, she knelt on the floor next to him, seeking a final assurance of his safety before reattempting sleep. Her hand came to his chest and rested there, his skin feeling especially warm against her pool-chilled flesh. The sweetness of alcohol scented his exhalations, and for a minute she was hypnotized by the steady rise and fall of his chest — proof of life. It wasn't a dream. He had survived.

In her idyll, her hand moved onto his belly and absently toyed with the fringes of his thick pubic hair. She savored the feeling — coarse and soft at the same time, like a pile of autumn leaves.

His penis lolled to one side, as if it, too, was in exhausted slumber, and she reached with her index finger to gently pet its blanched peak. Though she had no sexual intent in the action, the flesh awakened, slowly pushing from its collar and dragging across his inner thigh in an arc toward his belly. The response surprised her. She had assumed the drunk had rendered him temporarily impotent.

It was a novelty for her to so closely witness his erection. There had been countless times she had felt the flesh stiffen in her hand or against her leg or belly, but she had never actually watched that miraculous transformation.

Its growth stalled, and a slow contraction began. She repeated her caress, this one causing Mark to stir. He mumbled incomprehensible words, and his outstretched arm twitched, then fell still. She resumed petting the dragon, and it answered her touch with a stretch in the direction of his navel, then lifted, full and stone hard, from his belly. The dome was so tight its surface formed a ruddy mirror and dully reflected the image of the rotating ceiling fan. The spectacle filled her with a sense of feminine power — that with an almost imperceptible touch, she could command his body.

She watched the monolith, wondering how many other women felt as she did. Was *this* as important to them as it was to her? She thought of her many friends — astronaut wives — who had made careers for themselves. They were lawyers, dentists, doctors, real estate agents. Some were NASA employees and could claim their share of the glory of putting America — their husbands — into space. Others had achieved moderate levels of success in the arts as painters and musicians. One had even published a book of poetry. Sometimes it seemed to her she was the only one who really needed her husband for fulfillment.

Do they rejoice, as I do, when they harden their men?

She could not believe it. She was different, deficient. She depended on her sex and beauty to arouse a transient need within a man who really had no wants beyond the sky.

The leaden thoughts that had been with her at the breakfast table had crept past her guard to again weigh her. She squeezed her eyes shut and vowed to cast them off. It was a new day, a new life, and she would close the door on the past.

She rose, kissed *both* of Mark's heads, then climbed into the bed. A deep, refreshing sleep took her.

❖

Friday, 2 September
Cheyenne Mountain, Colorado

"So, what's up with the world's greatest hacker?" Haswell placed his lunch tray on the table and took a seat next to Mason. The men had been separated for a day and a half. Another lieutenant had called in sick, and Haswell had been asked to assume the absentee's duties in the Intelligence Division. "Have any new angles on our problem?" He pointed his fork upward to more clearly define the problem he had in mind.

"No, I've given up on that. I modified my program to try and make some sense out of the repeaters — the ones that were listed more than three times — but it was a bomb. Didn't tell me a thing. I just can't see any Soviet connection. And I don't have any time to screw around with it. Those conjunctions are a time sink."

"How far have you gotten?"

"We finished number seven this morning. Eight and nine ought to be done by this evening. If not then, tomorrow for sure."

"Shit! Another Saturday down the tubes." Haswell's temporary duty ended that evening. He would have to rejoin the conjunction-analysis team for any weekend work.

Mason peeled open a carton of milk and filled his glass. "So, how are things in Intelligence?"

"Same-o, same-o… trying to figure our what Ivan is up to. They launched number eighty-seven this morning. You know, that's a record pace for the commies. They sure don't have any budget problems. They've launched eighty-seven satellites for the year, and we've launched six… no, seven."

Everyone working in the Mountain was familiar with the robust Soviet space program, which averaged a hundred satellite launches a year. Mason did the mental arithmetic to calculate that the current year pace would mean one hundred and twenty launches. Haswell was right — a new record.

"What was this morning's bird?"

"Intell isn't sure yet. Looks like a geosync communicator. Chile reported seeing an apogee kick motor fire. They sure must have a lot of pay TV with all the transponders they've been putting up."

"What do you mean?"

"This garlic bread is great." Haswell stuffed his mouth with a piece, then talked around it. "Well, what I mean is, the Intell folks were telling me that the Soviet record launch rate has been due mostly to an increase in communication relay satellites... four or five more than they did in all of last year."

"Maybe they've finally found the ultimate weapon to keep their people pacified... two hundred channels of TV to watch. That ought to turn their brains to mush."

"Or, maybe something is shooting down *their* spacecraft? Hey, did you ever think of that, wonder boy? An alien spacecraft, sporting a death ray, is sweeping the heavens clean of our birds *and* theirs." Haswell knocked over the salt shaker with his fork. "Zap, there goes an American recce bird." The pepper shaker was his next target. "Zap, a *KOSMOS* takes it in the shorts. Yea, I like that theory. Maybe there're some butter-bars over there having their Saturdays screwed for them by some Major Jakeski. We're all on snipe hunts."

Mason laughed at his friend's imagination. "And how many people in Intell subscribe to your flying saucer theory?"

"Just thought of it. I'll have to go back and tell them. But I'll bet they stick with their own theory. You know how it is, Mike, great minds are never appreciated."

"Yea, especially great lieutenant minds. So, what's their theory?"

"Well, today's best guess is that these extra birds are taking up the slack for transponder failures on their *KOSMOS* 2069 platform. They all head straight for it... same spot in the sky."

"Straight for 2069?"

"Yea, that's their big comm relay platform that was supposed to consolidate most of their geosync transponders in the western hemi-sphere... cut down on the congestion and clean up the frequency interference. Intell thinks that it's a very sick bird. The commies shouldn't have had to launch any supplemental free flyers for a decade if that thing was working right. Yes, sir, 2069 is another fine product from the worker's paradise… a piece of shit that broke after only a couple million miles on the road. All these other launches, Intell says, are to fill the comm gaps in TV and telephone and recon satellite data relay. Not to mention that 2069 is also the primary comm relay for the Soviet Pacific Fleet. All their subs get target info from that bird. They can't allow it to go tits up."

"Sounds better than your UF…" Mason abruptly stopped.

Haswell looked up from his pasta. "What's wrong?"

"Blaine, what's the parking longitude of 2069?"

"I don't recall exactly. Just off the west coast of South America. Over the Galapagos Islands, I think. Why?"

"I wonder if it would have been in line of sight of that recce bird?"

For a few seconds, Haswell was bewildered by the question. Then he remembered who he was talking to — a guy whose brain held onto something like a pit bull terrier held onto a leg. "Mike, I know what you're thinking and it's bullshit — Bullshit with a capital B." He lectured him with his fork.

"My program didn't look at geosync birds. I needed to cut down on the CPU time, and I figured anything that far away couldn't be a threat, so I didn't include them in the search."

"And you can bet your ass nothing at that distance *is* a threat. Jesus, Mike, that's *twenty-two fuckin' thousand miles away*… a hell of a long way off to be nailing a recce bird that's at eighty miles altitude."

"Yea. Yea, you're probably right." Mason mulled over the idea a moment longer. There would be no better place to park a weapon than geosync. And "park" was the functional word. Satellites at twenty-two thousand miles above the earth's equator orbited at exactly the earth's rotational speed. They were geosynchronous, parked at the same spot in the sky. The phenomenon was a boon to the communications industry, because geosync spacecraft acted like stationary electronic mirrors and reflected signals to any spot in the hemisphere that they viewed.

But a weapon at geosync! If it could be done, what a field of fire it would have! An entire hemisphere! But how could it be done? What kind of weapons could shoot across twenty-two thousand miles?

Mason considered the questions. For lasers and other directed-energy weapons that fired at the speed of light, the distance was trivial. Their beams would span the gap in a mere tenth of a second — if such weapons existed, which Mason doubted. And even if they did, the recce bird had not been hit by a laser. Something solid had struck it — a kinetic hit.

No, a death ray at geosync was a ridiculous idea, he concluded, as ridiculous as Haswell's UFO joke. The Intelligence assessment of *KOSMOS* 2069 was sound. It was no weapon. It was a sick communications relay platform, and the Soviets were trying to get well by sending up several smaller satellites. That was the logical explanation, and he was a logical man.

"You know this cafeteria food is great." Haswell shoveled another fork full of spaghetti into his mouth.

"Yea. One of the great perks of working under a mountain."

Saturday, 3 September
Houston, Texas

Pettigrew was unconscious on top of the sheets, his breathing shallow and fast. His face was contorted in fear, and he mumbled incoherently. A stain of sweat grew outward from his torso, and his extremities twitched spastically. The nightmare had returned.

"Gunslinger Three, break right! Break right! You've got a MIG on your ass!"

Pettigrew jammed the throttle into afterburner and yanked his aircraft into a high-g turn. The acceleration crushed him into his seat and sent rivulets of sweat coursing into his eyes. The anti-g suit automatically responded to the increasing forces and tried to pinch his stomach to his backbone and tourniquet his legs in a painful squeeze. But it was not enough to keep the blood from being pulled from his brain, and his vision faded toward blackness. To stave off unconsciousness, he tightened his gut muscles, making animal grunting sounds in the process. Even a second of blackout could be fatal in a supersonic dogfight.

Artificially weighted to a thousand pounds, he struggled to look aft for the enemy. "I've got him, Fred! He's overshooting! He's going to eight o'clock!"

"I've lost you, Bob! Say your altitude!"

"I've reversed! I'm in a hard left, climbing turn… going through seventeen thousand! Ha! I've got you now, you slant-eyed prick!" Pettigrew steepened his climb to aggravate the MIG's overshoot, and it moved farther to his front. An electronic growl signaled that the guidance system of his heat-seeking missile had locked onto the engine exhaust of the target.

"Okay, motherfucker. Let's see how you like a Sidewinder up your ass! Gunslinger Three, fox two!"

His call announced to the rest of the now-scattered flight that an air-to-air missile had been launched. Similar calls from other pilots filled the airwaves in the churning struggle.

"Goddamnit! It missed the fucker!"

The panicked MIG pilot had made a violent turn, successfully evading the lethal projectile.

"Okay, dink! See how well you can dodge some twenty mike-mike."

Continuing to follow the enemy's desperate maneuvers, he closed the range and armed his twenty-millimeter cannon. The T-tailed speck moved closer to his gunsight pipper — the electronic dot that marked the focus of his cannon.

"Come on, baby, just a little more. That's it! Hold it! Take this to Uncle Ho!"

The cockpit floor vibrated as the Gatling gun spun to life. The battlefield smell of burned cordite came to his nostrils. One hundred rounds per second of high-explosive shells lashed out in a mile-long whip of red tracers. The line streaked over the enemy's left wing, and Pettigrew began the vernier corrections necessary for the kill.

It never happened. Instead, the sound of his own imminent death came as a rattlesnake buzz — his threat detection system had sensed an enemy I-band radar locked onto him. In his concentration on the MIG in his gunsight, and with no wingman to protect his rear, he had failed to see the other enemy maneuver into firing position.

Instinctively, he pulled on the controls to break out of the deadly beam, but the aircraft had barely begun to respond when the first cannon fire exploded into his aircraft. Acrid smoke filled the cockpit and burned his eyes. The engine fire-warning light glowed steady, and the controls froze as hydraulic power was lost.

"Bob's been hit! Gunslinger Three, eject! Eject! Bailout, Bob! You're on fire! Bail out! Bob... Bob."

"Bob, Bob, Bobby, baby. Wake up, honey. Wake up."

Pettigrew snapped upright, screaming.

"Calm down, baby. Calm down. You were just dreaming. Jesus, you're soaked with sweat." The woman sprang from the bed and hurried to the bathroom for a towel. Pettigrew remained sitting, gasping for breath, his brain fighting to come back to the present.

"Here, baby." She rubbed the fabric across his back in soft, caring motions.

"Thanks, Di... Denise."

He caught himself almost calling the girl by the wrong name. There had been a Diane in the recent past.

"Feel better?" The nude girl massaged his knotted deltoids, moving close so that her breasts rubbed against his back.

"Yea, thanks. I guess I had a nightmare."

"Nightmare isn't the word. You were shaking and shivering like an epileptic. What was it?"

Pettigrew took the towel and wiped his face . "Nothing. Just the war."

"That war really fucked you up." She reached around his front and gently caressed the mass of scar tissue that disfigured his left pectoral. She was fascinated by the fact that most of the nipple was gone.

"Does it hurt?"

The question was lost in his still-turbulent mind, and she repeated it.

"Does it hurt, baby?"

"Huh? Oh, no. No, it doesn't hurt."

Hurt? No. That pain ended long ago. But the other — Jesus, will it ever leave me?

Pettigrew climbed from the bed, slid open the patio door, and stepped, naked, onto the decking. His privacy was assured by a high fence capped with a riot of honeysuckle.

The dawn had progressed to only a gray haze, but the remnants of yesterday's heat were still there to draw a clammy sweat from his pores. The perspiration made the sounds of bubbling hot water from an adjoining spa exceptionally repulsive. A litter of underclothes decorated the patio and refreshed his memory of last night's aquatic copulation.

Other debris included several beer cans, and he touched these with his toe to locate one with some remaining fluid. One resisted, and he picked it up and drained its warm, bitter contents. The empty was released into the company of the other dead soldiers.

The woman joined him on the patio, and he silently wished her gone. He wanted to be alone. The dream had opened a fissure in his memory, and the hot magma of pain bubbled from it. Similar fractures in past years had taught him that a recipe of alcohol and solitude made the only mortar suitable for repair.

"Denise, I've got to work today. Why don't you help yourself to the shower and then head on back to your place? I'll call you this evening." He had no intention of doing so.

"Bob, today's Saturday. You don't have to go to work on Saturday, do you?"

The marine was glad he had a valid excuse to hurry the girl out of his life. Mark had called yesterday afternoon and asked him to come in to clean up some items on the RTLS report. He accelerated the ten o'clock appointment to suit his purpose. "I've got a seven-thirty meeting."

That was two hours away — ample time, the woman decided, for her to take the man's mind off his dream. She moved closer to run her fingers through the remnants of chest hair that grew from the unscarred areas. The smell and feel of his perspiration lubricated her, and she buffed him with her body in long, lazy strokes, like a cat rubbing against a post. Moving to his side, she spread her legs and did a series of languid pelvic thrusts into the steel hardness of his quadriceps.

Pettigrew remained mute.

She side-winded her way to his back. Fingers came around to his chest and converged on his right nipple — she did not believe that the damaged left one could still be erogenous. They dallied to tease the dusky disk into a miniature peak, then crawled down his belly to grab handfuls of flaccid penis and hanging testicles. Pettigrew was uninterested. He craved solitude, not sex. But the girl considered the loose flesh a challenge and began a skillful massage. In a minute she was proud of her success, running her hand the length of a warm shaft. She moved to his front to look at it.

"Well, at least a part of you still thinks that Saturdays are for fun. Does that floating around in space make all men this big? I thought you'd split me in two last night."

Still, he made no reply.

Stepping backward into the hot tub, she pulled him down to sit at its edge.

"No, baby. Not there. Move over here." Last night she had learned of the ecstasy of hydraulic masturbation, and the slight change in his position brought one of the bubbling jets of water to bear on her pubis.

"Oh, yea. *This* is the place."

With her own pleasure now guaranteed, she directed her attention at the pink rod stretching for her face. She teased it, first with water-lubricated hand strokes, then with light kisses, then with her tongue. In quick, darting motions, she lapped at the sensitive keel of the shaft's prow and, like a cobra spreading its hood, the crown widened. She took it into her mouth and dwelled at the apex in an exploration of the opening.

The male animal within his body applauded the maneuvers, but Pettigrew, the man, remained sadly unfulfilled.

There is more to a woman than this!

He watched the top of the girl's head rhythmically moving back and forth.

There is more, so much more. I've lived it. I know. But the hurt! Why did she do it? God, why? I loved her! I loved her!

He closed his eyes. His cream was trading bodies, and he was glad. He wanted to be left alone.

❖

Monday, 5 September
Cheyenne Mountain, Colorado

Mason sat at his desk in a slow boil. He had arrived at work several hours earlier to find that he had been designated the savings bond drive officer — one of the little shit details that had been falling on the shoulders of lieutenants since the time of the Roman legions. The conjunction analysis had been completed on Saturday, with no new revelations. The hold-the-presses urgency had passed, and it was back to the boredom of business as usual — reviewing contractor computer programs and, now, playing Fuller Brush salesman and going office to office trying to convince several hundred officers and NCO's to buy U.S. savings bonds.

And I got a master's degree in computer science for this?

Disgustedly, he brushed aside the instructions on his new job and turned to the computer keyboard. If the air force was going to give him bullshit, then they owed him some time on the machine. At least that's how he rationalized this latest round of hacking. The coast was clear, the office empty.

In less than five minutes, he had bypassed the several locks on the system and "Priority Access" was flashing behind the cursor.

C:LOAD DRAG MODEL.

He tapped the return key.

SEARCHING, was the answer. He had previously stored the program in an unused portion of the computer's memory and now awaited its retrieval. When finally finished, it was software he intended to submit as part of his Ph.D. thesis work.

NO RECORD.

"Son of a bitch! Somebody wrote over it." He had been reluctant to put software guards in the program to prevent such an erasure, knowing if a legitimate user was locked out of *available* memory, it would raise too much suspicion. Better to let his program go up in smoke. It had happened before — just one of the routine hazards a hacker faced. He maintained a hard copy of the work so the overwrite was only a nuisance. Later, when he had more time, he could locate another spot in memory and reload it.

C:LOAD STATE VECTOR.

It was another of his personal projects.

SEARCHING.

NO RECORD.

"Shit! They must've done some type of purge on this thing." As he often did when he was mind-mating with a computer, he talked to himself. "Did anything survive?"

C:LOAD SATELLITE LOSS.

SEARCHING.

It was the program he had demonstrated to Haswell, the one he had abandoned. But now it might be the only game in town.

READY.

"Hot shit! It's there! Now..."

LIST.

The screen filled with the program instructions, and he began his search. "It's somewhere in this subroutine. Somewhere… somewhere… here. Just change these two variables."

MINIMUM ALTITUDE = 22000.

MAXIMUM ALTITUDE = 23000.

The change instructed the computer to look only at satellites between twenty-two and twenty-three thousand miles altitude — only geosync satellites.

RUN.

WAIT.

The machine pondered the question: out of hundreds of pieces of Soviet hardware in geosync orbit, was there a single satellite that had a direct line of sight to each of the American losses?

The cursor remained static. He looked at his watch and had a brief worry about CPU time. If it was too high, the contractor might get curious and do some sniffing around. Then it crossed his mind that the contractor programmers were probably too lazy to bother. He would be safe for a while longer.

The door opened, and he swung in his chair, expecting to see Haswell. It was Major Jacobson. "Mike, I want to talk to you about this bond drive. I want you to really hit this hard. See if you can't break motor pool's record of three years ago." He continued straight for Mason, straight for the flashing unauthorized "Priority Access."

Mason had a panic attack that included visions of Leavenworth at the worst and permanent bond drive officer at the best. His lunge for the off switch was so violent his head almost smashed the screen.

"Are you okay?" Jacobson was still ten feet away, bewildered by Mason's knee-jerk response.

"Oh, yes, yes, sir. I'm just finishing up here. The bond drive? I was just getting ready to work on that." During the babble, Mason tried to shield the screen with his body while simultaneously hunting for the off switch. It was on the back of the terminal, but his spastic fingers couldn't seem to locate it.

The computer chirped its alert that output was imminent. Jacobson came to stand by him. Mason surrendered. He was caught. He would be selling bonds for the rest of his life. Then the speeding cursor deposited the yellow lines of text that would change the world.

CANDIDATE SOVIET SPACE OBJECTS IN LINE OF SIGHT OF

FAILED AMERICAN ASSETS: KOSMOS 2069. END.

"God! It's not possible!"

Jacobson was thinking the same thing. When had he authorized Mason a "Priority Access"?

❖

Wednesday, 7 September
The White House

"Mr. President, Mr. Killingsworth is here to see you."

"Please, send him in."

"Hobie! Come on in." The president dismissed an aide, rose from his Oval Office desk, and stepped forward to greet his visitor. He followed the handshake with a momentary clasp around the fat man's shoulders. "I'm glad you could make it. Have a seat." He motioned him to one of two facing sofas, and Killingsworth lowered his blubber onto the cushion. The president took the opposing couch.

"Thank you, Mr. President. That's a very beautiful arrangement."

"Yes, it is. One of my favorites."

He referred to the background stereo music — a harmonica solo of "Ghost Riders in the Sky." The president was a Texan who loved the outdoors and who had carried the trappings of the campsite — recordings of western ballads and log fires — into his White House office. He was also dressed for the trail, wearing jeans, a wide leather belt, and cowboy boots. Together with his John Wayne frame and craggy, weather-worn face, he projected a fine image of a frontiersman — strong, independent, courageous. Killingsworth had superbly marketed that image when he had been directing the president's election campaign.

"How's Ann?" The president reclined into the sofa corner.

"Fine, Mr. President, just fine. She sends her best wishes."

"Tell her hi for me… and Hobie, how many times am I going to have to tell you to cut the Mr. President crap. I think a thirty-year friendship ought to keep us on a first-name basis, even in this house. Hell, I wouldn't even be in this house if it hadn't been for you."

Killingsworth smiled. "Ah, Mr. President, it is your *office* that I address. With a knowledge of the history of this house, of the heroes who have occupied it, I would feel terribly uncomfortable without maintaining the formality of title. Please indulge me, *Mr. President*."

President Corbin laughed. He counted the friendship of the fat man among his most treasured possessions. While Killingsworth's physical appearance and mannerisms were gluttonous and soft, his brain was electrically quick and unfailingly accurate.

In one of life's fortuitous quirks, the two men had been randomly thrown together as roommates at Yale, where both had majored in political science. But any similarity had ended with their common academic interest. The president, then merely *Mister* Corbin, had a soft Texas drawl, a Texan's gregarious manner, and a cowboy's body. Killingsworth, on the other hand, had a Vermonter's brogue, an academician's seriousness, and a laughable physique. He was five feet, five inches short, and everything about him was round — the crown of his head — which had achieved total baldness by graduation, his face, his belly. Even his glasses were of a wire-rimmed, circular-lens design. The striking physical differences between the men had earned them the predictable college handles of Mutt and Jeff.

It had taken the president only a short time to learn his roommate was exceptionally gifted — his greatest talent being his organizational abilities. Nobody was better at turning chaos into order than Hobart P. Killingsworth, and there had been many occasions when the president had relied upon that genius to push him up another rung of the political ladder.

In one of his first calls for help — when Killingsworth had organized his campaign for the Senate — the president had watched him closely, hoping to discover his secret and plagiarize it. But the secret had turned out to be nothing less than the man himself. It was his very appearance — his disarming, almost feminine demeanor and his circuitous conversational mannerism. It was a conspiracy of body and mind that made people drop their guard and allow him to very accurately assess them — to find those who were skilled leaders, those who followed, and those who impeded — and put each in his proper place.

"Hobie, I need your help."

"Certainly, Mr. President."

"It's not just an opinion or advice this time. What I have in mind is going to take considerable time… several months, a year maybe. I'm not sure how your bosses will like that."

"Mr. President, I am certain that the university will have no objections. They'll relish the idea of one of their staff being called away by the president of the United States. It'll be a mark of prestige for the institution. No doubt when I return, they will ask me to share my experiences… my *inside* stories… at a reception for our most important donors."

"You won't be able to share this story with anybody, Hobie. This job is going to put you right in the middle of a possible national security crisis."

The fat man's eyes widened in surprise. He had expected to be tasked with a job of laying the groundwork for the president's reelection campaign. He had never before been involved in national security issues.

"National security? That's not really my forte."

"Your forte, Hobie, is getting people organized and the job done… done right and done fast. I need that. I need that badly. The country needs that."

Killingsworth did not miss the gravity in the president's voice.

"Of course, Mr. President. I'll do whatever you feel is necessary. What job do you have in mind?"

The president laughed cynically. "Right this moment, Hobie, I haven't a clue. I just know that I'm going to need you."

The fat man's face was a question mark.

"Let me fill you in." Corbin shifted forward in his seat. "Over the past several months, this nation's military satellite fleet has suffered some inexplicable losses. Nine satellites have just… quit. Died. And, with one exception, nobody knows why. The damn things are in orbits that make a retrieval or inspection impossible. The exception was a reconnaissance satellite that dropped a film-return capsule with marks indicating that the spacecraft was hit by something."

"Hit?"

"Yea. By what, nobody knows. There are *experts* saying it was a meteor hit. There are *experts* saying it was a piece of space debris. And now there are *experts* saying that the Soviets had a hand in it."

The last comment piqued Killingsworth. He leaned forward, his thighs disappearing under his belly.

The president continued. "The day before yesterday, an enterprising young air force lieutenant, who works at our space-defense center in Colorado, was doing a little checking on these losses and stumbled across a rather remarkable coincidence. It seems that of about five thousand pieces of Soviet hardware in orbit around the earth — the good stuff and the junk — there was only *one*, just *one,* that had a view of all of our dead spacecraft at the moment of their deaths. And that satellite is parked in an orbit twenty-two thousand miles high that commands a view of the entire western hemisphere. Now, the long and the short of it is, is that just a coincidence, or have the Soviets deployed a Star Wars type of weapon and they're using our birds for a little target practice?"

"Is that possible, Mr. President?"

"If there's one thing I've learned in the past thirty-six hours, there isn't a man alive who can answer that question. As soon as word of this lieutenant's findings reached the top brass, they confirmed them with more computer tests, then came knocking on my door. That precipitated our first Security Council meeting on Monday evening. Meeting, hell... it was more like a fist fight. And yesterday morning's meeting was hardly any better. After those fiascos, I told everybody to take twenty-four hours, comb through whatever intelligence we have, and come back this morning prepared to make their recommendations." The president looked at his watch. "We start in a few minutes in the Roosevelt Room. I want you there."

"Certainly, Mr. President. About these fist fights... which organizations are taking which positions?"

"You could pretty much guess. The CIA stands to lose in a big way if it turns out that the Soviets have snuck something by us, so they are very adamant that the findings are nothing more than a coincidence... that our losses can be explained as acts of God or screw-ups by men. The organizations responsible for building the satellites are, of course, screaming that the Soviets are responsible. Except for the air force, the Chiefs of Staff have been neutral. General Lawson, however, is pushing for an attack on the damned thing... an air force operation, of course. The State Department thinks they can negotiate with the Soviets for the answer, and if we don't like it we can stop grain shipments or boycott the Olympics. Somehow we've got to hammer out a plan of action out of that mess. And somewhere in that plan, whatever it is, I'll need you." The president stood. "Come on, let's see how round three goes."

He continued to talk as he escorted Killingsworth toward the door. "There's only one thing, Hobie, which everybody agrees on. *If* the Soviets have somehow parked a satellite killer above our heads, we are in serious, *very* serious trouble. If they can kill satellites, they can probably kill missile warheads. How many? How reliably? Who knows? But *any* capability calls into question our entire land and sea based missile forces. It's a terrifying thought, Hobie. Jesus, it scares the hell out of me."

They exited the Oval Office, stepped through the hallway, and opened the door to the Roosevelt Room to be immediately hit by the cacophony of multitudinous, intense, opinionated voices. The meeting participants had begun arguing the relative merits of their individual solutions to the *KOSMOS* question while awaiting the president. Killingsworth noted a four-star air force general locked in a particularly loud debate with the director of the CIA. The scene evoked the president's fist fight comment.

The room fell silent as the men noted their boss's arrival. Those who were seated began to stand but were motioned down by the president. "Please, gentlemen, take your seats." Holding Killingsworth at his side, he remained standing at the head of the elliptical table. "I believe you all know Hobie."

The fat man scanned the audience: the president's national security advisor, his chief scientist, the secretaries of defense and state, the director of the Central Intelligence Agency, and the five members of the military Joint Chiefs of Staff. At one time or another he had met all of them. It was obvious from their stares that the group wondered why he was there. "Gentlemen, it's a pleasure to see you again." Killingsworth added a nod to his salutation, then took a seat in one of the chairs against the wall. There were empty places at the table, but he considered that an arena for the players. For the present, he was still a spectator.

The president turned to his pipe-smoking chief scientist, Dr. Ernest Wells. "Ernie, what have you found out about possible weapons?"

"Mr. President, the experts I have consulted agree it is theoretically possible to build a kinetic kill weapon that could engage targets from an equatorial parking orbit. Our own Star Wars research has pointed us toward rail guns as just such weapons. These are devices that accelerate projectiles to tremendous velocities in short distances by waves of magnetism. The only power source is electricity. In laboratory tests we have demonstrated rail guns with muzzle velocities of twenty kilometers per second... that's about twelve miles per second. However, you would need speeds many times greater than that to make the weapon practical for geosynchronous altitudes. The community opinion is it would require a breakthrough in design, possibly a breakthrough in superconductivity that would allow more efficient use of electricity and more intense magnetic fields."

"Could the Soviets have made such a breakthrough?" He directed the question at the director of Central Intelligence, Harry Cahill.

"They do have considerable talent in that field, Mr. President. And their budget for superconductivity research is very large. But we have no intelligence to indicate there has been any type of breakthrough."

"You've had time to analyze the transmissions from the thing?"

"Yes, sir. They are your standard TV, radio, telephonic communication signals. Some of them are encrypted, and those links are certainly for military use, but that's standard practice... nothing that would indicate a weapon."

"Have you been able to take a picture of it?"

"We had a modified C-141 aircraft with an airborne telescope take photos of it, but the resolution is too poor to tell anything. Ground-based telescopes are no better. It's too close for the really big ones to image and too far away for the small ones to see anything."

"What about these other satellites that have been going up there? Does that suggest it might be a weapon?"

"They could be tankers taking propellant needed to keep the satellite in position, or it's possible that the spacecraft is suffering some equipment degradation that these other machines could correct. The platform is an expensive and important asset to the Soviets. It's their central switchboard for all western-hemisphere communication, civilian and military, so if it did have a problem, I'm certain the Soviets would go to great extremes to correct it."

"Then what's your overall assessment, Harry?"

"Unless our research turns up something new, I would have to say the *KOSMOS* is what the Soviets say it is... a communications platform, nothing more. I think the Mason findings are a coincidence."

"Coincidence!" Air Force Chief of Staff General Ron Lawson echoed the word derisively and leaned forward for the attack. "Do you realize how fantastic a coincidence that is? The Soviets have been pushing anti-satellite work for decades! And now they've got something up there! Goddamnit man, wake up!"

"General, I've got an army of experts looking at that spacecraft! It's clean!" Cahill came half out of his seat in a counterattack.

"Goddamnit, Ron, I want to keep this thing from degenerating into another free-for-all!" The president was next to shout.

"Excuse me, Mr. President, but it is just insane to believe that nine satellite failures, all watched by the same Soviet spacecraft, are a coincidence!" The general didn't pull his throttles back, even for the president.

"Then what would you have me do?"

"Kill it, Mr. President! Kill the goddamn thing! I've talked with some of our missile contractors, and they could slap together something that would reach it. Put a nuke on it and that'll be the end of the damn thing!"

"A nuclear weapon?" Now it was the secretary of state's turn to join the fray. "That would be a test-ban treaty violation."

"Who gives a shit, Bill. There's a treaty on shooting down each other's satellites, too, and that didn't seem to stop the Soviets."

"You have no proof, General!" The CIA director was back.

"And Ron, how do you know the *KOSMOS* couldn't defend itself from your missile?" The chief of naval operations asked the question. "If it's killing satellites, couldn't it shoot down anything approaching it?"

Before the general could reply, the president also struck at the idea. "And what if you're wrong, Ron? What if the *KOSMOS* is just a communications platform? What if the Soviets see your missile as an unprovoked attack, a prelude to a first strike on their country? What if they decide to retaliate? What if we start World War III going after a goddamn telephone switchboard?!"

The general was finally challenged into silence. He had no answers for the scenario the president had painted.

"Instead of building a rocket to go after the *KOSMOS*, why don't we use it to retrieve one or two of these other dead satellites of ours?" National Security Advisor Charles Talbot made his first entry into the conversation. "If they turn out to have holes in them, then I would have to agree with Ron… the *KOSMOS* must be a weapon and we should kill it."

The idea was digested for a moment, and a few heads bobbed in tentative agreement. Then, General Bachman, the chairman of the JCS, torpedoed it. "If we try to retrieve any of those satellites, the Soviets will know. Now, if there are no holes in them, then the Soviets are clean and it doesn't matter that they see us. But, if there are holes, then we have just forfeited the element of surprise. The Soviets would know that we were onto them. Forewarned like that, I would assume they would watch us like hawks for an attack. We'd never get close to the thing. I think it is extremely critical we hold onto the element of surprise, and that means we can't do any inspections or retrievals."

The president mulled over the comments. Bachman was right. They couldn't risk losing the element of surprise. It was another dead end.

The secretary of state was next with an analysis. "Gentlemen, I think it important to remember that if the Soviets have made a breakthrough, and if they do have a killer up there, there would be a terrestrial objective behind it. Shooting down our satellites and never saying anything about it would serve no purpose."

"Blackmail." The single word was growled by General Lawson.

"Precisely, General. They would use their killer to threaten us into some concessions. So? Where are the demands? Where is the blackmail? Is there anything different about the way the Soviets are conducting business today than before we lost these satellites?" The room remained silent and the secretary answered his own question. "No, there isn't. I would have to agree with Harry that there is nothing up there, that it is just coincidence the *KOSMOS* umbrellaed our failures."

"And what if *you're* wrong, Bill?" Now it was the president's turn to paint an unanswerable scenario for the other camp. "Suppose the Soviets aren't ready to make their demands? Suppose we just canter along like it's all a coincidence, and then one morning the phone rings and Belidov tells me my missiles are as useless as slingshots and to get the hell out of Berlin? To get the hell out of Europe? The way I see it, it would be just like the Cuban missile crisis. The Soviets had to knuckle under to our demands, because they knew we had all the offense. Now I'd have to blink, because they would have all the defense. Can I just sit around and hope that doesn't happen?"

Silence.

"So, gentlemen, I'm stuck in an impossible situation. If I risk ignoring the *KOSMOS*, I risk this country's survival. If I attack the *KOSMOS*, I risk provoking the Soviets into a nuclear war. I can't overtly challenge them on the issue, because if it is a weapon, I would have tipped our hand and forfeited the element of surprise. For the same reason, I can't even inspect my own satellites."

The silence persisted. Finally, Chief Scientist Wells broke it. "Mr. President, there is another alternative that has not been discussed."

Killingsworth's jaw was just one of eleven to unhinge in shock at the suggestion that followed.

❖

Three hours later, the fat man was no longer a spectator. He sat at the table as a player, thinking he was living a scene from "Twelve Angry Men." Coats and ties were gone, collars unbuttoned, sleeves rolled back. Ashtrays were smoldering gray-white mountains. For three hours the arguments had raged, and now it was done. He had his job.

Job? It was a challenge like none he had ever had before. For the first time in his memory he was terrified he would not be up to the task. What did he know of such technical matters?

"Mr. Killingsworth will head up the project."

"Mr. President! I…" General Lawson began yet another objection to the assignment. It was a project that rightfully belonged under the auspices of the air force.

"Enough, Ron!" The grueling marathon had reduced the president's temper to a hair trigger. "My mind is made up! I appreciate your candor in challenging me. I don't like *yes* men, but I will not debate this matter any longer. You have all demonstrated your parochialism on this issue. I can't have that! The project leader has to be free of axes to grind. Hobie is the only man in this room who doesn't have an agency or department to protect. He's the only one who can approach this objectively. I will not hear anything more about it! Do I make myself clear?"

The silence said that he did.

"Now, Harry, I will concede to your demands that the CIA be represented. You have a big part to play in this, and Hobie is going to have to rely heavily on you. And Ernie is right. To do the job right, we'll need somebody fluent in Russian and who has the smarts to learn about rail-gun design. Find one of your people to fit the bill."

"Yes, sir."

The president sagged in exhaustion. "I want everybody to continue searching for an answer to what this *KOSMOS* really is. Maybe we'll get lucky and not have to commit to this… this project. I pray that turns out to be the case, because it scares the hell out of me. It's too dangerous. We could kill people, then find out it was all for naught. But I have no choice except to press forward with it." The president spoke with his head down, his fingers massaging his temples. He appeared to be talking to himself, trying to convince himself of the rightness of his decision. "I can't just sit back and *hope* the *KOSMOS* isn't a weapon. The risk to the country is unacceptable. An armed *KOSMOS* leaves us naked." He looked up. "Time is of the essence, gentlemen. Until one of you can positively determine the *KOSMOS* is not a threat or this project determines it isn't, we won't be able to take a breath without the worry the Soviets are going to spring a trap on us. And once they do that, the element of surprise is gone. Time is critical. We must get an answer as rapidly as possible.

"Hobie, you'd better get to Houston."

CHAPTER 5

Wednesday, 7 September
Houston

Mark took a drag on his beer, leaned against the patio railing, and stared across the dark expanse that was the country club golf course. The muted din of the party crept through the wall behind him to mingle with the serenade of night insects. For Houston, it was a comfortable evening. The first cool front of the season had pushed through the area, taking ten degrees of temperature and twenty percent of the humidity with it. Seventy of each had been left.

He had sought the solitude of the patio to collect his thoughts. In a few minutes, he would present Pettigrew with his astronaut pin. It was a landing party tradition that rookies received the golden prize from their commanders at the function. He pulled the device from his pocket, thinking how close it had come to being swallowed by the Atlantic seven days earlier. It had been part of *Discovery's* cabin cargo — intended to have been sanctified by passage through a magical fifty-mile-high gate.

In his idleness, he studied its detail — a three-tailed shooting star passing through an ellipse. Such a small device, he mused, no bigger than a fraternity pin, yet, after years of watching the antics of the elite community of men and women who wore it, he knew it represented treasure beyond King Solomon's comprehension. The pins were the merit badges of space flight, given only to that select handful of humans who had placed their asses on the line to ride a controlled explosion into the heavens. This unique qualifying event made it the most powerful skeleton key on earth. Not only could it open any door to business or politics, or gain admission into the loftiest castles of the rich and famous, but it was also capable of opening the legs of a significant number of the female population. He suspected Pettigrew would find it useful in its latter application.

As he toyed with the piece of gold, the marine stepped around the corner and into Mark's company. "What're you hidin' from?" His speech was thickly slurred. "Judy's in there showin' a Grand Canyon cleavage and if you leave her alone for much longer I'll have my face in the Colorado River."

Mark laughed. He wasn't offended by the remark. The marine had earned the right to get blitzed on this special night.

"I think Judy's safe. Denise would tie your dick in a knot if you started chasing anything else. Where is she anyway? I'm surprised you'd let stuff like that out of your sight. Another *hero* might make a move on it."

Pettigrew had pulled a cigar from his pocket and was lighting up. Between several hard pulls on the weed he answered the question. "I saw Judy and a group of the other wives watching us dance, so I thought I'd be a real *gentleman* and introduce her." The emphasis made it clear his motive had been anything but gentlemanly. "They're in there talking now. I think Judy got a kick out of it, but some of the others looked like I'd just shoved a turd under their noses."

"I can believe that." Mark had to laugh at the idea of the twenty-seven-year-old, health spa poster queen taking her place as an equal among size-14 mothers.

He left the subject and held out the pin. "You ready for this?"

"After four years? You bet your sweet ass I am. I'm gonna tell Denise that beauty will make my prick grow another inch."

"That'll make two, huh?"

He exhaled a cloud of smoke with his chuckle. "You bastard. I'll get even in a few minutes."

Mark knew he would. Nobody ever won a war of wits with Pettigrew, and when he was drunk, nobody could even come close. He turned for the party but Pettigrew stopped him.

"Before we go back in, take a look at this." He pulled a blackened and twisted six-inch rod from his pocket.

Mark took it and moved to the light. "What the hell is it?"

"It's what almost killed us last week. Pfeifer just flew in from the

Cape with it. The propulsion people found it in the left engine oxidizer turbo pump, or what's left of it."

"What is it?" Mark repeated himself.

"You'll probably need a couple more beers to swallow this, but that's a GSE liquid oxygen temperature sensor."

"GSE?" Mark knew the term—Ground Support Equipment—items that remained on the ground.

"Yea, GSE. Apparently this temperature probe broke off of its mounting inside the launch pad liquid oxygen plumbing and was pumped into the orbiter engine guts during the prelaunch fill-up of the tank. It must have gotten stuck in a bend somewhere in the orbiter's pipes. When it finally did come loose, it got sucked into the turbo pump and... bang! No engine."

Mark cringed. The pumps were the most delicate pieces of equipment on the engines. Designed to feed liquid oxygen and hydrogen to the combustion chambers at a rate of a thousand pounds per second, their turbines turned at hellish RPM's. The tiniest piece of foreign material could destroy such precision machinery. It certainly could never survive the digestion of a six-inch stainless-steel rod, any more than a garbage disposal could swallow a spoon.

Pettigrew continued, "So, this piece of shit caused the left engine turbo pump to come apart, which then flung hot steel everywhere in the engine compartment. Some of the shrapnel punctured the center engine helium supply, and that's what almost turned us to bait."

"Christ, you'd think they would have a filter or something on the GSE to prevent crap like this from being ingested." He felt like he was handling a bullet that had been removed from near his heart. In his many years of flying high-tech machinery, it never ceased to amaze him how the most bizarre events could conspire to kill a man.

"Well, you can bet your ass there'll be a filter on that equipment now... probably three of 'em."

Just as those who had already heard the story before him, Mark saw the obvious. "Then there's nothing wrong with the engines. Whatever they do to fix the GSE should be a piece of cake. We'll be back in operation in no time." The words were out of his mouth before he realized he had included himself in the statement. It was a painful error.

"Yea. That's the word goin' 'round the party and our booze bill is climbing. Everybody's celebrating." Pettigrew drained his bourbon and flung the ice into the dark.

"Mark O'Malley! You out here?" The call interrupted them.

"Yea, around the corner."

A third man appeared. "Sorry to interrupt, Mark, but Dr. Powers wants to see you. He's in that empty room at the end of the building… the one across from the bathroom."

"Thanks, George. We were just coming in." They began walking. "Powers? I wonder what he wants?"

"Probably to thank you for saving *Discovery*… and NASA and JSC and his ass in the process."

It seemed unlikely to Mark the request by the JSC director was merely to acknowledge his airmanship. He had done that at each of their several meetings over the past week.

They reached the door, and Pettigrew flipped away his cigar and turned for the bar. Mark called after him, "Don't get lost. I want to make your pin presentation after I see Powers."

"I'll be with the women… discussing babies and headaches and feminine deodorant spray." His laugh was swallowed by the party.

A minute later, Mark found Powers and two other men in his company. He recognized one as the Secretary of the Air Force, George Casey. His presence added to the mystery of the summons. The other man was unknown to him. He was short, fat, and bald — a butterball.

"Mark, sorry to steal you away from your party, but I wanted you to meet these gentlemen. I believe you know Secretary Casey?"

"Yes, good to see you, Mr. Secretary." They exchanged a handshake during which Casey was lavish in his praise of Mark's skill in landing *Discovery*.

"And this is Mr. Killingsworth."

"Hobart Killingsworth, Colonel. I'm most honored to meet you."

Mark's eyes widened at the squeaky pitch of his voice and the equally feminine handclasp. He waited for a job affiliation to be given, but none was. Instead, the man gushed his praises. "Please excuse my insistence on meeting you. I'm sure you would like to mingle with your guests. It was just that I could not resist this rare opportunity to meet a genuine hero. You did a marvelous job in landing the space shuttle, Colonel. I was at breakfast when the news broke, and I totally forgot about my meal. I just sat watching the television. I don't think I even breathed, I was that engrossed in your flight."

Mark thought it must have been high drama indeed to have separated this man from the table. And he was shocked to hear his page had apparently originated with Killingsworth. He could not imagine what VIP label he wore to allow him that prerogative — and an escort by the center director besides. The gnome was too fat to be a general or admiral, and Mark finally assumed he must be one of Casey's civilian deputies. Whoever he was, Mark wanted no more of his slavish worship. He turned back to Secretary Casey. "What brings you to town, sir?"

"Just a short meeting with Dr. Powers to discuss some changes to the shuttle manifest."

The gathering of eagles suddenly made sense. Although there was no design problem with the shuttle, it would take time to replace the damaged engines. The flight rate would be slowed, and the entire launch manifest would have to be juggled. The air force was a heavy user of the shuttle and would, no doubt, be anxious to protect its launch slots.

Powers spoke. "Mark, Mr. Killingsworth was asking me if you might be available to make an appearance at a Friday night function in Los Alamos."

"Yes, Colonel. My audience would find it fascinating to hear an account of your mission."

"Friday? *This* Friday?"

The fat man nodded. "I realize it isn't much warning, but it struck me today that you would be the perfect celebrity for my group."

"I think you'd find the trip interesting, Mark." Secretary Casey endorsed the request in what Mark perceived as a veiled order.

Inwardly he groaned. An evening with the talkative blimp would be an evening in purgatory. Yet, it was now obvious Killingsworth was a man of some position, and it would not be in Mark's best interests to refuse the request. "Ah, yes, I think I could do that."

"Wonderful, Colonel! Wonderful! I'll meet you at the Los Alamos airport." He pulled a package from his breast pocket and handed it over. "I believe you'll find all your travel needs taken care of."

After several more minutes, in which Killingsworth babbled continuously about the RTLS, Mark was finally excused. He resigned himself to his fate. It wasn't the first time he had been ordered to be the tinsel at some feather merchant's fraternal club.

He found Pettigrew where he had promised — with Judy and her friends. His centerfold-figured date was now waxing eloquent on dieting. Mark could tell by the icy smiles of her audience she was being wished an early and severe case of cottage-cheese thighs.

"What did Powers want?" Judy had heard of the meeting from the marine.

"To send me to Los Alamos."

"What?"

"I got volunteered to give a speech to some fat bureaucrat's club in Los Alamos on Friday."

"This Friday?"

"Yea."

"But that's when the movers are coming!" Judy was ready to kill.

"I don't like it any more than you do. The last thing I want to do is spend an evening with this guy. He's a real toad. But Secretary Casey was there, too, and he virtually ordered me to make the trip."

"Shit!" She had been counting on Mark's help.

"I'll get back to town as quickly as I can." He looked to Pettigrew. "Ready?"

"Yea. Let's do it."

The men excused themselves and walked to the front of the dance floor. On the way, Mark signaled Dave Hammernick, the chief of the Astronaut Office, to join them. To him fell the job of making Rush's award — a NASA Space Flight Medal. The astronaut pin was an exclusive recognition by the Astronaut Corps of their peers. It was never given to outsiders. Instead, shuttle passengers were honored with a NASA headquarter's token.

Mark and Pettigrew waited behind Hammernick as he called on the politician to come forward to the stage. A polite applause welcomed him. Like the others before and all those pretenders who would follow, the fact that he had actually strapped his ass to a rocket and ridden it into space changed nothing. To the pilot astronauts he was as far removed from being an astronaut as airline passengers were from being pilots. Although the press would call him one and MC's around the country would introduce him as one, the true members of the fraternity would never consider him one.

After a minute of remarks, Hammernick pinned the award to Rush's lapel and offered him the podium. But the senator declined. He was in a hurry to escape the upturned faces. He had screamed! How many knew? What of the intercom tape recordings? Who would listen to those? The Press? What of his career? The flight was supposed to have helped it. But he had screamed and those with the aura had heard! It wasn't supposed to end this way. He fled to his wife and counted the minutes until he could make a polite exit from the agony.

Mark stepped forward to do Pettigrew's presentation. He began in the typical manner of a member of the brotherhood of aviators — with facetious slander.

"Last week, Bob was part of a unique first — the first RTLS — and tonight he's enjoying another first that should be acknowledged. This is the first time he's ever come to a party with a *woman*." The crowd cheered the implication.

"Actually, it was probably that time he spent with the marines that caused his sexual identity crisis. At least let's hope that he doesn't *really* like sheep and young boys."

More hoots flooded the stage.

"There was obviously some terrible trauma in Bob's childhood, otherwise why would he have really wanted to be a helicopter pilot?"

The crowd chorused a low "ooh." It was the ultimate slam. Everybody was well aware of the marine's fierce fighter pilot pride. *If you ain't a fighter pilot, you ain't shit!* read a plaque that hung in his office.

Mark continued, "And there's other evidence of brain damage... he joined the marines."

More cheers. A few cries of *semper fi* came as a protest from a handful of other marines. Mark dodged a sandwich roll hurled by one.

"That reminds me... you know Bob is so dumb that even some of the other marines have noticed."

That comment brought a maelstrom of laughter and a barrage of carrot sticks.

Finally, he put aside the jokes and began his sincere praises of a man whom he considered a better pilot than any in the room. He loved Pettigrew, as much as a man who shunned closeness could love. They were of the same blood, brothers of the sky, siblings of the wind, kin of machines.

Judy watched the performance thinking how typical it was of Mark, that in public or private he would not allow the slightest glimpse of his emotional soul. In the frivolous joking, his speech had been fluid and relaxed, but now the genuine accolades were stuttered and barren. It took a lifetime of intimacy with the man to know he was struggling to say *I love you, Bob. We are the same. I will miss you.* Instead, he found words like "admiration" and "respect" and "appreciate" to hide behind.

He pinned the piece of gold to the marine's collar, and an energetic applause filled the room. Swept up in the moment, Denise ran onto the stage to kiss her man, like a teenager throwing herself at a rock star.

Pettigrew excused the woman with a pat to her ass, then swaggered to the podium. "Ladies and gentlemen… and all you navy girls." The navy pilots hollered their complaint. "First of all, I want to make sure the record is set straight." He paused for a long moment until a very hushed crowd was awaiting his rebuttal to Mark's libel. "BaaaAaaaAaaa!" With a superb imitation, he bleated like a sheep. The crowd roared. "Hey, what are you laughing at? Sure… I went out with a sheep once. I picked her up at an air force officer's club." Another wave of laughter swept the room.

Pettigrew continued. "Now, you can ignore the rest of Mark's comments. He's been delirious for some time. I'm sure you've seen the symptoms. For example, he really believes that wearing air force wings makes him a pilot." The comment precipitated a fusillade of air force-launched vegetables which Pettigrew deftly dodged. "In fact, Mark is just like all other air *farce* pilots, pretending to be a real pilot… a marine fighter pilot." More jeers. "Hell, he even pretends to have male sex organs." Another salad came at him. "You don't believe me? It's true! I'm serious!" The ear-to-ear grin said he wasn't. "I've got proof!" The claim was ridiculous enough to momentarily quiet the riot to see what bullshit was next. "One day I went in to use the WCS trainer. Mark had just finished with it." He referred to the waste control system trainer — the toilet trainer. "And you know what he had left behind?" Nobody had a clue, and Pettigrew let the question hang for maximum effect. "He left this!" Reaching into his pocket, he tossed a female urine collection funnel into the crowd. The function of the plastic device was known to every astronaut present, and word spread to the uninitiated at light speed. The marine had even stuck an air force logo on both sides of the gadget.

It was tossed around the room, and with each new examination, a fresh wave of laughter and joking insults lifted the roof.

Pettigrew had officially joined the brotherhood, and his aura was blinding.

❖

Friday, 9 September
Los Alamos, New Mexico

Mark stepped from the twin-engine commuter plane and into the eye-squinting glare of the New Mexico high country.

"Good afternoon, Colonel O'Malley. It's wonderful to see you again. Can I help you with your luggage?" Killingsworth greeted him.

"This is it." Mark hoisted a garment bag over his shoulder and followed his host towards the car.

"I must apologize again, Colonel, for interrupting your party the other evening. It appeared you were quite busy with speeches and… and… what did you call it? That medal?"

"Medal? Oh, the astronaut pin."

"Yes. That was it. Dr. Powers explained its significance. I felt honored to have witnessed the propagation of such a tradition. I'm sure there are few people who can say they have seen such a memorable event."

"They're not all that memorable. Pettigrew made that particular one stand out."

"Yes, his acceptance speech was… unforgettable."

They had reached the car and Mark tossed his bag in the trunk. In a minute, Killingsworth was steering them through stands of ponderosa pine and Douglas fir. Mark watched other roads turn off into the evergreens. Windowless, concrete buildings, barbed wire, and armed guards hinted of the top-secret work that was the essence of the Los Alamos laboratory complex.

"Everything is ready for your appearance."

"Thanks. What organization did you say I would be addressing?"

"Oh, just some business associates of mine."

"And what business —"

"Colonel, look!" Mark's question was interrupted. "That sign. The Anasazi Indian ruins are just ahead. Have you ever seen Indian cliff dwellings?"

"No, I…"

"Then we must stop. I was looking at them earlier in the day and they are just marvelous. Do we have time?" He glanced at his watch. "Yes, yes, we have plenty of time."

Mark immediately regretted his answer. He had been intending to hole up in the motel until the last minute and escape back to it immediately after his speech. He wanted a solitary hike with Killingsworth as much as he wanted the clap.

"I'd better catch the tour some other day. I'm not dressed for a hike." He motioned toward his dress shoes.

"It's hardly a hike… more like a short walk. And the path is well maintained. We can talk about your visit along the way."

Shit! Mark was trapped.

The fat man turned into the parking lot. "And here we are. The trail begins just beyond that gate."

Within moments they were following an asphalt path through scattered groves of piñon trees. The sky was a dome of pristine blue, and they had a godly view of the Rio Grande valley to the east. A thunderstorm darkened the peak of a distant mountain.

"Behind us is the Jemez caldera. A million years ago, a massive eruption…" Killingsworth's commentary never ceased. Mark slowed his walk to open greater distance between them.

A quarter mile farther, the trail terminated at the base of a near-vertical, ten-foot rise. A ladder of rough-hewn logs rested against it.

"Colonel, you'll be astounded by the view from the top of this plateau. We'll terminate the walk up there. Notice these indentations in the pumice rock. They were excavated by the Indians to serve as their means of ascent."

Mark immediately stepped to the ladder, afraid that if he hesitated, Killingsworth would begin a dissertation on the geologic epochs the cliff face revealed. As he reached for the top rung, a hand came to assist him.

"Let me help, Colonel."

He was stunned by the voice. There had been no other cars in the parking lot, and until that moment, he had assumed he and Killingsworth were the only ones in the park. And the unidentified speaker knew him!

"Who are…?" Mark's question was aborted as the man bent to help Killingsworth up the final step.

"Thank you, Frank. Well, what do you think, Colonel? Isn't the view spectacular?"

The view was the farthest thing from Mark's mind.

Killingsworth read his question. "Colonel O'Malley, this is a business associate of mine. Mr. Darling... Frank Darling."

Mark shook the extended hand thinking how misnamed the man was. Darling was *big* — Pettigrew-big — but younger. Probably in his early thirties, was Mark's guess. He was wearing a short-sleeved T-shirt advertising a triathlon, and Mark was certain it wasn't just a token. The man looked like he was ironman material. The raised veins of a weight lifter mapped his biceps. The face was unmistakably Nordic, with fair skin, already tinted red with sunburn, and ice blue eyes. Long, blond, surfer-style hair covered his ears. But it was the eyes that Mark found most captivating. They were cold, expressionless — an assassin's eyes. It took Mark a moment to draw his attention away from those and notice the other facial features — a sharp, triangular nose, thin lips, and a squared-off jaw. The right cheek bore a small, ragged scar just below the eye.

"Isn't the view spectacular?" Killingsworth repeated the question while drawing a deep breath and assuming the pose of a conquering explorer — hands on nonexistent hips, eyes squinted at the horizon. "The Anasazis certainly built on the choice lots. I imagine..."

"Mr. Killingsworth, let's cut the bullshit. You didn't just happen to bring me out here. You planned this." Darling's presence made that much obvious. "Why am I standing on a hot desert mesa with you and your *business associate*?"

The fat man smiled and excused Darling with a head nod. The ironman began an indifferent stroll up the trail. "Well, yes, I do owe you an explanation. You are correct in assuming I brought you here for purposes other than a tour of the ruins." He mopped his brow with a handkerchief, took a breath, and faced Mark squarely. "Colonel, I am on a special assignment for the president of the United States."

Mark could not have been more shocked if the fat man had stood on his toes and tried to kiss him.

"We are here at Los Alamos, and specifically at this site, so that I may discuss this assignment in complete secrecy. Your shock is understandable. Please, let's continue this discussion in the shade. My naked palate is frying." He made another dab with his handkerchief at his reddening forehead while leading Mark toward a shadowed bench.

"Colonel, what do you know about kinetic energy weapons?"

It was another thunderbolt.

"I can assure you, the question is relevant to our meeting."

Mark shrugged his shoulders. "Kinetic weapons? Not much. I know they were part of Star Wars research into a missile defense shield."

"Have a seat." Mark accepted the offer. Killingsworth took the empty space next to him. "Until several days ago, my knowledge of these devices was also limited… in fact, nonexistent. But I have since had the privilege of talking with the experts in the field, most of whom work here in the Los Alamos laboratory facilities. It's a fascinating subject. Did you know that it has a vernacular all its own? Rail guns, smart rocks, KE rifles, hypervelocity?"

"I've heard the terms."

"To imagine… a weapon that can accelerate an object to speeds of miles per *second* in a hundred feet or so, and using nothing but electricity! Incredible!"

Mark began searching his memory on the discussions he had had with General Healy, certain this bizarre meeting was somehow related to his new job in Los Angeles.

"And, yes, Colonel, you are correct. Our experts did examine such a system in the Strategic Defense Initiative… Star Wars. It was thought that perhaps a rail gun could be based in space and shoot down ballistic missiles. "The theory of operation, I'm told, is really quite straightforward. Small objects are pushed by an invisible wave of magnetism."

He turned to Mark. "As an engineer, I'm sure you can understand the theory. For myself, a layman, I liked the analogy that one scientist presented to me. The object rides the crest of the wave like a surfer and is accelerated at those tremendous velocities. Have you ever seen a demonstration?"

"No."

"I did yesterday. Until that moment, I thought it was all science fiction. But the technology is really quite well developed. It was a political decision that ended the work at the laboratory level — a decision, I'm afraid, recent events have shown may have been flawed — seriously flawed."

For the first time since meeting Killingsworth, Mark detected a grave tone to his voice.

"Events?"

"Within the last couple of months, this country's military satellite fleet has suffered some inexplicable losses." The fat man recounted the story of the satellite failures and the film-pod damage, then began to tick through the theories on the causes. Mark's confusion deepened. It made no sense whatever that he should be a part of this.

"And, Colonel, there are experts who believe all of these losses were the result of a deliberate Soviet attack... a rail-gun attack."

"What?!"

"Yes. Shocking, isn't it? But the story doesn't end there." In five more minutes he had explained Mason's work.

"A Soviet rail gun at geosynchronous orbit? Is that what you're saying?"

"What I'm saying, Colonel, is that we are faced with choosing between two equally improbable explanations for our cosmic problems. The failures either were merely statistical aberrations *or* they were due to Soviet mischief. If the latter is the case, then the implications are staggering. Throughout history, the armies that have commanded the high ground have won the battles. The Soviets will be in command of the highest ground available. Our nation's very existence would be in jeopardy. Our entire strategic missile force could be as useless as a bucket of stones."

Mark could only shake his head in disbelief. Was he dreaming? Did he have heatstroke? Was the little fat man a hallucination? All scenarios seemed infinitely more believable than the story of *KOSMOS* 2069. And for the hundredth time he asked himself, *Why am I hearing this?*

"There are some advocates for destroying the *KOSMOS* with a nuclear weapon, but that option carries enormous risks. Keep in mind, thus far, our only evidence of foul play is circumstantial. What if the satellite is exactly what the Soviets say it is — a peace-loving, electronic monument to socialism? What if all of our losses are explainable as acts of God? How would the Soviets react to an unprovoked attack on one of their communication assets?

"And, if we decide to attack, who is to say the satellite could not defend itself by shooting down any approaching threat?"

Mark stood. "Ty didn't waste any time, did he?"

"I beg your pardon, Colonel?"

"General Healy... Ty Healy. He called me just a couple of days ago and said he had something hot for me to work on in Los Angeles. He wasn't kidding. I'm surprised he just didn't wait until I was there to tell me himself."

"Colonel, I am not an emissary of General Healy, and the job I've come to discuss with you does not involve an air force assignment to Los Angeles." Killingsworth rose and confronted his confused guest. "The day before yesterday I was at the Johnson Space Center in a search for the best astronaut that NASA has to offer. You, Colonel O'Malley, are that astronaut. I am here at the direction of the president of the United States to ask you to command a space shuttle mission that will conduct a clandestine rendezvous with *KOSMOS* 2069, perform a survey of it, and then, if it is a weapons platform, retrieve some items from it for analysis and destroy it."

Somewhere a cicada screeched. A peal of thunder drifted over the mesa. A breeze stirred the evergreen branches. They were the only sounds. Mark was as stone silent as the long-dead Indians. He could only stand and stare, his brain replaying the fat man's words over and over and at each replay finding them more ridiculous, more laughable, more insane — so insane that he was certain he had misunderstood them.

"What did you say?"

"I know this must come as a shock, Colonel, but a manned mission is our only alternative. We need to know what *KOSMOS* 2069 really is. Only a man can do that. If it is a weapon, then a breakthrough has been made. Only a man has the dexterity and reasoning powers to determine what components should be photographed and scavenged."

Mark didn't know if he should laugh or cry. Disgust finally dominated. "Mr. Killingsworth, I hope this is some type of joke, because if it isn't, this country is in trouble. What you have just suggested is the most insane, stupid, idiotic plan I've ever heard!" The fat man accepted the tongue-lashing without comment. "For starters, there is no way... none, zero... to get the shuttle to geosync orbit! Carrying nothing but OMS fuel, we *might* get to six hundred miles, which is only about twenty-two *thousand* miles short! And, as for *clandestine*, how the hell do you hide a space shuttle? The Soviets aren't idiots! They track us just like we track them. And aren't you the one who just told me that the *KOSMOS* may be capable of defending itself against any attack? What's to stop it from firing on the shuttle? And, even if we could get up there, how do we dock with it to do all this *retrieving and destroying*?"

Killingsworth pleaded his defense. "Colonel, I can understand your skepticism. I, myself, am doubtful. However, please consider that, at this very minute, the best minds in NASA, the air force, the CIA, and industry are working on ways of solving the problems you have enumerated."

"I'll bet they are. And they're going to find they're wasting their time. It's crazy. Impossible." Mark shook his head.

Killingsworth was undaunted. "The project will be similar to the Manhattan Project which was headquartered at this very installation. Now, as then, the people selected to solve the unsolvable are the very best. I am not a scientist or engineer and am still trying to come to grips with the technical aspects of the mission, but the experts believe it is possible to approach the KOSMOS, make the inspection, and perform the necessary operations... without detection by the Soviets."

"Jesus!" Mark scoffed. The rest of the counterattack died in his throat. Killingsworth was an engineering illiterate, and it was as much a waste of time to argue with him as it would have been to argue with the bench. He wanted the bloated bureaucrat out of his face and rudely dismissed himself by walking to a nearby piñon tree. He ripped a small bough from it and began to shred its greenery. The motions were angry, bitter. The country was facing a possible Pearl Harbor, and the civil servants responsible for national security were proving themselves to be mad. The bough was reduced to a bare stalk, and he plucked another.

For a minute he was like this, blinded by knee-jerk anger. Slowly, though, the red heat began to abate and reason crept back. For the first time he began to really hear the words.

The very best minds — a team of the best was capable of remarkable things. How many times had he seen that? The entire space program was a monument to American ingenuity and teamwork. Still, this particular project seemed harebrained.

He dropped the evergreen. "Tell me more."

Killingsworth smiled, happy that he had made inroads on Mark's objections. "The effort is only several days old, so there is little more that I can tell you. As the director, I have been consumed with the organizational aspects of the project. I have had no time to become literate on the technical details. I apologize for that. But I needed to identify an astronaut to command the mission."

Command the mission! The words were slowly pushing to the front of Mark's consciousness.

"Who's the contractor?"

"Omega Company of Denver."

Mark's heart rate moved higher. The Omega Company made the most powerful rocket in the air force inventory — the *Nova*. It had been a frequent carrier for geosync payloads.

Command the mission! It had become a scream.

It could be done! It could! Just like Apollo! Just like the Manhattan Project! It would be a crash effort, but with the right people and unlimited resources, it could be done! And it's being offered to me! Command the mission!

To see the earth from twenty-two thousand miles! To see it as a globe! Only those who have been to the moon have been any higher! In my lifetime, no one is likely to ever duplicate the feat. To fly that high! To command the mission!

Killingsworth misinterpreted his hesitation. "Colonel, I realize what you must be thinking. The dangers will be extreme. The Omega engineers think that, with considerable shortcuts in design and construction, they will be able to make a late November launch. I must emphasize, those were their exact words… shortcuts in design and construction. The risks will be enormous. I will certainly understand if you refuse my offer."

Mark had heard none of his comments. He was engrossed in the coarse mental math of evaluating options for an inspection craft.

"Colonel? Do you wish to refuse?"

"Refuse? No! No, I *want* the mission! It can be done. I'm sure of it! I'll bet the Omega people are planning on augmenting a *Nova*, assembling something in low orbit. One won't be enough. Weight is going to be critical. We're going to have to strip everything. We could…"

Mark paced in a tight oval, delivering an impromptu technical dissertation that was Greek to Killingsworth. The fat man could only marvel that the pilot would so enthusiastically embrace an offer that had every possibility of killing him. He had expected an acceptance to be made with somber misgivings, doubts, fears, a worry about family. But the man in front of him showed none of these.

"It can be done! I know it! I apologize for my earlier outburst. It was just that I was taken by surprise. But I want this mission. I want it!"

"It's yours, Colonel."

"And I want to pick my crew." As Killingsworth had done, Mark's first priority was to form his team.

"Certainly. But one crew member has already been selected… Frank Darling."

Mark was thrown back into the same shock he had experienced a half hour earlier. "What?"

"Frank is…"

"No! I will not allow that, Mr. Killingsworth. This mission will be dangerous enough without taking along some goddamn passenger!"

Killingsworth was surprised by the intensity of his reaction. "Please, Colonel, listen. Frank is a CIA employee."

"I don't give a shit who he works for. This flight is no place for amateurs!" Mark stood his ground like a baseball umpire defending his call.

"Let me explain, Colonel." To the limits that his dolce voice allowed, the fat man's tone became authoritarian. "The president is responsible to a nation of two-hundred and thirty million souls. The CIA is his right arm for securing their safety. They are *the* critical agency in this project. Frank is their representative. I selected him as I selected you, only after a careful review of every qualified individual. He is the best and brings to your crew talents that you may well need."

Mark's expression said he was still a disbeliever.

"He is fluent in the Russian language. And it is possible such fluency will be critical to your flight. Remember, just getting to the *KOSMOS* does not define a successful mission. We have to understand what it is and, if it is a weapon, bring back key components. What if there are placards or markings on the *KOSMOS* that reveal the function of various modules? Could you, or any other member of your envisioned crew, read those? I have already checked the records of all astronauts. None speak Russian. Would you have time to learn in the next couple of months? I think not. And Frank holds a master's degree in physics and has begun study on rail-gun design. By your own admission, Colonel, you are totally ignorant of such weapons. If you are worried about his mettle in dangerous situations, I can tell you he has served as a CIA field agent and has distinguished himself in mortal combat."

Mark could rally no meaningful defense to the arguments. It slowly dawned on him; he was extrapolating his Senator Rush experience — the man has *screamed,* for crissake — to include all outsiders.

"Colonel, believe me. The president and I are just as concerned as you about the composition of your crew. Our nation's security will turn on how well you and your men perform. I believe my justifications for selecting Frank are inarguable."

They were.

"Okay, okay. I'll accept Darling... on one condition."

"That is?"

"If I see anything in his training that suggests he can't hack it, I leave him behind and pick my own substitute, no questions asked."

"Agreed, Colonel."

Killingsworth waved over the man who had been maintaining a discreet distance.

"Frank, Colonel O'Malley has volunteered to command the mission. I've explained your unique qualifications, and he has agreed to your presence on the crew."

Mark extended a hand in a contained but sincere welcome. For now he would give the stranger the benefit of the doubt. But Darling would be history the instant he revealed the slightest incompetence — or incapacitating fear.

"Thank you. I will be a good pilot and engineer for you." Mark noticed a trace of Northern European accent in the speech, and his diction was English-class exact — no contractions. He was also struck again by the eyes. They were robotic, mechanically lifeless. If they held any joy or fear at the thought of flying a sixty-day wonder to geosync, Mark could not detect it.

"Let's go to the laboratory, Colonel. I have a team of rail-gun experts ready to give you an overview on the theory of operation." Killingsworth led the expedition along the asphalt. "NASA and the air force will make this press release on Monday." He handed across a piece of paper.

Mark read a text that contained his name. It made him wonder what the fat man's backup plan had been if he had said no to the mission.

"The flight will be billed as a classified Defense Department mission. Because some flights will have to be slipped because of a shortage of engines, there will be nothing remarkable about a manifest change that puts the Defense Department first in line. Your delay in retirement from NASA and assignment to the mission will be explained as necessary because you are the most recently flown commander and, therefore, are in the best position to complete the accelerated training program." He continued with details of a cover story for Darling.

Command the mission! Mark's gait was lifted by the echo.

It was on the drive to the lab that he finally thought of Judy. He knew she would be disappointed. But she had always understood before and would this time, too.

CHAPTER 6

Saturday, 10 September
Houston

Mark was so distracted with thoughts of the mission he was actually surprised to see the van in front of the house. Moving had become a trivial nuisance, shoved out of a brain crammed with a thousand questions and details.

He squeezed past three sweating and swearing movers who were manhandling the refrigerator and found Judy packing the fragile items of his flying memorabilia — plastic space shuttles and aircraft models.

"Good. You're back." She walked to him, brushed his lips in a familiar kiss, then returned to the work, completely missing the too-serious look he wore. She grabbed an F-4 Phantom model and bobbed into a box. "Things have gone better than I expected. The rain has held off so they have really been able to go nonstop. This is the last room. They'll be done in an hour. God, I can't wait to get out of here and into a shower."

She brushed her forehead of the latest wave of perspiration, then began to wrap the shuttle model.

"I put some of your grubs in the bedroom closet. Could you start vacuuming the other rooms? I don't want the new owners to think we're…" It suddenly dawned on her that she was talking to herself. Mark was a mute spectator. "What's wrong?"

A swallow rippled down his throat. "There's been a change of plans."

"Change? Change of what plans?"

"Well, this trip to Los Alamos wasn't exactly what I expected. I found out there's going to be a little delay before we go to L.A."

Judy was actually relieved. His strained look had given her a brief panic attack that he was bearing tragic news — a NASA aircraft accident or a family illness.

"I, well… Judy…" Words fled him, and after uncomfortable seconds he pulled the press release from his pocket. "Here, this probably explains it better than I can."

Judy unfolded the paper and began reading.

For release at 8:00 A.M., Eastern Daylight Saving Time, Monday, 12 September:
Because of the engine damage sustained in Discovery's recent launch abort, the space shuttle flight rate will have to be reduced for an approximate twelve-month period while replacement engines are manufactured and tested. Per long established agreements, Defense Department missions will be given priority on the launch manifest. The first post-Discovery flight will be a DOD mission aboard the shuttle Atlantis. Launch is tentatively set for late November. For training optimization, Colonel Mark M. O'Malley will command the flight. His previously announced retirement from NASA is being delayed….

She read no further. Her stomach contracted to a marble and began a fall to the center of the earth.

"Ma'am, we're ready for that." The movers appeared from around the corner and indicated the desk. A last shuttle model rested on it.

Judy didn't answer. She couldn't answer. Her legs had been rubberized, and it was all she could do to keep standing.

"Ma'am, excuse me, but we're…"

"Take it," Mark directed them. "Just put that model on the bookshelf."

Judy's head remained down, the paper still in her hands. "Why?" The question was barely audible.

"I can't tell you everything. Security prevents it. It's just that, well, I was offered the mission, and…"

"Offered?" She still addressed the paper. The movers grunted the desk toward the door.

"Yea. Since I'm so far up on the training step, they felt I would be the best guy for it." She was going to cry, Mark thought. He could hear it coming in her voice. Getting her to accept the reality of the press release was going to throw him into the dark den of feminine emotions, a place where he had always felt naked, helpless.

"You could have refused?"

The question prompted another dry swallow. "Yes." A pause lengthened to ten seconds. "No, no, I couldn't. I couldn't refuse, Judy. You know how much I wanted another flight. It was a dream come true for me. I couldn't refuse it."

She finally looked up, a meniscus of tears clinging precipitously to her bottom eyelids. "Mark." Her voice was cracking. "You knew how much I wanted to leave. Didn't that matter?"

It hadn't. Not really. When Killingsworth had presented the offer, he had not given it a thought.

As soon as it was out of her mouth, Judy knew it was a stupid question. Of course she hadn't mattered. She had never mattered when she was standing next to the shuttle. Never.

"Listen, Judy, these guys are almost done. Let's make a quick sweep of the place and get a room at the Hilton. We can clean up and go out for a nice dinner. We'll find an apartment tomorrow. I know you're disappointed, but this isn't the end of the world or anything."

She didn't hear him. She was blind and deaf to everybody and everything — except the sights and sounds of the LCC roof: shrieking women, crying children, her own screams, *Discovery* disappearing around the VAB wall in a steep, plunging turn. Those were the sights and sounds that came to her — the sights and sounds of Mark's death, of her own death. And now she would have to die again. It was too much. Too, too much.

Unable to think of anything else to say, Mark reached to gather her into his arms.

"No!" She screamed like a rape victim, sending him jumping back and causing the movers to nearly drop their load. "Don't you touch me! Don't you dare touch me!"

"Judy, please, listen. It's only for this last time. Just one more time. We'll be in L.A. by Christmas. What's another couple of months?"

"Another couple of months? *Another couple of months?!* I'll tell you what another couple of months are! It's another trip to the LCC roof!

Another countdown! Another couple of months of worrying if I'm going to be a widow! Goddamn you, Mark! Goddamn you to hell! You don't love me! If you had even a shred of love for me, you could never do this!" She wadded the paper and hurled it in his face.

The movers remained in place, the desk no longer heavy and voyeurism written on their faces. Mark cringed at their stares.

"Judy. You just can't understand. I…"

"You're right. You're absolutely right." Her voice was vile. "I don't understand. I wish I could. I wish I could understand how to compete with a machine. How do I do that, Mark?" Sarcasm dripped from the question. "How? Should I write to Dear Abby?

'Dear Abby, My husband is having an affair with a machine. What should I do? Signed, Don't Understand.'

"God… God… God… I wish it was another woman. I could understand that. I could compete with that. But how…?" She was pleading. "…How do I compete with this?!" She snatched the shuttle model from the bookcase and brandished it in his face.

Mark was silent. He had no answer. He was born the way he was. Flight was life. "Let's not argue about this now. You're tired. I'm tired. Why don't you get in the car and go on down to the Hilton. I'll finish everything here and meet you later."

"Oh, I'm leaving, Mark."

He was relieved by the statement. The sooner she got to the hotel, took a shower, and got some rest, the sooner she would calm down and understand.

"Yes, I'm leaving. But don't look for me at the hotel." The shuttle model fell from her hand and shattered on the floor. She shoved the movers aside and walked from the door, her ending words tossed over her shoulder. "I'm driving out of your life, Mark. You can fly ten more times… a hundred! I don't care! I'm going to Peggy's!"

"Judy, please… just…" He followed after her, but she ignored him. At the car, she jerked his previously packed suitcases from the trunk and angrily dumped them on the cement. Mark let her. The moving van was blocking the driveway. She would have to stay. In the delay, reason would return.

"Judy, there's a truck behind you!" He shouted the obvious as she climbed behind the wheel. But it didn't stop her. She dropped the transmission into reverse, screeched the tires, turned the car through the grass, bounced over the curb, and drove out of his life.

Sunday, 11 September
Houston

"What the hell is all this about, Mark? I have better things to do on a Sunday afternoon than come to a nature center for a tour by some midget, faggot guide. Who the hell is Killingsworth? And who the hell is the Nazi he's with?" Pettigrew had pulled his friend a discreet distance behind the others to ask the questions. Mark's telephone call of last night had been cryptically empty of information. *Don't ask any questions, Bob. Just be there — one o'clock.*

"You'll find out in a minute."

Fearing that Sunday work at a government installation would draw too much attention, Killingsworth had insisted on having the meeting somewhere other than the Johnson Space Center. He had suggested a park. Mark had picked the Armand Bayou Nature Center, a nearby preserve of southeast Texas swamp and forest. And now the fat man led the group, including the new initiates, Pettigrew and Anna Rowe, over a boardwalk trail. As he had done in New Mexico, he maintained a nonstop babble about the glories of nature. No one listened.

"Why is Anna here?"

"In a minute, Bob. Everything is going to make sense in a minute."

The trail bridged a swampy, lily-padded pond, and Killingsworth slowed to look at the turtles stroking their way through the reeds and grasses. "Do you come here often, Lieutenant?" He addressed the woman.

"No. This is only my second time." Anna held the same wonders as Pettigrew about this strange little man and Mark's baffling phone call, but she had the patience to wait for answers.

"A pity. It seems so quiet, peaceful." He watched her, becoming angry at Mark again at what he was seeing. *How could he select a woman for this mission!* Had he known, he would have argued vehemently against the choice. He was a staunch supporter of the feminist movement, but only up to the point where women would be exposed to danger. Women were always to be protected. And now, Mark had endangered one — a young and beautiful one.

He had already correctly guessed her age as twenty-eight. She was taller than he, but then, who wasn't. Five feet, six or seven inches was that guess. Her clothes, loose-fitting slacks and a high-buttoned blouse, made it difficult to gauge her figure, but, in certain of her motions, the fabric would tighten enough to hint at a Venus beneath. Her face was definitely a work of a master — flawless skin, soft, rounded features, a slight cleft in her chin, a rapacious mouth with a vermillion of lips that stirred up long-dead boyhood images of sweet, desirable femininity. *And her eyes!* They sparkled with a green verdancy that, to that moment, he had only seen duplicated in gems. They were framed in thick, blond lashes, and above them were eyebrows of long, feathered, golden filaments. Her hair was of the same gold, cut boyishly short, parted on the right, and waved across her forehead.

"How long have you been in the astronaut business, Lieutenant?"

"Three years."

"Have you flown in space yet?"

"Yes, once... a year ago on a mission that Mark commanded."

He had discreetly maneuvered her to the question that was most on his mind. "I have never met a woman astronaut before. What do your husband and children think of your career?"

"I'm not married."

At least that aspect of Mark's choice gladdened him. He wished it was true for O'Malley himself — for all of them. If it was possible, he would have had an entire crew of spouseless, childless orphans. There should be nobody but him and the president to grieve if the group failed to return.

They had entered a forest of oak and pine. Armadillos scratched in the dirt. The staccato hammering of a woodpecker echoed emptily. The day was gray with a threat of rain, and few others shared the trail — just an occasional bird watcher.

Killingsworth finally called a halt at a bench set under a massive, moss-laden oak. It satisfied his security requirements — there was a clear view of the approaches to the site. He motioned Pettigrew and Anna to the seat. Anna accepted. Pettigrew chose to lean against the tree and light up a miniature cigar. He clamped the tobacco between his teeth and crossed his arms in a body language that said he didn't particularly like the fat man.

Killingsworth cleared his throat, puffed himself, and squeaked out the same preamble he had given to Mark in Los Alamos. "Colonel Pettigrew, Lieutenant Rowe, I represent the president of the United States."

As the fat man plunged into the *KOSMOS* story, Mark watched their eyes widen with the same amazement he had experienced. He used the time to once again consider his choices.

Pettigrew. The marine was the best pilot he had ever met — fearless but not foolhardy. The kick-the-tire, light-the-fire, scarf-in-the-wind character was a facade. Behind it was a professional who knew the intricacies of the shuttle systems as well as the engineers who had designed them.

Anna Rowe. The woman had Pettigrew's natural piloting skills. But she was not his equal yet. His much greater breadth of experience gave him the edge. But someday she would be. Mark had seen enough pilots to recognize those who didn't really *learn* to fly, but rather came into the world with an unconscious knack for it. Pettigrew and Anna were two of those. In the air, they blended with their machines, became extensions of them.

Like Pettigrew, Anna was a test pilot. She was also the first military woman pilot to have been selected for the astronaut program. At the time of that selection, she had been assigned to the navy's experimental aircraft testing facility at Patuxent River, Maryland, and had accumulated more than twelve hundred hours of flying time in high-performance, fighter aircraft. Mark felt her credentials were as good as some of the males who had been selected as pilot astronauts, but NASA had chosen her as a mission specialist. He believed the rumors that, after proving herself, she would be designated a pilot astronaut and would eventually become the first woman to command a shuttle. From personal experience, he felt the promotion was already overdue.

That experience had come on the earlier mission he had commanded with Anna aboard. Then, they had flown to rescue a tumbling, twenty-ton satellite. Anna had been responsible for the fifty-foot robot arm — their only means of capturing the spacecraft. The arm's primary operating system had failed, and she had been forced to utilize a severely degraded backup system. Mark had been certain the mission would end as a half-billion-dollar failure, but Anna had captured the machine, succeeding where many others would have failed.

Killingsworth was finishing his story. "A manned mission is our only recourse. It will be exceedingly dangerous, but we need a man to inspect the Soviet machine. Colonel O'Malley's retirement from NASA is being delayed, and he will command the flight."

As Mark had before them, Pettigrew and Anna had been struggling to make sense of why they were sitting in a forest listening to a gnome tell them things they could not possibly have any reason to know. Now they understood. Mark was commanding the mission. They were going to be offered a place on it! Each wanted to accelerate their babbling benefactor to the question, each wanted to lunge at the opportunity, uncaring of the risks. Only the fat man did not understand the astronaut ethos — to fly! To fly higher and faster!

Killingsworth continued with a pitch for CIA participation. "Mr. Darling will be a crew member. He brings some special talents."

Pettigrew straightened at the announcement, his focus burning into the interloper. Darling had gotten a military-short haircut since the Los Alamos meeting, and the buzz amplified his look of a jackbooted, Aryan-pure storm trooper. Mark could tell the fat man's justification wasn't playing well with the marine. But he was certain that Pettigrew, as he had, would eventually warm to the idea.

"Colonel O'Malley has nominated you for the other positions of the crew." Killingsworth stared at Anna as he continued, as if what he was saying was intended especially for her — which it was. "You are under no obligation to accept. If the *KOSMOS* is armed, the mission will be *extremely* hazardous. Though it is important we form our team as rapidly as possible, I am prepared to wait until tomorrow morning for your replies. That will give you time to think about…"

Pettigrew tuned out the fat man, ground his cigar butt into the dirt, and stepped to Mark. "Thanks, Mark. I'm aboard."

Anna was a step behind him. "Me, too."

Killingsworth found the bench his only audience for his dissertation about the dangers of design shortcuts. *How could she do it? She's just a young woman! She could die! How can any of them accept the mission so casually? Don't they understand what I'm saying?!*

"Okay, Hobie. We've got ourselves a crew. Let's go. I want to get to Denver as soon as possible." The group started moving along the trail, and Mark issued his orders to the new hires. "Whatever the Omega engineers are planning, it will have to involve earth-orbit assembly. Bob, Anna, a training team is already being assembled to help us. We're going to have the best of everything. I want you two in the simulator practicing rendezvous and capture. Bob, you take the orbiter controls. Anna, I want you to handle the remote arm. I've already told Frank to get smart on the EVA procedures." He referred to the spacewalk procedures.

They arrived back at the parking lot with Killingsworth rushing to catch up, waddling like one of the nearby ducks. "I'm returning to Washington for consultations with the president and his advisors, but I'll be in daily touch. Before we part, however, let me caution you about security. If we are to have any hope of success, surprise must be total. In the future, when you have reason to discuss the *KOSMOS* connection to your flight, do not use Johnson Space Center facilities. They are almost certainly targets of Soviet agents. Instead, gather at randomly selected public locations. Invariably, you can find isolation in the midst of crowds."

Mark nodded his understanding, then directed another fifteen-minute exchange of ideas on the mission. More orders were given. Finally, handshakes ended the meeting and the others returned to their cars. Mark and Pettigrew were left alone.

"Why did you pick Anna?" Pettigrew's question was not prompted by any male chauvinistic prejudices. He had none. Anna was a pilot. In fact, she was an alumna of the same navy flying schools he had attended. They wore the same wings. In his mind, that was the only discriminator in life. Gender, religion, color, race, money, power — all were meaningless differentiators. *If you ain't a fighter pilot, you ain't shit*. The adage formed the foundation of his predilection. Wings were all that mattered. Gold navy wings were the best. Even the air force's silver were okay. Anna's were the best. They were gold.

But he knew little about the woman. Until this day, he had traded only passing pleasantries with her. She had been in a different group of astronaut recruits and had an office on the opposite side of the building, and they didn't frequent the same social haunts. Their paths rarely crossed. In an office of ninety people — all head down in the never-ending urgency of their own training — it was easy for a fellow astronaut to be a stranger. It took a crew assignment to bring people into the long term closeness that would ultimately produce friendships or antipathy.

Mark answered the marine's question on Anna's selection with a recount of her performance on her first mission, concluding with, "There's no one better, Bob. I picked her because she's the best with the arm."

Pettigrew silently accepted the explanation. If Mark said she was best for the flight, then she was.

They began walking to their cars. "Bob, I've got an apartment now. Here's my new phone number."

"How did the move go?"

Mark wished he knew the answer. He was still assessing the personal damages of yesterday. Did he still have a wife? He suspected that he did, that Judy would cool down and come to realize her place was with her husband, but her response had been so extreme, so shocking, he couldn't be absolutely sure. She had said, *I'm leaving*. But what did that mean? Leaving town? Leaving him? How long? A week? Forever?

He had called several of the local hotels and motels to see if she had been bluffing about driving out of town, but none had her on their guest list. A call to Peggy Marlow in Mountain View, California — her announced destination — had only served to alienate him from another woman. She had not yet heard from Judy, but his question had begged an explanation and that had left her solidly allied with Judy. *Asshole* was the epitaph she had closed with.

She was driving to Peggy's, he had finally decided. The woman was her best friend of more than twenty years — the widow of one of his pilot-training classmates — so it seemed logical she would turn to her. He concluded that, in a couple of days, he would hear she had safely arrived, and then he would have the exact answer to Pettigrew's question on how the move had really gone. For now, he could only share his confusion with his friend. It was contrary to his personality to be so intimate — even with someone as close as Bob — but the separation would be impossible to hide.

"The move went okay... except for Judy. She left me."

Pettigrew stopped dead in his tracks, turned, and faced Mark. "Left?"

"When I told her about the mission, she went crazy."

Pettigrew listened to the story. At first, it was a confidence that bothered him. Judy and Mark were not only his best friends, he had also seen them as proof that a loving and enduring relationship between a man and woman was not just a myth. Finally, though, with all of the facts on the table, his mood lightened. Judy had merely been frightened by her recent experience with the RTLS. It was a woman's transient hysteria and not at all serious. He told Mark as much. "She'll be back. Don't worry."

❖

Sunday, 11 September
Denver

It was 5:00 P.M. Colorado time before Mark arrived at the Omega factory and twenty minutes later before he had successfully transited the multiple layers of security. The final guard gave him directions to Dr. Striegel's office, and he was nearing it when he heard the shouting.

"Veight ist the problem! Veight! Veight! Veight! You must make zest design simple! Verstehen? Understand? This is too heavy! Vun hour! Vun hour! I want you back in *vun* hour with a simple design! A hundred pounds lighter! Nein! Two hundred pounds lighter! Now, get out! Out! Out!" A chastened-looking engineer in his late twenties was pushed into the hallway by the barrage of accented English. In his nervousness, he dropped a sheaf of blueprints that Mark had to step around to get into the shouter's doorway.

The legend was sitting at a conference room table. Mark had never met him. Ernst Striegel had been long retired from the space business before Mark had come to NASA. A rocketry genius who had labored his entire life in the shadow of the late Dr. von Braun, he had been as instrumental as that more recognized celebrity in putting America on the moon. Even now, twenty years after last setting aside his slide rule, there were no rocket designs flying that didn't bear some signature of his prodigy. Killingsworth had heard of his reputation from the president's chief scientist and had recruited him out of retirement to head up the design of the *KOSMOS* rendezvous machine.

Now, Mark stood before him — a man in his early seventies with a wild, white, Einsteinian hairdo and a liver-spotted face that was vagrant-scruffy with a two-day growth of beard. His teeth worked over the stem of a brown pipe, while his eyes glared impatiently through thick reading spectacles.

"Well, don't just stand there! We've got a rocketship to build! What's your problem?" The growls around the pipe were less fierce than had chased the previous visitor and held only a trace of accent. Still, Mark felt like a plebe at the academy being dressed down by an upperclassman.

"I'm Mark O'Malley. Mr. Killingsworth…"

In the distraction of his work, Striegel heard only the fat man's name and assumed Mark was one of his minions. "You tell Mr. Killingsworth I'm doing the impossible as fast as I can. The only thing that will slow me down is visits by you bureaucrats. Now… you know where the door is." He returned to his work. Mark immediately liked the man.

"Dr. Striegel, I'm not from Washington. I'm Mark O'Malley… Colonel O'Malley. I'm…"

No further explanation was needed. The name finally registered. The pipe came out of the doctor's mouth. A wide smile welcomed. "Colonel O'Malley! Of course! Our astronaut! I was told you would be coming. Please, be seated. Excuse my rudeness. It's just…"

"No need to apologize, Doctor." Mark shook the offered hand and took a chair. "I liked what I heard." Neither man had time for extended pleasantries and they ended there. "How is the work going?"

Striegel took a deep breath and leaned back. "For the first time in my life, Colonel, I have a blank check. I have the best of the best in my employment. That little fat man has worked miracles. We will build your rocket. Of that, I am sure. But, I must be honest. There is only so much that can be done even with such vast resources. We will have to cut testing to a minimum." He thought for a second, sucking on his pipe. "No, Colonel, that is not an honest enough answer. Much testing won't be done at all. We will make our best design, assume our numbers are correct, and fly with it… or rather, *you* will fly with it."

"How far have you gotten on the design? Friday, when I talked by telephone with some of your people, they could only say earth-orbit assembly would be needed."

"The design was finalized earlier today." He searched through a litter of papers. "Four days, Colonel. Four continuous days of computer work and arguments and we have a *final* design. If there had been no urgency to this project, that process would have taken a year. That should give you some idea of how corners are being cut. Here." He found the page. "This is an artist's conception of the KRV."

"KRV?"

"Excuse me, KRV stands for *KOSMOS Rendezvous Vehicle*. You

know how this business is. Nothing is done without abbreviations."

The conceptual print depicted an orbiting shuttle rendezvoused with a *Nova*. Elevated at a fifty-degree angle from the payload bay was another rocket booster. The shuttle's remote arm was grappled to the *Nova* and holding its base to the front of the elevated machine.

Striegel explained. "A few days prior to your launch, we will orbit a *Nova* into a low orbit... a shuttle orbit. On its front will be accommodations for two men. We could get you to geosync with just that machine, but you would run out of fuel on the way back. So, the shuttle will carry another *Nova* first stage in her cargo bay. That will be mounted on a yoke that can be tilted upward, as you see in the drawing."

Mark was familiar with the design. A tilt table was commonly used to elevate satellites and their booster rockets for release from the shuttle.

"You will rendezvous with the separately orbited *Nova*, grab it with the remote arm, move it into position, and bolt it to the shuttle-carried *Nova* first stage. You and your copilot will then move into *Freedom's* cockpit... that is the name the workers have given her. I hope it meets with your approval."

They were free men in a hell-bent rush to ensure their freedom was still secure. Mark could not imagine a more appropriate name. He nodded his acceptance.

"Once you are at the front, your fellow astronauts in the shuttle cockpit will throw the switches to pyrotechnically separate the assembled *Freedom* from her tilt table. The arm will then lift her clear of *Atlantis* and release her. The transfer burns to geosync will then proceed.

"You will be riding a four-stage, one hundred and sixty foot long, one hundred and eighty thousand pound vehicle. By the time you reach the *KOSMOS*, *Freedom* will be a two-stage, sixty-foot vehicle. If you find that the *KOSMOS* is a weapon, you will dock with it and perform your work. If the machine is benign, well... you will have made a dangerous trip for naught. In any event, you will fly *Freedom* to lower orbit for a pickup by the shuttle and return home."

It sounded so simple, Mark thought, like describing a drive to the store, omitting the fact the carburetor would have to precisely mix fuel and air, the intake and exhaust valves would have to open and close in the correct sequence, the cylinders would have to compress the gas, and the timing system would have to fire the spark at the exact millisecond. If any of those, or a hundred other critical events, did not occur, the car would not run and the driver would be inconvenienced. If *Freedom* failed, he and Darling would suffer the ultimate inconvenience... death.

"How do we explain away our rendezvous with the *Nova*?"

Striegel shrugged. "That is a detail yet to be worked out."

"And how do we hide a one hundred and sixty foot long vehicle from Soviet radar?"

"Another detail, Colonel, I'm afraid nobody yet has an answer to. All I can say is, we are working on those problems."

Mark forced himself to remember the project was only four days old. Give the whiz kids a chance, he lectured himself. He went on to other things. "There's no cockpit detail in this drawing. Do you have another drawing of that?"

"Better than that... a full-scale mockup of the cockpit, another miracle, is sitting on the factory floor. I can better address your questions there."

Striegel rose to lead the way, and for the first time Mark noticed he was a cripple. After each step of his left foot, he would make a deep bobbing motion and swing a useless right leg in a wide arc. The squeaking noise of a prosthesis accompanied the locomotion.

Exiting the elevator, Mark was immediately struck by the sense of urgency. Nobody walked. Like Christmas Eve shoppers rushing to beat the store closings, people hurried from point to point. Baggy-eyed men worked at drafting tables with the silent intensity of monks copying Old Testament scripture. A second shift of workers dozed on cots that had been deployed around the factory perimeter. He had found the front lines of the *KOSMOS* war.

At the rocket, Striegel continued the lesson. "We were very fortunate there was a *Nova* in the final stages of construction. This vehicle was to have launched a communication satellite in February, so it's well on its way to completion."

They began a walk of the length of the gleaming, stainless-steel tubing of the missile. It rested horizontally on wheeled cradles, and its fifteen-foot diameter dwarfed the men. Twin, ribbed bells — the engine nozzles — protruded from the back of the first stage.

"It's the modifications that are killing us. Like this one." He indicated the break between the first and second stages. Scaffolding covered the area, and a crowd of men and women worked from it. "The first stage will be jettisoned during the *Nova*'s launch and orbit circularization achieved with a partial burn of the second stage. You will rendezvous with everything forward of this point. Then the trick will be to attach another first stage...the one you will carry in the shuttle. These people are working on the changes necessary to allow that joining."

"And exactly how will I do that?"

"Explosive bolts, Colonel. You will have to align the two pieces with the shuttle's remote arm and then thread twelve bolts into place to secure the stages. Controls will be placed in the cockpit to allow you to fire those bolts and separate from the first stage after its fuel is expended."

They passed the divides between successive stages, with Striegel pointing out key features. Finally, the forward end came into view. "We've just finished removing the communications satellite adapter. The cockpit modifications will start immediately."

The amputation had left bundles of wires and tubing protruding from the blunt top of the final Nova stage. Workers armed with drawings and multimeters were making sense of the spaghetti.

"This will be our toughest challenge... turning an unmanned rocket into a manned rocket. And weight is our biggest enemy, Colonel. From the low orbit you will depart, it takes eight pounds of propellant to put each pound of payload into geosync and eight pounds to bring it back. That's about three thousand pounds of fuel just for your flesh and bone. Then we have to provide you with a life-support system. And, if you are to rendezvous with an object, you will need a radar. Then, you will need a means of docking. And tools. And storage space to return any parts from the *KOSMOS*. All of these requirements translate into weight... weight we cannot lift. So, it will be impossible to build a conventional cockpit."

Mark turned his head in a search for the mockup.

"It's over here, Colonel." Striegel bobbed and squeaked his way around a partition. "The cockpit design we have selected is the essence of simplicity. As I said, weight gives us no choice. On the down side though, it will expose you to even greater danger."

They rounded the wall and the mockup came into view.

"This?!"

Monday, 12 September
Houston

Mark's right. She's good. Very good. Pettigrew made the observation while standing shoulder to shoulder with Anna in the aft station of the shuttle simulator. They were in the final moments of a practice rendez-vous and capture — a real-world task that could only be completed with the crew facing aft into the cargo bay. Only from that position were all three components of the delicate ballet simultaneously visible — the orbiter, the satellite, and the remote arm.

Pettigrew was on the starboard side, his left hand resting on the black-knobbed stick of the translational hand controller — the THC — and his right hand grasping the rotational hand controller — the RHC. With these, he was gently nudging a simulated quarter-million pound orbiter to its simulated quarry — a tumbling, sixty-foot long satellite. On the port side of the cockpit, Anna held identical THC and RHC controls for flying the arm.

"I'm coming aft a little." Pettigrew announced his intentions. There was no shuttle task that demanded greater coordination between crew members than the satellite capture task. It was critical each person knew what the other was doing. Mistakes could result in a collision and death.

Pettigrew pushed in on the THC. The control was designed so the orbiter would fire thrusters to move — to translate — in the direction of its displacement — up and down, forward and aft, left and right.

"Now, a touch of right yaw." A twist of the RHC fired the correct combination of jets that swung the orbiter's payload bay into alignment with the satellite.

They alternated their attention between the overhead and aft-facing windows. Near lifelike scenes of the satellite, the orbiter cargo bay, and the remote arm were being generated by the simulation computers and projected onto these windows. Although they were standing in a machine in Houston, the out-the-window view was of a rendezvous with a spacecraft in a two hundred mile high, eighteen thousand mile per hour orbit. The scene was being continually updated by the computers to reflect their inputs to the orbiter and remote arm controls — a billion dollar video game.

"That looks good, Bob. You just need to come up about fifteen feet."

Pettigrew tapped the THC to the up position, and the satellite image grew larger in the window. He stabilized the vehicle with a down tap. "Close enough?"

"Yea, that's good. Hold it there." She watched the spikelike grapple fixture on the satellite image rotate into view and began maneuvering the arm toward it.

"Those rates are too high. You'll never get it." Pettigrew referred to the tumbling motion of the spacecraft. Throughout the morning, the simulation operators had been increasing the difficulty of the capture task by giving the satellite successively higher tumble rates. On this run, he was certain the rates were too high and a capture would be impossible.

"Maybe. But I'm going to give it a try."

There! It happened again. Twice already, he had felt it — in her speech and actions — a strange feeling of déjà vu, of having lived these moments, of having known Anna Rowe. But that was not possible. Until four hours ago, he had never exchanged five sentences with her. He shrugged it off, checked the satellite's position in the overhead window — it looked good — then glanced to his right to watch her work.

All morning he had been taking these moments to do so, to measure her talent. He suspected she was making the same assessment of his. It was a fundamental precept of airmanship — to know the limits of your wingmen. The timid, the weak, the incompetent could kill you. So far, nothing in Anna's behavior indicated she was any of these. Quite the contrary. As she was doing that very moment, she had demonstrated a consistent and fierce will to succeed. Aggressiveness, sound judgment, and expert motor skills were all cherished qualities in a pilot, and Anna seemed to have an abundance of each.

"Missed!" She shook her head in self-chastisement. In spite of her best effort, the rates had been too high to complete the capture. The grapple spike rotated out of view of the TV camera.

"Nice try, Anna, but you're not going to get it. Those sim people will have to turn down the rates."

"No. Not yet. I want to give it another shot."

Like the tiniest speck of sand blown into the eye, her words seemed to find some strangely sensitive crevice in his soul and irritate it. But in a heartbeat, it was gone, blinked away.

Within a minute, the spacecraft tumble had brought the spike back into view, and Anna launched another attack at it. The marine returned to his surreptitious assessment of the woman and was again pleased by Mark's choice. Her concentration was intense. Her eyes flitted between the windows, the TV monitors, and the arm displays, and her hands remained in a continuous fluid caress of the controls.

Then, slowly, he began to see Anna Rowe, the woman. A fluorescent light glared just inches above her left ear, and the cramped cockpit kept him less than two feet from her. Imperfections would have been impossible to miss, but he saw none — just softly rounded cheeks of milk-pure flesh, a perfectly formed nose and chin, a delicate neck. Her mouth was the only exception to the image of youthful innocence. It was full and suggestive of all the latent power of her sex. In the intensity of her concentration, the pink tip of her tongue darted to wet her lips.

As far as he could tell, she wore no cosmetics. Not even lipstick. And no jewelry. Her ears were not even pierced. She radiated the simple, subtle beauty of a Norman Rockwell girl-next-door subject. And that, he decided, was why he had not previously noticed her. Hers was a different beauty than that of the high-cheekboned, long-haired, painted, and adorned women whom he normally bedded.

She jerked back on the THC. The grapple fixture had again rotated out of view. Another miss. Her right thumb came to her mouth and she nervously chewed its nail. It was the only chink he had seen in her armor of self-confidence.

"Give up?"

"One more time."

She was back on the controls, and Pettigrew was back in his study. He had no worry about discovery. It was easy to hide the true focus of his eyes. The robot arm TV monitors were on her far side, and it was part of his piloting task to watch those.

His gaze roamed across her front, but her blouse had baggy, pleated pockets that completely disguised the size and shape of her breasts. Loose-fitting slacks did the same for her legs and ass. If there was a curve below the neck, he couldn't find it. A nun could have taken a dressing lesson from her, was his thought.

He left her body and returned to work, watching her third grapple attempt. At first, the control inputs confused him. She had the arm moving before the spike had even rolled into camera view. Then, he understood her plan. She was attempting to lead the target, commanding full translation rates with no direct view of the grapple target. On her two previous attempts, she had watched the markings on the spacecraft image and mentally calculated the point at which she should make the control input.

When the spike finally did tumble into view, the arm was aimed just slightly to the right, but most importantly, the relative motion between arm and spike was near zero. She quickly corrected the lateral misalignment and drove the robot onto the image of the steel shaft. A squeeze of the capture trigger commanded the mating device on the arm to twist a snare of simulated cables around the probe. In less than fifteen seconds the capture was complete. The simulated spacecraft was welded to the simulated arm.

"Got it!"

"Great job, Anna!"

"I'm going to stow it this time. It's good practice."

Pettigrew understood. For the *KOSMOS* mission he could not envision a requirement to stow anything in the cargo bay. But the challenge of doing so — of putting an object the equivalent of two Greyhound buses in a space only inches larger than two Greyhound buses — would hone her skills for whatever robot arm tasks the mission would ultimately require. But it was a job that did not need him, and he moved forward in the cockpit, took a seat on the center instrument panel, and began reviewing the rendezvous checklist.

A moment later the study was interrupted when her work finally brought him a view of her curves. To get a better view of the position of the satellite, she rose on her toes and leaned forward into the aft window. The effect was to draw the fabric of her trousers tightly across her buttocks and surprise him with a pair of perfect, taunt mounds. And the revelation did not end there. She turned sideways to type to the orbiter computer keyboard and then stood reading the display while absently reaching behind her back to tuck in her blouse. For an instant, the pleats of the pockets disappeared — stretched button-bulging tight across the high, full curves of her breasts. He laughingly kidded himself that maybe he had finally discovered the source of his familiarity with the woman — just last night he had dined on a marvelous pair of tits, just like hers.

"I'm almost..."

Caught!

He had been caught in the stare. Her turn to him had been completely unexpected, and his eyes were a millisecond too slow in their rush back to the checklist.

She sensed what he had been doing, and it caused her to stumble in the completion of her sentence. "…done. Another couple of minutes." Her words were cooler now.

"Take your time. I've got things to look at… I mean, ahh, the checklist. I mean…" *God!* He felt stupid and knew he sounded the same. When was the last time he had cared that a woman saw him visually undressing her? When was the last time he had found a woman who didn't enjoy the stare? For both questions the answer was — a very, very long time ago.

Why was it different with this woman? That, he couldn't answer.

Tuesday, 13 September
Denver

Mark was exhausted when he stepped into the motel room at 8:00 P.M. In the past two days he had managed only six hours of sleep, and all of that had been on a cot at the factory. He desperately needed a shower and a few hours of rest in a real bed to become productive again. Nonstop work on *Freedom's* cockpit had driven him to his knees. Controls had to be designed for the engines, for stage separation, for the laser radar, for the navigation computer, for the docking mechanism, for the life-support system, for twenty other functions. And that was just the tip of the iceberg. Somehow they had to find room to mount the knobs and switches and sticks of those controls. There would be little real estate on which to do so. Striegel's design was a motorcycle. No, he corrected himself. It was a kite.

He sat on the bed, picked up the phone, and dialed Peggy Marlow's, praying as he did so this call would go better than the last. That had been on Sunday when he had made another check to see if the woman had heard from Judy. This time she had and, in the process, had acquired Judy's perspective of Saturday's debacle. It had earned him another tongue lashing, *You're a selfish prick, Mark!* He had no friend in Peggy Marlow.

But at least the call had relieved his worries about Judy. She was going to Mountain View. And the more he thought about that, the more he thought perhaps it was for the best. It was obvious now he would be spending little time in Houston. Judy would have been left alone in an apartment. At least in California she could enjoy the company of her best friend.

"Hello." Peggy answered.

"It's Mark, Peggy. Did Judy get in?"

There was an impolite pause. "Yea. She's here." The voice told him he was still an asshole and a selfish prick in Peggy Marlow's estimation.

"Can I speak to her?"

"Sure, Mark. Just forget about that goddamn space shuttle and you can come out here and talk to her for the rest of your life."

Mark's fatigue pushed him over the edge. He was tired of taking shit from women, particularly this one. "Peggy, this is none of your goddamn business! Just put Judy on!"

"The hell it isn't my business! I know more about what's going on with your wife than you'll ever know! You're just like Bill was… in love with yourself and your career and your flying! You're a selfish bastard just like he was! You don't give a damn about the agony you inflict on Judy! Nobody is ever going to walk up to *you* and tell *you* that your spouse is… is… is a grease spot on the end of a runway! Don't tell me this is none of my business! I've been where Judy is, but I made a mistake! I didn't walk out the door like she did, and I got to see the chaplain walk in! Goddamn you! Don't you dare tell me this is none of my business!"

His plan to go on the offensive, to assert himself, went up in smoke. Her mention of Bill Marlow's death did it. How could he counter that?

"Peggy, listen. Let me just…"

"It's me, Mark." Judy's arctic-cold voice came on the receiver.

"Judy, thank God. Peggy is being a real bitch. Listen, I…"

"Are you going to quit the mission?"

If she had asked if he was going to cut off his testicles, the question would not have had a greater effect. "What?"

"Are you going to quit the mission?"

"Quit? No. No, I can't quit."

"Then we have nothing to talk about. Good-bye, Mark."

"No! Listen, don't hang up! Judy? Judy?"

There was a pause. "I'm still here."

"Listen, there are things about this mission that I can't talk about. You don't underst——" He aborted the comment, remembering the explosion it had produced in Houston. "All I can say is it's critical that I fly it."

"And the next one?"

"What?"

"What will be your excuse for flying the next one?"

"A next one? There won't be a next one. This will be my last."

"Sure it will." The words were cold sarcasm.

"No, Judy, I mean it. I really mean it." An eavesdropper would have thought he was swearing off the bottle.

"Mark. Mark." Her voice fell into sad resignation. "Do you want me to go through the list of how often you've broken that promise? I've had two thousand miles to think about it. Remember Vietnam, Mark? The first time you went, there might have been a shred of patriotism in your motive. But the second time? What about the second time? You didn't have to go. Nobody asked you. You volunteered. I can remember you and Bill standing at the O'club bar and reminiscing about your first tour. *Shit hot! Combat rules! No rules! Two missions a day! Yankin' and bankin' all over the sky! Going for the kill!* I believe those were just a few of the terms you two used to describe the *fun* you missed. You had hardly been home six months and then left me with two babies and a kiss and walked out the door. And you know what I remember most about that moment, Mark? I remember your smile. You were like a little kid on Christmas morning. It wasn't patriotism driving you over for the second time. It was *you*, Mark, *you!*

"And your extension at Edwards? You had orders in your hand, Mark. You had laid your life on the line for three years flying some mad scientists' crazy inventions… machines that hardly looked like they belonged in this century. Machines that killed, Mark. How many memorial services did we go to? I'll bet you don't have a clue. You want to guess?" The sarcasm was back.

"Judy…"

"Four, Mark. Four times we buried friends. Four young widows. Thirteen fatherless kids. And then we had orders to leave. Our time was up. We had orders! But what happened? You begged and pleaded and worked the system to get an extension, to stay another two years, to fly more crazy, insane machines, to bury a couple more friends. You knew how badly I wanted to leave Edwards, but that didn't count. Not at all.

"And then, we come to NASA."

"Judy, stop. This isn't going to solve…"

"Oh yes it is, Mark. It's going to solve a lot of things. It's going to make you see that you're kidding yourself when you say there won't be another mission. Tell me. Tell me right now… yes or no. If they came to you this very second and said you could stay at NASA to have a sixth mission, would you take it? Yes or no, Mark. What's your answer?"

Silence.

"I thought so. Just like this time, I wouldn't count. You would take the mission in a heartbeat. Good-bye, Mark."

"Judy!" The phone went dead in his ear. "Goddamnit!" He slammed the instrument into its cradle, then leaned his head into his hands and wearily massaged his face, thinking that things couldn't have gone worse. Maybe, he thought, it was Peggy. Maybe it wasn't such a good idea that Judy was staying there. Maybe the woman was fueling her rage.

It was too many *maybes*. He narrowed the problem. A sixth flight was make-believe. The issues were Judy and this mission. And what were the resolutions? He would never give up the *KOSMOS* mission. Never.

Even if it means losing Judy? It was beyond his comprehension to believe she would leave him over this. Marriages didn't end on things like this. At least he had never heard of it. Couples split because one or both found someone better. He had no one else. Judy had no one else. They loved each other. The facts were that simple. There would be no permanent dissolution. He had been wrong about the depth of her anger, but that was all he had been wrong about. She would eventually get over it, and in three months they would be living together in Los Angeles.

He rose from the bed, picked up his bag, checked out of the motel, and drove back to the factory. The phone call had stolen any hope of sleep.

CHAPTER 7

Thursday, 15 September
Volokolamsk Forest

Kobozev lay prone in the snow, studying the bull elk through binoculars. It was a magnificent specimen, a world-class trophy — over three hundred and fifty kilos and with a rack span of almost one and a half meters. The four other conspirators stood behind him, each suffering from the cold and wishing that Kobozev would end his hunt and get on with the meeting. None had come prepared for a lengthy outdoor recess. They had assumed another hunting-lodge rendezvous. But, as each had arrived, the KGB guards had escorted them into the field, to silently wait in a cold, dry snow while their leader indulged his ego in another kill.

Kobozev set aside the glasses and reached for the American-made, three-hundred-magnum Colt rifle. It would be a difficult shot — greater than four hundred meters — through light snow and a brisk crossing wind. He brought the stock of the weapon into his shoulder and his cheek tight into the lay of his right thumb. The animal, now bugling a challenge to other males, came into focus. *Marvelous! Marvelous!* he thought. *A wonderful addition to my collection.* He leveled the cross hairs on the animal's vital area, just behind the shoulder, then made a one meter high correction to account for the drop in the bullet. He willed his respiration slow and even, took a final deep breath, let out half of it, and slowly squeezed the trigger. The weapon rocked upward, but in half a second, he had it releveled and the target back in the scope. He was just in time to see the remnant of a dust cloud that marked bullet impact on the animal's body, twelve centimeters below the aim point. He cursed himself for the error, for not having compensated enough for the extreme range.

The deep thudding sound of the hit, like the sound of a fighter's fist hammering into a sand-filled punching bag, joined the echo of the rifle firing. The animal bounded through ten steps, hesitated, foamed blood from its mouth and nostrils, then collapsed in a leg-twitching heap.

"Excellent shot, Comrade Kobozev." Yazov made the comment, hoping to curry enough favor to avoid the man's venomous tongue for the remainder of the meeting. He particularly wanted no more insinuations about his loyalty to the group. He had become paranoid that Kobozev's agents had a bullet aimed at his head every second of the day.

"No, Comrade Yazov, it was *not* a good shot." Kobozev rose from the defilade of rocks and operated the bolt action to eject the spent shell and rechamber another. Yazov withered at the sarcasm. "Had I hit the animal where I was aiming, it would have dropped in its tracks."

Yazov merely nodded, wishing he had kept his mouth shut.

A large, four-wheel-drive vehicle arrived, and the city-garbed visitors welcomed its heater. Kobozev sat in front and signaled the driver to proceed to the fallen elk. Other guards were already approaching it in separate vehicles. He turned to his guests. "So, Comrades. Does all go according to schedule? What of Red Sky?" The question was directed to Defense Minister Zhilin.

"We are nearing readiness for a last test. General Chernavin is confident the pointing problems have been corrected. Two American satellites will be engaged within a several-second period. If the test is successful, then Red Sky will be ready for the one-hundred target demonstration."

"*If*, Comrade? Chairman Belidov's cancer will not wait for us. The test *must* be successful. The Iranian Initiative *must* be a *fait accompli* before his incapacitation… before Sorokin's ascendancy. Do I make myself clear?"

Zhilin understood. They all did. Failure would mean their collective necks. "Very clear."

"Now, Comrade Ryabinin, do the Americans suspect anything?"

Just this morning, the KGB chief had received messages from North American agents on that very subject. "Nothing. They are blind to our plans. They continue to think that equipment malfunctions are the cause of their problems. There are reports of increased activity at their major missile factory… a *Nova* factory, I believe it is called… but such activity is to be expected. The Americans will want to speed up their missile production so as to replace their damaged spacecraft."

"Excellent. They give us more targets. And are Belidov and Sorokin still ignorant of our work?"

"I have had them under continuous surveillance. Their phones, living quarters, and automobiles have all been wired for monitor. They suspect nothing."

"The stars shine on us, yes, Comrades?" The weakest of smiles curled Kobozev's lips. "And what of the American-targeted terrorist attack. Is that plan proceeding satisfactorily?"

"An agent at our London embassy awaits word to continue."

"And will the attack be sufficiently heinous to rouse the Americans to retaliation?"

"American civilians — women and children — will be the principal casualties. Their citizenry will be screaming for blood. The president will oblige."

"Can you be sure the focus of their retribution will be Iran?"

"Absolutely. The explosives are North Korean, a weapons supplier of Iran. It will take them some time, but the Americans will be able to make the identification in the residue of the plastique. And a host of other subtle clues will similarly point to Iran. We need not worry. American bombers will be launched to punish the Iranians for the butchery."

Their lorry braked to a stop. Guards had already passed the bumper-mounted cable of one vehicle over a tree limb and were winching the elk off the ground by the base of its antlers.

Kobozev stepped from the truck and motioned for the others to join him around the trophy. "A magnificent creature! Don't you agree, Comrade Yazov?" He had noted the man's aversion to the scene and tormented the weakling by demanding he look again.

The minister of economics nodded. He had never seen an animal killed by gunshot, and his stomach turned at the copious amounts of blood. It dripped from the wound and from the animal's muzzle and melted the snow beneath it into a bright crimson mush. Steam rose from its body, and droppings fell from its relaxed bowels. Yazov could not help but imagine his own end in similar circumstances — his blood dripping from a firing-squad wound, stinking feces flowing from his body. He choked back his nausea.

Kobozev pulled a large hunting knife from his belt and began to estimate the width of the rack using the blade as a ruler. "Do our Teheran plans move forward?" Again, it was a question for KGB Chief Ryabinin.

"Explosives for the car bombs are being delivered via diplomatic pouch. The cars themselves will be stolen the day prior to the assassinations. Falsified documents will be left at the scene to implicate the Americans, though I doubt such a sign will be necessary. With a completely unjustified American attack fresh in their minds, the masses will instantly attribute the murder of their beloved patriarch and his progeny to the Great Satan. They will be screaming for American blood."

"Fantastic!" Kobozev had finished his measure and turned to face the group. "I suspect, Comrades, that you are looking at a world record!"

At the outburst, the others stared incredulously, wondering if Kobozev's preoccupation with the beast had deafened him to the discussion. It hadn't. He immediately finished the scenario Ryabinin had been tracing. "And an aggrieved Ayatollah Hashemi will welcome us into his ports to defend the Iranian homeland from any additional American aggression." It was a brilliant plan, fueled only by hate and mistrust — the most plentiful, reliable, renewable resources on the planet. "The American president will immediately demand our withdrawal, and we will laugh in his face. Red Sky will make him, and Sorokin, as vulnerable as this beast."

He plunged the knife into the elk's belly and unzipped it from anus to throat. Great masses of red and pink offal spilled from the cavity. Yazov grabbed his mouth and fled to the truck.

"Comrade Ryabinin, tell your London agent to proceed." Kobozev continued to expertly field dress the animal.

❖

Saturday, 17 September
Houston

"A toast. To the Amelia Earhart of the space age, Anna Rowe. May her second journey to the stars be as successful as her first."

The bespectacled, slightly built, fiftyish man raised his champagne glass in a salute, then delicately sipped from it.

"Thank you, Richard. That's sweet of you. This whole evening has been sweet of you. I've really enjoyed it."

Anna lied. She had been keeping company with the man for more than two years and normally looked forward to their weekly outings. But tonight's dinner date — to celebrate the announcement of her flight assignment — had been a bust. She had other things on her mind.

"Did you? I didn't think so."

"What?" In her preoccupation, she had lost the direction of the conversation.

"You said you had enjoyed the evening. I didn't think so. You've looked troubled and tense all night. Was the week that bad?"

She seized the excuse. "Oh yes. Yes. It has been bad. I've just had so much to do, Richard. I'm sorry if it appeared I didn't enjoy this. I really did." She patted the man's forearm in an emphasis of her sincerity. In the motion, her attention was drawn to her well-chewed fingernails, and she immediately hid them by curling her fingers into a fist. The action further upset her.

For God's sake! Richard knows I bite my nails! He knows everything about me. We sleep together! So why, all of a sudden, am I aware of the unsightliness of my hands?

The answer came, but she vehemently tried to deny it — *Pettigrew*. Throughout the week, she had detected his eyes engaged in a critical examination of her body. The invasion of privacy had been maddening. In fact, on Thursday, it had caused her to badly botch a capture attempt. During that sim, she had glanced toward the pilot and found his gaze dwelling on her left hand. The remote arm THC control was just inches from his position and it had been impossible to hide the evidence of her nervous habit. And yet that was exactly what she had tried to do — hurry her control inputs to limit the time her fingers were visible. The results had been disastrous. She had rammed the simulated arm through the simulated satellite.

And *why*, she kept asking herself, did she care if Pettigrew found her fingernails repulsive?

"I certainly hope things lighten up for you."

"I'm sure that won't happen. Once you get assigned to a flight, things only get more hectic."

"Well, in that case, we'll have to plan a long vacation after you get back... Anna, darling..." He grabbed her hands. "...Would you like to go to Colorado for Christmas? I can get a condo in some resort. We could have a wonderful time." The man's eyes were pictures of expectation.

Anna wished the question had not been posed while she was so unsettled. "Oh, Richard, that's so nice of you. But let's not plan anything that big for awhile. I'm not sure how much free time I'll have after the flight."

The man's face sagged in disappointment.

She was confused, almost frightened, by her rejection of the offer. For inexplicable reasons, she was trying to distance herself from a very dear and close friend. Had the plan been offered at the beginning of the week, she was certain she would have jumped at it. What had changed? She quickly supplied herself with twin excuses; she was tired and her period was due tomorrow. It sometimes played havoc with her emotions. Colorado would be fun.

"No, on second thought, let's do it. I haven't taken a vacation in a long time, and right after a flight is the best opportunity to break away from the office."

"Wonderful! Wonderful, darling! I'll call a travel agent on Monday and see what's available. I'm so happy you changed your mind."

Anna was happy, too. She had subdued her hormones and taken control of the situation — something she should have done in the simulator on Thursday. Staying in control — *that* was the most important thing.

Her dinner partner dreamed aloud about the trip. "I've always wanted to sit in a lodge by a roaring fire, with a beautiful woman, and watch skiers come down the mountain at night with those torches in their hands. It must be magnificent. The photos certainly are."

She smiled at his vision and the flattery embedded in it. Though she didn't say so, she preferred the idea of being one of the skiers in the scene, not an observer. But she knew that was not part of his fantasy. Richard didn't ski. He was a frail, non-athletic man — a surgeon — afraid of any sports that might hazard the source of his livelihood — his hands. She also accepted the fact that, at fifty-five, he was probably too old to be taking risks on a ski slope.

"Okay, Richard. I'll leave the planning to you. Wherever you want to go will be fine. But for now, I'm going to have to ask you for a ride home. I know it's Saturday, but I have training tomorrow. And... well,

I'm sorry, but would you mind if we ended tonight at the door?"
Typically, they would spend Saturday nights in bed together. But this
night she craved solitude — an effect of her period, she was sure.

"Well, all right, my dear. As brokenhearted as it makes me to part
company with such a beautiful celebrity, I guess I'll have to. As a
taxpayer, I should do my part to ensure all government employees are
well rested. I wouldn't want you to fall asleep on the job." He smiled at
his own weak humor.

An hour later, Anna was in her nightgown standing in front of her
mirror brushing her hair. Its shortness made the repeated sweeps unnecessary, but the ritual was a stubborn remnant of her childhood. Then, like
a golden waterfall, her tresses had reached to beneath her waist, and each
night, her mother had stationed her in front of the mirror to brush the
satin. With long, loving strokes, she had brought each rivulet of yellow
to a glistening hue.

In the idyll, her eyes touched on the framed photo of her parents that
sat on the bureau. Her mother had been captured as a big-bosomed
woman in her early fifties. Her father stood beside her, supporting
himself with a cane. He was the antithesis of the woman — feeble, infirm
looking, and, at seventy-one, so much older than his wife that the casual
observer would have immediately concluded they were viewing two
generations — father and daughter.

She stared at her father's image and tried to recall loving memories
of him, but none came. She could only remember him as the photo
depicted — a weak and silent man. Even before his death, he had been
invisible to her. And afterwards — from age eight — she had been
encapsulated in a maleless world, the boundaries of which had extended
even to her schools. At her mother's insistence, those had been Catholic
and all-girl. As a result, Anna had walked off the stage at her high school
graduation as a beautiful woman carrying cum laude honors and her
mother's oft-repeated commandment — *Stay in control. Don't let things
happen to you. Make them happen for you* — and an abysmal ignorance
of the male animal.

It was an ignorance that had quickly extracted an emotional toll. She
had been a sophomore at Stanford University when a boy had carried her
too quickly to the portals of sex. When she had seen the blood-engorged

shaft growing from his crotch, she had tried to end the encounter, but her frenzied date had seized her hand and forced it into a blurring stroke of the beast. Her first experience with "love" had ended with hot semen exploding over her scream-opened mouth.

It was three years later, after she had completed pilot training, that she had sufficiently recovered from that incident to again make herself sexually vulnerable to a man. That time, the male animal had been guilty of fraud. A charming pilot, on temporary duty to her China Lake squadron, had deceived her for three months with promises of commitment. It had been only after he had returned to Norfolk, Virginia, and her calls and letters had been ignored, she learned he had been engaged.

Twice burned, Anna had shackled and gagged her sexual muse — the other being living within her that craved to love and be loved and who had made her so vulnerable to heartbreak. She had sealed her in the deepest recesses of her soul and had guarded her body with the vigilance of a religious novitiate. There had been other relationships, but those never progressed beyond the level of adolescent dating. After two or three attempts to penetrate her defenses, men had not called back — that was, until Richard had come into her life.

In him, she had finally found a man who was sensitive and caring and honest. He enjoyed sex with her, but at a minimal frequency and intensity. That was fine with her. If the relationship was staid, so be it. It was far better than being used by men.

She did not love him. She was now certain she could never really love. She had learned enough about men to know that, to love one, would require her to somehow forget the lessons that had been hammered into her by her mother, by the nuns, by her religion — *Stay in control!* How could she ever release that other woman from her crypt and still maintain control?

She so dearly wished she had a friend to confide in, to seek their consul. But there was no one. It could never be a man. And what women could she share with? Other female astronauts? She had no close friends among them. They were civilian scientists. She was a military pilot. The difference in background overwhelmed the bond of sex. Her mother had been dead for four years, but, even if she were alive, Anna knew the woman could not have helped. Her mother had never loved her father. She had loved her career. She had married as her reproductive clock had been tolling midnight, and only for that reason — to have a child.

No, her mother could not have helped her love. But, Anna reminded herself, at least her mother had been content with her state in life. Perhaps she could have passed on the secret of achieving happiness without love. It made her wonder what had changed between mother and daughter. Certainly her first experiences with men had deeply bruised her emotional being, but she knew even those injuries were not deep enough to account for all of her confusion. She had walked into adulthood both needing to be loved and needing to stay in control and seeing the two states as mutually exclusive as fire and water. She was half a woman. Was it an evolutionary process, she wondered? If she ever bore a daughter, would that child be closer yet to a whole woman? A woman who could control her life out of bed, who could compete as an equal with a man, who could pursue her dreams into male-dominated bastions, then freely and wantonly release that control in bed? A woman who could step, without a thought, back and forth across the emotional abyss that separated those worlds?

She had no answers.

Her lazy brushing continued and her gaze was drawn to another photo, this one wedged in the lower corner of the mirror. It was of herself and Richard at the entrance to Disneyland. She took the photo and studied it. Abundant, unconditional love was written on the man's face. But there was something missing in the gaze. Something amorphous and impossible to put in words. What was it?

Richard doesn't look at me… like Pettigrew does.

She immediately cursed herself for letting that thought slip into her consciousness. Pettigrew's stares were a dime a dozen. She knew she could walk into any officer's club on a Friday night and find a score of Pettigrews. His attention was nothing special, and she felt men who lusted in his manner were nothing more than cattle. They certainly were incapable of loving or being loved. Richard *could* love her. The Pettigrews of the world, like the Stanford football player and the China Lake pilot, could only *use* her. In fact, the stories of Pettigrew's sexual conquests were legend in the astronaut office and revealed him to be an exceptionally talented *user*.

She replaced the photo and turned to switch off the lights. But, as she did so, the mirror image of her body in profile caught her attention. She stood still, fixed on her reflection, pondering the source of male attraction. In a reenactment of the scene in the simulator, she reached behind and pulled the fabric taut to the front of her body. Her breasts stood in relief. The mounds were too large for her frame, she thought.

She released the fabric, and then, with eyes darting like she was doing something nasty and feared discovery, she pushed the spaghetti straps from her shoulders. The gown dropped to the floor. She stayed in profile and examined herself — naked except for bikini panties.

Oh, God, yes! My frame is my father's and my breasts are my mother's! They're too big for me! And my legs are too skinny!

She turned to face the mirror, and the *real* imperfection of her body — her nipples — came into view. They were half the diameter of most other women's.

My mother's breasts — a man's nipples — Oh, God!

Then, just as suddenly as the impulse to drop her clothes had come to her, she became embarrassingly aware of her nakedness and her senseless abandon to the female worry of breast appeal. She quickly bent to pull on her gown and then scolded the image.

What are you doing, Anna? You're acting crazy! Why are you so suddenly concerned about your breasts? Richard has always found them satisfactory. Pettigrew's lustful stare? It's disgusting to even think about what goes on in that man's mind. Oh, God, I'll be glad when my period is over!

She again reached for the light switch, and this time her eyes touched on her fingernails.

Damn that man! My fingernails are my business! My breasts are my business!

❖

Monday, 19 September
San Francisco

Peggy Marlow walked into the restaurant and located Judy on the patio. She had left work early to meet her friend for lunch and some shopping.

"God, isn't this beautiful!" Peggy seated herself. The patio commanded a sweep of the bay, complete with Alcatraz in the foreground and the Golden Gate in the background. A fleet of distant sailboats and windsurfers seemed to skate across a plain of glittering diamonds.

"Yes. It is beautiful." Judy's attempt to imitate Peggy's breezy assessment fell significantly short.

A waiter came with a menu for the new arrival and filled her wine glass.

"What's this?" Peggy referred to a large tablet lying on the table.

"Oh, just some sketches I did to kill the time."

"Do you mind?"

"Help yourself."

Peggy sipped her wine while paging through the drawings. All were bay-area scenes — sailboats, fishing boats, bridges, trolleys, Alcatraz Island. "Judy, these are great! I had no idea you could draw."

"Thanks." Her tone said she didn't believe it.

"No, really. I'm not bullshitting you. You've got some talent. I don't remember you doing art when we were stationed together. Did you just start? Have you been taking lessons?"

She snuffled a self-deprecating laugh. "No. The last time I did any drawing was before this." She raised her left hand and frowned at her wedding band. "I never had time when we were together. The kids and moving were my hobbies. You remember those days." Their earlier lives had been parallel — living at the same air force bases, pulling up stakes and moving every couple of months as their husbands had gone from one training program to another, sitting out two Vietnam tours together.

"Yea, tell me about it. I thought I had married a goddamn Arab nomad. If I never see another moving van, it'll be too soon."

The waiter came to take their orders. After his departure, a silence persisted and both women stared into their wine glasses. Finally, Peggy spoke. "Are you ready to talk about it?" On many a night, while waiting for their husbands to return from Vietnam, they had sat over a wine bottle and confided in each other, sharing their souls. She thought it would be appropriate therapy now. Judy had talked about the split, but Peggy sensed she was poisoning herself with something else.

Judy kept her head down, her fingers twirling the wine glass. The liquid rocked from edge to edge in a hypnotizing wave. Twice, it appeared she would answer, but each attempt ended with her lip bitten back. Then, it came — the rise of the demon. Tears began to fall in soft taps onto the tablecloth. "Peggy…" She did not look up. "Peggy, I'm scared. I'm so scared. Mark isn't coming back from this flight. I know it."

Peggy pulled tissues from her purse and passed them across the table. "Oh, Judy, you don't know that. That last mission has got you paranoid, that's all."

"No, I do know it. He's not coming back." She mopped at her cheeks and nose. "Do you remember when we both had that feeling... at Nellis. The feeling that someone had... had been killed. Remember? We both left our houses to go over and see each other, and we both held each other and cried because we were so scared. Well, I feel the same way now."

Peggy recalled the episode. A crazy, psychic feeling had simultaneously come over each of them, and they had rushed out of their houses and met on the sidewalk. When their men had come home safely and the incident had been recounted, Mark and Bill had laughed and teased them — *Jeanne Dixon doesn't have to worry about losing her job to you two.* All of the Nellis Air Force Base planes were back, and nobody had died. It was the next day that word came of the accident in Turkey that had killed one of the squadron pilots who was on temporary overseas duty.

"Judy, that was just coincidence. You remember. How many times did we have those same feelings and nothing happened? Remember when they were in Vietnam? We'd just *know* that one of them had been killed. Hell, we had that feeling at least twice a week for two years — almost turned us into goddamn alcoholics — and both Bill and Mark survived. And what about the day Bill died? Neither of us had that special feeling then. It was just coincidence. Mark will be okay this time."

"No, Peggy. He's not coming back." Judy finally looked up. Hers was a face of the damned. "I'm so scared. I'm trapped. I can't leave him. I love him. Being here... I mean, it's just a bluff. I know now that it's all a bluff. I could never leave him. But I'm going to lose him. I know it. All along, the sky has had a claim on him. He's never belonged to me. He's belonged to the sky and it's going to take him. And I'm going to be left alone. I'm going to die, Peggy. I'm going to die, too."

Peggy grabbed her hands, squeezed them forcefully to stop their shaking, and launched a blitz of words. "Nobody is going to die, Judy. Not Mark, not you. Everything is going to be just fine. Now snap out of this. If you can have feelings, then I can too. And my feelings say everything is going to be just fine. Mark is going to be an asshole and go fly his goddamn rocket. He's going to come home safely, and you guys are going to move to L.A., where you'll live out the rest of your lives in traffic and smog. Your feeling is nothing but a little gas." The comment brought a hint of a smile to Judy's mouth. "Jesus, you sure had me fooled. I thought you were really thinking of leaving that son of a bitch and I was going to have to console you in a divorce. I can't tell you what a relief it is to hear this is a bluff. Mark's a good guy... for a man, I mean. But that doesn't mean you have to make it easy on the bastard. I'll hold your hand while you run up his credit card bill so high he'll need a shuttle to reach it."

❖

Wednesday, 21 September
Houston

"Welcome back. What time did you get in?" Pettigrew motioned for the waitress to bring another beer.

"About two."

"You look like shit. Don't they sleep in Colorado?"

"Not where I was." Mark peered through a miasmic fog of cigarette smoke and atomized hamburger grease in a study of Pettigrew's selection for a crew rendezvous point. The tar-paper walls were covered with automobile license plates. Exposed electrical wiring vined its way upward through two-by-four studs to the ceiling fans, where connections were made with bright yellow wirenuts. A family of stuffed armadillos surveyed the scene from a ledge over the bar. The motif was primitive country-western, and the majority of patrons were attired in the uniform of the urban cowboy... jeans, boots, and cowboy hats. A steady fare of the latest C&W hits was being punched up by a group of kickers gathered at a corner jukebox.

"Jesus, what a dump. Is this one of your regular haunts?"

"I've passed through here on occasion. Don't drink the water and you'll be okay."

Mark laughed. If it burned down, the place would look better. But it did meet Killingsworth's security requirements. Ladies' night and the lure of four-bit long necks was bringing in a crowd. By the time Anna and Darling arrived and they got down to business, the din would easily cover their conversations. And Pettigrew had come early to claim a rear corner table that further guaranteed their privacy.

The waitress returned with a bottle of Lone Star.

"How have the sims been going?"

"Fine. Anna's shit-hot with the arm, just like you said she'd be." He made no mention of the crazy feelings he had been having about the woman. Men — not even the closest of men — shared such wonders.

Pettigrew was the first to notice her entry. She paused at the door trying to adapt her eyes to the dim interior, and her head ratchetted from side to side in a search for their table. The movement was too fast and gave away her nervousness at being unaccompanied in a predominately male lair. A group of barflies was already appraising her, and the marine wondered if it was lust or laughs they were sharing. She was attired in another frilly, balloon blouse and baggy trousers — about as far removed from the spray-on jeans and body-paint tops of the other cowgirls as Texas was removed from Manhattan. A cowboy with a massive beer belly and no ass tucked a long neck in his back pocket, hiked up his Levi's, and sauntered to her.

"Excuse me for a second, Mark. I've got to save Anna from a redneck."

He hurried to her side. "Sorry, Buffalo Bill, she's with me. We're over in the corner, Anna." He grabbed her arm and led her away, the cowboy glaring after him at the curt dismissal.

"What do you want to drink?"

"Huh? Oh, ah, a Coke would be fine. Thanks." Anna was rushing to catch up. The marine had touched her — a meaningless, gentlemanly, five-second escort to the table — and yet she could think of nothing else. How did her little finger get to her mouth? She jerked the hand away.

"Hi, Anna. Bob tells me you haven't lost your touch with the arm. I'm glad to hear that. None of us is going to have much time to practice."

"Yea, thanks. Well, he's been... he's... a lot of help."

Darling's entry interrupted them.

Drinks were ordered and delivered, and Mark began to bring his crew up to date on the Denver happenings. In ten minutes he had described Striegel's plan to rendezvous with the *Nova*, capture it with the shuttle arm, and bolt another stage to it. There were few questions. The marine was well on his way to being an expert on shuttle rendezvous procedures, and Anna's proficiency with the arm was assured. She and Pettigrew would be ready. It was *Freedom's* flight to geosync that would be breaking new ground. Mark continued into those details.

"*Freedom* has no pressurized cockpit. We're going in our EMU's."

"*What?!*" The exclamation came in a chorus from Anna and Pettigrew. Mark paused to ensure that the outburst hadn't attracted any attention. It hadn't. They were still an isolated, invisible island in a noisy, expanding body swap.

"There's no other way. The machine has to be simple and it has to be light. A pressurized cabin is a luxury we can't afford."

"Jesus Christ, Mark! Simple is one thing, but your EMU? You're dead if it leaks!"

Mark turned to Darling. "Frank, I want to make sure you understand what we're planning here. We'll be making the entire trip to and from geosync, all forty-eight hours of it, in our EMU's... our space suits. Every space machine this nation has ever put a man in has been pressurized. *Freedom* will be the first to fly without that protection. All we'll have is our space suits. If a leak occurs..."

Pettigrew finished the scenario. "Your blood boils inside your body."

"But the training people have told me that the suit can only support life for about twelve hours. How can we stay in it for forty-eight?"

"*Freedom* will carry the extra oxygen and cooling water that we'll need. While we're attached to it, our EMU's will be supplied from that source through an umbilical."

"What about our batteries and lithium hydroxide? They are also limited." It was another Darling question that indicated he had already acquired a fluency in the suit design. Mark was pleased.

"None of our consumables — oxygen, water, batteries, or LIOH — will be on line while we're aboard the *Nova*. Our umbilicals will be supplying us with everything. Anytime we're off those, we'll be eating into the suit reserves. I would estimate it'll take us two hours to do the space walk to bolt *Freedom's* two pieces together. Then, when we get back from geosync, it might cost us another two hours to transfer into *Atlantis* anything we strip from the *KOSMOS*. Those are four hours we'll definitely be using the EMU consumables. That leaves us with about eight hours to crawl across the *KOSMOS*."

"Mark, you're talking about flying to geosync stuck on the end of a rocket like a bug stuck on a pin! You're talking about *living* in a space suit for two days! How are you gonna eat, drink, *shit!*"

"We'll extend the drinking water by tapping into the cooling supply coming through the umbilical. That'll be a simple modification. And we'll carry a high-calorie liquid mix for food."

"Where?"

"Velcroed to the inside of the suit chest cavity, just like our water bag. We'll have two straws at our chin to drink from… one for water, the other for food."

"And waste?" Darling repeated Pettigrew's question.

"A low-residue, prelaunch diet will help take care of solid waste. We'll also take an enema and some cement pills before leaving the shuttle to guarantee no bowel activity. For urine collection, our UCD bladder will be enlarged." Mark referred to the male urine-collection device, a waist-worn plastic bladder with a condomlike sleeve that attached to the penis.

"What about sleeping? Will that be possible?" As a rookie, Darling could not imagine how sleep would be affected.

"In zero gravity you can sleep anywhere. We'll take turns on the glide up and back. Oh, and we're also going to have some amphetamines on a tab next to the drink straw. If we need an upper, we can pick one off with our tongue."

As Mark had done at Denver, Pettigrew searched for a reason the plan would not work. But he could find none. The modifications to make the suit habitable for two days would be trivial compared to the construction of a pressurized cockpit. But the risks still terrified him. There would be no protection against a suit leak. During shuttle space walks, a crewman could always retreat into the airlock for that emergency. Where would you run at geosync? He knew the answer — nowhere. You died. The end would be mercifully quick if it was a large leak, torturously slow if small.

Mark continued with details about the communication system. "*Freedom* will have an encrypted two-way radio link to *Atlantis* and Mission Control, but, to minimize the possibility of detection by the Soviets, we'll be running silent… in the *listen* mode only. We'll transmit only to report our findings on the *KOSMOS*. Otherwise, no one will hear anything from us.

"Frank, we'll be locked in position, side by side, on the front of *Freedom*. I'll be on the left. There'll be a pedestal of controls between us and on our sides. The *Nova* guidance system should get us within a couple of miles of the *KOSMOS,* and then we'll use a laser radar to finish the approach. We'll plan to come in from above — from the space-facing side of the machine — to avoid any earth-pointing sensors it might have. From that point on, our actions will depend on the *KOSMOS*. If it's a weapon, we'll latch onto her with a mechanical claw, climb off of *Freedom*, go on our scavenger hunt, string some demolition explosives, and leave. If she looks benign, we won't even stop. Once we arrive back in the shuttle orbit, you two…" He indicated Anna and Pettigrew, "…will pick us up."

"What type of fuel reserves will you have?" Anna asked.

"Not much… maybe a couple hundred pounds."

"How are you going to hide from any Soviet radar?"

Just yesterday, Striegel's team had finally answered that question. "They're adding some rocket-propelled decoys for us… metal-skinned balloons that should confuse any watching radar operators. And we'll know if they're watching. We're going to have a radar detector. If I see we're being painted, I'll pickle off one of the decoys. On a scope, the balloon will appear larger than the *Nova*. It might be enough to sucker an operator away from us."

Anna was shaken by the entire plan. It was desperate, primitive.

"Bob, I want you trained for EVA… the generic contingency stuff… payload bay door closing, RMS stowage, K-band stowage." The significance of the directive was obvious to all. Pettigrew and Anna were to possess the expertise necessary to recover from any orbiter malfunction and fly *Atlantis* home — by themselves.

Covered by the crooning of Willie Nelson and Hank Williams, Jr. and a posse of other singing cowboys, they delved deeper and deeper into the mission details.

Hours later, Pettigrew laid in bed, his hands interlaced behind his head, his eyes fixed on the ceiling. Worry about Mark and the mission had finally faded to allow wonders about Anna to enter his mind. He saw the jade in her eyes, the gold in her hair, her lips, neck, breasts. What would she be like in bed? What would her breasts feel like? Her nipples? Her legs? Thighs?

A teenage-hard erection rose to join him in the thoughts. He looked at it, trying to remember the last time he had achieved a hardness with merely a thought. He could not. He never thought of women. When he needed them, they were always available. He had no reason to *think* about them, certainly no reason to fantasize about them.

What is it about her?

CHAPTER 8

Wednesday, 5 October
Johnson Space Center

"Are they ready?" Pettigrew looked up the stairway of the shuttle mockup to see a technician handing an EMU helmet through the hatch. The activity was in support of his first lesson in EVA — dressing in the space suit.

"Bill said it would be another five minutes. They're still working in the airlock." Anna immediately returned to her study of the EVA checklist. Over the past two weeks, she had been doing a good job of maintaining a purely professional relationship with the marine. It helped to never have a spare moment for idle talk.

"I'm going to watch them finish setting up."

He climbed the stairs and peered through the side hatch. The mockup was a high-fidelity replica of the shuttle cabin. Stowage lockers, toilet, galley, sleep stations, lighting, control panels, the airlock — everything was configured exactly as it would be inside a real orbiter. From the interior of the airlock came sounds of men struggling to hoist the two-hundred-pound EMU — the space suit — into the wall-mounted stowage position.

Several minutes later, the technicians exited and Bill Kaplan, their instructor, called that he was ready. Pettigrew relayed to Anna and they climbed inside.

"Good morning, Bob, Anna. Let's start in the airlock."

Pettigrew rotated the inner hatch handle and lifted the door into a retaining clip. The action exposed an opening from the orbiter mid-deck into a four-foot diameter, seven-foot high cylindrical volume. An identical hatch on the exterior wall, which remained closed until airlock depressurization, was the exit path into space.

Kaplan waved them into the chamber with the joking comment, "Behold... Pharaoh's tomb."

It was a descriptive analogy. Like a guard intended for a high-tech afterlife, the helmeted space suit hung from one wall. Stowed as it would be for launch, the arms and legs were trussed up in a canvas covering, giving the appearance the suit was designed for an amputee. The lettering for the chest-mounted controls was written in mirror image, like the lettering on the front of ambulances, so it was readable by the suit occupant when viewed with a wrist-mounted mirror.

Kaplan began the lesson. It was a refresher for Anna, but Pettigrew was a first-time student. "Bob, undo those stowage straps and we'll take it apart."

Pettigrew followed his instructions, and within a few minutes they had disassembled the device into its component pieces. With the exception of the now-handless arms dangling at each side, the boxy-looking torso was unidentifiable as an article of human apparel.

"Shove the pants outside. We'll do as much of the dressing as possible in the cabin." They stooped from the cramped volume and into the roomier mid-deck.

"The first step in getting dressed is to put on a urine-collection device, a UCD. Then, you get in the liquid cooling underwear, the LCVG. You'd sweat to death without that." Kaplan handed him both items and he began to undress.

Anna had no desire to remain in the cabin with the pilot nude but knew it would be a laughable display of girlish modesty to retreat to the outside. She darted a glance at Pettigrew, hoping to see he had stopped undressing and was awaiting her exit. It would be the perfect resolution to her dilemma. But he continued to shed his clothes as nonchalantly as a football player in a locker room. Already he was down to jockey shorts and was working on his shirt buttons.

She resolved to not let the situation affect her and, in a single, fluid motion, set down her checklist, turned her back, and crouched to straighten the LCVG. The maneuver reeked of casualness.

Pettigrew cast aside his shirt, pulled off his shorts, and stood naked

behind her. He searched the UCD package for the assortment of prophy-
lactic-like sleeves that were used to attach the penis to the device. The
thick-walled rubbers came in three different diameters and were open on
each end. One end attached to the one-way urine valve of the bladder,
while the other rolled onto the penis. The pilot grabbed for the largest cuff
— he needed it — and began work.

"Hey, Bill, you've got a call downstairs. It's your wife… says it's
important." A technician stuck his head through the hatch and made the
announcement.

"Okay, I'll be right there. Bob, after you get the UCD on, go ahead
and climb into the cooling garment. I'll be right back." The instructor
disappeared out the hatch.

Quiet.

Graveyard quiet.

An abysmal silence came to refrigerate the cabin and its two remaining occupants. Like Adam being confronted by his Creator, Pettigrew
was suddenly and embarrassingly aware of his nakedness. By some
incredibly baffling process, at Kaplan's departure a sense of modesty he
hadn't felt since puberty came crashing down. No longer was the
situation professional. He was alone. With Anna. Naked.

For a moment, he watched as she tried to extend the ten-second task
of straightening the LCVG into a second minute. She looked as if she was
searching for a lost contact lens. Seconds ago, the sight had struck him
as hilarious. Now, her obvious discomfort only intensified his own foot-
shuffling nervousness.

He quickly stepped through the leg straps of the UCD and pinched the
device between his thighs. Stretching open the mouth of the rubber
produced a squeaking noise, like the sound of someone rubbing his
fingers across an inflated balloon. In the oppressive quiet of the metal-
walled cabin, it was deafening.

Snap! The sharp crack of the collapsing rubber echoed. His sweating
fingers had slipped.

Squeeeek! He stretched the rubber open for a second attempt and
hurried it toward its target.

Holy shit!

Like a frightened turtle, his appendage shrank backward into a hairy
shell. The maw spread before it yawned ridiculously large.

Christ! If I shrink any smaller, I'm gonna have a pussy!

In an unconscious, nervous response, he cleared his throat. The cough, as the sounds that had preceded it, screamed of his anxiety. He tried to cover it with casual conversation.

"I really enjoyed the Monday night football game. Did you watch it?" For a microsecond, his schoolboy jitters disappeared with the faked aplomb. Then, he remembered they were *both* in the simulator on Monday night.

Anna was still on her knees, pouring over the LCVG like an archeologist excavating the Dead Sea scrolls. At hearing the question, she sighed with relief.

Finally! He's ready to get into this damn thing. I thought I would scream with that quiet. Now, just act professional and help him dress. Oh, what did he ask? Yes, the football game. Be cool.

"Ah, yes, I did. Good game." While speaking, she grabbed the LCVG by the shoulders and turned to stand. The turn was faster than the stand.

Never! Never in her life could she remember being more shocked and embarrassed! There — at eye height — not two feet in front of her, was Pettigrew's penis! Worse yet, he was touching it!

She dropped the LCVG as if it were radioactive and jerked away, stuttering an apology. "Oh, I'm… I'm… sorry Bob. I… I thought that you were ready. I… I… thought… You asked… the football game, I mean, I thought you were ready. I'm sorry."

Pettigrew wished the rest of his body could perform the same disappearing act as his penis. When she had surprised him, he had been using his thumbs to coax the head of the diminished creature into the rubber. It had hardly been an awe-inspiring sight.

Great fucking job! Monday night football — idiot! I'm sure she was impressed by what she saw, too. In a minute, I'm gonna need a tweezers to find my lizard. Why does that woman have such an effect on me?

With an Academy Award-winning performance, he acted unaffected by her *faux pas*. "Forget it. If we ever did this for real, there sure as hell won't be time for any modesty. We'll be floating all over the cabin."

Fearing another misunderstanding, he turned his back. They were now both facing opposite walls.

Like a reluctant Cyclops, the beast peered out of a foreskin cave. He was circumcised, but the current sight made him wonder if the birthing doctor couldn't have trimmed another inch from his body. To compound matters, he was suddenly aware of the cold of the cabin. The mouse hunched deeper into its hole.

There was a different weather report where Anna stood. She was on fire. Blood burned her face. Sweat rained from her armpits. She was certain that stains were already showing on her dark blouse.

I've got to get hold of myself! Pettigrew is right. This is a professional situation. I'm acting like a high school girl. Modesty has to be forgotten. I've got to put the whole incident out of my mind.

It was impossible to meet the challenge. Like demanding of oneself not to think of elephants, that's all that floated before her — elephants — or at least images of their flaccid trunks.

Where the fuck is Kaplan? Why does it have to be so goddamn cold? Why does it have to be so goddamn quiet? Why am I letting that goddamn woman drive me nuts!

As he fumbled at a third attempt to get his pencil to stay in the hula hoop, the words of the last woman to enjoy his rod came sarcastically to mind. "You about split me in two." It was a thought that brought a burst of genius. *That's it! I'll send a little blood to that anemic midget!*

He searched his memory for the most depraved sexual encounters of his life, and, within seconds, his mind was choked with more pornography than Times Square. Images of soft, perfumed tits, hard projecting nipples, firm, humping asses, and warm, moist pussies teased his libido.

Anna tore at a nail with her teeth. *What is keeping that man? Does it take that long to put on a — a — condom? Oh, God, I hope we never have to do this in orbit! Where is Kaplan! This quiet is driving me crazy! What is Pettigrew doing?*

She searched for a diversion. The LCVG lay disheveled on the floor, but she had no intention of resuming her idiotic dwell on it.

In a glance to the floor, she noticed the checklist was behind her, and she shuffled backward a step to retrieve it. She would put her face in that. While bending, her peripheral vision took in Pettigrew's feet.

He's turned his back. I — No, Anna! Don't!

As if they belonged to another being, her eyes ignored the protest and swept up his naked form. The drum of her heart deepened and made a squishy sound in her ears. Simultaneous sensations of intense heat and a skin-tightening shiver gripped her. Her nipples stiffened to nail-like sharpness. A fingernail came back to her mouth. *He is so… so… different.*

Muscled legs rose to muscled buttocks. On the occasions she had seen Richard's naked back, the vista had been forgettable. Richard's legs were spindly and birdlike, and the flesh of his bald ass sagged into a crease at his upper thigh. Pettigrew had no such crease. Like coiled-spring steel, his ass bulged with masculine power.

Other details caught her eye: a tanned, hairless back; shoulders that were as massively proportioned as his legs; an unusual birthmark of several lightly pigmented lines that arched around his left side; a ragged, three-inch scar on his left calf.

What is he doing?

Her indecent scrutiny was snapped by the realization that he was no longer working with the UCD. His arms hung motionless at his side, and his attention appeared to be fixed on the wall.

The marine stirred. It was the impetus needed for her to retake control of her senses. She jerked her head away and buried it in the checklist.

Goddamnit! Nothing is gonna bring that little fucker out of there! The half minute of triple-X rated memories had done nothing. His penis remained shrinkingly bashful in its pale sheath.

Finally, acknowledging the emasculation, he disgustedly tore the large-diameter rubber from the urine valve and grabbed for the smallest one. A moment later, he had pulled the recalcitrant from its hiding place and imprisoned it in the new sleeve.

Thank God that's over! He felt like he had just had a root canal.

Anna heard the velcro attachment of the waistband being made and sighed with relief.

"Okay, Anna, I'm ready."

She turned, only to again be shocked by the sight of his body.

Pettigrew was used to the reaction. "Oh, this?" His hand scratched at the scars. "Just a little bamboo tattoo the North Vietnamese gave me for a keepsake."

The comment refreshed her memory that he had been a POW, but she had never realized he had been so grievously tortured. It was apparent, now, what she had thought was a birthmark was really part of the scarring. A network of thin, white trails snaked across the left part of his chest and around his side. The left nipple was the terminus of many of the routes, and, as a result, it appeared he had no nipple. The fact that his chest was otherwise covered with dark hair tended to amplify the mutilation — none grew on the scar tissue.

"I'm sorry, Bob. I... I didn't mean to act so... so..."

"Repulsed?" He supplied the word.

"No, please. I didn't find... I mean, I don't find the scars... I don't find them like that at all. You're very..." She caught herself almost saying *attractive,* but the appeal of his body was an emotional quicksand to be avoided. She nervously cast her eyes to the checklist and shoved the conversation back to the lesson. "After you get in the LCVG, I have to put on your bio leads. There's a photo here that shows their placement."

She referred to the EKG transmitters that were taped to the chests of EVA crew members. The flight surgeons maintained they needed heart-rate data in Mission Control to determine if a space walking crew member was exerting him or herself to a level that exceeded the cooling capacity of the space suit. But, like the other astronauts, Anna and Pettigrew dismissed that explanation as so much bullshit. They suspected the real purpose of the instrumentation was to allow the surgeon to pronounce the victim dead in the event of an accident. EVA was a dangerous adjunct to a dangerous business.

With her assistance, Pettigrew stepped into the cooling garment. The UCD bladder covered his crotch, but his movements briefly exposed a mat of pubic hair. She modestly averted her eyes.

He noticed the demure response and wondered how many times in her life she had not looked away. How many men had she slept with? He hoped his had not been the least memorable of her visual experiences, although he couldn't imagine any man purposely displaying a smaller penis than the Lilliputian specimen he had brought to the lesson.

She worked to untangle a knot in the EKG wire bundle, a task made difficult by her well-recessed fingernails, and the struggle gave him cause to wonder anew at what inner turmoil sustained her nail-biting habit. It seemed so out of place with a personality that otherwise exuded strength and confidence.

"There. I think I've got these wires straightened out. Let's see... the photo shows that I tape this red one a hand's width beneath your..." She had again trapped herself. The placement was supposed to be a hand's width beneath his left nipple, but the disfigurement made her reluctant to use the word.

"Nipple." For the second time, Pettigrew supplied the missing word and, for the second time, it embarrassed her.

"Yes, a hand's width." She peeled the paper from the adhesive back of the sensor, then took aim with her left hand, placing it so the heel covered the remains of his areola.

The touch was magic.

It had been intended only as a landmark for measurement, just five fingers, just a palm lightly pushing into him, but, in a heartbeat, that insignificant encounter affected his body as certainly as a hot, writhing embrace. His penis continued its rebellion and now roared from its foreskin tunnel like a bullet train.

Christ! I don't believe it! I'm getting a fuckin' hard-on! How can she do that?

Within seconds, the expanding flesh was being further aroused by the provocative squeeze of its covering. The floodgates of blood opened wider, and a pounding heart rammed more fluid into the appendage. He winced with discomfort.

"I'm sorry. Did I hurt you?"

"Huh? Oh, no. It's okay. I… I just have a… a cramp in my leg. I'll be okay." To add some credibility to the lie, he stretched his right leg and massaged the thigh. "There, it's okay now."

She resumed her work.

Pettigrew gritted his teeth. The discomfort had progressed to pain. The UCD was strapped tightly enough over his crotch so there was no way the erection could assume a skyward aim — he was thankful for that. But the constraints to diameter and direction were watering his eyes. At any moment, he was certain he was going to hear a loud *pop* — the head of his weapon exploding.

In a reversal of his earlier psychological warfare, he began to concentrate on the most debilitating scenes he could imagine — the extreme fatigue of a marathon, lifting weights at the gym, swimming in an ice-cold mountain lake. But this effort to quiet the monster proved no more successful than his previous attempt to awaken it.

More squeeze, more blood, more squeeze, more hardness.

He shuffled his feet. Anna was certain she was somehow hurting him and tried to be even more delicate with her fingers. They barely brushed his skin. Pettigrew wished she would use a hammer and nails to make the attachments. The continuing caress was agony, and a weak groan snuck from his throat. He reattempted the deception. "It's my leg again... the muscle... it cramps sometimes. An old high school football injury."

"I thought it was your other leg?"

"What?!" His eyes widened in shock. Her "other leg" comment had made him think the true source of discomfort had been discovered.

"A moment ago you were rubbing your right leg."

Panicked, the marine looked down to see this time he was massaging the thigh of his left.

"Oh. No, it's my left leg. I mean, it's both legs. I get cramps in..."

Just as he thought death from embarrassment or penis strangulation was imminent, Kaplan stepped through the hatch. The pilot sagged with relief — all of him. Like a band of Indians retreating before a troop of cavalry, his netherworld antagonist was sent into full retreat by the instructor's arrival. He was saved.

Anna, too, wilted in her deliverance. She couldn't remember ever having lived a more stressful fifteen minutes.

"Sorry I took so long. It was my wife. She locked herself out of the house and I had to run back to my office to leave my key with the secretary." He examined the placement of the EKG sensors. "Good job. Doesn't look like you two had any problems getting this far."

Anna lied first. "Yea, no problem." *Oh, God! Don't ever make me have to do this again!*

Pettigrew followed suit. "It was a piece of cake." *Just ask my dick!*

As Kaplan continued the lesson, Pettigrew glanced at the woman. She had become a sorceress. Modesty, embarrassment, spontaneous arousal — sensations he had not experienced in countless years — she now commanded with a touch, a glance, with merely her presence.

❖

Sunday, 9 October
East Anglia, UK

The KGB agent stopped the car, lit up a cigarette, then turned to his passenger — a dark-skinned, bearded Palestinian. "The Israelis are launching another attack on your homeland." He spoke in fluent Arabic with a tone approaching boredom. The ritual had become tiring. This was the fourth consecutive day he had made the trip to one of the American NATO bases of East Anglia. Today, it was RAF Alconbury behind the chain-link fences.

A flight of two F-4 jets taxied into takeoff position. They were unarmed reconnaissance versions of the Phantom, but the Palestinian's mind was too warped to separate that reality from his tortured past. His brain saw only the Israeli jets whose bombs had decapitated his twenty-three-year-old wife and severed his five-year-old daughter's legs at the hips. She had died in his arms while he had watched the flight of Phantoms speed out of sight. The American warplanes had become triggers for his psychopathic hatred of the Jews, and now he focused that hate on the formation of F-4's roaring down the runway.

The KGB officer stayed until the aircraft were dots on the end of greasy strings of smoke, then drove his passenger the five miles to Brampton village. On the trip, he marveled anew at the power of hate. The mind-altering drug and the repetitive trips to view the jets had probably been unnecessary. Hate alone was a sufficient wind to bear the man on the suicide mission. He would kill Jews. He would avenge his wife and daughter. He would be cradled in Allah's bosom. He was as pliable as a child.

The Soviet drove slowly through the parking lot of the apartment complex that housed the American air force officers and their families. "Here is where the Jews live that killed your wife and daughter."

The man remained mute, merely staring his hate with coal black eyes.

They parked in a deserted alley, and the guide helped his subject into the backpack. It contained twenty-two kilos of North Korean plastique explosives, a sufficient mass to atomize every piece of flesh and bone within five meters.

"You will kill many, many Jews when you pull this, but you must wait until you are with them." He indicated a rip-cord-like handle that was connected to a detonator.

"It's just as I've told you for the past week. Walk straight up the street for two blocks. Two! Then turn right. The path will end at the apart-ments… at the nest of Jews. Understand?"

The man nodded.

"Good. Now give me your hands." The agent guided him in multiple touches of the steering wheel. His own hands were gloved, so the only fingerprints that would appear on the wheel would be the kamikaze to his left.

"Here is the pistol." He slammed a clip into the nine-millimeter weapon and pulled the slide mechanism to chamber a round.

The Palestinian jammed it into his waistband, bid his mentor good-bye with the blessing, "Allah akhbar," then climbed from the car and hurried toward oblivion.

"Allah akhbar." The Soviet blasphemously echoed him as he disappeared around the corner. *Yes, indeed. A god would have to be great to give us such fools as yourself.* He then stepped from the vehicle and began a casual stroll toward the village center. He would be able to make the six o'clock train back to London.

The martyr proceeded as instructed — straight into the apartment commons and into the Sunday afternoon leisure activities of the Americans. A man played softball with his eight-year-old son. Another waxed his sports car. A five-year-old girl pedaled her tricycle around a group of other preschoolers. Two mothers sat in lawn chairs and traded gossip. One bulged hugely in advanced pregnancy.

With the same confident gait of a postman about his duties, the Palestinian walked to the car waxer, pulled out his gun, and calmly put a bullet into the man's wondering face. Brain tissue splattered onto the glistening hood and beaded in ruby droplets. The women screamed their terror and raced to gather the children. Three rounds stitched one's chest. A gut shot mortally wounded the pregnant woman. The ball player scooped his son, but the escape was terminated with a bullet to the spine. The Palestinian came to him, ignored his paralyzed body, and emptied the clip into the boy's skull. He then walked to the shock-rigidized girl on the tricycle, gathered her into his arms, kissed her cheek, and pulled the backpack rip cord.

❖

Sunday, 9 October
San Mateo Coast

Judy walked off the path, took a seat in the shade of a wind-flagged cedar, and opened her tablet. For a moment, she searched the surroundings, trying to decide which segment of the panorama she should draw first. It was not an easy choice. The state park was situated on the top of three-hundred-foot-high Pacific coast cliffs, and her vantage within its boundaries was one of the best. A broad plain of wind-rippled, California-golden grasses stretched for a half mile to the precipice. Islands of grandfatherly evergreens stood their centuries-old watches among the headlands. The Pacific intimidated the land with its heaving immensity, and, at its limit, a cloudless sky lifted through ten shades of blue to finally appear azure at zenith.

She focused on a particularly wizened cedar a hundred feet distant, and her pencil began to capture the ancient soldier.

She thought of Mark. They spoke by phone once a week now. Meaningless talk. The mission was never mentioned. She had resigned herself; he would never give it up and she would never leave him. As it had always been, she would have to endure. Like a cancer patient coming to grips with the inevitable, she had made the transition from denial, to anger, to resignation. But there were still frequent, fearful falls into the deepest depressions. Mark was not coming back. The sky and the shuttle were demonic conspirators that would not be denied his life. In waves as regular as those that hammered the beaches, that dread would come to hammer her. She would bolt awake at night with *the feeling*. It would attack her at meals, in the shower, when she was shopping, or drawing, or writing letters. There was no escape from it.

She had captured the outline of the reaching cedar and was just beginning to replicate the finer aspects of its nobility when the young lovers walked into its shade. It didn't surprise her that a couple would seek out the site. It looked as if, from the moment of creation, God had intended it for such intimacy.

The boy spread a blanket and helped the girl recline. It was obvious they had not seen her, and Judy's first thought was that she should rise to make her presence known. But she didn't. She was no voyeur. She just wanted to finish her drawing, and besides, she thought, it would be cruel to spoil the couple's escape. They would not find a more private location. She had searched earlier, and there was a sizable Sunday crowd on the lower trails. Here, it was just them — the lovers, her, and the arthritic cedar — all solitary in their mutual company.

The pencil continued to work the paper, and only absently did she watch the new arrivals. The boy — she guessed he was nineteen or twenty — laid on his back beside the younger girl, and for long moments he seemed content on watching the sky. Finally, though, he rolled to one elbow and began to play the game of love — staring into his beauty's face, alternately talking and laughing, and kissing the kisses of carefree youth. Minutes passed, and ever so slowly, Judy's eyes fell from the evergreen and dwelled on the lovers. Ever so slowly she became a voyeur. Ever so slowly the boy and girl took her back… back… back.

❖

To the first time. To the bicycle trip. It was July. High school was finished, and in the fall she would enter the University of New Mexico. Mark's sophomore year at the academy was complete and he was home on his summer leave.

"Do you want to go back?" Mark sat on the step of the country store, idly picking pebbles from between his feet and flicking them away.

"No. I want to keep going. This is fun." *Go back?* Judy could no more go back than she could stop breathing. She was joyous! She wanted to run and kiss the complaining girl who had caused the early disintegration of the expedition. She and Mark would now be alone for two days — and nights! She didn't yet know how she would trap him, but tonight she was determined she would make love to Mark O'Malley. She was sure he was as virgin as the forests that greened the nearby mountain and equally sure a sample of her body would change him forever.

The plan had been for their foursome to complete the bicycle ride around the Sandia Mountains — the ten-thousand-foot, limestone hulk that dominated Albuquerque's eastern border. But the prissy coed who accompanied a classmate of Mark's, lasted only three hours before camping out lost its appeal — until the first time she had to squat behind a tree to urinate. When she sighted the store phone, she cried for daddy. Now, Judy and Mark watched as the bicycles were being loaded into Daddy's station wagon.

"Last chance, you two." The coed's father stood by the car door and offered them the same rescue.

"Thanks, Mr. Rowland, but we're going to keep going."

The man and the other couple waved their good-bye, climbed into the vehicle, and drove away.

"Ready?" Judy nodded, and they mounted their bikes to resume the adventure. Two years ago, she could not have imagined herself on such a journey, but love had transformed her into a chameleon — she would color herself whatever brought her closest to Mark. Early in their relationship, after detecting his interest in backpacking and camping, she had faked a similar passion. But the counterfeit fascination had soon turned genuine. She had discovered that, like him, a piece of her could only be satisfied when she was surrounded by the virgin earth and its glories.

In the silence of the ride, her entertainment was the boy's twenty-year-old body. He was shirtless, wearing jean cutoffs and low-cut tennis shoes, and every exposed piece of flesh was bronzed by the July sun. It was flesh turned lean and hard by the rigors of the academy, with bulging fillets at the neck and swollen muscles broadening his upper back. At the steeper rises in the road, he would stand and thrust at the pedals with all of his weight, and she relished the unobstructed view of his buttocks and thighs. Muscular bulges and the rhythm of male sinew, and the fantasy of being only hours from touching them, were a wonderful distraction from her own labor.

The sun burnished her body to the same copper as his. She had exposed as much of it as possible, wearing jean cutoffs that were much briefer than his and the smallest bikini top her mother had permitted her to buy. Her waist-length hair was tied into an auburn ponytail.

For hours they rode northward on a high-desert road leading into the empty vastness of the Cerrillos plain. The route was paved, but few vehicles passed them. Long ago, an interstate highway had ended the commercial importance of the trail. They rode easy, with no timetable and with frequent stops to rest or explore a relic of abandoned adobe. Judy felt as if they were the last humans on earth. Mile after mile their audience was nothing but piñon and juniper trees — evergreen islands floating on a desert sea. Widely scattered columns of spiraled tan — dust devils — bobbed and weaved among the green like football running backs dodging tacklers. Overhead, a parade of cotton candy clouds invaded the blue, while thunderstorms randomly decorated the horizon with slanting, gray curtains of rain. In some places, the desiccated air sucked the fluid from the sky before it touched earth.

"That's called virga," Mark explained. "It's so hot and dry, the rain evaporates in its fall."

Judy watched, fascinated by the phenomenon — rain that died in the sky. There must have been virga before she had met Mark, but she had never seen it. It had taken him to open her eyes to the beauty above.

Another time, they stopped and watched the nearly effortless glide of a hawk. Only the very tip feathers of its wings would occasionally flex to command a turn. "I've done that, Judy. I've glided like that. At the academy they teach us to pilot gliders, and we learn to do what that hawk is doing... ride the thermals."

"Thermals?"

"Yea. You can't see them, but the sun's heat causes columns of air to rise from the earth. They're called thermals. In a glider you fly straight until you enter one of them and then immediately begin a circle so you can stay in the column and let it lift you. Watch. The bird is doing the same thing."

She watched as the creature glided forward a short distance, then banked sharply into a tight turn.

"There! It's found one. Now it'll stay in a circle to gain altitude."

Without a single beat of its wings, the bird spiraled upward until it was a faint black dot.

On another stop, the lesson was on clouds. "The cumulonimbus are starting to build over the mountains."

"The what?"

"The cumulonimbus clouds. The thunderstorms. See?" He pointed to a line of the anvil-headed, stratospheric mammoths that rose fifty thousand feet above the mountains to the east. "Those smooth white tops are cirrus clouds. Most people call them mare's tails. I don't think they are as pretty as the nimbus part that has all the rain. But they're sure more fun to watch than stratus clouds. Those are the flat, boring clouds you see mostly in winter."

It was the conversation of a nerd, a geek. But Judy couldn't have been more captivated if it had been the serenade of a teen rock idol. This boy was so vastly different from all the others — and she would have him.

Shadows were lengthening when Mark finally called a halt at a primitive dirt road turnoff. "We'd better start looking for a campsite."

Even though they had seen only two cars in the last hour, the plan to move farther from the main thoroughfare pleased Judy. She wanted absolute privacy for what she was planning.

Within a hundred yards, the road deteriorated to a trail, and they dismounted to push their bikes along it. It climbed a small hillock, led deeper into the evergreens, and finally faded away.

"This looks good. I'll put up the tent. Why don't you..."

"Listen! What's that?" Judy silenced him. A rhythmic squeaking noise floated on the breeze. Her stomach plummeted in sickening disappointment. All day, they had been alone, and now, when she had most wanted isolation, they had inadvertently chosen a campsite that was already occupied.

Mark propped his bike against a tree and walked toward the sound. Judy followed. In a minute they rounded a knoll and found the source of the mystery.

"A windmill!"

The rusting structure had long been abandoned and was near collapse. Several fan blades were missing, as were pieces of the rough lumber tower that held it in place. A rusting pipe extended from the well head and rested on the lip of a concrete holding tank. Water trickled from its end, coming in greater volumes each time a breeze was captured by the turbine. There had been sufficient wind to fill the four-foot-deep tank, and water now spilled from its uneven lip.

"It must have been the water supply for whoever lived here." Mark pointed to a crumbling adobe wall that still held a door frame.

Judy was awed by the oasis and dipped her hand in the cool wet, rubbing it on her face. She would never have imagined the desert earth could hold such bounty and that it could be so easily mined with the wind. "Mark, this is so beautiful! Let's camp here! We can walk our bikes down."

"Yea. This is a great place. I was thinking that we were going to have to be careful with our water, but we've got all we want with this."

Thirty minutes later both bikes had been stripped of their stores, the tent had been staked, and Mark was unrolling their sleeping bags and foam underpads. Judy was tempted to tell him he was wasting his time — they would only need a single bed tonight. But she held her tongue. She would allow him no preparation for her assault. As cleverly as a predator maneuvering downwind of its prey, she would hold the element of surprise to the last.

He looked up from the work. "I'm going to sleep outside. You can have the tent."

"Thanks." She almost laughed at him.

The encampment continued. Mark stacked stones to bank a fire and began to set out cans of food for supper. Judy scavenged for wood. During the work, a wind rose and the sluice gushed a response.

"I'll fill the bottles while the wind is up."

"Good idea."

She rummaged through his pack, found the plastic containers, and disappeared behind the tank. A minute later, he heard the splash.

"Gawd! It's freezing!"

"What are you doing?" He stopped the supper preparations and turned to see her fully immersed in the tank, her head under the spigot and water sheeting her face. It never occurred to him she might be naked. Her clothes were out of sight on the far side of the tank, and she crouched low enough to put the water line at her neck.

"I'm taking a shower… a freezing one! How can the water be so cold in the desert?" As she spoke, she plied her fingers through the tresses, then tilted her mouth to the stream. "It tastes wonderful!"

Mark had intended to use a cloth to wash off before bed, but Judy's full-immersion approach was too appealing. He added a piñon log to the fire, emptied his pocket of his wallet, and stepped to the tower. The sun had dropped below a nearby cedar, and its shadow had fallen over the tank. The water had become an opaque dress for her body.

"Come on in. It's great!" Like the serpent in the tree, she tempted.

Shedding his shoes, the gullible Adam delicately climbed the wood-work and hung his legs into the tank. "Damn! You're not kidding! This water is cold! How could you just jump in?" He swung his feet back to the tower.

"Where are you going?"

"I'm not getting in there. It's too cold. I'm just going to wash off with a cloth."

"Chicken!" Before he could get clear, she launched a fusillade of water splashes with the palms of her hand.

"Stop it, Judy! It's freezing!" A speedy escape was impossible. To the sensitive soles of his bare feet, the knotted wood was like broken glass. "Damnit, Judy!"

His howls only increased the fury of her attack, and she laughed at his struggle to simultaneously shield himself from the shower while tenderly probing at the tower with his feet.

Finally, the provocation was great enough to send him on the offensive. He had nothing to lose. He was already drenched. He plunged into the tank and launched his own water-spray counterattack. She laughed giddily at her success and retreated backward. They were both blind to each other by the four-handed spray.

"I'm gonna… gonna…" He was now laughing and trying to form his own threat.

"What, Mark? What are you gonna do? Get me wet and cold?"

He trebled his hand motion, overwhelming hers, and Judy had to turn away.

"Ha! Give up?"

"Yes! Yes! I surrender! Stop! You win, Mark! Stop!" Then, in a lightning-quick motion, she turned and flung herself through the spray, between his arms and into his body.

In an eye blink, their voices stilled. The wind pump squeaked to a stop. The sluice slowed to a trickle. The last wave of their play crested the tank edge and splashed on the ground. The extreme quiet of the desert returned.

As in a trick of photography, Mark was frozen — his arms and hands arrested in midflail, his eyes dilated in fear. For the first time in his twenty years of life, the flesh of naked woman was against his skin.

Judy maintained a crushing grip around his waist. With her head on his chest, the pounding of his heart sounded like artillery in her ears.

"Judy! What? Where? Where are your clothes?"

Unabashedly, she smiled and pushed backward to point over the pool edge. "They're out here. You didn't think I'd take a shower with my clothes on, did you?" As she gave the answer, she came to a complete stand, and her drape of water fell to her lower belly. Mark tried to keep his eyes focused on her face, but they kept rebounding to her nipples — pink gems glistening on mounds of untanned breast.

"I… Judy… I…" He could make no sense.

She reached behind her neck and squeezed the water from her hair. By some incredible process, the action seemed to make the flesh even more naked and his eyes even more difficult to command. Judy noticed and maintained the pose in a continuing, ladies-locker-room-casual, ringing-out of her hair. Finally, she released the mane and waded back to him. He stood as paralyzed as a wax figure, his throat bobbing in multiple dry swallows.

"Mark." She took his hands in hers and began to slowly massage them. "I love you. I've always loved you. For two years, I've wanted you." She slowly raised his hands. "I wanted you so much. I wanted you to see me like this. I wanted you to touch me like this." She brought each palm onto her breasts and lightly guided them in a slow caress. He noticed none of the chill of her skin. It was fire that he touched — white fire, dangerous fire, fire that was spreading to his crotch.

"Judy, I... I... the fire is going out." He grabbed at the excuse and fled the trap, his feet suddenly capable of negotiating the rough lumber ladder with ease. While maintaining his back to the temptation, he hunched down and nervously fed sticks of wood into the coals. The fire blazed far bigger than necessary, and he stepped backward from the heat.

For a moment, Judy remained in the tank and watched him, wishing she could read his mind and see how he struggled — certain he *was* struggling. He was so poorly equipped to deal with her — with any woman, she thought. In a way, she felt guilty about what she was doing. Regardless of his seniority in age, it was child abuse. She was victimizing a boy. In a premeditated plan, she was shoving, pulling, dragging him into manhood, into love with her. But, if she was to have him, there was no other way. Another woman would certainly steal him if she did not.

Finally, she climbed from the tank, ignored her clothes, and walked to his back. He startled into another rigid fright as her arms came around his waist and warm breasts were pulled into him. She rested her cheek against the cool, smooth copper of his skin and again heard the deep thuds of his confused heart.

"Isn't it beautiful, Mark?"

"Huh?"

Judy smiled to herself. His voice was an octave higher.

"The sunset. Isn't it beautiful? Look at the mountains. They're red." Her hands began a slow stoke across his belly and chest, touching on tiny nipples that seemed hard enough to scratch.

"Ah, yes." Mark was happy to talk about anything. He gulped loudly. "The... the Spaniards named them Sangre de Christo... *Blood of Christ...* you know, because, you know, because of the red color they, you know, take at sunset."

Judy's hands swept across the corrugation of his stomach muscles and came to the snap of his jeans.

"Judy... don't... I..." His hands touched hers and resisted with all the strength of a newborn baby.

"I love you, Mark. It's okay. It's okay." She brushed her lips against the blade of his shoulder.

The sound of the snap filled the air like a gunshot and brought his body into a palsy. Judy worried. The trap was not fully sprung. He could yet escape. She began a continuous soft whisper in his ear, like a mother lovingly preparing her child for some unknown.

"Mark, take me. Make love to me." Her words covered the soft buzz of his zipper being lowered.

"Judy, it's, it's not… not right."

"It is, Mark. It is right. Nothing on this earth could be more right." Her fingers continued their work, spreading the jeans and slowly pulling them from his hips. They fell to the ground.

"Mark, no woman has ever loved a man as I love you. I don't know why, but you do something for me… something I can't imagine any man ever doing for me." Her fingers now came under the waistband of his jockey shorts and began their slow peel downward. His shivering intensified. "God intended us to be here, Mark. He brought us here. I'm sure of it. He made this spot for us to fall in love, to share each other for the first time." She felt resistance on the pull and suspected it was his erection. Without looking, without touching, she stretched the elastic wide to the front and continued to ease the underwear downward, squatting as she did so as to guide it past his knees, to his feet. She lifted his right foot and pulled the clothes completely from his body, then moved her cheek to the side of his thigh and began to run her face and hands up the length of his body in a long, delicate, feline stroke. "Mark, you are so beautiful." Her monologue never ceased. If she could hold him for just another minute she would have him. Her hands climbed upward along the sides of his thighs, then slowly onto the cheeks of his ass. Those bulged in Michelangelo-carved symmetry — firm, tight, muscular — and she lightly kissed each while continuing to straighten.

Ten more seconds. That's all!

Hands came under his arms, across ribs, across the washboard of his stomach, across the depression of his navel. His breath came shallow, fast, audible. "Judy…" It was the weakest of protests.

"It's okay, Mark. I love you. It's okay." Her fingers touched the first wisps of pubic hair. She paused for only a moment to relish the softness, then furrowed deeper into the thick mat. Her hands stayed in the curls and moved outward to avoid any contact with his erection. She had yet to see it, to touch it, but knew it was there, stretched and swollen in virgin splendor. She would save it for the very last.

Her fingers moved onto his thighs, then reversed and crawled upward to begin an exploration of his sac — of its softness, of its hardness.

Mark's groan was animal.

"It feels right, doesn't it, Mark?" Continuing as a temptress, she answered for him. "Yes. Yes, it does. It feels so right."

It was time. Keeping her left hand in the massage, she brought her right into a feathery grasp of the steel. His respiration became that of a sprinter's, and a low moan escaped his throat. The trap had closed. He was hers.

"Oh, Mark. Mark, Mark." She moved to his front and began to kiss him, almost chastely, with only the briefest flicks of her tongue teasing his lips. Between each wet dart, she whispered further invitations. "Touch me, Mark. Hold me. It's okay." To that moment, his hands had hung uselessly at his side. "Put them on my back. Yes, yes." His embrace was awkward, reluctant. "Lower, Mark, lower." Her own body shivered at the hesitant fall. It ended on the small of her back. "Go lower, Mark. Touch me."

He did, with the gentlest of petting strokes, across the little, split moon. It was a catalyst. The hands became braver and moved up her sides in a wondrous trace of all that was feminine — rounded hips, the deep curve of her waist, and the bulging sides of her breasts.

She separated from him, took his hand, and pulled him the three steps to the sleeping bag. It was like leading a child across the street. Soundlessly they reclined, Judy falling to her back and trying to bring him onto her. But he resisted.

"Judy, we can't. I mean, what if you get pregnant?" He knelt next to her, sitting back on his heals, nervously rubbing his palms back and forth across his thighs.

"I won't get pregnant, Mark. It's not the right time."

"Are you sure? Are you sure you can't get pregnant?" The voice was begging, pleading with aroused male passion that it *please, please* be so.

"A woman knows, Mark. It's not the right time of my cycle. I won't get pregnant." She lied. Her period was a week away, but she would not allow this chance to slip by. Someday, she would conceive his children.

If it was this day, so be it.

Mark gulped. She was so beautiful and so soft and so warm and so, so convincing. Fear of fatherhood evaporated like the virga in the sky.

His eyes devoured the things of dreams, of fantasies — a beautiful woman lying on her back wanting him; soft mounds of breast peaked with pink; a small, concave belly; a tiny triangle of curled, auburn hair capping smooth, flawless thighs.

She found his hand and, ever so gently, laid it on her mound. For a moment, his fingers remained as still as the evening air. "I'm very soft there. Feel me." She encouraged exploration, slowly cycling her hips in a pumping motion. His middle finger answered the invitation, slipping slowly into the wet silk, down, down, down, into the deep wet.

Her breath came faster. "Mark, Mark, Mark. That feels...*so* wonderful. But let me show you where it's best for me." She grabbed his other hand by the middle finger and brought it to the magic stone. "Feel here? Oh!" The short cry came as the most sensitive part of her body came under his touch. "When you touch me there, I think it feels like when I touch you… here." Her fingers came back into a gentle massage of the now-wet crown of his shaft. The instructions were instantly clear, and he began to slowly rock the nubbin of flesh back and forth, up and down, over and over. "You'll make me come, Mark. Oh yes, yes, you'll make me come doing that."

For the first time, Judy lost control. She was in some faraway magic kingdom, some place not of earth. Her eyes stared straight upward into the deepening blue of a crystalline twilight. Evening stars glared bright and cold and steady. Did the sky look like this from planet earth? No, it didn't. Mark had taken her away to a different place. A place of wondrous pleasure. How? She couldn't remember. But she was there, feeling his fingers dancing in her, on her, his cream wetting her own fingers. "Oh, Mark! Mark, I'm coming… I'm coming! *I'm coming!*"

In his ignorance, Mark was almost frightened by the words. It was the baffling wonder of all virgin males — what did a female orgasm *do*? And, as it had done for men since the time of Adam, the answer surprised him. There was only the slightest arch of her back and a pelvic thrust into his fingers and a very long beseeching moan to unhearing deities to signal its arrival and passage.

It was a lesson that emboldened him. He wanted to know everything about this wondrous, soft, wet, writhing creature. He wanted to suck her breasts, to join tongues with her, to read and understand the sexual intent of every movement of her body, to understand those wondrous dreams of puberty. And he did, in a foreplay that lasted through the yellows and reds of a dying sun.

Turquoise was coloring the horizon when she finally pulled him onto her, splayed her legs, and guided him in the joining. Mark was carried onto the shore of a new and glorious world of heat and wet and soft, while Judy sped away from planet earth at light speed, rushing to the pleasure palaces of the gods.

The twilight deepened to indigo. The air became cold. The fire died to glowing embers. Overhead, the brighter stars winked on to join the planets in their nightly parade. There were no insect serenades in the desert, no crying animals to disturb the stillness. Just peals of thunder rolled across the mesa — the bass voice of a faraway storm pummeling the Blood of Christ mountains. Its clouds glowed white with continuous flashes of lightning, and its wind, made gentle by the distance, stirred the evergreens around them. The aged joints of the pump creaked their response. Water trickled from the sluice and into the pool with the tinkling noise of a wind chime. These were the sounds that mingled with the moans and breathlessness and cries of their continued mating.

Judy watched over Mark's shoulder, smiling at the sky, at the fresco of stars in their slow pirouette about Polaris. No woman of any royal palace, no starlet, no celebrity of fame or fortune had ever had a more beautiful wedding bed. And this *was* her wedding bed. Although the man heaving above her didn't yet realize it, although he had said nothing of love, she knew this was a mating for life. Mark O'Malley would forever be hers.

Thirty minutes later, he lay exhausted on his back and Judy nuzzled into his neck. Her hand stroked the side of his face and combed through his hair. It was military-academy short, almost a bristle, and somehow it enhanced the hardness, the sheer male power of his body.

"Judy! Look! Quick! Over there!"

"What? What is it?" The urgency of the command so abruptly shattered the stillness she was momentarily terrified someone had invaded their Shangri-la. She pulled the sleeping bag to her neck and quickly searched the camp. No intruders were visible in the starlight.

"Up there, Judy! Almost right over us!"

She could now see his arm was pointed upward and turned to follow its extension.

"What?"

"It's a satellite! See… it's moving past that bright star. It's in a polar orbit. God, I'd give anything to fly that high!" A faint dot of light glided silently northward.

At the mention of *satellite,* Judy's fear of visitors vanished. She collapsed to her back, laughing at the mistake. She should have known. This was the boy who had earlier pointed to the virga, to the thermal-soaring hawk, to the clouds. She should have known that his preoccupation with the sky didn't end at sunset.

She continued to laugh at his excitement over such trivia and crawled onto his front. "Mark, I can lift you higher than that." She moved forward to touch a nipple to his lips.

❖

Judy put down her pencil. In the reverie, she had made four sketches. None had a cedar. All had a windmill.

She watched the lovers. The *tête-à-tête* had gone no farther than an unbuttoned blouse, and the girl knelt next to the boy, smiling and laughing and tempting him with her small breasts. Judy watched and wondered. *Is she thinking the same thing? I can capture this man. I can lift him out of this world.*

Even when I had everything — When I was like you, with a body that was new and hard and perfect, and it was his first time — even then, I couldn't steal him. I never had him. I never changed him.

CHAPTER 9

Saturday, 5 November
The White House

Killingsworth was ushered into the president's personal office on the third floor.

"Please have a seat, Mr. Killingsworth. The president's meeting with the Joint Chiefs of Staff has been extended. He will be with you shortly."

"Thank you."

The aide glided out, leaving the fat man alone.

It didn't surprise him that the president was tied up with his military advisors — getting a briefing on the results of the retaliatory air attack on Iran was his guess. He ached for his friend. If the *KOSMOS* crisis hadn't been enough of a strain, now he had the additional burden of dealing with the madmen of Teheran.

Fifteen minutes later, the door opened.

"Hobie, sorry for the delay." A preoccupied president walked briskly to him and shook his hand.

Killingsworth could not miss the damage the burden of office had so recently wrought. The president's bloodshot eyes were ringed with fatigue, his mouth grimly set.

"We can talk *KOSMOS* in a minute. First, I want to see how the networks are covering this Iranian thing." On the wall across from the desk was a large cabinet holding a battery of television sets. He turned on three, collapsed into his chair, and selectively listened to each news anchor. There were scenes of him making the nationally televised announcement several hours earlier: "We have positively identified the government of Iran as responsible for the heinous attack of October the ninth that left eleven Americans dead, including six children and three women. As I promised, retribution would be swift. At this very moment, air elements of the United States Navy are attacking key Iranian military installations."

There were other cutaways to pirated Iranian television broadcasts showing burning oil storage tanks at the Bandar Abbas Naval Base and dead and wounded being lifted into ambulances. Extended coverage was given to the extraction of the bloody body of a woman and her baby from a demolished car.

The president muted the screen. "With just a phone call, Hobie, I can do that." The words were bitter. "People who woke up this morning are now dead at my command."

"Mr. President, you had no choice. The evidence was irrefutable."

He scoffed derisively. "Yes. Evidence excuses all."

Scenes of a sea of humanity crowding the streets, beating their breasts, and demanding vengeance on the Great Satan came onto the ABC monitor. "I pray to God the message got through to those lunatics." He picked up the remote control and blanked everything. As difficult as it was for him to believe, there was an even greater crisis awaiting his attention.

"I got your message, Hobie. Two more dead satellites?"

"It was more than that, Mr. President. The machines, both of which were within the *KOSMOS*' view, failed within *seconds* of each other. General Lawson believes it is proof positive the Soviets are refining a weapon and could be very close to fully operational status. The fact that the satellites were on opposite edges of the *KOSMOS* hemisphere suggests an exceptional ability to engage missile warheads. Those were the general's words."

"I don't suppose there was anything in the way of *evidence* the Soviets were behind these latest failures?"

"No, sir. The failures followed the same pattern of the others. The craft are unreachable for an inspection."

"So, I still can't risk an attack." The president stood and paced. "I'm frightened, Hobie... really scared. We've got to get to that thing."

"Mr. President, *Freedom's* manufacture is complete. Tomorrow, its components will be flown to the Kennedy Space Center. Its booster rocket will be installed in *Atlantis* and the rest will be placed atop a *Nova* rocket. Every conceivable shortcut is being taken, but the earliest the *Nova* can be launched is November eighteenth. The shuttle will lift off November twenty-second. The rendezvous and assembly should be completed on the twenty-fourth — Thanksgiving Day. If all goes well, O'Malley and Darling will be in the vicinity of the *KOSMOS* on the twenty-sixth. That's when we'll know the true mission of the machine."

The president examined the calendar that the fat man laid before him. In the twin distractions of the England terrorist attack and the *KOSMOS* unknowns, he had forgotten how close the Thanksgiving season was. "The twenty-sixth, huh? God, Hobie, I hope that's soon enough."

❖

Monday, 7 November
Johnson Space Center

Pettigrew finished reading the checklist for the second time but had yet to comprehend a single word. Despairing he would do any better on a third attempt, he grabbed a coiled-spring exerciser, stood at the window, and squeezed out a two-minute workout with each hand. The drill came with the job. On a space walk, hands and fingers were the instruments of life itself, and the rigidity of the pressure suit gloves made even trivial finger motions exhausting. He vigorously pumped the spring to bring endurance to seldom-used muscles.

It was a magnificent Indian-summer afternoon. The air was still and crisp, the sun warm, and the sky snapping clear, and he was tempted to adjourn his study to his backyard spa. He couldn't remember the last time he had been at home when the sun was still shining.

Launch was three weeks away and the training had become murderous. He rarely saw Mark or Darling. Denver had swallowed them. In Houston, he and Anna had become Jonahs living in the bellies of a pod of simulators. Every minute of the planned mission, as well as every imaginable contingency, was repeated over and over until the procedures were flawlessly performed. And then they were repeated again.

But the labor was not enough to keep his mind off the woman. She was always there, always torturing him, always unwittingly summoning the questions into his brain: *What would it be like to fly with her? To hold her? To sleep with her?*

The same questions afflicted him now and frustrated his study.

Finally, he tossed aside the exerciser and pulled the weekly training schedule from his pocket. It showed she was in the MDF, the Manipulator Development Facility, for another hour — until 5:00 P.M. After that, there was nothing — a rare night off for both of them.

He stared at the page, wondering, would she accept an invitation to dinner? With a little office sleuthing, he had determined she was dating a lawyer or doctor or some such professional. He wondered how serious it was. Was she sleeping with him? Engaged to him?

He tossed the schedule aside, muttered a self-directed curse for allowing the distractions, and resolved to complete his study.

It was a resolution quickly forgotten. Five minutes later he was on a mission to find Anna and ask her to dinner.

At the MDF, he found her engrossed in the robot arm operation of lowering a fifty-foot-long helium balloon into the payload bay. The giant cylinder, replicating space weightlessness with the gas, came within inches of completely occupying the fifteen-foot diameter of the cargo volume. Her eyes were welded to the television monitors at her right, and she was unaware of his arrival.

Pettigrew approached from behind to ask his question. He hoped to appear disinterested in whatever reply it generated.

"Hello, Anna. How's the sim going?"

"Oh, Bob, hi. Well, this run is going better than the last. What brings you over here?" She had allowed herself only a brief glance in his direction before returning to the TV monitors.

"It didn't take me as long as I thought to look over those rendezvous changes." He nervously jingled his pocket change. "I came over here to see, to ask you… I was, well, I was wondering if you'd like to go, well, to go to dinner with me tonight."

Nice fuckin' job, Pettigrew! You sure sounded cool and disinterested. Shit!

"Hey! Anna! Watch it!" A technician screamed the complaint as she jammed the balloon into the port side of the bay. The question had so startled her, she had spastically jerked at the controls.

"Dinner! I mean, dinner? I… I… yes, I would love… that would be nice." Afraid to face him, she directed her answer to the television.

"I thought I'd make reservations at the Clipper Ship for seven o'clock."

"Seven? That'll be fine."

"Good. I'll pick you up about six-thirty."

"Okay, six-thirty."

"Well, see you then." He had to concentrate to keep his exit poised and confident. His legs wanted to accelerate to the speed of his pounding heart.

❖

Anna stood at her bedroom mirror and worried. On the way home from the MDF, an overpowering wave of femininity had pushed her into a lady's boutique. There, an aggressive saleswoman had convinced her she had the perfect dress for the evening.

Now draped in it, Anna turned in profile for yet another critical examination, still not convinced it was perfect for her. As promised, the emerald green color did emphasize her gold hair and jade eyes, and the high collar was modest enough. But the interlock-knit material adhered to her body like a sheath. It was so contrary to every other dress that hung in her closet. Every curve was on display.

She turned her back and twisted her head for a rear view. Like the neckline, the hemline was modestly located, coming to midcalf. She was happy for that. It would hide her too-skinny legs.

Completing the turn, she again faced her image. She had lightly mascaraed eyelashes and thinly shadowed eyes. A hint of blush reddened her cheeks, and she wore a raspberry lip gloss. All were recommendations of the boutique staff.

Her eyes inadvertently touched on the photo of Richard.

Richard!

Not a single thought of the man had crossed her mind since Pettigrew's invitation. The man who worshipped her, who brought her gifts, who invited her on trips, who took her to bed — that man had been shamelessly evicted from her mind.

Pettigrew!

He was the new occupant. She had been frustrated with thoughts of the man for weeks. Even sleep had not always shielded her from his presence. Twice, she had awakened from intensely pleasureful dreams that had included visions of his naked back.

She dabbed perfume to her neck and wrists in another rare act of preening, while repeating her litany of warning. *Stay in control! Remem-*

ber Stanford! Remember China Lake! Remember Pettigrew's reputation! Remember Pettigrew's lustful stares! God, remember those! Men will use you!

But the other being challenged. *Pettigrew will not use you. He is afraid of you.* Anna had seen it, too. Over the past weeks, he had run from her on every occasion a computer glitch had momentarily idled the simulators. His excuses had been transparent — use the bathroom, get some coffee, place a phone call. Even his flight from the MDF, just hours ago, had been obvious. Why would a man who was afraid of a woman ask her to dinner? And why should he be afraid?

The door bell startled her from the wonders. She made a last brush of her hair, walked to the entryway, took a calming breath, and pulled open the door.

"Hi."

Pettigrew's eyes widened noticeably. *Jesus!* The woman before him was not the same one he had spoken with at the MDF. He had been expecting Anna Rowe — a pretty woman with chewed nails, no makeup, and wearing baggy slacks and a loose-fitting blouse. This woman was nothing less than stunningly beautiful, and in his attempt to address her, his mouth made unproductive gaping motions like a beached fish.

Anna wondered what she had botched. Makeup? Her clothes? What? She burned with embarrassment. "I... I... I guess." She was retreating inside. "Please, just give me a minute and I'll..."

"No!" Pettigrew's exclamation startled her. "I mean, no, Anna. Please, I'm sorry. I didn't expect... I mean, I thought you would... I mean you're fine... fine! You're beautiful!"

Goddamnit, Pettigrew! Nice way to start the evening! Will you ever learn how to talk to this woman?

Thirty minutes later they were standing alone at the end of the Clipper Ship dock waiting for their table. Their body language was a study in first-acquaintance jitters. A yard separated them. Pettigrew leaned backward on the dock railing while Anna faced the same railing and looked over the waters of Clear Lake. They each twirled a wineglass between nervous fingers. No one could have guessed this man and woman had been cohabitating for fifteen hours a day for the past six weeks. They would have thought they were seeing just-introduced strangers. But the circumstances of the simulator and the dock were as vastly different as being together at a crowded party verses being strangers in an elevator. In the cocoons of the machines, in the comforting security of flashing lights and warbling tones, communication had been no problem. But now…

"Not many days you can enjoy an evening like this in Houston." Anna addressed her wineglass.

"Yea, it's cool enough to scare off the mosquitoes." *Brilliant, Pettigrew! Just fuckin' brilliant! Jesus, why did I do this?*

"Yea, it would be a nice evening anywhere. For Houston, though, it's nothing short of fantastic." Anna glanced at her watch. Time seemed to have stopped. She was in hell. Then, she noticed something else. *My watch!* She had forgotten to remove it! The multifunctional, stainless-steel, wide-band pilot's watch, bristling with push-button controls, glared from a petite arm that was naked to the shoulder. Another millimeter of fingernail found the saw of her teeth.

"It sure is a beautiful sunset." Another pearl of witticism, Pettigrew thought.

"Yes, it is. I just wish they could all look like orbit sunsets."

"What do those look like? Are they the same to the eye as the photos show?" *Finally!* For the first time since meeting her at the door, he had formed an intelligent question. He turned to watch her answer.

"Oh, Bob, they are so magnificent. This is… is… nothing." She referred to the *Gone With the Wind* sunset that was streaking the horizon with shafts of flamingo and scarlet. "In orbit, when the sun falls below the earth's limb, each color of the spectrum appears separately, distinctly. It's a perfect rainbow that cuts across a… a perfect black." Her eyes were alive with the memory.

Pettigrew was staring now, captivated, wanting so very much to fly with her, to share that intimacy with her. "When did you first want to fly?" He surprised himself with the question. It was blurted out and totally irrelevant to orbit sunsets.

Anna didn't care about the sudden change of topics — anything to sustain the conversation. "I think my mother was responsible. Her company had a sales contest and one of the prizes was a ride in a hot-air balloon over the wine country. She won and took me along." Her face brightened, her smile widened. "I was changed that day, Bob. Everything was so beautiful, so quiet… the earth, the clouds, everything. We launched just before sunrise, and in some areas there was a low ground fog and only the hills were visible, like islands in a white sea. For a while, the pilot stabilized just over the fog... the top was as flat as this lake... and we seemed to just hover there, totally motionless.

"I must have been seven or eight then and decided that very day I wanted to fly. I couldn't imagine there was anything more wonderful than to be a pilot."

In the storytelling, she emitted unseen waves — like magnetism — that pulled Pettigrew's soul closer. In vastly different circumstances, he had felt those waves before — over beers in an officer's club bar, waiting out the weather in a squadron ready room, leaning against an aircraft on the flight line, in all the gathering places of men of the brotherhood — the brotherhood of the air — where stories had been recounted of childhood longings to fly. On so many occasions, the waves of these kindred spirits had tugged on his soul. But never had the pull been as it was now, generated by a woman of extraordinary beauty, tainted with sex, over-powering.

"How about yourself, Bob? Was flying something you always wanted to do?"

He turned into the railing to tell his story as she had hers — in a gaze across the lake. "Yea. It goes a long way back. I grew up on a farm in Idaho, and my uncle owned a nearby crop dusting company. He was an old World War II marine pilot. After my chores were done, I would ride my bike over to his field. It wasn't much of a field, really. Just a barn for a hanger, a grass runway, and a couple of biplanes. Well, he sort of adopted me. I think it was because he didn't have any kids of his own. Anyway, when I was about ten, he built a set of blocks out of two-by-fours and strapped them to the rudder pedals so my feet could reach them. Then he began to teach me to fly in his old Piper Cub. In five minutes I was hooked for life. It was just like you described, such a feeling of freedom. I never wanted to do anything else. I'll bet I had a thousand hours of flying with him before I was a teenager."

"When did you first solo?"

"You mean legally?"

She laughed. "There's only *one* first solo."

"I must have been, let me see, fifteen. No, fourteen. I remember because I couldn't even drive a car... legally. My uncle stayed with me for an hour while I did touch-and-go's in the Piper. Then he jumped out and said, 'Don't tell your momma. She'll have my hide,' and walked away. It was the most wonderful day of my life... the wind rushing by my head, the feel of the stick and throttle. I think I even let out an Indian-style whoop. I never wanted to come down."

Anna's heart skipped at his smile. She had never seen it, not a smile like that, not a smile of such rich joy.

He sipped from his glass. "After I had made a couple of landings, my uncle got in another plane and led me through a mountain valley. It was September and the aspen groves were in full color and we just skimmed above their tops. A wind was shimmering their leaves so they looked liquid, like we were flying over lakes of gold." He turned to face her. "I doubt if even a sunset from orbit could have a gold color like those aspens. It was like... like..." Suddenly the easy memory was over-whelmed by the extreme beauty of the woman. She was watching him, smiling comfortably at the story, the last blush of the day twinkling in the green spokes of her irises, her skin rouged by the burnt-orange in the west. The lightness in his face evaporated as the analogy was completed. "It was like... your hair."

Anna's smile collapsed. In an eye blink, the intimate, beautiful simile had turned the moment heart-attack serious. The only intrusions of sound were the lapping of the waves on the pier pilings and the far-off cry of a gull. Pettigrew ached to hold her, to run his fingers through the gold of his metaphor. Anna was a tumult of emotion — embarrassment, fierce attraction, gut fear.

The moment passed as suddenly as it had come when a patio loudspeaker announced their table was ready.

Pettigrew looked toward the restaurant. "I guess it's time to go." It was said with all the enthusiasm of someone facing a tooth extraction. In spite of what had just transpired, the dock had become a sanctuary.

"Yea." Anna had no appetite and feared what Pettigrew feared—that the table would be another awkward transition for them. "I'm really not too hungry, but..."

"You're not? Then why don't we stay out here? We can always go in later after the crowds are gone." Pettigrew jumped at the escape.

Anna thanked the saints above for the minor miracle. "Sure. I'd like that. I feel like I've been locked in buildings for weeks now." A passing sailboat gave her an immediate transition. "Do you sail, Bob?"

"No. There weren't a lot of places to sail in the part of Idaho I come from." He didn't add that as a child he had almost drowned in a canoeing accident with his older brother. The experience had given him a psychopathic phobia of the water.

"San Francisco was a wonderful place to learn. I love it."

With the statement came jealous visions of her cuddled in the cockpit of a lawyer's or doctor's private yacht.

"When you have a nice breeze and the rigging is singing, it's almost as much fun as flying. Would you like to come sometime? I could show you. The apartment complex where I live has rentals." It was an invitation straight from the other being, and Anna wanted to take it back as soon as it was offered. But that was impossible.

"Sure. That sounds like fun." The other being within Pettigrew, spelled c-o-w-a-r-d, silently howled for him to keep his goddamn mouth shut, but it was too late.

"After the mission, then. We'll do it."

"Sure."

The conversation waned, but now there was no sense of urgency that it be continued. The promise of the future date had an instantly calming affect on the current one.

Slowly, the spinning earth drained the last color from the western sky and lifted a blanket of stars from the east. Jupiter, and Saturn brilliantly ruled the twilight.

They silently enjoyed the spectacle, raising their faces to it like a farmer might study the soil at his feet or a sailor survey the seascape. The limitless black was their element, and they spoke of it.

"There's Aldebaran." He pointed to an orange star forming the eye of Taurus the Bull. "Sirius will be up soon."

"Yea. You can already see Bellatrix and Rigel."

They were fluent in the Arabic names and positions of the fifty navigation stars used by the shuttle star trackers. To others, they were merely random points of light, but to astronauts, the stars were life itself. Without them, the orbiter would be blind to its attitude, and without precise knowledge of attitude, reentry would be a three-thousand-degree funeral pyre.

"I used to take one of my uncle's open cockpit planes up at night and lean my head back and watch the stars. It never occurred to me that any had names except Polaris."

"I love night flying. Sometimes I'll take along my portable tape recorder and plug it into the intercom and listen to music while..."

"What?!" He interrupted her. "Anna, you really do that? I mean, you listen to music while watching the stars?"

She was taken back by his sudden excitement. "Yes. Neil Diamond, John Denver, some classics."

"Anna, I do that! Sometimes I'll come out here at night and take a '38 over the Gulf and watch the stars and listen to music. I never would have believed anyone else did that." He felt like a Robinson Crusoe sighting the imprint of a human foot in the sand — there was another being on a remote island of his soul. The waves that tugged him toward the woman were no longer of magnetic intensity. They pulled with the fierceness of stellar gravity.

Anna's own excitement grew. "Have you ever listened to Pachelbel's Canon? Do you want to trade tapes? Do you..."

The earth turned to deepen the black and bring the things of dreams over their heads. Supper was forgotten.

Saturday, 12 November
Johnson Space Center

Mark sat at his desk in the crew quarters, a small, motel-like facility near the astronaut gym. Rather than renew the lease on his apartment, he had moved into the NASA quarters. They were normally used by crew members to maintain a one-week, preflight health quarantine from young children living at home. The facility would not be needed by his childless crew. He would be the lone occupant.

It was Saturday evening, and he picked up the phone for his weekly call to Judy. Normally, by unspoken agreement, the conversation would be devoid of any mention of the mission. But this one would be different. In keeping with air force policy, *Atlantis's* launch date had finally been released to the public. He could tell her the date — November twenty-second — and make his request.

"Judy, it's me."

"Hello, Mark." The greeting was bland.

"Listen, I've moved out of the apartment. I'm living in the crew quarters now." He gave her the telephone number.

Dangerous ground laid ahead, and he took a breath before continuing. "Judy… the launch date has been set. It's the twenty-second, in ten days. We'll be leaving for the Cape on Sunday, the twentieth."

Silence.

In a childish act, Judy thought that she could postpone the inevitable by refusing to discuss it.

"Judy?"

"I heard, Mark… the twenty-second." The voice was unsteady.

"I've arranged for a NASA jet to pick you up at Moffet Field on the twentieth and bring you to the Cape. Peggy can come along, too. I've cleared that with management." Killingsworth had given him a blank check to do whatever he wanted with his family. He had already talked with the kids. They were steel. If anything happened to him, they would be fine where they were. It was Judy he feared for. At Mountain View she would be too exposed. In a disaster scenario, the press would eat her alive. He continued his sell. "We'd be able to see each other. And I'll make sure you're kept up to date on how the flight is going. The air force won't be able to go into details, but they can reassure you. You could stay at the beach house. I think you'd find it more comfortable there."

The feeling came upon Judy with a demonic vengeance. Her knees weakened and she collapsed backward onto the hallway wall, sliding slowly downward until she was a sheet-white, sitting heap. She had easily seen through the camouflage and to his hidden agenda. It wasn't her comfort that concerned him. He wanted her protected by NASA in the event of a disaster, protected by the barbed wire of a government installation, protected by a casualty assistance officer, by flight surgeons, by a platoon of public-affairs mouthpieces. The extremes to which he had gone — the NASA jet, the inclusion of Peggy as an escort, the billeting at the beach house — said it all. They were unheard-of concessions by a bean-counting bureaucracy that had typically appeased wives with the barest expenditure of resources.

He wasn't coming back. *The feeling* sickened her physically. A dry heave rippled her throat. "Mark, don't go! Please! Don't go on this mission! I don't want to die!" It was the begging, tearful plea heard by executioners.

"Oh, Jesus." He shook his head in despair. She had turned back the clock two months. Would she never understand he had to fly the mission? That he would never walk away from it? "Judy, you're not going to die. Nobody's going to die. It's just another shuttle mission. After the bad press of the RTLS, NASA is looking at everything with a magnifying glass. Flying *Atlantis* will be safer than walking across the street."

"No, Mark! The sky wants you! The shuttle wants your life! They're going to take you! I can feel it!"

"Goddamnit, Judy, enough! The sky, the shuttle... you're talking like they're... like they're alive or something! You're talking like an insane person! I *can't* quit! The country needs me! It's as simple as that!" He hid behind the shield of patriotism.

"*I* need you, Mark! *I* need you! And if you fly this mission, I'll lose you! I know it!"

He heaved a huge sigh and smeared his hand over his face in a struggle to compose himself. "Okay, Judy, okay. Listen, I can understand your fear about coming to the Cape. I mean, I can understand how the RTLS scared you. So forget about that. Just forget about the Cape. But how about coming here, to JSC? It would be so much easier for you to be kept up to date on what's going on."

"Oh, Mark, stop lying! Don't lie anymore! I know why you want me there! You want NASA to hide me!"

"Judy, I'm not..."

"No, Mark, I won't come back there! I won't! You're asking me to walk into hell and I can't do it! I can't! I won't!"

He was whipped. There was nothing else he could say. He would talk with Killingsworth and make sure that he had people discreetly positioned in Mountain View to protect her.

❖

Thursday, 17 November
Red Sky Control Center

Kobozev watched the control room activity from the elevated, glass-enclosed command room. He understood nothing of what he saw — the huge Mercator projection of the Red Sky hemisphere, the scroll of data across adjoining screens, the multiple digital clocks counting backward to unknown events, the amphitheater of computer consoles. No, he understood nothing of it. Nothing, except the power that it represented. It would be from this grand, bustling monument to socialist genius that in seven days a new world order would emerge. For almost four decades, the most powerful nation on the face of the earth — the United States of America — had built a great wall of nuclear armed missiles. And behind that wall, their economy had flourished and the poison of their democracy had spread like a cancer around the world. He silently laughed. Even Mikhail Sorokin had been infected with the disease of democracy. The man who would assume the Party chairmanship would, himself, orchestrate the destruction of the Party by returning power to the people.

Power! The idiot would give it back to the people! But I will not allow it! America will be taught a lesson in power! Sorokin will be taught the same lesson! Power is to be acquired, coveted, used — never given to the people! Lenin understood power! Stalin understood power! Power is everything! And Red Sky is the source of ultimate power! Red Sky will reduce the American Maginot Line of missiles to a trillion-dollar mirage. From this very room I will show them that! I will show them the power!

Yes, he thought, Sorokin had seven days remaining to preach his new gospel of reform to the Politburo. Yes, the American president had but seven days to wield his power.

Smiling, he turned and faced the other four conspirators. "Seven days, comrades. Just seven days." All understood. None replied. Kobozev walked to the table and took a seat at its head. "Now, are we ready?" He nodded to Anatoliy Ryabinin to proceed with a review of KGB activities.

"The Iranian situation could not be more exploitable. The disinformation program of our Teheran agents has made the city rife with rumors of an American invasion force massing in the Gulf of Oman." He chuckled. "And the American president has been extremely accommodating in giving substance to those rumors. His response to the England terrorist was more than we could have ever hoped. Iranian casualties approached almost eight hundred dead and two thousand wounded. It was an incredible stroke of good luck that one of their errant bombs demolished a mosque, burying over five hundred worshippers. The zealots are screaming they will turn the Persian Gulf red with American blood. It is a population so blind with rage it will be easily duped by the assassinations of their leaders. The Americans will be blamed. Hashemi's ascension to power will be unquestioned."

"*If* the assassinations are successful." Andrey Yazov chased the statement with a swallow of a green antacid liquid, then wiped his mouth with the back of his hand, smearing some of the chalky substance on his cheek. The man's stomach had become a caldron of ulcerous fires. He could see a thousand ways the coup would fail, that they would be discovered and executed. Images of the dead elk were constantly in his mind — its staring glass eyes, the blood streaming from its mouth and nostrils, its waste flopping from its death-relaxed bowels. That would be his fate. Slumped over the ropes of an executioner's post, blood bubbling from his nose and mouth, urine staining his pants, his open sphincter passing feces to fill his black market, silk underwear.

But maybe there was a way out. Maybe he could get to Sorokin to warn him of the plot. Maybe a tearful confession would win him amnesty. If he could only escape his KGB followers! He must find a way! Another flare seared his intestines.

"I see, Comrade Yazov, you still suffer a lack of faith in our plan." Only a flickering forked tongue could have given Kobozev a more reptilian look of evil, of danger.

"Yes, I do, Comrade Kobozev!" Yazov slammed his fist on the desk. There was steel in his spine today, but only because Kobozev could not intimidate him with his weapons.

"Then, let Anatoliy continue, and maybe your fears will be laid to rest." His voice and demeanor were calm, level — the antithesis of Yazov's chalk-stained, tic-blinking face. He nodded to the minister of state security.

Ryabinin pulled a Teheran street map from his briefcase and spread it on the table. "The assassination team is already in place, living in a high rise apartment… here." He pointed. "On the twenty-third, as they do every Wednesday, the ayatollahs will conduct a staff meeting and a prayer service at the Hamadan Mosque… here. The entourage typically departs by the same route." He traced it with his finger, a boulevard that passed directly in front of the apartment. "The car bomb will be located along that route, visible from the apartment window. As the subjects motor past it, our agent will detonate it by remote control. It is a massive bomb. Casualties will be extremely high. The faithful know of the routine and invariably jam the streets seeking a blessing from their shepherd."

Yazov scoffed. "And how can you be certain that Hashemi will be spared? If you kill him we have done nothing but hang ourselves!"

"Hashemi will delay his departure. As the junior spiritual leader, he frequently remains behind to officiate at their religous court."

"And if the fools choose this route" — Yazov jabbed a fat finger at a boulevard at right angles to the first — "*then* the plan has failed!"

"We have covered that possibility. Another bomb is being parked along that avenue, and if the group should pass in this direction, it will be detonated by other agents living in an apartment that overlooks it."

Kobozev smiled at the weakling. "See, Comrade Yazov, the plan will not fail."

Yazov's blubbery lip quivered while his brain tried to find a flaw. But another intestinal eruption distracted him. He gulped at the bottle while Ryabinin continued.

"Evidence will be left at the apartments that will implicate the Americans, though I doubt Hashemi will need it. The masses will need nothing to blame the United States."

Kobozev turned to the defense minister. "Musa, will your forces be ready?"

"The *Kiev* carrier battle group is on routine maneuvers in the northwest Indian Ocean. They will begin their approach to the Gulf of Oman on the twenty-first and will be in position to arrive in Iranian territorial waters on the twenty-fourth, within an hour of Red Sky's demonstration."

"Does this schedule meet with your approval, Comrade Skripko?"

The minister of foreign affairs leaned forward. "It does. Tomorrow, I depart for Canada, and my published itinerary has me returning to Moscow on Wednesday. That will not occur. Instead, on Saturday, I will notify the American state department of my desire to visit with the president on the twenty-third."

"Excellent, Comrades. Excellent! Red Sky is ready. Iran is ready. Our navy is ready. And our timing is perfect. I have talked with the chairman's doctor, and our beloved leader is within two weeks of death. Next week he will be virtually incapacitated with pain-killing drugs. Sorokin will, no doubt, remain in the Kremlin for the death vigil and to put the finishing touches on his case to assume the chairmanship."

"What if the Americans are ready for Red Sky?" Yazov again tried to throw up a roadblock.

Ryabinin answered him, "The Americans know nothing of Red Sky."

"How can you be so certain? We have been killing their satellites! The Americans are clever! They must suspect us!"

"They do not. They have announced their intention of launching a space shuttle next week, a secret military mission on the twenty-second. That can only mean..."

"What?" Kobozev interrupted. "Why was I not told?"

"I, myself, just heard of the plan this morning."

Yazov leaped at the opportunity to spread doubts. "See! The Americans do know! We must abandon this idiocy! Forget the Iranian Initiative!"

Kobozev shot him a scathing look. "Silence! This is a godsend!"

Ryabinin agreed. "Yes, a godsend. As I was explaining, the Americans would never launch a manned space shuttle if they suspected Red Sky. It could not threaten Red Sky and would be totally defenseless from attack."

"Exactly!" Kobozev's eyes glowed with excitement. "And what better way to show our resolve to the American president than to kill their shuttle." He turned to Zhilin. "Ensure that after it is launched, the shuttle is included as a target in the Red Sky demonstration firings."

CHAPTER 10

Friday, 18 November
Over the Gulf of Mexico

The five g's weighted Anna to nearly six-hundred pounds and crushed her into the steel of the ejection seat. Her neck muscles ached in fatigue to hold erect the extra pounds of helmet. Sweat crawled from her scalp and ran across her brow and into her eyes, stinging them with salt. All she could do was blink away the tears. The oxygen mask gouged the bridge of her nose as it, too, was tugged by the artificial gravity. Her stomach muscles, in a continuous contraction to restrict the flow of blood from the brain and stave off blackout, futilely begged the brain for relief. So did her breasts. The g's were torturing them. Invisible claws were pulling the masses from her chest.

Had she known the day was going to include acrobatic flight, she would have worn her jogging bra for the extra support. But the trip to Ellington Field had been spontaneous, and now she was helpless to do anything about the pain-inducing g's. She was in close formation with Pettigrew's aircraft and had to exactly mimic his maneuver, which was currently a five-hundred-knot, five-g pull-out at the bottom of a loop.

Her left hand was in a continual fore-and-aft motion as she jockeyed the throttles to keep her line of sight along the leading edge of his wing. The tip was only two yards from her canopy, trailing a ghostly vortex of condensed water vapor.

Pettigrew could feel the elevator control surfaces of his own aircraft being tickled by the turbulent wake of her wing and glanced over his right shoulder to check her position.

God! She's welded to me!

Their morning training session had been cut short by a computer malfunction, and she had concurred with his suggestion they take a pair of T-38's for a therapeutic spin. It was a perfect day for formation flight. A cold front had washed the sky to a spotless cobalt.

Pettigrew completed the loop and entered a barrel roll, watching Anna follow with Blue Angel precision.

It was impossible for him to tell the flight-suited figure was Anna — that it was even a woman. He could see nothing of her face. The dark helmet visor and the oxygen mask covered every bit of flesh, and the ejection seat harness camouflaged the female swell to her chest. But he knew the swell was there, the green eyes were behind the visor, that golden hair was under the helmet, and an exquisite mouth was behind the oxygen mask. He could strip everything from her and see her as he had seen her on the dock — a woman of incomparable beauty.

He turned forward, made a slight correction to the controls — they were upside down in the roll — then snatched another quick glance to the right. It brought an intense feeling of intimacy. No lawyer or doctor lover, staring at her naked body, lying on her, pushing himself into her flesh, had ever been closer to Anna Rowe than he was now. Wing tip to wing tip, fully clothed in their machines, dancing with the wind, they shared souls.

Back at Ellington Field, the duty officer relayed the message, "John just called. Said to tell you the sim is still hard down. It'll be at least four hours before they have it fixed."

"Four hours. Okay. Thanks, Charlie."

They started for the parking lot.

"I think I could fly this mission blindfolded." Anna made the comment.

"Yea. I'm ready to launch, too. A day off from the sim doesn't break my heart."

"What are you going to do?" Anna's heart pounded. The other being was stirring in her crypt. She wanted to ask him — to extend these moments.

"I think I'll go back to the office and look over the fuel-cell shutdown procedures." He laughed. "I'd probably go into shock or something if I actually went home while the sun was up."

"Yea. I know what you mean." Her mouth was cotton.

"See you back in the office." He turned for his car.

"Bob?" The other woman seized Anna's tongue.

"Yea?"

"I was wondering… Well, I did promise to take you sailing."

The point of the statement eluded him. "Yea, that's right. You did."

"Well, if you want, we could go now." Woman within cheered her success.

"This?" Horrified, Pettigrew looked down from the dock at the catamaran. "I thought you said a *boat*… a sailboat?"

"Well, I said *sailing*." Misreading his reaction as one of disappointment, she quickly added, "But don't worry. These cats are a lot of fun. On a day like today, we really ought to get some speed out of it. It's perfect weather."

Pettigrew looked to the wind-churned waters of Galveston Bay and then back to his flimsy transport. It had no cockpit, no motor, no seats — just two aluminum hulls and a nylon tarp. He had a bad feeling — a very bad feeling. It wasn't that he disliked water. He *hated* it. The childhood canoeing accident had so terrified him he had never again engaged in any type of water recreation. Only after joining the Marine Corps had he been forced to learn some rudimentary swimming strokes — just enough to pass the qualifying test.

For a tenth time he questioned himself, *What the fuck am I doing here?* He knew the answer. He had been victimized by male ego. An hour ago, when Anna's invitation had been hanging pregnant over the car lot, his testosterone had set him up. If some old fart of a lawyer or doctor could go sailing with her, by God, ol' Bobby Pettigrew could sure as hell do it!

At the moment, ol' Bobby Pettigrew was wishing his balls had stayed out of it. The craft looked no more capable of surviving a trip into the tempest than he looked capable of walking across it.

"Ahh… Anna, don't you think it's kinda windy?"

She had crawled aboard and was busy checking the rigging. "Windy? Yea, isn't it great!"

He looked back to the whitecaps. *Yea, just great. Just fuckin' great!*

Goddamnit, Pettigrew! You sure can fuck yourself sometimes. What are you gonna do now? Tell her you're sick? You gotta go home? You've got a bellyache? A headache? Cancer? Remember — better dead than look bad.

Yea... but drowning? Christ!

"Bob, have you ever been on one of these?"

"If it's not an aircraft carrier, I haven't been on it."

She laughed. The humor escaped him.

"Well, it's definitely not one of those. But you'll get the hang of it. I'll sit at the stern and take control of the tiller and the sheets and talk you through what I'm doing. Then you can do it. Just stay next to me, on the same side. Okay?"

"Yea. Okay."

"You'll see... It's just like flying. It's really simple."

Pettigrew had no intention of touching any controls. He had already resolved that his only objective for the afternoon was to survive — hopefully without screaming.

As she was skittering under the boom to take her place on the port side, a voice interrupted them. It was the apartment manager. "Hey, Miss, you two have to wear life preservers before you go out — company rules. They're in that cabinet."

"Oh, yea, sure. We'll get them. I forgot."

Pettigrew hadn't forgotten and wanted to run and kiss the man. He had just been ready to ask for a life jacket when the shout had saved him from the cowardly act. He pulled two from the cabinet and tossed one to Anna. Strapping it on returned some semblance of calm to his mind.

"Okay, Bob, come aboard."

Taking a deep breath, he stepped onto the hull, his weight almost pushing it under water. Like a terrified cat clinging to a curtain, he fell to the tarp on all fours.

For the first time, Anna noticed that her passenger looked somewhat apprehensive. "Are you all right, Bob?"

For a fighter pilot, there was only one answer to that question and Pettigrew almost startled her with the urgency of his reply. "Me? Oh, sure! Yea, fine, fine."

"Okay. You're gonna *love* this."

Yea... about as much as Custer loved the goddamn Indians.

Scrambling back and forth across the tarp with the ease of a veteran seaman, Anna cast off the lines, pulled the tiller hard to port, and reefed in the sheets. The sail caught the air and they began to glide through the relatively calm waters of the marina.

"Listen, Bob, isn't it quiet? Just the slap of the water on the hulls and the wind in the rigging. I love it."

"Yea. Nice." He lied. But, in spite of his white-knuckle fear, his brain still had room for her beauty. At her apartment they had changed into heavy sweat clothes, and even in that bulk, she was stunning. A broad smile revealed small, straight teeth, and her eyes sparkled with emerald luster and childlike enthusiasm. The cold wind had buffed her cheeks to a rosy hue.

He was just beginning to relax his death grip on the tarp frame when they drifted into the unobstructed wind. Immediately, the port-side hull lifted — their side — almost throwing him backward into the water. In a panic response, his hands shot out. His left found a piece of the rigging and his right came across Anna's chest, almost knocking her overboard. She immediately slackened the sheet and the craft resumed a horizontal attitude.

"Are you okay?"

He was certain he was going to hear that question a lot before the trip was over.

"I am now… Jesus! We almost capsized back there. Don't you think it's too windy?"

"I'm sorry. I should've warned you. That's the fun with these cats. You play the wind and race on just one hull. You're lifted right out of the water. It's great! We weren't gonna tip over. Here, let me show you."

Pettigrew said nothing, afraid if he opened his mouth, a scream would find the exit. Anna measured the wind with a glance, then adjusted the sail and tiller. Within seconds, the vessel was again skating on the starboard hull.

"See, it's stable. And look how fast we're moving!"

The craft accelerated rapidly, making a whining sound, and at each split of a wave, an ice-cold spray rained over them. Pettigrew felt like an acrophobic doing a wing walk and turned his face forward. He answered her shouts of excitement with a head nod and one-word replies of "great," "terrific," and "wonderful" — all pushed through clenched teeth.

Fifteen minutes later, she signaled an end to their first tack. "At that buoy we'll turn back toward the marina. No reason to go too far out."

"Yea. Good idea." Pettigrew thought they were already far enough out to be in danger of falling off the edge of the earth.

The buoy came nearer. "Okay, Bob, I'm gonna turn into the wind. When the bow comes through, we'll have to switch sides. Ready?"

"Ready." As much as he hated the thought of giving up the security of their current configuration, he had no choice. The only thing ahead was a horizon of water. Salvation, in the form of terra firma, lay to the rear.

She pushed full-right rudder and tightened the sheet. The bow began to swing and the sail exploded over their heads, like laundry cracking on a clothesline. The sound and the wallowing loss of headway sent new tremors of fear up Pettigrew's spine.

"That's it, Bob. Let's move over to starboard."

She ducked under the boom. He followed. "Now, all I have to do is... watch it!"

A fluke of wind snapped the sail full, and the boom swung violently toward them. Anna ducked. Pettigrew reflexed backward, his hands windmilling in a blind search for a hold but finding only air. He splashed into the water.

"Bob!" Lunging for him, she grabbed a handful of sweat shirt. "Quick, get up on the tarp!" But the rescue ended two seconds later when the sail took wind — she had forgotten to slacken the sheet. The catamaran accelerated away, tearing her fingers from him.

"Bob! Bob! Are you okay?" She cupped her hands and shouted.

From behind a wave, she saw an arm fly up and took it as an affirmative response to her question. But Pettigrew was definitely *not* okay and opened his mouth to say so, only to have the scream smothered by a face-slapping whitecap. He choked on the inhaled fluid. The feeling of suffocation threw him into a blind panic, and his arms and legs thrashed so wildly he looked like four men overboard. In the terror, he forgot he wore a life jacket.

Anna willed herself calm and adjusted the controls to establish a return tack. Rescue was going to take several minutes of maneuvering.

The ferocity of his panic had turned Pettigrew's arms into cement pipes. He began to sink lower. *So, this is it. Not wrapped in the cockpit of an aircraft... not in the shuttle... but in the water! The motherfuckin' water is gonna take you!* He felt like an Indian warrior, dying a squaw's death.

Then, just as he was certain his next breath would be all liquid — a miracle!

God's a marine!

He was buoyant! His hands jerked to his chest for the reassurance it wasn't a predeath hallucination. The life-saving bulk still encased his torso.

From thirty yards away, Anna watched her target and came about for her final run to the rescue. Her plan was to maintain speed until the last second, passing just upwind, then dumping the air from the sail and letting him grab the hull.

"Are you okay, Bob?" She shouted forward.

Fuck no, I'm not okay! I'm in the goddamn water freezing my balls off. "Yes!"

Three yards from his head, she made her move and slackened the sheet. The port-side hull smacked onto the water, and the craft came to a wallow just beyond his reach.

"Here, Bob, swim to my hand."

Swim? What the fuck's that? Do I look like Mark Spitz?

His legs kicked in a spastic scissor motion that produced little propulsive effect. Anna perched on her knees, hyperextending her right arm.

"Hurry, Bob! Hurry! The wind's shifting!"

She knew if she missed this time, it would be another ten-minute tack for a second attempt, and by then he could be incapacitated by hypothermia. The water temperature was in the fifties. She would never be able to pull him aboard by herself.

Pettigrew groaned and stretched to reach her fingers. Finally, by random chance, his legs coordinated their action enough to push him through the last foot of separation.

"Gotcha! Here, grab the… Ayeeeeee!"

A wicked gust pushed the cat from under her, and she fell headfirst into the water.

"Grab the boat, Anna! It's drifting away!"

"I've got it, Bob! I've got it!" She had been smart enough to coil the sheet around her left hand. "Hold onto my body. I need both hands."

Pettigrew released her right arm and encircled her waist. She quickly pulled hand over hand to the hull.

Pettigrew's body was in a quake, his lips purple — hypothermia at work. Even though she had only been in the water for a minute, Anna could already feel it stealing her strength. "We need to get out of the water... fast. Do you think you can climb onto the tarp?"

"Yea, let's go." The chatter of his teeth made speech difficult.

"You first."

Throwing his arms up on the frame, he laboriously pulled and wiggled his chest onto it. His knee came over the edge, and with a loud groan he was finally able to heave the rest of his body aboard. He flopped spread-eagled on his back, gasping for air. But the reprieve was only five breaths long. Anna was still in the water.

"Let me help you."

"Okay." Now, her teeth were clacking.

"On the count of three. One, two, three!" With the grunts and groans of desperation labor, he pulled her aboard, and they collapsed in a sodden heap on the canvas.

Fuck me in the heart! I will never, never get on a goddamn boat again! Never! I don't give a fuck if the damn thing is loaded with naked Hollywood starlets that want to fuck my eyes out — never!

Pettigrew's body was in such a tremor he found it difficult to even twist the shower controls. Anna had gone to the master bath and sent him to the guest bathroom.

Sailing! What an idiot you are, Pettigrew! A fuckin' idiot spelled with a capital fuckin' I!

He pulled off the soggy sweat shirt and flung it into the corner.

How can anybody call that fun? Flying is fun. Drinking is fun. Fucking is fun! Sailing, rowing, swimming, skiing — that water-sport shit is...

He pulled off his underwear, and the sight of his crotch interrupted the silent diatribe on things nautical.

Christ! Your balls are probably in your armpits!

The extreme cold had emasculated him. Barely visible in a tangled mass of dark hair was a bloodless-pale, shriveled piece of foreskin — the only remnant of his gender.

He stepped into the stream of hot water and sighed with relief.

Now this is how God intended water to be enjoyed.

The feel of the warm liquid cascading over his body was nearly orgasmic, and he turned down the cold control to make it even hotter.

R—I—N—G!

What?

He pulled his head back to listen.

R—I—N—G!

The phone. Anna can get it. Freezing to death was her idea.

Returning to the waterfall, he adjusted it to a still hotter temperature. But the hallway phone continued to demand an answer.

I'll bet it's John. They probably got the goddamn simulator fixed and want us back. And I'll bet Anna doesn't hear it. She's probably still in the shower. Goddamnit!

R—I—N—G!

Oh, this water feels so good. Anna, answer the fuckin' phone, please!

R—I—N—G!

Okay, okay. Fuck it!...Goddamnit!

Angrily, he closed the shower controls, wrapped a towel around his waist, stepped from the tub, and jerked the door open.

R—I—N—G!

"Hel——" He stopped when he heard Anna's coincident 'hello' from her bedroom phone. She had finally answered.

Goddamnit! Wouldn't you know!

He slammed the receiver onto its cradle and made an immediate turn for the bathroom. The shakes had returned, and he was bound for the liquid heat. Whatever schedule Anna was receiving, he was determined it would wait until he was warm again.

Then... it happened. He was paralyzed in midturn, like a biblical character struck into a pillar of salt, and for the same reason. He had glimpsed the forbidden. Anna's bedroom door was not completely closed, and his position in the hallway was perfect to see the reflection of her back in the bureau mirror. She wore only a pair of bikini panties.

He could feel his heart. It thundered in his chest. It drummed the vein of his neck. It pulsed in his ears. Gone was any sensation of cold. Now, fire filled his veins.

She was standing by her nightstand, one hand holding the phone, the other shaking a towel through her hair.

Pettigrew... Jesus!

For the briefest of moments, his conscience tried to rally a condemnation of the sinful spying, but it was bulldozed aside by the male animal.

She's beautiful! God, she's so beautiful!

Like a theater spotlight, a shaft of sun came through the bedroom window to illuminate her form, and his eyes touched on every curve. The lower part of her legs was blocked by the bed, but he could clearly see her thighs. They were lean and muscular, with not the slightest dimple or sag. The panties failed to cover the first inch of the shadowed split of her ass. His mouth went to cotton at that sight. Her buttocks bulged gracefully outward and blended into her thighs without a crease. Her hips curved in hourglass symmetry into the narrows of her waist. He was certain he had never seen a more superbly proportioned woman.

Anna's phone conversation continued, and he could hear enough of it to know it was somebody from the simulator. She turned, and he had to lock his knees to keep from collapsing at the sight of her front.

Breasts. They were moderately large and set high on her chest. Her motions with the towel caused them to shimmy in tight oscillations. The nipples were small and bright pink from the heat of her shower, and, in the sunbeam, they cast tiny shadows on the adjacent flesh, like the peaks of mountains at sunset. He could feel life returning to his crotch.

His eyes searched lower and consumed her flat belly and the vertical slit of her navel, coming to rest on the V of her panties. His mouth dried some more. The underwear was not sheer, but his imagination had little trouble dispensing with the obstruction.

"Yes, okay. Yes, seven A.M. I'll tell him. Thanks, John. Good-bye."

Even though discovery was imminent, he could not turn away. Shame, embarrassment, guilt — things that should have been consuming him were not even whispers in his brain.

She was in the process of cradling the phone when her eyes finally touched on the mirror. He heard the gasp. The phone fell from her hand and she clutched the towel to her chest. Chaos ruled.

Oh God, no! He's been watching me! He's seen my breasts! Run! Now. Now! NOW!

But the other being nailed her to the floor and screamed at her heaven-sent good fortune. *Yes! Yes, Anna! Let him take you! He loves you!*

Their eyes maintained lock. Elsewhere in the universe the measures of time continued — pendulums oscillated, springs unwound, sand fell, atoms vibrated, planets turned. But in the house, time ceased. Was it a minute they stared? Or five? Or an hour? They had no sense of the span.

In the bedroom, only the steady tone from the disconnected phone invaded the silence. In the hallway, the soft tapping sound of water dripping onto the tile floor was all that could be heard.

Still holding the towel around his waist, Pettigrew began a slow walk toward the image, not even conscious his legs were moving.

He's coming to me! God, no! No! He'll use me! Just like the others, he'll hurt me!

But the other woman would not release control of her body. *Remember the dock, Anna? Remember seeing him naked, Anna? Remember the dreams? Oh, Anna, yes. Remember those dreams? Him lying on you, loving you?*

Three steps to her door.

Her heart choked her.

Two steps.

Pettigrew could not find saliva to swallow.

One step.

Silence thundered.

He stepped into the threshold, pushed the door fully open, and turned to face her. She had been so fixed on the reflection, the sudden reality of his appearance startled her.

The noise from the phone changed to a warble, and he glanced at the source. It was the first time he had broken lock with her eyes.

"It… it was John. They… they still haven't fixed the simulator." She made no attempt to pick up the receiver.

He stepped into the room and began walking to her.

"John said, that… that they would work on it through the night."

He was around the end of the bed.

"They… he wants us to come in tomorrow at seven."

He stopped a foot from her.

Oh, God, God, God… Anna! You are so beautiful!

The ray of sunlight slanted across her face and turned her eyes into starbursts of green. He looked into them — saying nothing, touching nothing. She matched the stare, her focus alternately skipping between his eyes, as if one might reveal something the other did not.

He loves you, Anna! Embrace him!

No, I can't! I can't! He'll use me! He'll...

She did not finish the protest. His left hand reached to straighten a tangled lock of damp hair.

"Anna." It was the first word he had spoken — barely a whisper.

Her eyes soundlessly encouraged him to continue, but he said nothing more. Instead, the hand came down the side of her face, caressing its satin, his thumb gently tracing her pale lips.

Oh, God, Bob! Don't — I'm not strong enough.

She closed her eyes and squeezed the towel more tightly hoping it would stop her shaking.

The feel of her softness brought Pettigrew an explosive erection. Even the weight of the wet towel was insufficient to arrest its growth, and the spike raised the cloth, like the center pole of a tent.

Anna flinched. His other hand reached to cradle her face. She felt his towel drop on her feet and knew he was now naked. Her heart beat in explosions. A dry heat burned her skin while her legs trembled as they had in the water. The voice of caution — of the nuns, of her mother, of Stanford, of China Lake — gasped a last, feeble objection. Fingers opened. The towel fell. She stepped to embrace him.

"Bob, Bob, Bob." She clutched him, surprised to feel the stab of his erection. It took more than just sight to arouse Richard. A warm, glorious high came with the press of the sandwiched shaft. She had created it.

Pettigrew enveloped her and pulled her cheek into his chest. They collapsed onto the bed and he rolled on top of her, pushing himself lower to be level with her face. In the dimming light, her eyes had dilated to become space-black pools ringed with emerald needles. He cupped her temples in his hands and furrowed her hair with his fingers, wishing the silk was longer, wishing it was a golden cloak he could pull over his body.

They said nothing, each wondering if the room, the bed, the strange flesh touching their bodies were still just wishes, just dreams. There had been no plan, no scheming, no preparation to gain the ecstasy under their hands. It was as if there had been a ripple in time and space. In one moment they were showering in a house in Houston, Texas. In the next they were in a distant Eden.

He kissed her mouth — gently, chastely, a feather's touch — then moved his lips across her neck and onto the rise of her breasts. The flesh was cloud soft and infant smooth and capped with tiny promontories of rock hardness. There, he pulled back to see. Her nipples were petite — hardly bigger in diameter than his own — and the flamingo of the outer edges faded through ten shades of pink to appear almost translucent at the centers. He touched them, bringing each between thumb and index finger in a delicate twisting and pulling motion. Anna's chest heaved in deeper respiration, and the worry of weeks past — about her freakish breasts — was nowhere in her brain. She was flying into orbits never before visited.

He lowered his mouth to the left summit, flicking it with his tongue, then drawing it into a gentle suction. Her magic spaceship sped her to a place where she had no thoughts, only feelings. Richard had never kissed her like this, touched her like this, nursed her like this. Bob was so delicate, so gentle, so loving — so different than she had ever imagined.

He returned to her mouth, but this time the kisses were not chaste. Lips parted and tongues touched — tentatively at first, each inviting the other into deeper explorations until they danced in long, slow, coiling embraces. Heated breaths were exchanged. Moist exhalations mingled with inhalations. He moved across her cheeks and neck with delicate bites. Saliva wet her.

Her hands covered his back, stroking the hair of his neck, moving lower across the massive plain of his shoulders and down to the mounds of his buttocks. She shivered with the novelty of the feel, of the latent power in the muscles, of their smooth, scalloped cheeks, of the crevice that separated them.

Then, they began a slow rise and fall, a slow compression and relaxation that brought his erection into a grinding massage of the juncture of her thighs. Though her cotton panties remained a barrier, she could feel the hardened point of his body stroking along the upper reaches of her crease. It was a stroke into Valhalla. Richard never did this. Richard was gentle and sweet — and very clinical. Richard only inserted. Pettigrew's motion was touching her in virgin places, places that wanted more pressure, more friction, more weight, faster oscillations, places that told her brain to pump her own hips to facilitate the contact.

Her eyes closed. Her head lolled from side to side. Gasps replaced breathing. Her hands gripped his buttocks. Her hips tried to lift him. She was coming.

Pettigrew was joyous. He never wanted the moment to end. He wanted to bring her supreme happiness — now, always. For so many years, in countless relationships, he had cared nothing of the pleasure women received from his body. They were to be used and discarded — disposable relief. Now, he cared only about the woman beneath him. It was in her fulfillment his own resided.

Anna floated in deep space. The orgasm had been intense, totally foreign to her. The others in her life, if orgasms at all, paled in comparison to the one just passed. Her mind drifted in a semiconscious rapture.

I'm weightless... I'm floating... Bob is on me... He's sucking my nipples... His tongue is fondling them. Don't stop, Bob. Don't stop. Don't.

But he did, pushing upright into a sitting straddle of her thighs.

For the first time, she saw his erection — a sight that made her wetter yet. It was much larger than Richard's, projecting upward from a thick jungle of dark hair and ribbed with swollen, purple veins. His heartbeat gave it a weak nod, and the rubbing against her panties had reddened it. The tiny slit glistened with his own wetness.

Then, she looked beyond his sex — into his eyes. There was no mistaking it. She could still see the fear in them. It was now heavily camouflaged with animal passion, but it was still there.

What, Bob? Why are you afraid of me?

She could wonder for only a moment.

He stood to the side of the bed and guided her panties off her hips, down her legs, and from her feet. It was an action that returned a flicker of fear. She would next have to open herself for a man. It was the ultimate loss of control, the ultimate surrender to the dangers of dependency and to the pain of rejection. But the other woman struck like lightning to vaporize the worries. Nothing would be allowed to interfere. Nothing! She would have Pettigrew.

He remained standing and staring. She was pure woman — no jewelry, no eye shadow, no lipstick, not even a hint of perfume adorned her body — yet she was more beautiful than any woman he had ever seen. Like an orchestra, every feature was in perfect harmony — the gold of her hair, the emerald of her eyes, the creamy whiteness of her skin, the fiercely aroused pink of her nipples, the wispy yellow delta of her thighs.

Then, he covered her. There was the merest hint of hesitation before her legs splayed open. The tip of his body fell naturally into her crease, and with the primordial whimper of woman receiving man, she received him.

He began his trip to Eden.

Anna's legs drew higher and came around the back of his calves, then higher still and around the back of his thighs. Her arms encircled him, her hands coming to rest on his buttocks and enjoying their rippling contractions. Their mouths mimicked the mating as his tongue cycled in deeper and deeper probes of that wet.

Minutes past — five, ten, twenty. The room darkened. Gasps, sighs, moans filled it. Those came quicker now. The oscillations, too. They were approaching the end. Hard and soft began to demand more of the other. Slow gave way to haste, and that, to urgency. Pettigrew's withdrawals became more complete, his penetrations deeper. The woman writhed under him, gripping his body, encouraging its heaving.

Finally, it came. Simultaneously, the ripple — the reward of their labor — began to move through their bodies. It freshened into a swell, then a wave.

Their coupling became frenzied. The wave rose higher, curling at the top, poised to crash. Floating, flying, drifting, Anna was higher than she had ever been.

"Anna, Anna. Oh, God, Anna, I need you! I love you!"

The words, the first he had spoken since their embrace, were delivered in pulsating gasps coming from his lips in the same stuttering rhythm as the cream that jetted from his body.

An hour later, mated again, Anna laid motionless on top of Pettigrew. Her cheek rested on his chest and his arms draped her. Those were still. Each could feel the even, steady tide of the other's breathing, and each assumed the other was asleep. Each was wrong. Each grimly faced the consequences of passion.

In his meditation, Pettigrew stared at the darkened ceiling. It had been eighteen years since he had last professed his love, his need for a woman. But it could have been yesterday, so clear were the bitter memories. Those flickered across the invisible screen above the bed, and he watched and despaired.

TRAVIS AIR FORCE BASE WELCOMES HOME OUR POWS.

The banner decorated the hanger where the throng of relatives waited. A red carpet stretched from the aircraft stairs, through a gauntlet of American flags and to the crowd's front. A thousand more of the red, white, and blue pennants fluttered in their hands. Under a hazy, California spring sky, an air force band played *America The Beautiful*. The crowd cheered.

Loudspeakers blared names, and each man came down the stairs — a parade of thin, pale men. Men old beyond their years. Men wearing medal-bedecked tunics. Some were borne on stretchers. Others hobbled on crutches or canes or dragged broken limbs that had never been set and had healed at grotesque angles. Some wore eye patches or had burn-scarred faces or other evidence of neglected wounds. But, within the limits of his handicaps, each man saluted his nation's flag and a waiting general, then limped, walked, ran, or was carried down the red carpet. At its end, shrieking wives broke from the crowd and raced to hug their husbands. In the blind flight, purses were dropped, hats blew away, heels broke from shoes, dazed, young children were left behind — and still they ran without pause. And ran. And ran until their men were in their arms and the nightmare was ended.

Then, it was his turn. *Robert J. Pettigrew, First Lieutenant, United States Marine Corps.* The speakers proclaimed his exit, and he stepped onto the stairway platform. Like a lost child searching for his parents in a busy department store, his head swung insanely in all directions for Karen. He was mad to find her! But it was an impossible search. A sea of thousands waved and screamed and cried.

Karen, Karen, Karen, Karen! Sweet Jesus, where are you? Tears gushed from his eyes. He had to hold her. It was an agony to delay even the five seconds to salute the general.

Then he bolted down the carpet, screaming, "Karen! Karen! Karen! Karen!" The woman was life itself. For more than seven hundred days her memory had sustained him. When the bamboo whips had been flaying his chest, when his vocal cords had grown numb from screaming, when he had been left hanging by his wrists until his shoulders were dislocated, when he had been cast into a lightless, pestilent hole for sixty-six days, when he had awakened on seven hundred and forty-two mornings — it had been visions of Karen that had sustained him.

And then she was there, stepping from the crowd. Golden hair, blue eyes, painted mouth, rouged cheeks, cream skin, long legs, full breasts. Even in his wildest fantasies, she had never appeared more beautiful.

"Karen! Karen!" The flags flickered by his sides. The red road disappeared under his blurring feet. Another name was announced. The band stuck up the *Marine Corps Hymn.* And Karen waited. He hurled into her, grabbing her in a crushing bear hug, lifting her from the ground. His nightmare had ended. "Oh, Jesus, God! God! God! God! Karen!" He cried into her neck, great heaving, stuttering cries. Cries that choked. Cries that blinded. Cries that made children curious and adults embarrassed. Cries of joy! Joy! JOY!

Kisses followed — to her lips, her cheeks, her eyes, her hair, her ears. The model-perfect makeup was demolished.

For a half hour he could do nothing but cry. He cried as she led him to the car. He cried on the drive to the officer's club. He cried as she sat him at the patio table.

Then she began to cry. Oh, she was sorry. She was so very sorry for tearing his heart out.

"Bob, it was only five days ago I found out you were alive. Until that phone call, for *two* years, I thought you were dead.

"A day after your plane was shot down, I got the message you were missing in action. You can't know what that's like… to not know if you're a widow. To wonder what to do with the rest of your life. I wanted to die.

"I wrote letters, made phone calls, but the marines could only say you were missing. The Red Cross couldn't find out anything. I wrote to Hanoi and they wouldn't answer. I wrote the president. My congressman. The pope. Everybody. But nobody could tell me if I still had a husband."

She blotted a Niagara of more tears and stuttered in an attempt to go on. Oh, she was so, so sorry.

"I met a man. He was… is… highly placed in a New York advertising agency. He saw some of my modeling photos and called me for an interview. He was nice to me. More than nice. He opened doors for me, Bob, important doors. You knew how badly I wanted to go to the top with my modeling, how hard I worked for it. You remember… I never gave up. Never! It was so important to me. I studied and learned and practiced… the exercises, the clothes, the makeup, the diet, the camera work, the resumes, the interviews. I never gave up trying to be perfect. Well, he's helping me to the top, helping me in a very big way… the top fashion companies, good contracts."

She averted his gaze, his agony. Oh, she was sorry all right.

"Bob, please understand. In my mind, you were dead! I mean, it had been thirteen months and not a word!

"Missing. Missing! Missing! God I hate that word! I hate it!

"I thought you had died. And he… he… God, Bob, I didn't know it would turn out this way! I didn't! I thought you were dead!

"He asked me to marry him.

"His lawyer helped me with… our divorce. I got it in Tijuana. You and I, Bob. We're not married anymore. We haven't been for eleven months. I've been living another life with another man.

"There's nothing more to say, really. I love you, Bob. I'll always love you. I never wanted to hurt you. I never wanted it to come to this. I'm sorry. But it's done. I can't undo it."

Then his begging and pleading came.

"Divorce *him*? Remarry you? No, Bob, I can't do that. You see, he had a… a condition to our marriage. Before I went too far in my career, he wanted a… a child.

"I'm pregnant, Bob."

And he howled the words, "No! No! I need you, Karen! I love you!"

I need you. I love you. The words echoed in his brain, across the years, across space — from the tarmac at Travis Air Force Base to Anna's bed. From eighteen years ago to one hour ago. He understood now, so clearly, the source of his familiarity with Anna. She was Karen. It didn't matter their careers were so vastly different. The women were the same. And he had allowed himself to be captured, blinded by their beauty, intoxicated by their strength of will. That Anna's passion was the sky was even more intensely compelling. Beauty-wrapped passion for flight — Anna had come into his life as the perfect conspiracy, the *only* conspiracy of female body and soul that could draw from him those most insane of words: *I need you. I love you.* Words he had last spoken to Karen. Words that could only lead to pain. He could never love again. The memories of Travis Air Force Base, of Karen, were just too vivid to allow it.

❖

I love you. I need you. The words echoed in Anna's brain, too — and terrified her. She had heard them before — at Stanford, at China Lake, and from Richard — but never had she heard them as Pettigrew had cried them, with such soul-baring passion, such urgency. They were terrifying. Even now, an hour later, they hung in the room demanding an answer. But she had given none. Even when it had seemed her very being was possessed by the other woman, when her brain had been choked and distracted with the pleasures of paradise, when his body had been riding her into a carnal heaven, she could not bring herself to mouth the words the other being pleaded, even now, for her to speak — *I love you.* They were so terrifying. They demanded she become another person, an alien person, a person who had not been formed by a mother who had counseled *control*, by a father who had been a masculine shadow, by a feminine, Madonna-oriented religious order that had preached fear of man, by a woman deceived by man at Stanford and China Lake. They demanded she become a woman untouched by the lifetime of conspiracies that had created Anna Rowe.

If, she wondered, she could not now speak the words, when could she? If they would not come spontaneously to her lips while she was in the consequence-numbing throes of passion, if they would not arise from her soul as she laid naked on this man, while she felt the heartbeat of his shaft inside her, while his seed swam in her, when, then?

Never. Never, she was certain.

CHAPTER 11

Saturday, 19 November
Cape Canaveral Air Force Station

Killingsworth stood by his car and watched from the Banana River causeway as the *Nova* preempted the dawn. Like its namesake, the machine took on the appearance of an exploding star. For a moment he was terrified it had blown up, but then the fire began to rise in a perfect arc to the east. It was blinding, arc-welding white, and rushed toward a purpled, morning-starred horizon. Fifteen seconds later the noise exploded over him, the pulsating crackle of solid rocket boosters superimposed on the screech of the twin liquid engines. Again, he erroneously assumed disaster, not believing anything making such a sound could be under the control of humans. The noise punished man and animal alike, making him stop his ears with his fingers, tapping his body with palpable shock waves, sending a flock of pelicans into a lumbering escape. But the light and noise faded quickly. In a minute the machine's fire diminished to join Venus as another morning star and the noise ebbed to silence.

Ten minutes later, his car phone rang. "Mr. Killingsworth, the hospital called. Your friend will be okay." It was the code to tell him everything had gone well with the *Nova*'s ascent, although the Soviets would not see it that way. To disguise the true purpose of *Atlantis's* impending rendezvous, telemetry from the missile had been modified to reflect a malfunction.

The fat man paused for a moment before returning to his jet. *Atlantis* had captured his eye. She was only three miles north of the *Nova* pad, and with the end of that machine's sound and light show, she once again commanded the morning. The great xenon lights bathed her cradle in shafts of wedding-white light and she appeared as a dazzling monument to man's primordial yearning to see beyond his horizon.

The sight gripped him with melancholy. The next roar to shatter a Florida dawn would be from *Atlantis* and he feared for his heroes and heroine. They would possibly be the first to experience the horrors of a new combat, a soundless battle zone where there were no whistling shells or bombs, no explosions, no cries from the wounded. Only the quiet of death would be the same. It was beyond his comprehension that men and a woman could so willingly fly into such danger.

Sadly, he contemplated the significance of the moment. If not in three days, the time could not be long off when man would engage in mortal combat in space. He was too much a student of history to believe otherwise. In every alien environment that humankind had conquered — the deserts, the mountains, the jungles, the air, the sea surface, the sea depths — had it not been so? Why, he asked himself, should space be different? Because of the treaties, the promises of men? He scoffcd. They were valid only as long as it took for the weapons and machines to be developed. It had always been so. It would always be so.

He got in his car and sped to his waiting jet.

❖

Saturday, 19 November
Johnson Space Center

Judy watched him. Mark was sitting alone on a bench behind the astronaut gym, cooling down from his run. His back was to her and he was unaware of her presence.

In their last telephone conversation, she had said nothing to him of her plans to come to Houston. Really, there had been no plans. It wasn't but eight hours ago she had made the decision — one that had taken every remaining reserve of emotional strength. In the steps to Peggy's door, in the cab, in the walk along the jetway — along every step of the trip, she had to consciously will her body to continue. Her constant companion had been *the feeling*, the all-pervasive premonition this would be the last time she would ever see her husband. She had held out to the end with the ridiculous thought that if she did not make the trip, fate would somehow be confused, that if she never said good-bye, it would be a piece of unfinished business that would bother the gods into sparing Mark. But, as the days had vanished from the calendar, the dread of not seeing him had slowly overtaken the dread of the final good-bye.

The shadowless day was an additional burden. The sky was overcast, and a cold, gray mist fell from it. The scene was a black and white photograph.

She watched as Mark stretched supine on the bench, staring skyward. It was just like him, she thought, to look at the sky even when it was a featureless dome. It never stopped calling him. Never. *The feeling* was there to remind her of that fact.

She walked toward him, and he heard the crunch of her steps on the cinders and rolled to investigate.

"Judy!" He bolted to his feet and rushed to envelop her in a hug.

Her own hands swept over his back in a reacquaintance of his form, and she burrowed into his sweaty neck to remember his taste and scent. The sensations were heaven-sent.

"Why didn't you call? I would have sent a plane for you." He stood back beaming at the surprise.

"I'm not going to the Cape, Mark. Tomorrow I'm going back to Peggy's." The statement was forceful, full of resolve. She had vowed to make that fact known immediately. She would never go to the Cape — never — and wanted no further arguments on the subject.

Mark had no trouble reading the message and complied. He wanted nothing to spoil their reunion. He would conduct this visit as they had been conducting their phone calls — ignoring tomorrow.

"Come on, let's get inside. It's getting cold out here. Where are your bags?"

She took him to her rented car, and he carried a single suitcase into the crew quarters. A cook was just beginning supper preparations, and he asked her to include an extra steak for Judy. At the refrigerator, he shoved a ten-dollar bill in a cash box and retrieved a bottle of wine. He was alone in the quarters, and after the cook was gone they would be able to enjoy a very private and relaxing evening. He had already been riding a high with the news of the *Nova* success, and now Judy's visit had made him even more lighthearted.

It turned out to be a two-wine-bottle meal that left Mark intoxicated and Judy certifiably drunk. As the alcohol numbed her and blurred tomorrow, she rushed more of it into her body until she was mindlessly giddy. Her antics brought a few disparaging looks from the cook, but Mark made no effort to caution moderation. He suspected she needed a drunk. He had seen combat veterans with the same need — to drink away thoughts of tomorrow's targets, of tomorrow's fears.

The cook finished cleaning the kitchen and announced her departure. Finally, they were alone.

Mark went to the shower — he had yet to clean up from his run — and Judy joined him. She carried the rest of the wine in a plastic glass and set it in the soap dish. She was living a lie, a Roman enjoying an orgy while the city burned. Drunk or sober, tomorrow would come.

It was a shock for him to see how much weight she had lost, but he never had the chance to comment on it. The body that remained was still strikingly beautiful, and two and a half months of celibacy instantly rigidized his body into a begging, pleading pose. Judy lathered her hands and began washing him, teasing him by covering every inch of his skin except that which wanted most to be washed. The shaft reddened, then purpled in its extreme distention.

Mark reciprocated in a petting, biting, sucking tease that exhausted a hot-water heater designed for ten people.

"So… it's finally bed time." As the stream chilled, she chugged the remaining wine, dropped the cup, then stood giggling like an idiot. Mark had never seen her so drunk.

"Yea. Let's get out of here." He had been ready thirty gallons ago. The foreplay had tightened his erection to the point he wasn't sure he had enough loose skin on his body to even blink his eyes.

But the bed was a quick ending, as Judy used the only power she had ever had over this man — her sex. She pushed him back and took him in her mouth and in seconds had him flying on the wings of orgasm. The rich, thick seed flooded her mouth, and she swallowed it away. Done, she curled into his back, her legs bent to match his, like spoons in a drawer, then fell into an alcohol-induced sleep. Her last conscious thought was that she wasn't drunk enough. She could still see tomorrow.

❖

Saturday, 19 November
Houston

Pettigrew sat naked on the edge of his spa, senseless to the cold rain. He ripped another beer from the second six-pack, popped it, and rushed it to his mouth. The wall in his mind, the wall that had contained the hellish memories, that wall he had labored for eighteen years to buttress into an impenetrable barrier, now lay breached and shattered, totally demolished by Anna. It had taken her just two months. Slowly at first, brick by brick, she had weakened it — with her emerald eyes, the golden sheen of her hair, her fierce determination to be perfect, her passion for the sky. Then, yesterday, the sight and feel of her naked body, the glowing peaks of her breasts, the soft, satin curves of flesh, the warm sheath that had enveloped his body, tickling, caressing, stroking — it had reduced the fortress to a heap of rubble.

And now, demons flew from the wreck like tortured souls from a netherworld, shrieking around his consciousness in insane, disjointed, batlike flight. In one moment he was running down the red carpet on the Travis Air Force Base tarmac, in the next he was flying with Anna. An eye blink later he was hearing the voices of the North Vietnamese militia. He was in his Uncle's Piper, flying over golden aspens. He saw a green-eyed Karen — not Anna — standing in the simulator, working the remote arm. He felt the lashes of bamboo, saw his nipple hanging grotesque and bloody on the end of a three-inch strip of flesh. He saw himself, eyes closed, rocking on Anna's body, felt her wet heat sucking on his steel. But when his eyes opened, the woman transfigured — her eyes turned blue, her hair visibly lengthened, snaked through his fingers, came over his shoulders, and covered his back in a golden cloak. In seconds, Anna had become Karen.

Another beer was consumed and then another and another as he sought oblivion, sought to escape the terror. But there was no escape. The alcohol only sharpened the memories. The demons came in clouds. He was under a canoe drowning. He was on fire, falling into the jungle. A blue-eyed Anna was telling him she was pregnant with another man's child. Her belly grew huge with it. He was running on a red carpet toward Karen, but he never drew close to her. The *Marine Corp Hymn* played. Flags flickered past his head. He ran until his lungs burned. But the pathway was infinite, and he never came closer to the smiling woman. Then, he collapsed and Anna magically appeared at his side. She lifted him with her smile and embraced him and kissed him and he proclaimed his everlasting love.

"No! Goddamnit to fuckin' hell! No!" With homicidal violence, he hurled a full can of beer into the wall. It impacted with a hissing thud.

He jumped up and stumbled drunkenly into the bedroom. In his panicked reach for the phone, he knocked over the nightstand lamp.

❖

Anna sat at her bureau, brushing her hair. In the reflection, she could see the bed — and yesterday.

It had been heaven. His arms crushing her, his mouth biting and sucking, his body melting into hers. And the words. *Oh the words! I love you! I need you!*

Did he mean them? Was it just passion? How can I know?

The other being was quick with her opinion. *It wasn't passion, Anna. He does love you. He does need you. Love him back!*

She set the brush aside and lifted the photo of the Rowes. *Oh momma. How do I love a man? How can I ever love? The words won't come.*

The phone interrupted.

"Hello?"

"Hello, Anna."

Guilt swept her. Her fingers came to her mouth. "Richard! How are you?"

"Fine, darling, fine. I thought you had forgotten about me."

"What? Forgotten? Of course not." She had erased the man from her mind.

"You said you'd call. It's eight o'clock."

"Oh, Richard, I'm so sorry. I… I had some last-minute things to take care of. I was just getting ready to phone."

"Well… Guess what I have in my hand?"

"I… I…" She was tongue-tied.

"I hold here some Dom Perignon that is aching to bid you bon voyage."

"Oh, Richard, that's so nice." Her teeth found another stub of nail.

"Break out the glasses and I'll be right over."

Her eyes widened in shock. She could think of nothing worse than a visit from the man. And he would definitely want to take her to bed! Her stomach tightened. She could never go to bed with him again. Never. Not after yesterday.

"Ah… Richard. You know, I'm in quarantine for the flight." She thanked God for the NASA health stabilization plan.

"Oh, that's right. The NASA doctors are trying to spare you from us lepers. Well, not to worry. Physician, heal thyself! As a doctor, I have determined I am disease free." He chuckled.

Her mind scrambled for another excuse.

"Richard, I... I really appreciate your thoughtfulness, but my pilot is coming over tonight. We have to review some late changes to our checklist procedures. I hope you'll forgive me." She pressed the lie. "It is important. You wouldn't want me to make any mistakes up there, would you?"

"Oh... no! Absolutely not! You go ahead and have your study session."

"I'll call you from Florida." It was a meager price to pay to escape his company.

"Okay, darling. I'll keep Mr. Perignon on ice until you get back. We'll celebrate then."

"Thank you, Richard."

"And, darling... guess what? Aspen had over a foot of snow yesterday. In just four weeks, we'll be up there, cuddled under a down blanket, watching a winter wonderland. I can hardly wait!"

The comment brought visions of her and Pettigrew making love in front of a fireplace in an Aspen cabin. More guilt weighed her.

"Richard... I... I... that'll be so much fun." She dreaded telling him otherwise. She could never make the trip. Pettigrew had changed everything. "Now, I have to go. I hear the doorbell... my pilot."

"Okay, call me. I love you."

Her reply died in her throat. At very nearly the same time last night, she had heard those identical words, and they had tingled every nerve in her body. Now, from Richard, they were just meaningless sounds.

"Good-bye, Richard."

She cradled the phone and returned to her bureau and the brushing. Then...

Like a bullet fired into a steel room, the lie about Pettigrew's visit ricocheted around her mind. *Why couldn't it be the truth?* The strokes of the hairbrush slowed. The other being was back to tempt.

She looked at her watch. It was nearing eight-thirty. A finger came to her mouth. They had to get up early for the flight to the Cape.

He could come over for just an hour... to study. But study what?

Rendezvous? No. We've gone over every word in that checklist. Ascent? Entry? No. We've got those down pat. Damn! There's noth... No! There is something!

In moments she found them — the weighty volumes of the shuttle malfunction procedures. The documents represented the engineers' best guesses on how a crew should respond to every conceivable system malfunction. Hundreds of pages of complex flow diagrams were contained within the covers of the two volumes.

Anna took one and hurriedly turned to the communications section. That system was particularly baffling, and even highly trained veterans could get lost in the maze. She found what she was looking for — the response to a pulse code modulation master unit failure.

This is it! I've never understood this. Bob could help me. Oh, I would so dearly love to talk to him — just talk to him.

She walked to the phone, chewed a finger, took several deep breaths to compose herself, then lifted the receiver.

The sounds of raw sex filled the room — the slap and suction of sweaty bellies joining and disjoining, rutting animal sounds, the grunts and gasps of intense labor.

"Uhhh... Uhhh... Uhhh... Bobby... Uhhh... Baaaaby... slow down."

Pettigrew didn't slow. The woman's voice had no more chance of reaching his brain than of being heard on the moon. The demons were in full possession of him.

"Bobby... Uhhh... Uhhh... are you... Uhhh... close?"

We're divorced Bob. I'm living another life with another man. I'm pregnant.

"Uhhh... Uhhh... Please... Uhhh... Bobby Baby... Uhhh... I'm sore." She tried to hold the flying buttocks, but like a pile-driving machine, the stabbing continued.

You knew how badly I wanted to go to the top. You remember. I never gave up. Never!

She gained some relief. Fatigue was finally winning. Sweat sheened him.

This is all a woman is good for — to fuck, fuck, fuck! Never to love! Never!

Like a boxer in the fifteenth round, the punches became weak and spastic, the grunts louder, the sweat heavier.

He collapsed as dead weight, gasping for breath. The woman assumed he was having an orgasm, but she was wrong. Total exhaustion had ended the thrusting.

The woman's hands swam in the sweat on his back. "Jesus, Bobby. You need to call me more often."

Pettigrew's only answer was to roll onto his back and labor for air. She slithered, snake-like, onto his front. "Oh, I love it when you're all sweaty like this." Languidly, she drew her tongue through the salty fluid, pausing to suck on his unscarred nipple. Unconsciously his arms closed around her and he stroked her skin.

"You're sure quiet tonight, Bobby. Are you okay?"

Still, he gave no answer. A face devoid of any satisfaction looked over her shoulder and into the ceiling.

Anna, Anna. Dear Jesus, I need you. Stay on me... sleep on me.

For another minute the alcohol deceived him — it was Anna's flesh touching his. But reality returned. He jerked upright, throwing the woman off like a blanket.

"Hey! What the fuck's with you?" She almost cracked her head on the nightstand.

Pettigrew ignored her complaint, jumped from the bed, and bounced off the hallway walls on his way to the kitchen. A moment later he returned with the remnants of another six-pack. He had already opened a can and was tossing it back.

"Well, shit! Couldn't you be a little more gentlemanly about getting us a beer?" She sat cross-legged on the bed, her hand extended in an implied request.

"You can leave now." Instead of the beer, he offered her the first words he had spoken since their coupling had begun.

"What?" She was certain she had not heard correctly.

"You can leave now." The voice was as expressionless as the face. He turned and pulled open the patio door.

"Who the fuck do you think you are?! You think I'm some goddamn easy lay you can just fuck and kick out?!"

Pettigrew walked onto the patio and closed the door behind him.

"Goddamn you!" She flew from the bed, grabbed the first object that came to her eyes — one of his shoes — and hurled it after him. It thumped harmlessly into the glass.

Maintaining his back to her, he stepped into the spa and accelerated his drinking. The woman shrieked. "Fuck you, asshole! Fuck you! And I was just faking it! I didn't come at all! I've had more fun with my fingers!"

She whirled around and started to gather her clothes from the floor, violently kicking and throwing his aside. "And I mean it! I didn't come once! Not once!"

She was stepping into the bathroom as the phone rang. "Fuck your phone, too!"

A second ring.

Pettigrew stared into his backyard fence, oblivious to the woman's epitaphs and the ringing. The closed door and the noise of the spa pump and the bubbling water insulated him from the bedroom.

The woman grabbed a towel, wiped it between her slippery thighs, then threw it into the tub. "Cock sucker!"

A third ring.

She pulled on her panties and walked to the irritating noise, jamming her middle finger in the air toward Pettigrew's back.

"Hello!" The salutation was a threat.

Anna was chagrined by her error. The female voice and rude manner indicated she had reached a wrong number. "Oh, I'm sorry. I must have dialed the wrong number."

"Maybe not! Are you looking for that asshole, Bob Pettigrew?"

Anna's pause said she was.

"Well, you got the right number, honey. This is big stud astronaut Pettigrew's place all right. And if you haven't found out yet... he's a fucking asshole!" The woman slammed down the receiver. "Cunt!"

A minute later, Anna was still standing over the phone, head bowed, hot, liquid pain stinging her cheeks. It was Stanford and China Lake all over again. She had been used and discarded.

Then it overwhelmed her — an acute, nauseating awareness of the filth, the dirt of his body, of his touch, of his obscene erection, of his tongue, of his fluids. Insane with grief and sobbing hysterically, she flailed her arms in an attempt to shed her nightgown. She had to wash herself! She had to sterilize her body of his! The need was urgent, blinding. One of the arms of the gown tangled, and she screamed while tearing it away. Already she was running for the bathroom, pulling her panties off. They caught on her right heel and she fell onto the carpet, burning her knees. Rolling to her back, she wildly scissored her legs trying to throw off the hobbling underclothes. Finally naked, she regained her feet and lunged into the bathroom and began to rifle the cabinets in search of the douches. A minute later she was sitting on the toilet, washing her insides. She used another of the syringes and another. Then she batted on the shower controls and adjusted the temperature to near scalding. In the careless rush to enter the stream, she slipped on the porcelain and ripped the shower curtain from its rod.

Like a rape victim wanting to wash away every trace of the animal that had abused her, she viciously scrubbed her crotch and breasts. She scrubbed with her hands. She scrubbed with the bar of soap. She scrubbed with a rag. She scrubbed until her skin was raw and rash-red. She opened her mouth to the water to wash it. And then she collapsed into the tub in a crying heap.

❖

Sunday, 20 November
JSC Crew Quarters

Judy awoke to the pains of alcohol abuse. Just above the bridge of her nose, a nail was being driven into her skull. Her tongue was a vile lump of spoiled meat. A Saharan thirst vied with a distended bladder for highest brain priority. She sat up on the edge of the bed and worried for a second she would vomit, but the wave passed.

Where was she? The room was dark and exceptionally quiet. The bed was not hers. How did she get here? Then the alcoholic haze lifted and the answers came to slap her sober. She was in the crew quarters — in Mark's bed. She had spent the last night she would ever spend with him. He was leaving her. The sky would take him. There was no more headache, no more thirst, no bladder awareness. Mark was leaving. It was a reality that made her wish for a bottle and another anesthetizing drunk.

Her eyes focused on a bedside clock — 6:32 A.M. Mark was to leave at 8:00 A.M. He would soon be getting up. Her hand felt backward into the sheets. He was gone.

"Mark?" She fumbled for an unfamiliar light switch, and when she found it, her hung-over eyes squinted against illumination that seemed solar-flare intense. The room was empty. For a moment she feared he had already left, but then saw his flight suit still hanging in the closet. She donned her robe and opened the door. Muted voices — Mark's and one other — drifted down the hallway from the direction of the conference room, and she walked toward them.

"...out of your fucking mind, Hobie!" She had had no intention of eavesdropping, but Mark's whispered rage made her pause out of sight.

"We have no choice, Colonel!" The voice, also whispered, was pitched boy's choir high. Judy did not recognize it. "The Soviet foreign minister has asked for a Wednesday evening meeting with the president. Such short notice for a personal audience — on the eve of a holiday, no less... gives cause for suspicion. It could be the day we've been fearing. You must have completed your inspection by the time of that meeting!"

"Fuck the foreign minister!"

"Please, Colonel. Watch your voice. This is supposed to jam any listening devices, but let's not try to test it with a shout. And you might disturb your wife."

"Okay. I'll whisper." He did. "Fuck the foreign minister! Tell the son of a bitch the president has something else on his calendar!"

"Colonel, the request was marked urgent and the subject was given as arms control. It would be extremely suspicious for the president to ask for a several-day postponement of such a request."

"Hobie, it's impossible! You're asking us to do three days of work in one! There's got to be another way! I suppose you've checked with the Cape about accelerating *their* operations?"

"I did. And their answer was an emphatic no. *Atlantis* will launch on the twenty-second. No earlier."

"Why did I know that! Goddamnit! We'd have to make the *Nova* rendezvous, perform the assembly, and leave on *Freedom* all in a single day! It'd be a rewrite of the entire mission plan! Jesus!"

"If the foreign minister is carrying a surprise for the president, it's our only hope, Colonel."

For several moments the room was silent, and Judy thought the conversation had ended. But just as she made the step around the corner, Mark sighed wearily and resumed. "Okay, Hobie. Okay. We'll give it try. It'll take a miracle, but we might be able to pull it off. I... Judy!"

Both men were startled at her sudden appearance. She could see the panic in their faces and the obvious question — how much had she heard?

"Judy, I hope we didn't wake you."

She said nothing and made no further move to come closer. Her eyes just took in the scene — Mark and a strange little gnome of a man standing by the table. A small, red-lighted electronic gadget sat on that. She took it to be the instrument the voice had said would jam listening devices.

"This is a friend of mine, Hobie Killingsworth. He's involved with the mission."

"Pleased to meet you, Mrs. O'Malley."

She only nodded. The room was uncomfortably quiet as Killingsworth was momentarily overcome with feelings of dread and guilt — dread and guilt that he had just been introduced to a widow of his making. "I'm terribly sorry for intruding at this hour, but goodness, this space business is so… well… I certainly don't need to tell you. There's just no end to the details." As he babbled, he grabbed his coat from the back of a chair and the electronic jammer from the table. "I've been working closely with your husband for two months now, and we're still trying to tie up some loose ends.

"Well, I must be going. Again, Mrs. O'Malley, it was very nice to meet you. Thank you, Colonel, for your help. I'll be in touch with you in Florida." He shook Mark's hand and hurried toward the door.

Judy was an accusing, emaciated, hollow-eyed statue. The boot of *the feeling* was grinding out the last glimmers of her spirit.

"Weird little guy, isn't he? He called early this morning to say he would be coming by. I guess you didn't hear the phone. You were out for the count. Come on, I've got to get packed. Why don't you shower?" He tried to tease her with a laugh. "You look like you were hit with a couple bottles of wine." He walked to her and brushed her cheek with a kiss, then hurried toward the room.

"Mark." The call stopped him. "I heard. You're doing something dangerous."

He turned and came back, a huge, lying, carefree smile on his face. "No. No… the mission is a little different, but not dangerous. We're going to be making some special tests, that's all. I don't know how much you heard." He paused, hoping she'd volunteer an answer, but she didn't. "We were just having a little difference of opinion on some things that happened in yesterday's simulation. I know it might have sounded a little strange, but there's nothing to worry about." He kissed her again and walked away.

Judy started to challenge him, then stopped. *What's the use? I can't beat the sky. He will only lie some more. He will lie, cheat, kill for the mission, for the shuttle, for flight. He will kill me.* The wave of nausea returned, and she stumbled into the bathroom and vomited.

An hour later they were in an embrace at the door, hidden from the world by a silent fog. Strangely, she could not cry. She had reached that point of despair where the soul knew the action was futile. Tears, as words before, would change nothing.

"I'll make sure someone stays in touch with you during the mission. Remember… just two weeks and we'll be sitting in the L.A. sun. And please, Judy, don't worry about what you overheard. I'll be safe. I'm more worried about you than I'm worried about this mission." He cupped her waist with his hands. It was like holding a sapling. "You need to eat more. God, I can almost touch my fingers around you. And get some more sleep." Fourteen hours ago a backlog of testosterone had blinded him to the devastation. Now, the body was too skinny, the face too drawn. Bags, the color of bruised bananas, slumped from beneath her eyes. He excused himself from a little of the damage, knowing she had self-induced it with last night's drunk.

"I'll give you a call from the Cape. I'll call the kids, too. I know this has been tough on you, but it's the last flight. I swear it." He kissed her full on the mouth, but Judy's passion was all in her arms. She crushed him to the limits of her strength — a last act of defiance of the mistress that was calling from Florida.

Mark separated, picked up his bag, and began walking to the car. He was touching the door handle when she called.

"Mark…"

He turned, appearing Hollywood-dashing in the colorful flight suit, a smiling cowboy dressed for the rodeo. She tried to form words, but none came. This moment was no different than the ones she had lived at the beach. Memorable, everlasting words were only in books and movies. He waited for a moment, then dismissed her with a wave and another smile. "Don't worry. I'll be back." The door slammed. The car started. He drove away.

"Mark… I loved you." The whisper was in the past tense. She knew he was gone.

She went inside and wept bitterly.

Sunday, 20 November
Ellington Field

"Is that you, Bob?" Mark was leaning over adjusting the crotch straps of his parachute when he heard the door to the flight equipment room open.

"Yea. Sorry I'm late. A goddamn train blocked traffic. Did you file the flight plan?"

"Yea. I'll take the lead. The Cape weather looks good… a lot better than the soup outside." He straightened to face the pilot. "Jesus. You look like shit. You're not sick, are you?" The question was prompted by Pettigrew's fatigued appearance. Red blood vessels shattered the whites of his eyes like cracks in a gun-shot window.

"Just had a little trouble sleeping last night. Thinking of the mission." It was a believable lie. "I'll be fine as soon as I can suck on some oxygen. What wing is Anna taking?" He lifted his own parachute from its peg and heaved it over a shoulder.

"She's gone."

"Gone?"

"Yea. She left an hour ago. Remember, she's got the first-period STA." Pettigrew had forgotten the schedule. He had the afternoon session. The staggered training flights in a plane that replicated the flying qualities of a landing shuttle would keep him and Anna separated until evening. The wait would be an agony. During the hellish, sleepless night, he had finally resolved he would talk with her. He had no idea yet what he would say. It was just that he had been overcome with the need to see her alone again. To talk with her.

The two men began the walk to their T-38's and Mark used their outdoor isolation to brief the marine on Killingsworth's visit.

"We can't do it, Mark. It's too much, too dangerous."

"I know. But we don't really have a choice. If the foreign minister is handing over an ultimatum and we try to make our move to the *KOSMOS* afterward, we're dead. I told Hobie we'd give it our best shot. The timeline is being rewritten right now. We rendezvous, assemble *Free-*

dom, and leave for geosync… all on launch day."
"Jesus."

CHAPTER 12

Pettigrew landed from his afternoon STA training — a dozen three-hundred-knot dives toward a runway — and hurried to the crew quarters. There, the secretary informed him Anna had gone to the beach house to jog. He changed his clothes and followed.

It was deep twilight by the time he pulled into the driveway. Already the whitecaps glowed with bioluminescence.

"Anna!" The building was empty.

Crossing the dunes, he found her tracks and began to trail them. She had gone north, probably drawn by the magnet of a xenon-lighted *Atlantis* was his guess. It was a sight no astronaut could view without wanting to get closer — a spotlighted center stage for dreams. He thought of Anna's dreams — of Anna, the little girl, riding in the balloon; of Anna, the woman, flying to music and watching the stars.

A brisk wind sidewinded snakes of sand toward his ankles. Foam blew from the tops of combers and raced across the beach like scudding clouds.

In his walk, he tried, again, to prepare himself. He loved her. He needed her. No matter of denial, of hellish memories, of diversions of drink and sex would ever change that. No woman — not even Karen — had affected him as Anna had. They shared souls. But what did she feel for him? The same love? The same need? *Yes!* He was sure of it. He had seen it in her eyes, sensed it in her body. But why hadn't she said anything of love? Was it the other man of her life? Did she love him more? *No! It can't be! Her eyes! Her body! I could see it, feel it! She loves me!*

He prepared to tell her — to tell her of the terror he had found at Travis Air Force Base, to tell her of his fear of love, of his attempts to run from her, to let the demons fly and shriek and be finally stilled, to open his soul for the first time in eighteen years to another human being. He prepared to open his soul to Anna Rowe.

Rounding a shoreline curve, he found her. Dressed in a sweat suit, she sat several yards back from the reach of the surf. Her legs were drawn up, encircled by her arms, chin on her knees. She stared seaward and was unaware of his presence. For a moment he merely watched, aching to hold her, aching to share the jeweled sky with her.

"Anna." She did not answer the call, and as he came closer he understood why. She was wearing headphones, listening to a portable tape player.

He stopped a yard from her side. "Anna."

She jerked her head in a startle, the headphones pulling from her ears.

"I'm sorry. I didn't mean to scare you." He took a seat next to her and assumed her watch of the horizon. "They told me you'd come out here."

Oh God, God, God! Why is he here? Make him leave! Oh please, God, make him leave! The stars blurred as tears began to form. *No! I will not cry! I will not let him see me cry!*

"The count's still going okay. Weather's supposed to be good. Should be a good launch." He picked bits of shell from between his legs and absently flicked them away. "I'm looking forward to seeing the stars from up there... seeing a sunset like you described."

He wants to use me again! That's why he's here! The beach house has a couch, privacy! He's come to use me! Nausea gripped her.

"It's going to be tough trying to pull off the rendezvous and assembly on day one. They're supposed to have the revised flight plan ready for us tomorrow. We're going to be buried in all-day meetings on that." He never looked at her. The words were spoken into the sand and to the sea. And his brain was so consumed with subverting the last fears of letting this woman into his heart he was oblivious to any meaning in her silence.

Anna crushed her bottom lip, resolving not to let him see her cry.

"I didn't think... well... tomorrow, we won't have..." The words came harder now. "...time."

Time? What is it, Bob? Is this the last TIME you could use me? Big stud astronaut Pettigrew! Is this the last TIME you could fit me into your busy schedule? You lied to me! You lied!

"Anna, there are some things that I have... that I want to tell you. They're not easy, though. They go back a... a long way. I never really thought I'd be able to tell anyone." He snuffled a laugh. "I would have bet my life on that." His fingers toyed with the sand. "But, I can tell you because... because..." He looked at her, a featureless shadow. "I love you, Anna."

Love me! Anna grimaced at the blasphemy. *Oh God, how can he lie like this! How can he be so cruel! So evil! And I believed him! I let him have my body!*

Pettigrew's attention fell back to the sand. "The other night... I mean, when you and I were at your place. I said it then, but I had felt it long before."

Dearest God in heaven, please make him stop! The sheen on her eyes grew thicker.

"I love you, Anna."

Liar!

"I love you so very, very much."

How could I have ever felt anything for him? How could I have been so blind?

"I haven't said those words for eighteen years. When I came back from Vietnam, I was hurt."

She could stand the mockery no longer. For the first time, she turned and looked at him, through him. "Bob, that other night, at my apartment. It really didn't mean anything to me... nothing. It was just one of those... accidents that happen to people." In a marvelous act of composure, she delivered the words in cutting apathy.

The surf thundered the passage of time. The wind buffeted his body. The sand stung his skin. The stars indifferently watched the mortals torture themselves.

It didn't mean anything to me! He was back at Travis Air Force Base. The shadow he was looking at was Karen's. *It was one of those accidents!* Like the hand of some satanic monster, the words flayed his skin, tore aside bone, grabbed his heart, and ripped it from his body.

It didn't mean anything to me! No! It's not happening! Oh, dear Jesus God, no! His head shook side to side in an involuntary act of disbelief.

They continued to stare at each other's dark-muted forms, each silently screaming their agony.

Then, she returned her gaze to the east. Remote suns rose from the blackness — stars that had captivated her as a child, stars she had watched from a spaceship, stars that had covered her that night, in a seemingly distant past, when she had loved this man.

Without looking, she knew that he was gone — now she could cry.

❖

Monday, 21 November
Kennedy Space Center

Normally, the day prior to launch would have been relaxing — a morning T-38 acrobatic fun flight, a beach house lunch with wives and friends, maybe a TV movie. But on this day, Mark and the rest of the crew remained sequestered in the quarters, reviewing the massive changes to their first day's activities. *Freedom's* only geosync injection opportunity would occur fourteen hours, twelve minutes after launch. If they missed that, they would not get to the *KOSMOS* prior to the foreign minister's meeting.

In the review, Mark became more convinced than ever they would not make it. The rendezvous would not be completed until the thirteenth hour, leaving them only an hour to assemble *Freedom*. In simulations, their best assembly time had been almost two hours. Was there a miracle that would save an hour?

There were no breaks to the work. Meals were served while plans were debated, modified, and debated again. A crush of experts filled the room. Arguments ebbed and flowed. Small groups splintered from the nucleus and held whispered caucuses in the corners. And through it all, Anna and Pettigrew remained at opposite ends of the table, speaking to each other only when necessary to clarify a checklist item, and then with rigid formality.

Finally, the day ended. Weary men and women agreed they could do no better. The revised checklists were taken away to be packed in the cockpit, and *Atlantis's* crew was freed to face their last night before the mission.

Mark went to the crypto-encoded telephone and called Killingsworth. The fat man was in Houston to observe the flight from Mission Control. "Hobie, if anything happens to me, make sure Judy's protected. She's naked out there. The press would eat her alive."

The fat man felt tears coming. *If anything happens to me.* It was a line that, until two months ago, he had heard only in movieland fiction. "I will guard her, Colonel."

"Thanks, Hobie."

"And Colonel, my prayers go with you and your crew. The president also sends his prayers and best wishes for a safe and successful flight. And forgive me for the presumption, but I wish you Godspeed on behalf of the rest of a nation that sleeps in ignorance of your heroics."

Even through the distortions of the encryption, Mark could sense the man's sincerity and was moved by it. The little fat man whom he had so offhandedly dismissed when they had first met had become *his* hero.

"Thanks, Hobie. I'll call you from the *KOSMOS*."

Mark next dialed Mountain View. Peggy answered. "She went to the beach to walk, Mark. She said she's not up to another good-bye. I think it would be best if I just told her you called."

He thanked the woman, thinking it probably was for the best. What else could be said?

He then made his last call to the children.

Anna, too, made a call — to Richard. Twenty-four hours ago she had been contemplating how she would break off that romance, but now she wanted to reinforce it — more than reinforce it — to cement it. Richard was the only man she had ever been intimate with who had not hurt her. And marriage would protect her, she was sure. A wedding band would have spared her from Pettigrew, would spare her from any more wonders of the male animal.

"Yes, Richard, that's right. When I get back, I want to talk with you about the future... about us. I want to spend more time with you... the rest of my life."

While Anna was on the phone, Pettigrew sought escape in a punishing run. He would have preferred a case of beer, but his loyalty to Mark and the mission forbade that. He turned down a narrow, overgrown road that led to an abandoned satellite test site and sprinted into the dark. Fireflies flashed by his head. Nocturnal creatures scurried from his approach. His legs became instruments of pain. Muscles cramped. Lungs burned. Sweat soaked. Thirst tortured. Coagulated saliva flicked from his mouth and stuck on his face. He was a madman taking flight from his torturers — the Vietnamese, Karen, Anna.

In the crew quarters gym, Darling pushed himself through thirty, one-handed pushups, then concentrated with weights and springs on the muscles of a space walk — fingers and wrists.

Tuesday, 22 November
Kennedy Space Center

The faint smells of breakfast — frying bacon and fresh-brewed coffee — wafted through the louvers of Mark's door. Though it was the subtlest of sensory changes, it was enough to tug him awake. No child on Christmas eve slept lighter than an astronaut on the eve of a space mission. Sleeping pills, alcohol, exhausting workouts, saunas, whirlpools, beach house sex — at one time or another, all had been employed as sleep aids, and all had been overwhelmed by the forces of gut fear and joyful anticipation.

He checked the clock — 2:22 A.M. Sleep was certainly ended, but he resisted the temptation to get up. It was too soon. The schedule was planned to the minute and did not accommodate early risers. The technicians would not yet have arrived with his clothes, the weather forecasters would still be gathering their data, reports on *Atlantis's* status would not yet have been compiled. A member of the launch team would knock when the countdown clock said it was time to knock — T-minus four hours and fifty-five minutes — and not a second before.

To kill the time, he interlaced his fingers behind his head, stared into the dark, and watched the poignant memories play — the reels of memories that turn for anyone embarking on a last, familiar, glorious journey — memories of space flight, of the vibrations of engine start, of the g's, of the star-flecked blackness.

"Mark, you awake?" Thirty minutes later, the knock interrupted.

"Yea, Charlie, thanks."

While dressing for breakfast, his eyes touched on the room artwork. It had been on the wall for years, a joke by some civil servant, but now it seemed a bad joke. It was a "Star Wars" movie poster depicting a tense Luke Skywalker preparing to do battle with a death star and a worried Princess Leia clinging to his arm. Was a death star waiting for him?

Breakfast appetites were muted. So were the conversations. Anna and the marine were stones. Even Darling had more to say. Mark was blind to the pain that joined them at the table.

After weather and countdown status briefings, he returned to the bathroom and administered himself an enema. The low-residue diet he and Darling had been following seemed to be working, but considering the consequences of *any* residue, he took the chemical purge also. As he curled into a fetal position on the tile floor and delicately probed at his anus with the plastic tip of the colonic, he laughingly wondered if Luke Skywalker and Princess Leia had made similar preparations before their space missions.

He showered and then dressed in the mission clothes, beginning with the modified jockstrap of the urine collection device. He pulled his penis through the hole in the cup, then velcroed the bladder around his waist. The rubber was left disconnected — he would make a last void at the launch-pad toilet. The ensemble was completed with the hallmark, sky-blue NASA coveralls. Lastly, he pulled his wedding band from his finger. The tight fit of the spacesuit gloves would make it an irritant.

For a moment he toyed with the gold, wondering — for the first time that day — about the woman who had put it on his finger. What was she doing? He checked his watch — 2:10 California time. *Good, she's asleep.* He zippered the ring into his pocket, and with it went any other thoughts of Judy.

Five minutes later, at exactly T-minus two hours and forty minutes, he led his crew from the building and to the waiting Astro-van. The vehicle, sandwiched between armed security escorts, turned left onto NASA Parkway and began the ten-mile drive to the pad.

Along the journey, Mark studied his crew. With mouths grimly set and gazes averted, they were more intense than others of his previous crews, but he attributed that to the unique dangers of the mission facing them. The silence that persisted was certainly unremarkable. He had witnessed that before — the product of fear and joy competing for a man's and woman's soul. Sometimes, as now, silence was the only signature of that competition. But there were others. Sometimes men or women, rookies or veterans, would try to conceal their nervousness by locking their hands in their laps, playing with a pen, tapping out a silent tune on their thighs, telling jokes, talking nonsense. They understood. There was no turning back. No one would ask again if they were ready. No flight surgeon would rescue them with a diagnosis of illness. They were going — stepping closer to death than they had ever been before.

And Mark had seen joy rule the soul. Tears would come — the gushing tears of joy at the realization that a dream of ten-thousand nights was finally coming true, that a yearning implanted by the Creator at birth was finally being satisfied, that a first mission into space was finally at hand. Tears would flood cheeks and embarrass men and they would mutter silly excuses. But Mark had known the cause — *joy! Supreme joy!* Joy beyond poetry, beyond song, beyond all joy known to that moment of the person's life.

Guards waved them through successive checkpoints. Shafts of xenon-white began to illuminate the salt air above them. The pad would soon be visible, and Mark shifted in his seat to look forward to the coming spectacle. Then the driver made a final turn and the shoulder of vegetation dropped away. *Atlantis* loomed before them.

Mark's heart pounded at his breast until he thought it would bruise the bone. No work of oil or marble or curved symmetry of naked female flesh was more captivating. The machine glistened as a solitary diamond on sable black.

The spotlights turned her black and white colors severe, as in the markings of a sea mammal. The towering white needle of the pad lightning arrestor served as a beacon for the spectacle. A ghostly flag of liquid oxygen vapor wafted from the top of the external tank and swirled around the engines. In the background, a flare tower blazed with liquid hydrogen waste — an upraised, wind-whipped flame that appeared as a torch marking an Olympian event. The entire scene struck Mark as fake, as the work of some over-zealous Hollywood special effects artist. Reality could not be this colossal, this dramatic, this beautiful.

The van lurched up the incline of the pad and pulled to a stop at the elevators. One was being held open, and they stepped into it for the ride to the one-hundred-and-ninety-five-foot level, where the crew access arm reached to the cockpit. Mark exited the lift and went immediately to the toilet.

A moment later Pettigrew called him, "Mark?"

"Yea? I'm in the head."

"Take your time. The techs are running about ten minutes late."

"Thanks."

The timeline was fat enough that the delay could be absorbed, so he was not concerned. In fact, he was glad. The commander — always the first to strap into the vehicle — was usually denied the opportunity for a final, leisurely look at his machine. He hurried the UCD cuff onto his penis, then velcroed and zipped his clothes into place and stepped outside. His crew was scattered across the gantry. Darling stood in the middle of the access arm. Pettigrew and Anna had found widely separate observation points on the main platform.

He sought the same privacy and walked to an empty part of the gantry. Now was a moment too precious to spend in idle chatter with any human. It would be the last time he would ever stand at this spot, and he wanted to burn the memories indelibly into his brain.

The pad had an air of ghost town desertion to it. The only sound was the steady, dragonlike hiss of the engine purge — the respiration of a sleeping leviathan. A fog of ground-hugging vapor boiled from a nearby pond of liquid oxygen waste and enhanced the suggestion he had intruded into the lair of a medieval beast. Mark was certain if he could somehow reach out and touch the beast, her skin would be warm, alive.

Finally, the call came that the technicians were ready, and he walked across the access arm and into the white room. In turn, the others followed him into the machine and were tied to their seats. The hatch was closed. They stroked the monster through her switches and she stirred.

Tuesday, 22 November
Mountain View

"Judy?" Peggy called through the door.

"Come in."

The woman entered with a bottle of vodka and two glasses. "I couldn't sleep either. Saw the light under your door and figured you might need some company. We can make it a threesome." She held the bottle aloft to indicate the third party. "All we need is a dirty magazine and a cigarette to be sixteen again. Here." She poured two fingers of liquor and offered the glass to Judy.

"Peggy, I don't think…"

"Take it. If I need one, you do, too."

Judy reluctantly accepted the drink but did not taste it. Her stomach was a volcano, and she was certain the alcohol would induce vomiting.

Peggy filled her own glass, sat on the edge of the bed, and idly sifted among a pile of sketches that had been Judy's time-killing diversion.

"I'm so sorry for doing this to you, Peggy. Coming into your home and making you a part of this... this... waiting." It was 2:30 and she waited for the phone call. Mark had promised that someone would call when they were safely in orbit. It would be her only source of news because the exact launch time was secret and the networks would have no coverage of it.

"Ah, waiting. It's what we do best, isn't it? Here's to waiting." Peggy lifted her glass and drank a toast. "Not to worry, honey. Waiting is just another curse we've inherited from Eve... like periods, cellulite, and facial hair. Waiting for men. That was God's real punishment for listening to that fucking snake. Come on. I'll show you the right way to wait. Mix up some chocolate-chip cookie batter and then eat it all before you bake a single cookie."

Judy protested she would maintain a solitary vigil in the bedroom, but Peggy would not be deterred. She grabbed her hand and pulled her from the bed and into the kitchen.

Fifteen minutes later a bowl of chocolate sprinkled yellow batter sat between them. "This is called stress strudel. Dig in." Peggy wrapped a large twist of the sticky mix onto her finger and brought it to her mouth. Judy merely dipped a fingertip for a taste. Food was as repugnant as alcohol. "I also have a recipe for crisis cake and trial and tribulation turnover. We'll try that later."

Judy chuckled. She was always amazed at Peggy's wit. When she was intoxicated, as she was now, it was rapier sharp.

"Just like the good ol' war days, huh?" There was sarcasm in the observation. "Remember those? Sitting around with the other wives in that dust bowl of an air force base, laughing and scratching over a couple bottles of wine and trading cookie recipes? God! Somehow that seems just like yesterday. Kids wailing, the smell of diaper pails and ammonia. Jeeesss! The kids! Seemed like everybody was pregnant. How was that possible?" She sucked another batter wrap from her finger. "I think the men must have masturbated in our panties before they left or soaked the sheets in their sperm... a plot to keep us fat and ugly so we wouldn't be tempted to find a replacement while they were gone."

She civilized the snacking with a spoon, chasing every third bite with vodka. Judy pretended collaboration by rubbing her finger through a smear on the bowl edge.

Peggy's monologue ended with the batter. "Well, there's another side of bacon for the ol' hips." She patted hers. "You sure didn't help much."

"I'm sorry. My stomach is just too upset."

"Yea. Yea, I know." Like an older sister, she threw an arm around her friend. To that moment she had avoided all mention of Mark. The conversation had been slumber-party light. Now, though, she turned and stared into Judy's face. Reality had to be addressed. "He'll be okay, Judy. He will be. I know it. I can feel it."

Judy tried to thank her, but her throat was too constricted for speech. *The feeling* was more intense than ever. Tears welled in her eyes and rolled across her cheeks and Peggy gathered her into an embrace and stroked the back of her head as if she were a child.

"Come on. Let's watch TV... no calories." Peggy led her into the living room.

They maintained their vigil through a half hour of mindless television dribble, until sleep finally claimed Peggy. Judy remained awake to watch a sad-eyed priest with a sonorous voice recite a closing prayer. The national anthem played and the broadcast ended. Static snow became her entertainment. She stared into it, and another show slowly began to appear. It was launch morning and she was at the Cape. She couldn't tell which launch it was, but it didn't matter. Now, they were all the same.

She saw herself sitting on the condo balcony listening to the Atlantic suck at the sand, smelling its elemental scents, watching the waves make their white charge across the black. She had always spent the night before a launch in a beach-front condo — a sleepless night, a night of waiting for the knock on the door that would tell her it was time to board the bus for the drive to the LCC.

The curse... waiting.

She watched lightning flash and the moon blossom to silhouette lovers walking the beach.

She waited, counting the minutes in the waves and the hours in the turn of the constellations.

Waiting... waiting... waiting.

"It's time, Judy." The summons finally arrived.

She joined the other wives and children to begin their mission amid the carnival atmosphere of a vacation mecca. Mobs of tourists jammed the highways to get closer to the launch site. Motor homes and tents walled the approaches. Jiggling, bikini-clad girls and muscled, swimsuited boys threw frisbees amid fat retirees who sat in the shade of their camper awnings or attended to smoking grills. Roadside entrepreneurs hawked shuttle memorabilia — T-shirts, buttons, photos. Others sold hot dogs and lemonade and ice cream. The marquees of the town businesses — realtors, banks, restaurants — proclaimed their best wishes. *Good luck Atlantis! Go Columbia! Godspeed Challenger! Fly Discovery!* It was Woodstock and Disneyland thrown together on a sun-scalded beach. It was The Supreme Happening.

In the naivety of her first launch, she remembered having fallen victim to the heady atmosphere of celebration. She had been Queen For A Day! When their police escort had been stopped by traffic, oil-smeared people had recognized them and rushed their bus with cameras in hand. They had wanted her photo! *Her* photo! They had wanted to shake her hand, to talk to her, to tell people they had met an astronaut's wife.

It had been fun that morning, she recalled. The brother of one of the astronauts had brought his guitar and on the drive had led them in an enthusiastic sing-along. *Off We Go into the Wild Blue Yonder, On Top of the World,* and *Rocket Man.* The bus had been electric with anticipation.

Oh, yes, it had been fun that day... until the LCC roof. Then, the reason for the gathering of the masses, for her sudden incredible rise to celebrity status, had slapped her from fantasy-land. It had been carried on the scream of the main engines, felt in the earth-moving thunder of the solid boosters, seen in the thousand-foot flames. The crowds were there to watch space-suited knights joust with fire and speed and height — the forces of death. They were there to pray for their heroes, to cry for them, to cheer them on, to live vicariously through them. But, in the end, they were there to see who would win the battle. It was the threat of death that had brought them, the threat of Mark's death that had made her a star. How ignorant she had been. At later launches she had come to hate the carnival, to hate the excited faces anticipating the celestial game as Roman citizens might have anticipated the entry of gladiators into the coliseum.

They were waved through successive roadblocks, past the crew quarters, onto Kennedy Parkway. The first time she had made this drive, Judy had thought she had stumbled into a lost world of giants, not believing it was possible for humans to have assembled such goliathan structures. Men walked on buildings and crawlers and gantries like ants on redwoods.

Finally, they were brought to the LCC and escorted into an executive's office to wait. The room looked out on the launch pad, and Judy saw herself standing at that window and staring and shivering at the thought of what was to come.

Then, the wait resumed. Children grew tired and fussy and diversions were attempted — coloring books and toys for the youngest, headphones and rock music for the teenagers. Sometimes motherly limits were reached, and misbehaving children were dragged into corners and disciplined in fierce whispers.

They waited.

VIP's streamed through to offer their best wishes.

They waited.

Trays of food and drink were passed.

They waited.

They watched on TV as their husbands shook hands with white-room technicians, turned, and climbed through the hatch.

They waited.

They waited for the weather. They waited for computers. They waited for bugs and gremlins and glitches. They waited for clearance's and okay's and go's. They waited for the final litany.

"APU?"

"APU is go."

"Booster?"

"Booster is go."

"DPS?"

"DPS... go."

"RSO?"

"RSO... go."

A dozen others answered the launch director's poll. The Launch Control Center was go.

"Resume the count."

"T-minus nine minutes and counting."

Wives roused dozing children and engaged in last second panics to find sunglasses and hats and insect repellent. Escorts hurried them from the room and onto the roof for the last, longest minutes of wait.

In Mountain View, the phone rang.

CHAPTER 13

Tuesday, 22 November
Atlantis

Atlantis's computers commanded her nose level with the horizon, and she ran silently to the east at full throttle. She held her top-to-earth attitude, and the cloud-flecked beauty of the Atlantic finally intruded into Mark's peripheral vision. He tried not to look, to stay on the instruments, but the temptation was irresistible. He rolled his head to the left — the g-forces prevented greater motion — and glimpsed a lacework of cotton-white clouds on Gulf Stream blue. At the relatively low altitude of sixty-two miles, their extreme speed was apparent. The spiral arm of a late-season tropical storm came into view and was gone. A line of thunder-storms, casting two-hundred-mile shadows, was seen for only a moment.

He returned to the instruments and watched the scroll of his velocity meter.

Twenty-two thousand feet per second.

Twenty-three.

"Eighty-seven percent... Eighty..." Pettigrew noted the engine power reductions. With little fuel remaining to burden her, the machine's engines would push her to destruction, and she protected herself with the ever-decreasing power settings.

Twenty-five thousand feet per second.

Twenty-six.

"MECO... Twenty-six-four-seventy. Up at three-eighty. Right on the money. A perfect ride, Houston."

The crush of three gravities was instantly replaced with weightlessness, and unrestrained items floated free. Small particles of dirt that had escaped the prelaunch vacuuming drifted from their hiding places. A pencil that had shaken loose of Anna's kneeboard now hovered in midspace. Checklists floated slowly upward on their tethers, looking like snakes being charmed from their baskets.

"Jesus!" Pettigrew startled everybody by ramming his arm forward to brace himself against the instrument panel glare shield.

"What?" Mark had seen nothing to justify the panic.

"I... I don't know. For a second I thought we were tumbling." The instruments said they were rock steady. "It's just a little vertigo. I'll be okay."

Vertigo. Mark had seen others affected by it. The instantaneous transition from the acceleration of three gravities to weightlessness had been known to cause the sensation of a head-over-heels tumble.

A dull thud signaled the separation of the external tank and *Atlantis's* RCS jets — steering rockets on her nose and tail — fired to move her away from the spent hulk. It was destined for a mid-Pacific grave — at least the part of it that survived the blast furnace of reentry.

Mark reached to his translation hand controller and pushed inward. A small acceleration followed, enough to settle the thousands of pounds of unused liquid fuel that remained trapped in the orbiter's engine plumbing.

"Get your propellant dump switches."

"Huh?"

He was shocked at Pettigrew's response. They had practiced a thousand ascents in the simulator, and the procedures were as natural to the marine as breathing. "Your dump switches, goddamnit! Open them!" Mark's temper was short. If they had any hope of successfully making the *KOSMOS* rendezvous, they had to maintain the crisp precision that had been burned into them by their training. A touch of vertigo was no excuse.

Pettigrew's hand groped unsteadily for the propellant dump controls, then immediately regrasped the glare shield.

Mark noticed and worried. The vertigo could be an early symptom of space sickness. Was Pettigrew susceptible? He was still untested by the physiological effects of weightlessness. The RTLS had been too brief an exposure to zero gravity to be an indicator of his body's true response.

"How are you doing, Frank?" The marine's condition prompted Mark to check his other rookie. He had heard nothing from Darling since launch.

"I am okay." The adrenaline-pumping thrill of the ascent and the incomparable beauty that now filled the windows had done nothing to animate the man. *Iceman* came to Mark's mind.

"The OMS burn target looks good."

"Thanks, Anna."

She and Darling exited their seats and began to remove them from the aft flight deck. "Move slower, Frank. Forget about your feet. Use your fingers." Anna coached the novice. A life in one gravity was impossible to quickly put aside, and the rookie reaction was invariably to try and move the body as it had always been moved — with the legs and feet. But those appendages were too coarsely muscled for microgravity, and the result was a continual fight with the ceiling and walls. Darling took a moment to study the precise body control that Anna attained with merely the tips of her fingers.

Still strapped to his seat, Pettigrew continued to struggle with a maddening dizziness. No amount of reference to the attitude indicator would convince his brain they were not in a violent forward tumble. He focused his attention outside, hoping the view of a level horizon would help settle him. It did not. Sweat boiled from his pores and saliva flooded his mouth. His swallow response became continuous. Then, a guttural cough grabbed everybody's attention. Darling snatched an emesis bag from his coveralls and thrust it into the marine's hands. Pettigrew wretched violently. Droplets of the fluid splashed from the bag, and a yellow gout floated onto Anna's cheek. She wrestled with her own nausea.

"Fuck!" Mark slammed his fist on the glare shield. Time was their enemy, and Pettigrew's illness — anybody's illness — could sabotage the mission.

"I'll be okay, Mark." Several deep coughs had emptied the marine's stomach, and he closed the bag.

"Anna, get him some Scopedex and water and some more bags."

"No! I can take care of my…" Pettigrew started from his seat. He had no intention of being a burden, especially to Anna.

"Stay where you are, goddamnit! The less you move around the quicker you'll get over this shit. Give me that!" Mark grabbed the bag of warm mess and passed it to Anna. "Shove that in the wet trash." Anna floated downstairs on the errands.

"Check the OMS!" Mark snapped the order and Pettigrew turned to the computer display. For the present, he felt well enough for the task.

Mark doubted the prescription of scopolamine and dextrin would be any more effective than a witch doctor's chant in curing the pilot. For two decades, the mysterious sickness that affected nearly seventy percent of space travelers had baffled NASA doctors. The onboard medical kit was stuffed with their guesses on treatment — drugs to suppress the vestibular system, drugs to stimulate the stomach, drugs to quiet the stomach, uppers, downers, pills, suppositories, patches, injections. They might as well have tried snake oil, Mark thought. The only thing that had ever worked was what they didn't have — time. Still, he was glad Darling seemed to have been spared from the curse. To vomit in the space suit would be almost certain death. The debris could be inhaled or could foul the suit's oxygen circulation system.

He returned to the demands of *Atlantis*, and ten minutes later a kick from the OMS engines circularized their orbit at a hundred and sixty nautical miles. Whatever lay ahead, Mark thought, they had at least achieved a momentary sanctuary. *Atlantis* would remain in orbit without any further activity on their part. She would also spend half of each orbit underneath the *KOSMOS*. Some sanctuary, was his next thought.

They began the hours of work to fully convert the machine into a spaceship. The digital heart of the giant — five IBM computers — were programmed for orbit operations. The payload bay doors were opened, the rendezvous radar was deployed and activated, and the remote arm was unlatched and extended. Downstairs, Darling attended to the hours-long checkout and servicing of the space suits. Anna labored at the work of two people as Pettigrew's condition gradually worsened. His vomiting increased in frequency and violence until he was inverting his gut in bouts of dry heaves. He became a prisoner of the illness, barely able to type to the computers or throw a switch.

Mark's mood darkened. They would soon reach a point where the marine would have to be more than functional. He would have to be computer-precise, flying them into an eighteen-thousand mile-per-hour rendezvous with the *Nova*. Anna could not do it herself. She would have the equally delicate task of snaring their target with the remote arm. And he and Darling, closed in the airlock, would be unable to assist.

Tuesday, 22 November
Red Sky Control Room

"The American space shuttle seems to be flying to a rendezvous with their previously orbited *Nova* rocket." General Chernavin stood at the podium and briefed the conspirators.

"For what purpose?" It was Kobozev's question.

"We know there was a malfunction during the *Nova* launch. It is possible that the Americans are attempting to correct it. Considering the staggering expense of these machines, if there was any possibility astronauts could repair it, the Americans would certainly attempt such a repair. Perhaps they will space walk to replace a malfunctioning component or merely use their robot arm to do some work. Maybe they will only photograph it for a failure analysis. It is impossible to say."

"And Musa, what is your opinion?" Kobozev turned to the defense minister.

"I agree with General Chernavin. The Americans have a long history of using their astronauts to make repairs of malfunctioning robot machines. If there is any possibility the space shuttle and its crew could effect a repair, they would attempt to do so. At any rate, the rendezvous, at an altitude of less than four hundred kilometers, cannot be a threat to Red Sky, at thirty-five *thousand* kilometers."

Kobozev paused in a contemplative stare at the control room's world map and the traces of satellites that snaked across it. *Atlantis* was depicted as a blue flashing star currently passing over Australia. He turned back to General Chernavin. "Could the Americans make the repair and then return to earth before the Red Sky demonstration?"

"That is highly unlikely, Comrade Minister. Their missions are never shorter than four or five days."

"Then our good fortune continues. The machine remains a target."

"But surely they will not stay in orbit after the demonstration is announced. They will rightfully fear we have targeted the shuttle." Ryabinin made the observation.

Kobozev pondered the comment, then offered an opinion. "They will not flee. President Corbin will see the manned machine exactly as I see it… a test of our resolve, a demonstration of his. If we spare it, he will know we are weak. The situation could not be better. Their launch of the machine was truly a gift. General, you are dismissed."

The man departed.

"Comrades." When the door closed, Yazov was first to speak. He tried to sound authoritarian, but the blinking tic of facial blubber, the fearful, darting eyes, and the ever-present bottle of antacid made a joke of the attempt. "The Iranian Initiative can succeed without an attack on the American astronauts. We should delete it as a target. To kill American robots is one thing. To kill her men is too precipitous. It irrevocably changes the situation. It will mean war."

No one replied. The only sound was the noise of the control center, which permeated the observation window as a faint bustle. Kobozev rose from his chair and strolled leisurely, hands clasped behind his back, to look from it. Minister of State Security Ryabinin drew deeply from his cigarette and toyed with the ash on the lip of a tray. Defense Minister Zhilin ignored the comments by repeatedly capping and uncapping his pen. Invisible, inaudible waves of a deeper conspiracy undulated between the three. Red Sky was ready. Yazov had served his purpose. His weakness was endangering them all. Something had to be done.

The silence panicked the minister of economics. Yazov had been a party to Politburo politics for too long not to sense the telepathy connecting the others. His usefulness to a Kobozev-ruled Politburo was being debated, and he nervously glanced to Zhilin, then to Ryabinin, hoping to make eye contact, hoping to read the degree and imminence of his danger in their faces. But neither raised their gaze. His hand shot out for the liquid chalk and he babbled between swallows. "Of course, I… I… fully support the initiative. My loyalty is steadfast, absolutely steadfast. Yes, unbending. I…"

Without turning from the window, Kobozev cut him off. "Comrade Yazov, are you afraid of… death?"

Yazov visibly startled at the question. "Death? I… I…"

"The death of Americans, of course." Like a cat batting a crippled bird between its paws, Kobozev tortured him with the dialogue.

"It is nuclear war I fear. You, we, we *all*" — he emphasized the inclusiveness of the word —"could rise to power on the success of the Iranian Initiative, only to find ourselves immediately threatened with an

American attack. We will have gained nothing. As I said, an attack on the astronauts is too precipitous, too irrevocable."

Kobozev finally turned. "It is precisely for that reason we must — and *will* — attack the American shuttle! In the end, there is only one message of resolve, only one message that says we will not go back, and that is to kill. Not to kill robots, but to kill men! Lenin killed the Romanovs to send that message. We will kill the American astronauts to send the same message. Only then will they understand our conviction. Far from precipitating a war, Comrade Yazov, the deaths of the astronauts will ensure the president will meet our demands. In the deaths of those Americans, he will absolutely know we are not bluffing. It is a clarity of intention that avoids war."

Yazov had no reply. His right jowl twitched as if a string was attached to it and was being vibrated from above by an invisible puppeteer. He was condemned! It was no longer a frightened man's paranoia. Kobozev had just revealed his fate — *only one message of resolve… to kill.* The deaths of the American astronauts would be a message to the president. *His* death would be a message to Sorokin and the others, if they were stupid enough to challenge the *fait accompli* of the Iranian Initiative. He swilled some more of the stomach salve, his brain lashing out for rescue. *Think! Think! There has to be a way of getting free to warn Sorokin! And Sorokin must grant me amnesty! He must!*

❖

Tuesday, 22 November
Atlantis

Something was wrong. For a moment, Pettigrew wondered if the sickness had caused him to misread the time or make a mistake with the switches, but a recheck showed there had been no error. The door had not closed. The zebra-striped IN TRANSIT position remained.

"Mark, the right ET door didn't close."

Mark and Anna snapped their attention forward, their eyes suddenly huge in a fear response. Mark floated to Pettigrew's side. "Recycle the switch."

"I've done that… twice." The marine paused and swallowed back a wave of nausea. Speech alone was a stomach provocation.

"Have you tried the software switch?" It was Anna's question.

"Yea. No joy."

Unwilling to believe it, Mark reached past the marine and repeated the actions. Nothing.

"It could just be a bad feedback."

"Yea. Yea, it probably is." Mark's words were devoid of faith. The threat was so enormous that for a moment he could only see the fatal outcome — death inside a white-hot fireball of superheated plasma. The tiled, heat-resistant, external tank doors covered two six-foot-square openings in *Atlantis's* belly — the cavities through which fuel plumbing passed from the external tank to the main engines. If they could not be closed, the three-thousand-degree temperature of air friction during reentry would cut through her exposed guts like a welder's torch. They would die as human meteors, cremated at fifty miles altitude.

Mark grabbed the mike. "Houston… *Atlantis*. We have indications the right ET door didn't close."

There was a delay in the reply as men on the ground coped with the sudden rush of adrenaline, the sudden realization there might be another enemy to contend with — the machine itself. For three months it had been everybody's greatest fear, a fear beyond an armed *KOSMOS* — a fear that, in the hell-bent rush to prepare *Atlantis*, human error would make its secret conspiracy to kill.

"We copy, *Atlantis*. We'll take a look at our data." Ever the guardian of crew spirits, the capcomm continued with exaggerated calm. "It's probably just the indicator."

"Yea, that's what we're hoping… Hobie, anything new on your end?" While he had the microphone, Mark took a moment to make the inquiry.

"Nothing to report, Colonel. NORAD is watching and there has been no unusual activity. And the *Nova* remains untouched. How are things progressing up there?"

We're behind the timeline! Pettigrew is sick! We may have a serious problem with the orbiter! Other than that, things are just fuckin' great! Mark suppressed the temptation to unload his frustration. It would cost too many seconds. "We're doing our best."

Six hours later, Anna watched the CRT timer counting the final seconds to a trajectory correction burn. She was floating at the aft cockpit THC, and as the digits flashed to zero she tapped the control. Though there was no air to transmit noise, the hammer of the forward jets was conducted through *Atlantis's* aluminum skeleton and banged the cockpit like a depth charge shuttering a submarine. Items velcroed on the walls — pencils, checklists, drink containers — momentarily waved from the impulse as if stirred by a breeze. Outside, the vibrations loosened ice from the main engine bells, and the particles swam in silent formation with *Atlantis*, like a school of silvery fish.

She studied the numbers on the computer, confirmed a good burn, then checked the rendezvous radar. Their closing velocity had increased by two feet per second. They were in the daylight portion of their orbit, and from the overhead windows she could see the sun-washed *Nova* — a bright, sixty-mile-distant star. It would not be long before she would need Pettigrew's help, but one look at that human wreckage made her doubt she would get it. He remained in his seat, dry-heaving with clocklike regularity.

Moved only by patriotism, she prayed for his recovery. The country needed Bob Pettigrew. She did not. He had used her as he now used the emesis bags — to relieve himself. She would never forget that. Never. After the *Nova* rendezvous, the illness could retake him — anything, as long as he stayed out of her life.

Houston called — they were uplinking the next burn target into the ship's computers. Ignition time was an hour away. The break gave her a first opportunity to change out of her launch coveralls, and she glided headfirst through the starboard interdeck passage and into the mid-deck. Here she entered the orbiter's living room, kitchen, bedroom, and bathroom — all contained in a volume no bigger than a generous walk-in closet. The front wall was covered from floor to ceiling with rows of lockers and, for this mission, two spare space suits. Strapped to the starboard wall were four sleeping bags, while the opposite wall was occupied with a refrigerator-sized galley. The airlock formed the rear wall. Even the floor was functional — lift-up panels exposed trash containers and allowed servicing access to the pumps and fans of the orbiter's cooling system. These whirred steadily, filling the room with the reassuring hum and vibration of the spacecraft's respiration.

She slipped her feet under floor-mounted canvas loops to hold herself, then twisted the locker wing nuts open. The tray she extracted was net covered to prevent the contents from scattering.

"How's Bob?" Mark asked the question while ripping into the plastic bag that held his liquid cooling garment.

"The same. He throws up everything. Maybe he should try one of the suppositories."

"No. Everybody who's used those things say the side effects are too severe. Scrambles their motor skills, puts them under. He might recover from the vomiting. He won't from one of those. Just watch him and do what you can for him… and pray for a miracle. We're going to need it."

"I already have."

She grabbed panties, shorts, and a cotton golf shirt from the tray, then floated to the toilet area to change. Squeezed into the port-rear corner of the mid-deck, it was the only place on the vehicle that afforded some privacy, and that was minimal. She closed the partial curtain, then removed her coveralls, bra, and soaked urine collection diaper. The bra served no purpose in zero gravity and had begun to gouge her as the fluid shift had swelled her breasts. It was a microgravity phenomenon that affected everybody — blood that had been pooled in the legs by earth's gravity was free to spread throughout a weightless body. The results were a miraculous reduction in the size of calves and thighs, while women's breasts assumed a mass and uplifted poise the hardest-bodied Hollywood starlet would have envied. Even the face was smoothed of wrinkles by the stretch of skin from the migrating blood.

After dressing, she returned to the upstairs cockpit and began to fly the robot arm through a series of maneuvers to confirm its health.

Mark remained downstairs, preparing his suit and cursing the clock. Time seemed to evaporate at twice earth rate. The *Nova* range decreased to thirty miles… twenty-five… twenty. Thrusters thundered more frequently as Anna converted the computer burn targets into finer and finer velocity adjustments.

It was while he and Darling were installing batteries in the backpacks that Mark heard it — the cry, the spontaneous gasp of a terrified human. It was Anna. He rocketed toward the flight deck, confused by the outburst. There had been no klaxon to warn of a failure in any of *Atlantis's* systems, no alien sounds suggesting an explosion or cabin pressure leak, no smell of fire. The *Nova* was still much too distant to be a collision hazard.

"What?! What Anna?!" He shot into the cockpit expecting to find her

and Pettigrew in a frantic response to whatever had threatened. Instead,
they were still. Anna floated at the aft console, her hands on the remote
arm controls. Pettigrew had left his seat and now floated behind her. They
both stared at the TV monitors.

"What?" Mark rose higher so he could also see. "Oh, Jesus!"

A view of *Atlantis's* belly was being projected. Anna had maneuvered the arm to bring its end-mounted camera under the forward
fuselage. Except for a single shadow, the picture was of a smooth expanse
of shiny black tile. She lifted the microphone and made the call.
"Houston… I've got the wrist camera looking at the belly. The right ET
door is open."

❖

Pettigrew stared from the forward window into his eighth earth-orbit
night. Nothing was visible, not even the stars. They could only be seen
by eyes that were dark-adapted, and the cockpit lighting was too bright
for that. A half moon had been visible earlier, but that had set. Only a cold,
deep blackness appeared beyond the thick glass.

If he moved his head slightly, and that was all he could do, he could
see Anna's reflection on the window. Her back was to him. She remained
at the aft cockpit panels flitting from control to control trying to save the
rendezvous, the mission, the *country* from his weakness.

He damned his body for its betrayal. Always, in the past, it had
obeyed on command, giving him speed and strength and endurance and
agility. In Vietnam, by sheer strength of will, he had made it survive a
torture that would have killed most men. *Always* he had been the master
of his body and held in contempt the soft and weak who could not rise
above even trivial physical adversity. They were prisoners of their own
flesh.

Now, he was just such a prisoner. By no strength of will could he
escape the sickness. His sense of equilibrium remained chaotically
tumbled in an Alice-in-Wonderland chamber where there was no direction.

His continuing view of Anna's reflection renewed the enormity of
that loss. Nothing he had yet experienced had removed her from his soul
— not the pain of her words, not her cold indifference, not the sickness,
not even the threats hanging over his life. He wondered if time would
ultimately be a deep enough grave. Would he someday wake in the

morning and live the entire day without ever thinking of her?

"*Atlantis*… Houston. Mark, we have some words on your door problem." The call from Mission Control ended the maddening wonder.

Mark floated to the flight deck to answer. "Go ahead, Houston."

"Mark, we've looked at the electrical current traces on the door drive. It's a jam… a *hard* jam."

For many seconds the only sounds were those of the machine. She purred softly, lying her security. They had been hoping the door problem would be electrical in nature — somewhere in the cockpit a wire had loosened to cause the stoppage. They were trained and equipped with the tools to remove panels and bypass such malfunctions. But no amount of in-cockpit labor would ever clear a mechanical jam.

"It's an EVA then." Mark's voice was a despairing whisper.

"Roger, Mark. It's the only way. Someone is going to have to get to the door and take a look. We're certain there's nothing that can be done in the cockpit. The strip charts show both motors turned nominally for nine seconds, then simultaneously drew maximum current. Something had to have jammed the linkage."

In his entire life, Mark had never felt more burdened by the responsibility of command. He was facing a dilemma of perfect symmetry, and the specter of disaster grinned from each.

There were no procedures for the door repair. Even if Mission Control invented some, there was no way to get to the door. There were no handholds on the belly. It was an absolutely featureless table of heat tiles. Movement across it in a space suit would be like climbing a sheer cliff with catcher's mitts on each hand. And how could Pettigrew ever survive his sickness in the suit?

He considered the other alternative — use *Freedom* to fly underneath *Atlantis* and dock on the exposed fuel plumbing. He and Darling could then do the repair. But it would mean losing their return ticket from the *KOSMOS*. *Freedom's* fuel reserves were insufficient to support work on the door. Besides, if they attempted the repair, they would have to delay their departure a day — after the foreign minister's meeting with the president.

The view from the window demanded an answer. The sun was rising and the *Nova* glistened like a steel torpedo. She was less than a mile distant.

"Colonel O'Malley, Hobie Killingsworth here." The fat man's voice, heavy with worry, came over the speaker. "The situation with the door has been explained to me and I understand your dilemma. *Freedom* could be used to fix the door. I'm told it may well be the *only* way to get to the mechanism. I want you to know this mission was never intended to be a suicide mission." There was a long silence. He continued slowly, gravely. "Whatever decision you make, we will understand. The country will understand."

Mark shot a glance at Pettigrew. The pilot was ashen, his eyes rheumy and red. Town drunks looked better. There was no other way. Anna would have to save them. "Houston… *Atlantis*. Darling and I will leave for the *KOSMOS* as planned. Anna will do the EVA."

"We copy that, Mark. We'll get working on a plan for her."

"*What?!* What the hell are you talking about!" Pettigrew exploded.

"Colonel, are you sure? Do you wish to reconsider the consequences of your decision?" Killingsworth was back on the radio.

Mark ignored him to deal with Pettigrew's baffling outburst. "Anna's going to have to do the EVA, Bob. She was EVA-trained on her first flight."

"I can do it." Anna confidently endorsed the order.

Pettigrew disregarded her and remained focused on Mark. "Yea… well she's never been trained to do an ET door repair. Nobody has. It's too dangerous."

Mark's temper flared. "What the hell do you want me to do? Use *Freedom*? If I do, it's the end of the mission. You know what's at stake. We can't quit this mission!"

"I'm not talking about quitting! We all knew what we were signing up for." The marine hesitated for a moment, fighting another rise of nausea. "You and Darling leave. But I'm doing the door repair!" He snatched an emesis bag from its velcro and readied it.

"Colonel? Colonel? Can you hear me? Do you want to take more time to think about the situation?" Killingsworth blindly competed for attention.

"I don't have any time left, Hobie! I thought about it! We're going to the *KOSMOS!* Anna's doing the EVA!" Mark's frustration spilled into the mike. He immediately returned to Pettigrew. "Bob, you can't even get out of your fuckin' seat! How the hell are you going to do an EVA?

Anna *has* to do it! There's no other way!" He turned and began a descent into the mid-deck.

"No!" Pettigrew released his seat belt and seized Mark's shoulder.

"What the fuck is wrong with you? I've got to get into the airlock!" Mark angrily shrugged off the hand.

"Anna's *not* doing the EVA!" The statement was a threat.

Mark was stunned by the mutiny. "Listen, Bob, I don't know what the fuck is wrong with you and I don't have time to find out, but you better get your fuckin' head screwed on straight! You will *die* out there! Do you hear me? *Die!* One vomit inside that suit and you could suffocate."

"Then I'll wait until I'm better."

"And while you're waiting, what if a *KOSMOS* bullet comes flying through that wall. Huh? And you have to get out of orbit now! You're *both* dead!" For a second time, he signaled the conversation was ended by turning for the mid-deck and, for a second time, he was stopped.

"Anna can't do it, Mark! It'll be suicide for her!" The wave finally broke and Pettigrew heaved into the bag. He came up yelling. "She'll have to wear your spare suit! It won't fit! The gloves will kill her! If she gets hung up on something, she's lost!"

"I can do it. I've been trained on the suit." Anna again confidently countered the marine's objections.

"Stay the fuck out of this, Anna!" Pettigrew lashed her with his tongue.

She was stunned by the viciousness of the order. Never had she been addressed in such a foul manner. She bared her right palm and hurled it into the side of Pettigrew's face. A sharp crack signaled a direct, full-velocity hit, but she had not taken time to brace herself and the reaction of the blow caused her to tumble. When recovered, she faced the pilot squarely with eyes narrowed to green slits. "Don't you *ever* talk to me like that again!" She was glad to see the red welt of her handprint rising on his cheek. It was the only color in his face.

As if he were made of stone, Pettigrew ignored her.

Mark was dumbfounded by the pilot's attack of idiocy. He wondered if the sickness had scrambled the man's brain. Any rational person could see that Anna had to do the repair. *Atlantis's* only defense to a *KOSMOS* attack, thin as it was, was to run, to get out of orbit. To delay the door repair would be to leave her defenseless.

"Bob, you dumb bastard! You're going to fuck this mission and kill us all! I've got to get in the airlock! I can't stay here and help you find your fuckin' brain!" Mark grabbed the marine's coveralls and pulled himself eye to eye. "Now listen to me and listen good! I'm giving you a direct order! You have until the end of the sleep period. If you're still vomiting then, Anna does the EVA. You will not… I repeat… will *not* wait longer than the end of the sleep period! Do you understand?!" The extra time was not a compromise. Mark was virtually certain the pilot's incapacitation would remain another day. It was Anna he was thinking about. She needed the rest. Pettigrew was right on that account. The space walk would be dangerous and physically punishing. Beginning it at the end of a twenty-hour day would add to its hazards. The delay would leave *Atlantis* naked for ten additional hours, but that could not be helped.

Mark continued to hold the pilot, glaring at him fiercely. He was prepared to pick up where Anna had left off and smash his fist into the man's face if that's what it took to restart his brain.

Pettigrew remained blind to the logic. He could accept the threat of the *KOSMOS*. He had accepted that from the beginning. They all had. And the door failure was just one of a thousand failures that could kill them and they had implicitly accepted when they had crawled into the cockpit. But he could not and would not allow *his* failure to threaten Anna. An EVA under the best of circumstances was dangerous. The one being contemplated would be on the razor edge of suicide. Anna would be alone, absolutely inaccessible. He could only see the ultimate horror — to be trapped in the cockpit, watching helplessly as she died. He loved her. Beyond his own life, he loved her. There was nothing Mark could say that would penetrate the irrational fog precipitated out of that love. He would do the EVA.

"Do you understand, Bob?!" Mark repeated his question.

"Yea. Yea, I understand." He lied.

Forty minutes later, Pettigrew and his abusive tongue were nowhere on Anna's mind. Her brain had no room for anything other than the rendezvous. She flew *Atlantis* while watching the *Nova* with all the intensity of a heart surgeon staring into an open chest cavity. Now, at a range of two hundred feet, it had once again assumed Promethean proportions — an instrument of their deaths if she made the slightest error and collided with it. She ducked her head into her shoulder to blot the sweat from her face. She was too busy to even key a microphone and had donned a headset. After the hours-long microcomputer wizardry of radar and star trackers and inertial measurement units, it had finally come, as it always did, to this — to the human eye and brain, to the skill of a pilot.

"We're at a hundred and fifty feet, Mark."

"Okay, Anna. I've started the airlock depress." Mark toggled through the dozen parameters that showed the status of his space suit — seen on a one-line LED window on the top of his chest pack. The numbers confirmed the neoprene sheath was holding a thin atmosphere of oxygen against his skin.

"Bob, I've got to get on the arm controls now. You're going to have to come back here and fly the bird."

Pettigrew unbuckled his lap belt and carefully floated from his seat. Anna watched, convinced the mission was over. There was no way this remnant of a man could be in possession of the catlike quickness that would be needed to complete the rendezvous. He clung to his emesis bag like a child holding a security blanket.

Hooking his feet under restraining loops, he grasped the orbiter's translation and rotation controls and slowly tilted his head upward to view the target. The motion opened his throat and encouraged his stomach to the exit. He gulped it back.

"It's got a slow tumble in the yaw axis." Anna stated the obvious, not sure if he was capable of recognizing it.

"Yea. I... I can see that." His stutter was hardly more than a croak.

The sweat was coming again and he closed his eyes. The preliminaries were always the same — a flood of saliva, an involuntary swallow response, a sensation of stuffy heat, a clammy drench of sweat.

"You're at ninety feet." Anna triangulated with *Atlantis's* TV cameras. They were too close for radar. "Looks like you're drifting forward."

"What?"

"You're too far forward. I won't be able to reach it with the arm. Keep the "T" of "United" centered in your window... eighty feet."

He tapped at the translational hand controller.

"No, Bob! That's the wrong direction!"

In the airlock, Mark was blind to what was happening, but Anna's half of the conversation was image enough. It was exactly as he had anticipated — the marine was going to fail.

Pettigrew's head was swimming, the *Nova* a blur, Anna's voice an echo.

"You've got to start rate-matching!" The long axis of the rocket had moved through a quarter revolution and was now skewed across the payload bay rather than aligned with it. Anna moved the arm clear.

A twist of the RHC brought *Atlantis's* nose to starboard.

"Good… seventy feet. We need to close faster." She glanced at the sun. It was approaching the horizon. God help them if they lost the *Nova* in the dark. Any contact with the monster could rip a radiator open or gouge out a swath of tile or smash a window — all mechanisms of death.

The marine banged out several sloppy commands in his chase for coalignment. One sprayed the rocket with effluent and induced motion in the pitch axis, further complicating his task.

"We've got an opening rate now… one hundred and ten feet. Stay in close, Bob! It's getting dark! Stay with it! Stop the yaw! Pitch! Pitch! Pitch!"

Nothing looked right to Pettigrew. He was a trapeze artist tucked into a flying somersault. He needed to anticipate, to measure with the eye and lead with his control inputs. But it was hopeless. His brain was no more capable of such dexterity than a house plant.

Without warning, he released *Atlantis's* controls.

"Bob, no! Get back on the controls! We're too close!" The rocket was a steel overcast in their windows.

Pettigrew ripped the plastic bag from the console, brought it to his face, and rammed his fingers down his throat to induce vomiting.

"What are you doing? Are you mad? Stop it! The *Nova!* It's going to hit us!"

She lunged for the orbiter's controls, but Pettigrew shoved her aside and took them himself.

"I've got it, Anna! Stay with the arm!"

She would have never believed it possible, but he was suddenly in control of the craft. With several twists of his wrist, he nulled the relative pitch rate that had been most threatening.

"The nausea was just hovering there. I… I couldn't do anything. But I always have a minute of relief after an attack. I had to make myself sick."

Anna didn't question. The man was giving her what she needed — flying *Atlantis* into a near perfect duet with the *Nova*. She lifted the arm and searched the scene of its wrist camera to find the grapple spike.

"I've got the grapple fixture on TV. I'm tracking. Give me some more roll. I'm running out of wrist pitch. More. More. That's it. Come forward. Good. Stop. I'm coming in." She steered the end effector over the shaft and squeezed the capture trigger. A snare of steel cables twisted around the spike, and panel indicators announced the finish of the chase. *Closed. Captured. Rigidized.* The *Nova* was now fixed to *Atlantis*.

"We've got it, Mark! We've got it!"

Mark was stunned. To that second, he had been expecting to hear a staccato of thrusters as Anna executed an emergency escape from Pettigrew's abortion. "How much time do we have?"

"Fifty-three minutes."

"Jesus! Start the first-stage elevation! Hurry! Take any short cut you can!" He was rotating the outer hatch handle as he gave the orders. "Frank, as soon as we're out, I want you to get to *Freedom's* cockpit, power her up, and load the burn targets. On the way, deploy the decoy rocket pack. Anna, where do you have the *Nova*?"

"I'm moving it to the pre-mate position." Mark visualized the scene. She would have the aft end of the rocket above *Atlantis's* cockpit, the massive tube tilted upward at a fifty-degree angle — appearing to project outward from *Atlantis's* forehead like the horn of a unicorn. In this attitude it would be aligned with the elevated first stage and would be ready to be joined with it.

"Keep it low for a minute so Frank can grab a handrail." He struggled to fold the airlock hatch to the floor, cursing the restrictions to his mobility. The suit's three psi of internal pressure had hardened it to the consistency of steel and left him with all the agility of the Tin Man of Oz.

With Darling holding his feet, Mark floated partially outside and connected their waist tethers to payload bay reels — their lifelines to *Atlantis*. To come free of these would be to begin a month-long fall into the earth's atmosphere.

"We're tethered, Frank. Let's go."

Mark jerked himself from the airlock. The iceman followed and immediately climbed the forward-bay handholds. At the top rung he stretched to grab a *Nova* handrail, then continued his hand sprint along the missile's body, his tether reel unwinding behind. Anna watched from the overhead windows, and when his transfer between vehicles was complete, she rushed to finish aligning the two rocket bodies.

Mark closed the airlock, then pushed himself into a glide across the twenty feet to reach the elevated tip of the first stage. He seized a handrail. "Okay, Anna, I'm in position. Start moving the *Nova* aft."

"Roger."

"Down six inches... starboard three. You need a touch of positive roll and negative yaw." Like a spotter calling corrections to a crane operator, he directed her.

She translated his calls into ever finer arm motions to null the misalignment. The mating of the monsters proceeded with glacial slowness. Mark readied the first bolt.

"That's it, Anna! We've got a soft-mate!"

She flipped on the arm brakes, and he threaded the first fastener into its hole and began to tighten it with the wrench.

"What's the time, Anna?"

"Thirty-five minutes."

Please, God, just one more miracle!

A second bolt was twisted home.

A third.

He released his chest tether and moved further around the circumference. The fourth, fifth, and sixth fasteners were tightened.

"Twenty-two minutes, Mark!"

In spite of the maximum-cold setting of his suit thermostat, the exertion lathered him in sweat. His fingers and forearms ached in fatigue.

Bolts seven, eight, and nine were wrenched into place.

The airwaves became a babble of numbers as Mission Control and Darling exchanged information on the final burn targets.

Bolt ten was seated and torqued.

Eleven.

"Six minutes!" Anna screamed the warning.

The last bolt was twisted into place. "Anna, blow the pyro!"

A shudder waved through the structure as the pyrotechnic clamp that held the first stage to the tilt table was detonated. Now the one-hundred-and-sixty-foot giant was held only by the remote arm. Anna began to lift it clear.

"Four minutes!"

Mark raced up *Freedom's* back.

"Three minutes!"

"Isolation valves… open. Helium reg pressure is good." Darling called the preburn checks.

"Two minutes!" Anna's announcements were now redundant. Mark had arrived at the left side of *Freedom's* cockpit and could see the countdown to engine ignition on the computer display. He moved between the port and center consoles and pushed back into restraining locks, then released his tether.

"One minute!"

"Release, Anna! Release!"

She squeezed the hand-controller trigger to open the snares, then drew back the arm. Mark and Darling were now free, commanding their own spaceship.

In both machines, hands shot for controls. At the close range, *Freedom's* engine exhaust could mortally wound *Atlantis*, and Anna moved her away in an emergency separation maneuver. Mark commanded maximum rates to steer his transport into the correct burn attitude — nose aligned directly along their orbit path.

"I'm clear, Mark! I'm a hundred and twenty feet away with an R-dot of seventeen! Burn!"

He was arming the *Nova* engines when the sound came — a buzzing noise — as if a mosquito had passed near his ear. Five seconds later the cue repeated. *Freedom's* threat-detection sensor was being tickled by the invisible beam of a Soviet search radar. Somewhere below, the enemy was watching.

"They're painting us, Frank." He squeezed off the first radar decoy and made his prayer. *Take the bait, you bastards! Please, take the bait!*

Valves opened, pumps spun to life, propellants mixed, *Freedom's* twin, first-stage engines silently blossomed fire. The journey began.

❖

Tuesday, 22 November
Soviet Tracking Ship, *Gagarin*

Senior Warrant Officer Vlas Bukharin was propped in his bed trying to divert himself from the blast-furnace heat with a cheap pornographic magazine and a bottle of vodka. As on every sail, the crew quarters' air-conditioning had ceased working before the harbor had been cleared. A noisy fan served as an ineffectual substitute, blowing stagnant, tropical air over his body. Except for a pair of shorts, he was stripped of clothing.

A photo of a woman guiding a hairless, oriental organ into her hairless, oriental orifice was his current object of fixation, and he tried to imagine what a fuck would feel like. It had been two and a half months since he had last had one, and then, the woman had been like the one in the picture — a Vietnamese whore.

His ship, the *Yuri Gagarin*, had sailed from Vladivostok more than three months ago and had provisioned at Cam Ranh Bay, Vietnam, on its way to a South China Sea station. The whore and the black-market vodka that scalded his throat had all been part of his personal provisioning in that port-o-call. In particular, the bottles of alcohol he had secreted aboard were necessary to survive the excruciatingly boring duty — tracking American spacecraft and data-linking the information to Moscow via satellite. Under the best of circumstances, the routine of the job was maddening. Now, idling in the fierce equatorial heat of their current location, it was a living hell.

"Senior Warrant Bukharin, are you there, sir?"

"What is it?" He answered the intercom while indulging himself in a photo of the same oriental couple now entangled in an imaginative position of oral sex.

"Sir, at acquisition, the American space shuttle had rendezvoused with the *Nova* rocket. There was but one target."

"So? Track it!" He cursed the inadequacy of the technicians that the training units provided. The rendezvous had been watched by the global network for hours. Even *Gagarin* had seen it in progress on the last orbit. It was hardly news that only a single target had come over the horizon.

"But sir, now there are *three* targets. Which should we track?"

Bukharin doubted the operator's observation, believing instead he had mistuned his radar and was seeing false returns. The equipment was old and, if not properly babied, could show squadrons of phantoms.

"Damn you, Manarov! Your orders were clear! Track the American shuttle!" A teletype message had arrived from Moscow shortly after the shuttle launch, directing all units to focus on the manned spacecraft.

"Sir, I... we are not certain which object is the shuttle. The three are rapidly diverging. One appears to be moving into a higher orbit."

The officer swung his legs to the floor and hurriedly began dressing. If he remained in the discussion, his men might miss getting any data and, considering the intense interest that Moscow held for the shuttle, that would certainly incur the wrath of his supervisors.

"Check your equipment, Manarov. I'll be there in a moment. And the stars protect you if I find you have botched this!"

The *Nova* flashed bullet-straight, increasing her speed nearly a hundred miles per hour for each second of flight. This first burn would not change the low point of her orbit. It would remain at *Atlantis's* altitude. But the increased velocity would slowly lift the machine to an apogee equal to that of the *KOSMOS*. She would trace an ellipse — the geosync injection orbit.

They were two minutes into the burn, and Mark could not yet see a change in their height or speed. Another sunrise was in progress, and the earth still appeared hugely close, its horizon curving only slightly. But that would soon change. The planet would shrink to a ball.

He found the ride similar to the late stages of a shuttle ascent — a soundless push, with only the g-forces to tell of something violent happening behind him. The exception was in the magnitude of those forces. *Freedom* had no throttle. She ran flat out, and as fuel consumption lightened her mass, she crushed her passengers.

But Mark was oblivious to the suffocating squeeze. It was the cyclic buzz of the Soviet radar, a beat in their headsets marking time to the nod of *Gagarin's* antenna, that occupied him. *Freedom* was a fly caught on the edge of a spider's web. She was slowly crawling toward safety — out of the operator's field of view — but the lethal insect could grab her at any moment. All the enemy had to do was spotlight them with a high-frequency track radar and stay with them until engine cutoff. They would then know precisely the orbit they had thrusted into and could pass that vector to the next radar, and it to the next, and so on around the world. They would never escape. Each site could have its sensors staring at an exact point on the horizon, waiting for him and Darling to rise into view. But, without the vector, those downrange operators would be blind. They would have to initiate a time-consuming search. *Freedom* might pass undetected while electronic fingers probed empty space.

Bukharin shivered in the frigid air of the radar control room. Men could live without air-conditioning. The electronics could not. The youthful rocket-forces technician that had paged him stepped aside and allowed Bukharin a view over the shoulder of another juvenile. He peered into the scope and knew immediately the glowing orange lines of phosphor were not phantom tracks. Sixteen years of radar experience told him that. As the conscript had reported, there were now three objects passing overhead.

"Sir, the objects are all on different trajectories and are expanding out of my search fan." The operator's voice was tainted with panic.

Bukharin's own panic began to rise. He grabbed the message clipboard and hastily paged through it to see if instructions addressing the fragmentation had arrived while he had been absent. None had. They were to track the shuttle. But which of the objects was that? It was a shell game with a ticking clock demanding a quick guess. He wished he had not indulged in the drink. A clear head was needed.

"Track the brightest object!"

The operator ran his hand over the slueball, placed the designate cursor on the target, then activated tracking. Above them, the radar stopped its sector sweep and steadied itself in a stare at one of the mysteries. It was the decoy. Senior Warrant Officer Vlas Bukharin had guessed wrong.

The threat warning tone ceased. Mark hesitated, afraid to celebrate lest his reprieve be only a momentary data glitch, but the quiet endured for ten seconds, twenty, thirty.

"Jesus!" The exclamation slipped from his throat. The distraction of the radar had caused him to miss the approach of engine cutoff. It was abrupt, just like that of the shuttle. He quickly recovered from the surprise and hurried through the postburn checklist procedures.

"Stand by for first stage jettison." He flipped the cover from a guarded switch, said a quick prayer he had made no mistakes in the installation of the explosive bolts, then pushed the button. A loud bang answered the prayer. They had shed the finished giant, a hulk that would endure for decades and, Mark thought, seed the sky with another decoy to confuse the Soviets.

They entered a weightless coast up an invisible hill twenty-two thousand miles high — a six hour climb. At the top they would fire the second-stage engine to tilt their orbit into the same plane as the equator. A full revolution later they would burn a final time to raise the low point of their orbit to geosync altitude, which would make their orbit a circle to coincide with the circle of the *KOSMOS*. It was an eighteen-hour charge to the enemy — across a potential battlefield that was, in every sense of the word, devoid of cover.

"Get some sleep, Frank. I'll take the first watch."

Darling adjusted his suit temperature, slaked his thirst with several pulls on the drink straw, then closed his eyes.

Mark twisted the rotational hand controller, and *Freedom's* steering jets pushed the vehicle into a slow end-over-end tumble. The idea had also been Dr. Striegel's — in all ways possible make *Freedom* look like a piece of junk. Typically, any unstabilized space object was somebody's refuse. If found between burns, the machine would appear electronically dead and uncontrolled. It might be enough to fool any searchers.

For the moment, the cream of the Milky Way was at his face, and Mark felt a brief sense of security in its immensity. How could anybody ever find them? With their vector unknown, they had become the proverbial needle in a haystack, swallowed by an all-encompassing blackness. Then the feeling departed as quickly as it had come. The enemy was clever. If they tried, they could find them. He wondered if, even now, a message announcing their departure was being passed up the chain of command? Were they under observation at this very moment? The threat detection sensor said *no,* but it only sensed the presence of radar energy. The enemy could also be searching in other parts of the electromagnetic spectrum — in the infrared or even in visible light. He imagined unseen beams probing around him — electronic pitchforks being stabbed into his haystack. His worry intensified with the thought the searcher's job would be getting easier. As *Freedom* rose higher, it would stay visible longer. And, he wondered, what type of early-warning sensors would an armed *KOSMOS* have? Maybe they were already in its sights.

He forced aside the worries. None were really new to him. In various degrees they had been on his mind since he volunteered for the mission. He would face them as they materialized, if, indeed, they ever materialized. For the present, only one threat was absolutely unambiguous —

Atlantis's ET door — and he turned his thoughts to it, praying fiercely that God would extend today's miracles to Anna's EVA. He tried to include a petition that Pettigrew recover enough to do the EVA, but it was fainthearted. The man had been so devastated by the illness Mark doubted if even God could command a miracle enough to make him fit. Anna was their only hope. If she failed, they were all dead, empowered with the ability to choose the manner of their death — a slow suffocation in orbit as their oxygen was consumed, or a quick, reentry incineration.

His body interrupted. The zero-gravity fluid shift had filled his bladder and he urinated, hoping as he did so he wouldn't soon see the fluid floating in his face. He didn't.

His stomach was next to demand attention, and he took several deep draws on the food straw. It was something he should have done earlier. The calories refilled his severely tapped energy well and lifted his spirits. He began to dwell on the day's success.

They had done the impossible. Under extreme duress, they had made the rendezvous, assembled *Freedom*, and made the first trans-*KOSMOS* burn. They could even still be in possession of that most life-guarding of all elements — the element of surprise. Then, there was Striegel's masterpiece — *Freedom*. It was functioning flawlessly, and the suits continued to hum and whir with unflagging obedience. There was a lot to be thankful for.

The cathedral of stars that covered him provided an even greater sense of well-being, reminding him of what he was doing, of where he was going — upward at six miles per second into an orbit that no man had ever circled. Even the *Apollo* astronauts, crammed in their capsules, could not have enjoyed the earth as he would soon see it.

Then it came. *Freedom* finally tumbled enough to reveal the planet. For a moment, he was afraid, overcome with the same sensation of awe as a commoner might experience in a king's throne room. He was an intruder in the sanctuary of God, seeing creation from the mightiest of seats.

The horizon now fell steeply away in a blue arc of sun-sheened Atlantic. Ahead lay the tans of Africa. The thin veil of earth's air was spotlessly transparent, and he could see the vast Namibian sand dunes. Eons of wind had rippled them like a disturbed pond of ocher water. There was no obstruction to his view — no walls or multipaned glass to limit the eye. He felt naked. The suit no longer covered his flesh, and the monster craft no longer grew from his back. He was a new Icarus with wings that endured, as much a creature of flight as any bird.

CHAPTER 14

Wednesday, 23 November
Mission Control

Killingsworth watched the lighted shuttle symbol slowly blink along the orbit trace. The map was the only item on the Mission Control projection that made the slightest sense to him, and he could see *Atlantis* was approaching western Africa. He had been told her crew was midway through the eight-hour sleep period, although he could not imagine anyone sleeping under the circumstances of this mission. On second thought, he decided Pettigrew was probably capable of sleeping before a firing squad.

The map also gave *Freedom's* position. It was moving steadily behind *Atlantis*, an effect of orbital mechanics that had been explained to him but that he did not understand. There had been nothing on the radios from its crew, which the optimists took as good news and the pessimists suspected. He was not sure in which camp he resided. The plan had been to run silent, but dead men were mute, too, and he had periodic seizures in which he envisioned a blast-riddled *Freedom* silently bearing corpses into the abyss. In another hour they would know — a second burn was scheduled. If the crew was safe, if the machine was functioning, the burn would be executed and the air force tracking radar would see the orbit change.

He continued to agonize over whether to notify Judy and the other next-of-kin of the door problem. Would it help prepare them? He removed her phone number from his pocket and laid it on the console, staring at the horror it represented. He could see the woman — auburn hair, attractive. She had a right to know. It was her husband. He was not God. But after another twenty minutes of the debate, he assumed a godly role and decided to withhold the information. The door could yet be closed and the crew saved.

Wednesday, 23 November
Freedom

"Something is coming." Darling reached across the center console to shake Mark's arm. The contact woke him from a shallow sleep.

"Huh?"

"Something is coming… twelve-thirty."

Mark was instantly alert and searching.

"It is glinting in the sun. There. It just flashed."

Mark saw it, a white burst just to the right of the nose. With no background for scale, it was difficult to judge distance.

"Get the laser on it. Check range."

Darling started with the switches while Mark twisted the RHC to stop their tumble and put the mystery on the nose. *Freedom's* thrusters shuttered their response and the machine steadied. Mark cursed. The effluent from the forward jets made a blizzard of ice crystals that flashed in the sunlight like a million shards of mirror. They were suddenly blind to the object. He slammed forward on the THC to push them out of the cloud.

There was no difficulty in seeing it now. The frequency of glint was higher, the flashes brighter. It was coming down their throats — fast. The iceman stopped work with the laser range finder. It would be a wasted effort.

"It must be the *KOSMOS* firing at us!" Mark was thrown back to Vietnam. A SAM was drilling toward him. He remembered the recipe for escape — put it on the nose, wait until you couldn't stand it any longer, then yank the aircraft into a hard turn the missile could not follow. This SAM was already on the nose, and a voice in his brain was screaming, "Break!" But that was impossible. Only the space machines of science fiction could climb and dive and turn with aircraft agility. It was impossible to significantly alter *Freedom's* orbit except by the enormous power of her main engine. And it was too late for that. Whatever was coming would be on them well before they could complete the complex second-stage start procedures.

The danger gleamed like the blade of a thrown knife. It was close enough he could see its rapidly rotating tubular shape. He was going to die, and in the microsecond reaction that came with that realization, his thumb mashed the decoy fire switch. A flash in the mirror and a quiver of the cockpit signaled release of the second rocket. It was their only chance — that the killer was radar guided and would be drawn off by the balloon. But it wasn't. It filled their faceplates.

He flicked the radio transmitter to standby and was preparing to make a deathbed call to Houston when a faded, but familiar pattern rolled into view. He aborted the call. "It's one of ours!"

There was no attack. The object was passing fifty feet over their heads — a spent upper stage from some long-forgotten launch, a ghostly derelict emblazoned with the American stars and bars. The flag was pitted and faded from decades of micrometeoroidal erosion.

Mark would have found his stupidity laughable except he had thrown away one of his two remaining decoys. "Goddamnit! I should've known! We're in a *transfer* orbit… a goddamn freeway! Everybody's been using it for years. I should've known there would be shit like that floating around! I wasted a decoy!"

"It is a small loss. The plane change burn is due in forty minutes. We would jettison the second decoy anyway."

Darling was right. The plan had been to leave one of the decoys in each vacated orbit — another fake for anybody who might be watching. And they would soon be leaving their current orbit. *Freedom* was approaching apogee — the crest of a geosync hill. Over the past six hours, her initial twenty-thousand-mile-per-hour impulse had been slowly nullified by gravity. She was now slow enough she could be turned, her orbit tilted level to the equator like the hoop of an inclined lamp shade might be adjusted to horizontal.

Mark punched up a navigation display, maneuvered to the burn attitude, then occupied the remaining moments before the firing with a study of the earth. *Freedom's* nadir was passing over the south-central Pacific, and that ocean filled the hemisphere from east to west and pole to pole. The extreme distance made the sea appear uniformly still and smooth — a blue disk on obsidian black. Only the white of the earth's weather systems and polar ice caps suggested the planet was more than a cosmic water drop.

The countdown toggled through one minute, and he continued the burn preparations.

"Thirty seconds."

"Helium iso valves are open. Good pressures."

"Fifteen seconds."

"Engine enabled."

"Five seconds." Mark pushed the THC to settle the main-engine propellants at the rear of their tanks. Without the shove of the thrusters, the fluid could be floating anywhere and the tank outlet could be dry.

"Ball valves are open. Looks good. Stand by." Another full-body slam announced engine ignition. As with the first-stage burn, the punishment was delivered in absolute silence and with no motion cues. The star field remained fixed. There were no spinning needles to record motion. No racing tapes. Nothing. Only the decrementing digits of VGO — velocity to go — said that a burn was in progress.

The shove ended. Lungs became functional again. The empty steel was jettisoned and the tumble restarted. Now the undertow of gravity began to suck them along a curve that would pass within a hundred-and-sixty-miles of the earth's surface — orbit perigee. It would be their final close approach to the planet before rendezvousing with the *KOSMOS*. At the next apogee, in twelve hours, a last burn would transform their ellipse into a circle — the same circle that the Soviet spacecraft traced. They would be on her heels.

❖

Wednesday, 23 November
Atlantis

Pettigrew bolted awake to the perception of great danger. A flash had filled the cockpit. Although black now painted every window and the cockpit was only faintly illuminated by the instrument lights, he was certain a brilliance had come through his eyelids to wake him. His first thought was that something had exploded, but *Atlantis* denied it. There were no computer alert messages, no red or yellow on her warning matrix. She was midnight-still, the steady rush of the cabin fan now an unsensed background noise.

A dream, he concluded. A check of the clock showed an hour still remaining in the sleep period, and he closed his eyes in a last chance at rest. The previous seven hours had yielded little.

He adjusted the hardness in his crotch, a condition that seemed grossly out of place on a body as miserable as his. But it was an effect of the environment. An absence of gravity and the abundance of displaced blood in the middle body produced wake-up erections that could cleave diamonds.

The flash came again a second time. Something earthward was the source, and he slipped his lapbelt to stretch back and investigate from the overhead windows. The next burst revealed the mystery. Tropical storms were pummeling southern India. The flashes were lightning. He watched jagged runs of electricity trace arterial patterns in the blackness. Some clouds fizzled continuously with pulsating gray-white luminosity, like malfunctioning fluorescent lights. In others, bolts were passed from cloud to cloud, triggering chain-reaction explosions that sped for hundreds of miles in one direction, then echoed back to the starting point — all in the space of seconds.

The scene receded from view, but he remained in a hover in the aft cockpit waiting for the hardness to melt. When it did, he turned to glide to the toilet to relieve his bladder. It was a maneuver executed slowly. Though it had been four hours since his last attack of nausea — a record — he knew he had not seen the end of it. A general feeling of malaise still pervaded him.

"What the… What are you doing?!" His assumption that Anna was asleep had been wrong. He had entered the downstairs to find her dressed in the liquid cooling garment and carrying a caddie of EVA equipment and tools into the airlock. Mission Control's teleprintered plan for doing the EVA floated nearby. The answer to his question was obvious. She was in the advanced stages of preparation for a space walk. She had already moved Mark's spare EMU into the chamber.

"I couldn't sleep. I'm getting ready for the EVA." She faced him with a severe look of determination.

"The hell you are! I'm doing it!"

Anna wanted to laugh. The wreck before her looked like an explorer who had stumbled into civilization after having suffered great privation. His bloodshot eyes were deep set in puffy purple rings, and a thick stubble of dark beard accentuated a waxy pallor. From just the manner in which he clung to the interdeck ladder, she was certain he was still in the grips of the illness. She forced her voice into a civil, rational tone. "Bob, look in the mirror and tell me you can do this EVA. There's no way. You're still sick." She resumed her work.

"I can do it, Anna! I *will* do it! Get out of the cooling garment!" He grabbed her arm.

"Damn you! Don't touch me!" She recoiled like a provoked snake.

Pettigrew drew back, realizing his mistake. Anna wasn't going to respond to orders. He made his own attempt at civility. "I can do the EVA. I'm better now."

This time, Anna did scoff. "Okay, okay. Prove it, Bob! Let go of the ladder! Turn upside down! Spin around!"

The challenge trapped him. He remained motionless, silent.

"What's wrong? Can't you do that?" Sarcasm hung thickly on the words. "You're going to have to do it out there!" Her arm shot out in a point. "Look at you! You've been vomiting for twenty-three hours! For God's sake, you haven't even been able to change out of your launch coveralls!" He glanced down at his clothes, stupidly surprised to see the accuracy of her observation. "And you're holding onto that ladder like… like… like you're afraid you're going to fall down. Don't be a fool, Bob! I'm doing the EVA!"

He refused to yield. He would not let his weakness threaten her life. She was too vulnerable. Outside, her hands would be her life. The suit would be agony, the gloves a torture. Even the ill fit of the cooling underwear portended danger. As small as Mark was, he still outweighed her by thirty-five pounds and was taller and had longer arms and legs. She swam inside the garment that was sized for him. It gathered in bulges on her body. Even her breasts, as swelled as they were, did not fill the chest. Through the loose weave, he could see the circles of her areolas bouncing freely whenever she moved. She would have minimal cooling from the device.

"Anna, I… Okay, okay. You're right. I can't do the EVA… now." His tone was conciliatory. "But I'm getting better." She shook her head in disbelief. "No, really. Please, listen to me. Really, I am. I can feel it. It's been almost four hours since I last vomited. In another day, maybe less, I'll be a hundred percent. I don't want you to go out there. It's just too dangerous. Let's wait. Please."

"Wait?!" She threw a hand up in frustration. "Wait?! God! God, Bob!

Every minute we wait, it's another minute we expose ourselves to the *KOSMOS*! For God's sake, we're *trapped*! *Trapped!* Can't you understand that?! We're a sitting duck! We can be *killed* if we wait!"

Pettigrew's anger flared, his pleading tone of seconds ago now history. "I don't give a shit about the *KOSMOS*! I'm not going to let you kill yourself!"

"Oh? You don't give a *shit*, huh?" The words were hissed. It was the first time he had ever heard her swear. "That seems to be your attitude about some *people*, too." In her rage, the innuendo on his trivial use of women — of her — slipped from her mouth. "Well *I* do care! There are two men out there who are depending on me and I'm not going to endanger them because of your stupidity! They could be on their way back right now! We may have to do an immediate deorbit after we grab them! I'm not going to wait around for a day and *hope* you get well enough! That delay could kill them! It could kill all of us!"

"Goddamn you, Anna! I'm not going to let you kill yourself!"

She glared at him. "Don't you talk to me like that! I told you! Never talk to me like that!"

"I'll talk to you any way I want to get it through that fuckin' head of yours, you're not doing this EVA!"

She slapped him. This time she had a good handhold and maintained her position. Her arm recocked and delivered another blow. Pettigrew didn't flinch. He, too, had a rigid hold and merely accepted the punishment.

For a moment, Anna matched his stare, her eyes searing his. Then she surrendered to the fact he would never be rational on the subject. It was like arguing with one of the lockers. She would ignore him. She turned, grabbed the tool caddie, and pushed it into the airlock.

"Anna, please, don't. I…"

"*Why?!*" His seemingly senseless badgering had broken her, and she whirled to face him. Tears were close. "Damn you! There's no other way! Why, Bob?! *Why are you doing this?!*"

"*Because I love you!*" He bellowed as madly as she. He had never wanted to say the words again, not after what had happened on the beach. But her resolve to do the EVA had gouged them from him.

Only *Atlantis's* droning intestinal murmur intruded on a sudden, library silence.

Anna was dumbstruck. *Why is he doing this? Why now, of all times, must he torture me? God, why is he doing this?*

This latest profession of love had come with the same urgency as when he had been in her bed, heaving on her, stabbing her with his obscene flesh, lying to her. Lies — then and now. She called on every emotional reserve she possessed but could not stop the tears. They filled her eyes, weightless drops that refused to run. They thickened and his image blurred beneath them. It was a lying image. The coal-black eyes that seemingly begged and pleaded and needed were just part of an expert lie.

"I love you, Anna." Quietly, he repeated the words.

She blinked, and the flicker ejected shimmering droplets of liquid. Anna was emotionally finished. She could form no reply. She just wanted to be left alone. She wanted the lies to end. He had other women. He could lie to them.

Too tired to care about the display of feminine weakness, she wiped her eyes, drilled him to the soul with a last pitying look, then turned to release the airlock hatch from its stowed position. She would close herself in the chamber and finish dressing. It would be difficult, but in her training, she had managed several solo donnings. She would do it again.

Pettigrew's own eyes began to tear at her latest silent rejection. "Anna, please." He released the ladder and grabbed for her, intending to turn her back into the conversation. The touch was too much. She exploded.

"Get your hands off me! Damn you! Goddamn you! Why do you want to hurt me?! Why do you lie to me?!" She released her hold on the hatch to force his hands away, and together they tumbled into the middle of the volume. Her shouts grew hysterical. "Leave me alone!"

Pettigrew's arms flailed in a desperate attempt to reattach himself to the wall. He was getting sick. A hand inadvertently brushed across her breasts and she screamed louder. "Don't! Don't touch me!" She tried to slap him, which only churned them into a more violent tumble.

Pettigrew finally separated from her and his back slammed against the lockers. He was upside down and used the floor-mounted foot loops to stabilize himself. Gingerly, he righted himself and tucked his feet under the straps. But the anchor was too late. His stomach was at the back of his throat.

Anna grabbed the airlock hatch and whipped around to confront him. She was now wailing like a damned soul, a shower of tears orbiting her head.

Pettigrew begged. "Anna, God, Anna, what's wrong?! Why won't you believe me?! I'm not lying to you! I love you! That's why I don't want you to do this EVA! If anything happens to you, I'll die! I'll die!"

"Love me? *Love me?!* Oh, God! Is that what you said to the other woman the day after you *loved* me?!"

Pettigrew went rigid, completely blind-sided by the accusation. He groped for an answer, but none came. Anna did not need one. There was admission enough in his eyes, and she attacked viciously. "Yes! Yes! I know! I called your house and she was there! *Big stud astronaut Pettigrew!*" She spat each word as if it was exceptionally obscene.

In a heartbeat, it all made sense to him. She had tried to love him. There had been a seedling of it growing within her and he had crushed it. His fear had crushed it. *No! No! Oh, God, no!*

Anna backed into the airlock and reached to swing the hatch into place. Pettigrew fought his stomach. "No, Anna, no!" He frantically searched his pockets for an emesis bag. There was none. The hatch was moving closed. "Anna, please. That woman…"

She ignored him. There was only one thing she wanted — to escape him, to escape into the airlock.

A first dry heave rippled up his throat. He snatched a nearby towel to his face and began hacking the wet waves that followed. Through the attack, he screamed an explanation. "The woman at my house… she didn't mean anything to me! Anna, she didn't mean anything! I was afraid! Oh, please listen, Anna! I…" She did not listen. The hatch handle was turning closed as he ducked his head into the towel for a third time.

Behind the door, Anna struggled for composure, trying to stop the sobbing, to arrest her tremble. She had to recover. Mark and Darling were depending on her. She had to forget about Pettigrew, endure the pain, see only the mission, only the EVA. Discipline! *Discipline!* Mental discipline would be her salvation — the discipline that had been drilled into her by her mother, by the nuns, by the navy, by her instructor pilots, by her astronaut training.

Pettigrew wiped bloody expectorant from his mouth, then hurled himself onto the hatch. He had insane intentions — to physically restrain her, to stop her from the EVA, to make her believe in him. But the dimmest flicker of reason penetrated the idiocy of emotion. The very root of his attraction to the woman was her strength. On so many occasions he had marveled at it. There was nothing he could do or say to make her abandon the EVA. Additional pleading would only distract her, and distractions could lead to mistakes — and mistakes to death.

The thoughts brought a self-damning curse. He had let his emotions take him — take Anna — to the brink of disaster. But he would end the madness now. When she was next able to hear him — after she had donned her headset— she would find him as mechanistic as Darling. He would follow her through the checklists with exacting precision. He would be her protector to the limit that was possible.

It took her the better part of an hour, but Anna succeeded in dressing herself. She remained hanging on the wall for an additional hour, washing the nitrogen from her blood and protecting herself from the bends by breathing the suit's pure oxygen.

Pettigrew used the delay to study the plan that Mission Control had uplinked — to study it and to grow even more fearful. Anna was to anchor her tether reel as far aft in the payload bay as possible and then attempt a superman-style dive toward the aft edge of the left wing. The reel would unwind behind her. Grabbing the elevon — a movable flap on the trailing edge of the wing — she was to translate inboard, hand over hand, along its perimeter, to the small gap between it and the fuselage. Hopefully, that gap would provide another hand path to the functioning left ET door that was to be reopened. She would use an additional tether to anchor herself to the exposed plumbing in that cavity. In her final configuration, she would be tied to the left door and free to float to the malfunctioning right door. Pettigrew would monitor her work from the remote arm TV camera.

"I'm ready."

"Go slow." The marine watched on TV as the outer hatch opened.

Anna remained hypersensitive to his voice, listening for any hint he was drifting back into insanity. There was none. Since she had slammed herself in the airlock, his radioed voice had been the model of professionalism, crisp and cooperative in every way. It was a change she prayed would endure.

She exited the airlock, moved up the bulkhead handrails, and traversed to the left edge of the payload bay.

"How are the gloves?"

"They're okay." She lied. Even the simple task of hooking the tether-reel eyelet had been difficult. Her fingers were too short and she had to jam them into the glove crotches to grasp anything. Whenever she did, the pain was severe, as if she were pushing the webs of her fingers onto dull ax blades.

"Good. I can see you from the windows now." She had moved far enough aft to allow the direct view, and he scrutinized her suit to ensure her chest-mounted load of tools was properly stowed and no lines were dangling to create a hazard. The tether reel slipped freely along the slide wire as she pulled herself hand over hand by the adjacent rails.

At the port aft corner, she moved the spool to a hard point, then paused to study the challenge — getting to the trailing edge of the elevon. Twenty feet of flat wing surface separated her from it. Beyond, there was a one-hundred-and-sixty-mile drop to the earth, but that view was not frightening. Even when she made her dive, her body could not fall. It was still in orbit and tethered to *Atlantis*.

"Be careful, Anna." Pettigrew's soul formed prayers like an auctioneer singing a bid. Even a sprained wrist could be disabling enough to kill her.

"I will. Here goes."

Grasping a handrail with both hands, she aimed herself, torpedo-like, at the elevon, then pulled. Within a yard of travel she realized her mistakes. Besides putting too much energy into the pull, she had not considered the great bulk of the backpack. It scraped the bulbous projection of *Atlantis's* maneuvering engine pod and deflected her downward. Three hundred pounds of flesh and machine slammed into the wing surface.

"Uh!" Pettigrew heard the breath-stealing grunt over the radio.

"Anna!"

Her body ricocheted from *Atlantis*, unconstrained until the tether unwound to its full length. At that point, it drew taunt and jerked her, like a dog being snapped rearward after a headlong run to the end of its leash. Unlike the dog, though, Anna had no ground to fall to and tumbled into a multiaxis gyration. Her arms and legs thrashed in an instinctive but futile effort to control her motions.

"Anna! No! Don't move your arms! You're getting tangled!" The tether was between her legs, under her right arm, and around the back of her neck.

She stopped the reckless flail, but her body motions remained — a rebounding yo-yo, continuing in an arc on an ever-shortening radius as the reel spring pulled her back. A handrail came into view and she seized it, but her momentum carried her onto her back, hyperextending her elbow and brutally jamming her left breast and ribs into the suit arm bearing. She kept a death grip on the rail in spite of the eye-watering pain.

"…side." Her answer was salted with static.

"Say again, Anna!"

Unintelligible garbage came from the speaker.

"Switch to your backup radio! Signal if you can hear me!" She flashed an OK sign and made the change.

"I'm okay. I just banged my side a…" Static smothered the rest.

Whatever the problem, it was affecting both radio transmitters. Pettigrew suspected damage to the antenna. The suit had taken a vicious hit on the sill of the payload bay.

"Anna, forget this shit! It's crazy! And your radios are all fucked up! Please come back inside! I'm feeling much better! I could do this tomorrow!" This time he was not exaggerating. As quickly as the illness had come, it was now leaving him.

"…must just be a transmitter problem. I'm hearing you loud and… not giving up. I just… too hard. I'll go slower…" Static chopped the sentences.

Damn that woman! Damn her!

Anna shivered from fright. She had a great urge to urinate and did so. Pettigrew's argument came back to slap her with a vengeance. The suit was an inquisitor's torture chamber. She had hardly even started the EVA and already her hands were in agony, her elbows and knees burned raw, and one breast deeply bruised.

Pettigrew directed her out of the tangle of steel cable. An occasional word mixed with scratchy hisses were all that came through the speaker, but her motions indicated she understood. She was finally ready for a second attempt.

"Slow, Anna! Very slow!"

She waved an acknowledgment, aimed her body — making certain this time it would miss the OMS pod — then pulled with a fraction of the energy of her first effort. The patchwork of thermal blankets slid slowly by, followed by the flicker of the painted red bars of the American flag. The aft portion of the wing rose toward her, and she lifted her arms to prevent any inadvertent contact. The slightest touch would produce an equal reaction and push her away from the surface. The elevon hinge line passed — six feet to go. The convergence was perfect. Three feet. She reached forward. The edge was at her fingertips. She grabbed.

"Perfect, Anna! Beautiful!"

The elevon was covered by glass-smooth tiling that would have been impossible to hold except its trailing edge was four inches thick, just barely within the span of her hands. But the success was not without cost. The palm bar, a piece of steel woven into the gloves and positioned incorrectly for her smaller hands, gouged the sides of her knuckles like an awl.

She began the fifteen-foot hand shuffle toward the fuselage. At the application of each new grip, the steel stabbed deeper. Pain corrupted her optic nerve with flashing points of colored light.

Pettigrew called her progress. "Ten feet to go... five... three. You better hold up there, Anna, and swing underneath."

"Yea." If she said more, it was lost in the static.

Thus far, she had been doing a handstand along the top of the elevon. Now it was necessary to move underneath and continue the traverse in a weightless hang from its edge. She moved carefully. To lose her grip would mean starting over, and she was certain she lacked the physical reserves to repeat what she had just accomplished.

She swung underneath the wing, and the black quilt of belly tiles came into view. They reflected an earth that was a million feet below. The island of Madagascar floated on the cobalt blue of the Indian Ocean, its northern half covered with a pox of thunderstorms. They cast long shadows to the east and reminded her sunset was near. The darkness would complicate her work.

She began the forward translation. The imaginary awl found the most delicate end of a nerve and twisted into it like an ice-pick being rocked back and forth under a fingernail. The pain inflamed her arms and induced a tremble.

I'm going to fail! Three men are going to die because I can't do this! For the first time in her life, she was faced with the reality that her skill as a pilot, her quickness of hand and eye and mind, might not save her.

Pettigrew watched her groping movements on the television monitor. Occasionally her transmitter would kick in and he would catch several cycles of heavy breathing. He said nothing. It was obvious she was at the absolute limit of endurance and the slightest distraction could force an error.

She reached the forward end of the elevon-fuselage gap but could not yet celebrate. A four-foot span of tile still separated her from the door cavity. She would have to stretch across it — float parallel to *Atlantis's* belly, holding herself by her right hand and reaching with her left.

Her pulse rose to one-sixty. A gasping respiration rushed oxygen to starving muscles.

She stretched forward with her left hand and it found the opening. She was so very close. All she needed was a handhold in the cavity. The door linkage and plumbing provided many of them, but she was flat against the belly in a crucifixion mimic and could not see. Nor could she feel. Pain was still being conducted to the brain, but not the sense of touch.

The anchor of her right hand began to loosen and she tried to remake it, but all muscle response had ceased. Like an amputee, the appendage was merely a memory. The hand came free.

No! She was crying — the sputtering cries of someone who had pulled up lame within sight of a finish line and was struggling to hobble the last yards.

Her only remaining body contact with *Atlantis* was the bend of her left wrist. It hung over the edge of the door cavity — not enough to hold her, but a reaction point to pull against. She did, and began a slow drift toward the opening. The movement gave her greater access to the cavity and she made a last chance thrust into it. A sharp pain was the only indication the open palm had jammed onto something. She squeezed — or tried to. She could not be certain the flesh had responded. But a pull inward brought an answering tug. She had a handhold!

"…at… door…"

"Are you tethered?" The darkness blinded Pettigrew to her progress.

"…doing…"

Goddamn these radios! Goddamn them!

Groping with the stump that substituted for a right hand, she used a spare tether to anchor herself on a piece of tubing, then collapsed into a zero-gravity drift. She had done it.

CHAPTER 15

Wednesday, 23 November
Teheran

Ayatollah Hashemi helped the aged, stroke-crippled patriarch to his seat, paused to receive a mumbled blessing, then fell to his knees in worship with the rest of the inner circle of Iranian leadership. As he bowed his forehead to the tiled floor, he prayed for the dead men that surrounded him — for they were surely dead. In minutes, their bodies would be charred atoms and he would be the master of the Iranian people.

Justice will be done. Less than an hour ago, his bodyguard had whispered the coded message telling him everything was in order for the car bombing. Like puppets, the Soviets would serve him, and, in return, he would... What? What would he do? Reward the infidels by opening his country to their navy? They certainly believed it. But he was not so certain. He would pray for divine inspiration on the question.

The service ended and the men rose from their pillowed kneelers. Robed, lesser functionaries appeared from an anteroom to carry The Most Revered Patriarch to his wheelchair. Hashemi leaned to kiss the man's cheek in a final act of respect. It was time the old man left this world, he thought. He had survived a dozen major operations, was down to a single kidney and lung, wore a catheter and pacemaker, and was a slave to a dialysis machine. Allah had called him long ago, but modern medicine had intervened to delay his departure. Now, the five hundred kilos of Czechoslovakian plastic explosives that were parked two blocks from the mosque would undo the miracles of the doctors and assist in his final farewell — as it would his chosen successor who was following the patriarch from the room.

Hashemi silently cursed the successor, certain he had wrongly influenced the patriarch's decision on the heirship. It was he, Hashemi, who had been most faithful, most devoted to the Law. It was he who would best lead the Iranian people, who would best do Allah's will. Allah had told him as much in his private meditation.

Even through the thick walls of the mosque, the roar of the crowd reached him. The Most Revered Patriarch had exited the building and been sighted by the people. It was sad, he thought, that so many of those faithful would also have to die. But it was God's will. Those who perished would surely be rewarded. They were martyrs — unwitting ones, of course — but martyrs just the same. They were sacrificing their lives so he could lead the greater masses closer to God.

He walked into an adjacent chamber, blessed those who waited, then took his seat as the presiding judge in the Court of Justice. Immediately, two guards roughly handled a sobbing, black-veiled woman into his presence. She fell on her knees and the prosecutor read the charge — adultery — and presented his evidence. Hashemi stroked his beard in what others saw as an act of serious judicial contemplation. But his mind was far from the proceedings.

The patriarch should be in his automobile by now.

The waving black mound before him beat her breast and begged for mercy, protesting that she was a good woman. Allah had blessed her with two infant sons. Was that not a sign of her devotion? Who would raise them if she was condemned? Her husband had been martyred in battle with the Iraqis. There were so few men left after that great slaughter, she cried. A woman cannot live alone. Loneliness had driven her to forget the Law. It would never happen again.

Hashemi had heard the story countless times before. Why did they bother?

The masses will be cheering the motorcade. The patriarch and his chosen one will be giving their blessing. The assassins will be watching.

He reached out with the scepter and moved the veil from the woman's face. Tears flowed. Eyes begged. For the sake of my children, spare me, was the sobbing incantation she maintained.

In slow, delicate movements, he traced the young and beautiful features with the ivory knob — up a flawless, olive cheek; around huge, dark eyes; across quivering, bloodless lips. She was certainly a gift from God to honor man, was his thought. But the Law was the Law.

The motorcade drivers will slow because of the throngs. In their zeal to glimpse the patriarch, the swarms will press in on the vehicles. They will slow to a crawl. The assassins will wait until the exact moment.

"Justice will be done... Death."

The woman's shrieking wails were covered by a deafening explosion.

❖

Wednesday, 23 November
Atlantis

Anna stayed rag-doll limp, accepting whatever attitude and position the two tethers allowed. She had yet to detach the line connecting her to the payload bay. That, and everything else, could wait for a more complete recovery — and for sunrise. The illumination provided by the remote arm spotlight and her helmet-mounted lights was too feeble to work by, even if she had had the strength to do so.

Thirst finally shoved its way through the crowd of other bodily abuse, and she ducked her head down for the plastic nipple of the water bottle. It wasn't there. In the haste to escape Pettigrew, she had forgotten to install it. Likewise, she had left the food bar behind. Both would have been godsends now. Her mouth was a desert.

Too quickly, the dawn came, the strata of colors briefly tinting *Atlantis's* belly.

With all the enthusiasm of a battered boxer rising for another three-minute pounding, she gritted her teeth and seated her hands fully into the gloves. "I'm ready to start." Uncertain of her radio, she supplemented the call by waving at the remote arm camera and then pointing to the jammed door.

"Roger, Anna. I've got the autopilot holding belly to sun so you'll have good light. Be careful — extra careful — when you stow your reel." It was her only means of return to the payload bay, and she had every intention of being cautious.

She pulled herself back to the left cavity, found a hard point for the bay reel, and removed it from her hip. Tether management — it was the religion of the EVA crewman, practiced as a God-given commandment that promised life.

Finally, she was free to maneuver to the jammed right door, and a gentle push propelled her there. It yawned obliquely open about seventy degrees, a fortunate angle because it allowed ready access to the inside of the hinge line. She hovered over the maw, steadying herself with a hand on the door edge.

"I don't see anything that's obviously jammed."

Enough syllables reached Pettigrew that he could understand. "If you don't find anything right away, come back in. I'll try tomorrow."

She ignored him and pulled nearer to study the forward hinge. *The motor. The linkage. There's nothing jamming it!* An exhausted adrenal gland managed to squeeze out a slug of stimulant. If the blockage could not be found, they were dead.

"There's noth——" She hesitated. A pinpoint of reflected sun had flashed from a crevice of machinery. A move to the side gave a better perspective. "...it! Bob... see it!"

It took six more broken transmissions to describe the find. A two-inch length of steel safety wire securing an adjacent nut — and left uncut by a worker during the rush to get *Atlantis* ready — had jammed the hinge.

She removed a needle-nosed pliers from her chest tool caddie and grabbed the tip of the wire, but it resisted as if it were welded to the hinge. After a painful and exhausting struggle, she abandoned the tool and looked for another. The choices were meager: a vice grip, a wrench, and a screwdriver. Only the screwdriver looked promising, and she removed it and began to jam it into the linkage, pushing and twisting, trying to insert it as a wedge to loosen the wire. But the thickness of the blade was just a fraction too great. It was another exercise in isometrics — steel against immovable steel with flesh and bone punished in the stalemate.

Thirst began to rule her brain, to even displace the pain. Her tongue was swollen, and a second urination burned as if pure salt was flowing from her.

She was twenty minutes into the torture before it happened. The blade found the crevice. Anna froze, afraid to believe it was true. But it was no trick. There was less than a quarter inch of penetration, but it was enough.

With the delicacy of someone setting nitroglycerin aside, she ungripped the screwdriver, reclaimed the pliers, and squeezed the jaws onto the tiny splinter.

Even over the distortion of the radio, Pettigrew could identify her shriek as one of joy.

"You got it?!"

She floated from behind the door and held the pliers for the camera.

"Good job! Now, move back to the left door and I'll close the right." With the repair complete, he had no thought except to get her back inside as quickly as possible. She was still vulnerable to a hundred different dangers.

She made the move, and Pettigrew threw the switches to finish the door closing.

"Wave when you've transferred back to the payload-bay tether."

Another thumbs up signaled she understood.

The sun was nearing the horizon, but now she was unconcerned about the approaching night. Compared to what she had just done, the tether transfer would be trivial — clip the bay reel to her hip, release the left cavity anchor, and be effortlessly pulled back to the bay. As pain-deadened hands fumbled with the tethers, she anticipated the glorious reward that would soon be hers — water. It was a dangerous distraction, a sin against the commandment of tether management.

She released the line from the left door and waved to the camera that she was returning to the bay. A hard shove started her. Pettigrew saw the signal and turned to the switches. The door began to move.

He never heard her scream. The radio failed to transmit it. He watched the door indicator flip to closed and then turned to look at the television. The belly was now a smooth quilt of glistening black, a shield impervious to the heat of reentry. If needed, *Atlantis* could run from orbit. He floated to the aft windows to cheer Anna's return.

But only the reel greeted him. Glinting silver in the last light of the sun, it rose above the wing like an empty fishhook drawn upward from the water. Obediently, it wound itself into the bay. The sun sank. Darkness ruled. Anna was gone.

"Anna!"

Wednesday, 23 November
Red Sky Control Center

One hundred meters underground, Kobozev entered the control

center radiation/germ-warfare airlock. Zhilin and Ryabinin followed.

"Where is Yazov?"

Zhilin answered Kobozev's growl. "Sorokin is delivering an address at the economics ministry on the need for market reform. Yazov feared his absence from such an important address would look suspicious."

A hissing rush of air signaled that pressure equalization was in progress. Kobozev shouted over the noise. "Yazov will betray us to Sorokin at the first opportunity. Your men..."

Ryabinin interrupted him. "...are watching and listening. Yazov will never be alone with Sorokin."

A light flashed to indicate they could proceed, and the trio stepped into tunneling that led to the control room. The passage was dimly lit and dank smelling. Even though all of the surfaces were finished in reinforced concrete, water still percolated through the walls, forming an occasional puddle.

"Give me the Teheran report." The hollow echo of Kobozev's voice joined with the sharp echoing *click* of the party's brisk steps.

"A complete success, though not without some moments of concern. The successor was killed instantly, but the patriarch survived the initial blast, in spite of the loss of both legs. He was rushed to the hospital but died moments after arrival."

"And what of Hashemi? Is his succession being questioned?"

"No. The state radios and presses are already announcing his leadership."

"Has he made any statements concerning the welcome of our forces?"

"None."

Kobozev stopped. For a moment, the only sound was the echo of dripping water. "None? Does he betray us?"

"The man is not a fool. He has to understand his vulnerability. If we leak the videos we made... which he *knows* we made... of his underling discussing the assassinations, the populace will tear him to pieces, literally. We *own* Hashemi, now and forever. He'll make the announcement. Skripko will not have his audience with the president for many hours yet. There is still time."

Kobozev considered the assessment and agreed. There was still plenty of time for the statement. He resumed walking. "What has been the response of the Americans?"

"They deny Iranian charges they were behind the bombing or are preparing to invade the country. Both are accusations that have taken a life of their own in the streets of Teheran."

"Has there been any sign of a military response by the president?"

The defense minister answered. "No. The disposition of their forces in the region remains unchanged... a guided-missile cruiser, two destroyers, and a mine sweeper."

"And their space shuttle?"

"It remains in orbit. The *Nova* also, although its orbit has changed."

It was a statement Striegel would have given his good leg to hear. The first rocket-propelled decoy was still leading the baying hounds. It had taken several hours, but the Soviet tracking network had uncovered the mistake made on the *Gagarin* — the object reported as the shuttle was not. Headquarters had made the obvious conclusion — it had to be the *Nova*.

"Changed?" Kobozev paused with his hand on the control room door. The dim lighting gave him the appearance of a caped Beelzebub standing at the portals of his subterranean hell.

"Yes. Initially, there was some confusion with our rocket forces, but they have sorted it out. The *Nova* has moved into a different orbit."

"Red Sky..."

Zhilin preempted the question. "Is not threatened. The *Nova*'s orbit is still inclined by twenty-eight degrees to the equator, and it touches a high point of only eight hundred kilometers."

"Then what mission is it performing?"

"There is no military mission from that orbit. In all likelihood, the astronauts made a best attempt at a repair, but it was not completely successful. The rocket again malfunctioned as it was thrusting away."

Kobozev appeared satisfied with the answer and Zhilin continued. "But there were also reports of a mysterious third object leaving the vicinity of the shuttle for a higher orbit."

"What? What is it?"

Zhilin had anticipated the response and rushed to calm his leader. "Such reports are not uncommon. Equipment malfunction or atmospheric disturbances could be the cause. And that appears to be the case for this report, because no other tracking site has acquired the mystery."

"And what if it is not some malfunction? What if the object is real? What if the shuttle has launched an attack on Red Sky? Musa, if you have failed me!" As he had come so temptingly close to complete success, as the mantle of the chairmanship hovered over his shoulders, Kobozev had fallen victim to the paranoia that something would bring disaster at the last second. The tone in which he now addressed his friend had previously been reserved for Yazov.

Zhilin stiffened. He was not a man accustomed to verbal abuse. He was as much a part of the conspiracy as Kobozev. A mistake by any would kill them all. And he had made no mistakes. His forces would find the mystery object — if it existed. He answered coldly, formally. "Then we will find it and kill it, Comrade Kobozev. I have given orders for a careful watch to be maintained."

"Kill the *Nova!*" His paranoia drove Kobozev to the immediate decision. He owned the skies. He would use the power.

"What? The *Nova* is no threat to Red Sky!" Zhilin was now shouting.

"I said, kill the *Nova!* There are things happening you cannot explain! Equipment malfunctions, atmospheric disturbances, unknown missions! You make *guesses* when our lives hang in the balance! Kill it!"

"Killing the *Nova* will occupy assets that could be used to search for the mystery. The *Nova* is already crippled. We should leave it."

"Kill it!"

A moment later, Zhilin was on the phone relaying the order. The decoy had done its job. A useless, metal-skinned balloon would occupy a world net of radar and draw the fire from a trillion-ruble death star.

❖

Wednesday, 23 November
Moscow

As Kobozev had been stepping into the Red Sky control room, Yazov had been hurrying to his limo. A guard held the door, while another waited by the driver's side. He was certain they were both agents of Ryabinin's ministry. His men were everywhere, denying him the opportunity to save himself. But he would trick them. He glanced at his watch. *Yes, there is time!* Sorokin's address had ended early enough.

"Take me home!" He chased the curt order by tossing back a handful of stomach tablets. A sour belch and loud flatulence acknowledged the arrival of the medicine. His intestines had become organs of constant pain. Nothing helped.

At his residence, he closed and locked the door, checked the security of every window, then searched each room and closet. Except for his wife, the apartment was empty. And he knew where he would find her — where she always was at this time of the day.

He came to the bathroom door and listened to ensure he had arrived at the right moment. Yes, the timing was perfect. With a deep huff of his chest he resolved for a final time he would go ahead with the plan, then entered.

"What are you doing here? Get out! You know I don't like company while I'm bathing!"

He faced a manatee-shaped woman who was poised with one foot in the still-filling tub of bubble bath. Pendulous breasts with huge, dark areolas stretched for the earth like giant drips of tallow. Yazov beheld his salvation.

"I said, get out!"

He ignored the woman and reached to turn up the volume of the portable TV that sat on a nearby table. It was a ritual for her, to bathe while watching an East German soap opera. Now, the sounds from the box would cover the listening devices Ryabinin's henchmen had certainly installed. He unplugged the drain and opened the taps fully to add more camouflaging noise.

"What are you doing? Are you insane?!" She reached to reverse his actions, but he batted her hands away.

"Sit down and listen!" He spoke in a fierce whisper, simultaneously pulling her into the water. The splash of her buttocks raised a tsunami that crested the tub and soaked his trousers. "Shut up and listen to me, you cow!"

The woman visibly startled at the viciousness of the address. Her husband had never talked to her in this manner. Quite the contrary, it was she who normally lashed at him with a barbed tongue.

Yazov knelt at the side of the porcelain and continued his whisper. "I am in mortal danger because of your greed! Kobozev knows of the embezzlements! He knows of your Swiss accounts and jewelry and gold! He knows of this... this despicable opulence!" He swept an arm to indicate the bathroom. The enormous tub was fashioned from Greek tile and had fixtures of solid gold. A nearby plate of the same metal held her midafternoon snack of rich, French chocolates. A gold-leaved bidet, accented with carvings of diving dolphins, sat in the corner.

"He knows and is blackmailing me into treason!"

The woman caught her breath at the word.

"Yes! Treason!"

"But… but… how? Why?"

"Belidov is near death! Sorokin has a majority of support in the Politburo and will succeed to the Party chairmanship, or at least he *thinks* he will. Kobozev has other ideas, treasonous ideas."

"Treason? I don't want to hear this! I don't want to know any more! Let me go!" She struggled to stand, but Yazov held her in the water.

"Frightened, are we, my dear? Good! It is because of you my life is threatened, and now I shall include you in the treason! Listen!

"The car bombing in Teheran… surely even the shit you watch on that box would have had the news… that was Kobozev's plot. He is mad for power. Mad! The new Iranian leader will invite our navy into their waters. Kobozev intends to control Persian Gulf oil and bring America to her knees. That will be his coup to usurp Sorokin. In just several hours, Skripko — he is also one of the fiends — is going to deliver an ultimatum to the American president, demanding the United States not interfere in our occupation. And tomorrow Kobozev will demonstrate Red Sky to the Americans to show their military vulnerability."

"Red Sky?"

"Yes, a space weapon that has bankrupt this nation and wetted Kobozev's lust for power."

"But I don't understand… I…"

"Shut up! I don't have much time! Just listen! Your greed has entangled us in this conspiracy! Kobozev threatened to expose me to Sorokin if I didn't cooperate with him. Red Sky was consuming so much treasure that my ministry had to be included in the plot."

"What? You yielded to treason with such a threat?" The woman rallied for a counterattack. She jerked her blubber around and faced her husband, in the process sending another tidal wave over the tub edge. "What is Kobozev going to tell Sorokin? That we used our Party privileges to acquire a few works of art, a few jewels? Idiot! Everyone in the Party has been doing that since the revolution began!"

"Woman, you are the fool! Are you blind to what is happening?! Do you not have ears, or has the fat blocked them?! At every opportunity, Sorokin preaches bold ideas of reform. The country's economy is a shambles, a joke. The nation is unraveling! Something must be done, and Sorokin has proposed unprecedented changes… returning power to the people, bringing Party members who abuse their offices to justice! A few works of art, a few jewels, you say! Fool! Do you know how many millions of rubles I have embezzled so you could afford your *few* trinkets? *Tens of millions!* Enough, my dear, to make us far and away the best examples of Party abuse and buy us a last trinket… a one-way ticket into the gulag!"

The speech momentarily deflated the woman.

"Yes, I think you see the situation. We are doomed! Doomed! Unless you can get to Sorokin and…"

"Me?"

"Yes! You! I cannot! The phones are tapped, the rooms are bugged, and I am constantly watched by Ryabinin's men."

"Ryabinin?"

"He is also one of the conspirators. Zhilin, too. So you *must* get a message to Sorokin explaining the plot. Tell his wife if necessary. Or one of the other ministry wives. But just get the message to Sorokin! We can appeal for mercy. He might grant us a pardon. Or reduce our sentence."

At the suggestion, the woman grabbed her husband by the collar, almost pulling him into the tub. "Now it's your turn to listen to me! I will not tell Sorokin! And neither will you!"

"What?! Have you not heard a word?!"

"Shut up, coward! You disgust me! Sorokin is the real danger to us! Appeal for mercy?! A reduced sentence?! Do you think I want to spend *any* time in prison?! Lose everything I have?!"

"Woman, you are…"

"Shut up! Sorokin *should* be displaced! He is the danger! He is the traitor to the Party! You will *not* tell him of the plot! You will cooperate with Kobozev in every manner! Do you hear me?"

"Cooperate? Are you mad?! If the plot fails, we are dead! Even if it succeeds, Kobozev will kill me! I can sense it! He is another Stalin. A ruthless, bloodthirsty madman. He doesn't trust me. Sorokin is our only hope. You must get the message to him! You must!" He was beginning to cry. The vision of the dead elk was again upon him. It would be his fate.

"Please, you must help me! Please!" He broke into stuttering sobs.

"You make me sick!" The woman shoved him away and he sprawled on the floor, adding his tears to the tub spillage. She stood and dressed in her robe, glaring at the despairing heap. "You've always been a disgusting weakling!"

Yazov raised himself to the edge of the bidet and beseeched her with crying eyes. "Please, my love, help me! Please!"

"I have heard nothing of this conversation. Nothing! I am not a party to treason! I know nothing of embezzlement!"

She stepped from the room, leaving Yazov to vomit his fear into the golden bowl.

❖

Wednesday, 23 November
Atlantis

At sunrise, Pettigrew searched from each of the windows but found nothing. He was wrecked by grief, a shell of a man. It had been his weakness that had sent her outside, his weakness that might have killed her. Mission Control was searching for her and was certain they would find her, but what condition would she be in? Nothing further had come from the speaker.

"*Atlantis*… Houston. Fifteen minutes to Hawaii. They're standing by to search, Bob."

"Roger."

He watched the little flashing sticks of light that formed the clock digits, tormenting him with their precise, lethargic, uncaring gait. He was powerless. Throughout the vehicle, silicon robots were in control and, in this, his most needed moment, he could do nothing. He had ceased to even pray. No just and loving God could do this — kill the single thing he most needed for life.

A new depression came to drown him — the realization Anna had never believed in him. She had never believed in his need, in his love for her, in its intensity, its purity. Because of the phone call, of the other woman, she had seen him as nothing but an obscene liar. The thought propelled him to the microphone and he spoke into it — haltingly, tearfully — uncertain if the words would ever be heard.

"Anna, please live. I love you. Please believe that. More than my own life, I love you. But I was afraid of you… running from you when you called." The story of Vietnam, of Karen, of Travis Air Force Base began to pour into the abyss.

At Mission Control, a scene of near chaos was transformed into confessional quiet. Men and women shared embarrassed glances as Pettigrew's soul came into their headsets.

Killingsworth was stunned by the marine's profession. He had had no inkling of this side of the man or of his relationship with Anna. As the words continued, he wished there was some way to give him privacy. But that was impossible. The radios could not be switched off for fear he might need immediate help. They had no choice but to listen, to unwillingly trespass in the most inner sanctums of a man's soul.

Pettigrew cared nothing that Mission Control was hearing him. If the world had heard, it would not have mattered. Anna was his only thought. She had to know.

"Anna. Please believe me. I love you. I need you."

"AOS Hawaii for six plus twenty."

"Roger, Houston."

AOS — Acquisition Of Signal. It was the call telling Pettigrew he had entered that island's radar coverage and would remain in it for six minutes and twenty seconds. There would be other tracking sites to follow, but he knew if Anna wasn't found on this pass, the chances of getting to her before her oxygen was depleted were remote.

The sun was rising and its glancing rays turned the Pacific to molten gold. The back-lighted Hawaiian Islands appeared as lumps of coal in the crucible.

One minute gone.

Atlantis's cabin fans droned. Outside, spinning particles of ice from the cooling evaporator flashed in the low sun like the mirrored balls on nightclub ceilings. They soundlessly ricocheted from the aft window.

Pettigrew was in a new blasphemy, challenging the God he had so recently denied. *Prove you are a God! Give her back!*

Two minutes gone. He confirmed — for the third time — he had the required checklists ready for the rendezvous and the cockpit was configured. Everything checked.

Three minutes gone.

Oahu passed beneath. Its volcanic spine would keep the dawn from

Honolulu for another hour. He imagined the ignorant gaiety of the
population below — people rising for another day of fun and laughter,
lovers rolling into each other's arms or toasting the sunrise with champagne or walking hand in hand in the surf; people oblivious to Anna's
terror, to his grief, to Mark's and Darling's danger. It was beyond his
comprehension how the world could still be the same.

Four minutes.

"Bob! They've got her! They've found her!" Around the Capcomm's
call he could hear a celebration. "We'll have a target vector in a couple
of minutes!"

"Hurry! For crissake, hurry!"

Three minutes later, the six numbers that uniquely defined Anna's
position and velocity were transmitted to Mission Control and then to
Atlantis. "Bob, the target vector is aboard!"

"Roger!" He typed to the ship's computers and heard a thump as the
K-band radar turned its dish to the point in the sky where she had been
electronically spotted.

The track indicator flipped to gray — a radar lock.

"I've got her! I've got her on radar, Houston!" Flickering LED's
steadied on the range. "She's at thirty-seven thousand feet. Jesus! Her
range rate is a negative five decimal two!" The latter number indicated
she was continuing to separate from *Atlantis* at five feet per second.

"Roger, Bob. GNC is working on your burn targets."

Pettigrew looked along the line of sight of the radar and thought he
could see a tiny speck of white, but without a background for depth
perception, it was impossible to tell if it was Anna at seven miles or a
piece of ice at seven feet. He watched through the binoculars trying to
convince himself there were humanlike dimensions to the object.

"Where are the targets, Houston? Range is running away!"

"In work, Bob. It takes time!"

The marine cursed his dependence on Mission Control. In an aircraft,
the rendezvous would have been trivial. He had done a thousand in his
life. He would merely lead Anna and fly to her. His brain could easily
handle the calculations of the intercept. But in space, the laws of orbital
mechanics ruled, not the human eye. He knew if he attempted to aim
Atlantis and thrust at her, he would rise to a higher, slower orbit and drift
even farther away. Until he got within a hundred feet, he might as well

not even have a window.

"Bob, the first target is onboard."

"Roger, I'm burning it now." The vehicle shivered at the jet firings. The radar range rate slowly decreased to zero, then turned positive. He was finally closing the distance.

The second target came fifteen minutes later. Then a third. *Atlantis* flew into darkness, but Pettigrew didn't notice. He only had eyes for his instruments. Successively finer targets came aboard. Shorter burns were completed. The range decreased to five miles... three... one. A braking target came aboard and he nulled it.

"I've got a visual, Houston!"

In the burst of a new sunrise, the white of Anna's space suit was a brilliant star, and he snatched the binoculars to look closer. She was in a slow tumble, a foot-long tether waving from her wrist. Her arms floated symmetrically in front of her chest. The body position was clearly one of relaxation — or lifelessness. "Anna, I'm less than a mile from you! I can see you in the binoculars!"

She remained absolutely still. "Wave at me, Anna! Wave!" *It's just her radio! Yes! It's failed! That's all!* His soul created hope where there was no cause for any.

Atlantis's minus-Z star tracker began to take marks on the human star, and Pettigrew typed to the keyboard to allow the data to be swallowed by the navigation software. More burn targets appeared in the green phosphor and were executed. Finer and finer they became, nulled with mere flicks of the controls. Range decreased to a thousand feet... four hundred... two hundred. Range rate slowed to three feet per second... two... one. He had finally entered the target bubble that allowed him to fly as an aircraft pilot, to beat the computers with his eye and brain.

He maneuvered *Atlantis* so Anna would strike the forward bay bulkhead. It would be the slightest of impacts, at inches per second.

She touched.

"Anna! Grab the handrail!" There was no response. Her visored face rolled toward him, but a mist of condensation coated the inside of the acrylic and kept her hidden.

In an attempt to shake her to consciousness, he backed *Atlantis* away and commanded another closure, this one at higher speed. An audible thump came through the structure as she hit the window.

The impact brought motion. *She moved! She's alive! Alive!*

"Anna! Grab the handrail! Grab it!"

Slowly, her right hand reached toward the anchor.

"She's alive, Houston! She just grabbed the handrail!"

The capcomm answered, but Pettigrew didn't hear. Overlapping, chaotic, unintelligible prayers of thanksgiving rose from his soul.

But something was wrong. She had moved down the handrails and out of his direct view, but he could see on the television she was in trouble, struggling to make a simple hand-over-hand translation.

"Anna, concentrate! You're okay! You can do it! That's it! Now the next hand! You're only a yard from the airlock." He coached her downward.

"You can swing your feet into the hatch. Swing, goddamnit! You're not trying! Try!" It took her several attempts to thrust her lower body into the opening, and when she did, he shot to the mid-deck to observe through the inner hatch window.

"No, Anna! Don't rest!" She floated in the chamber with the same stillness he had seen outside. "You can't rest, Anna! You have to close the outer hatch! Close it! Damn you! Close it!" There was a fifteen-pound-per-square-inch pressure across the inner hatch — seven tons of force holding it closed. He was powerless until she sealed the outer hatch. Then he could repressurize the airlock, equalizing the force.

"No! Anna, snap out of it!" Again she had fallen still. "Just turn the handle. That's all you have to do. Just turn it and then you can rest."

She twisted the handle and the latches gripped closed.

Immediately he opened the repressurization valve, and a shrieking hiss marked the rush of air into the airlock. The delta pressure needle began to swing.

Her body had limped at the instant the door had been seated. He could only imagine she was dying in these last seconds.

The needle touched zero. The pressure was equalized. He slammed the hatch handle open, jerked the door out of the way, grabbed Anna's feet, and pulled her into the mid-deck. There was no help on her part. He could have been pulling a drowning victim ashore.

He wedged his feet under floor restraints and spun her around. Her face was still hidden by the condensation.

"Be alive, Anna! Oh, God, be alive!" The supplication was simultaneous with his manipulations of the EMU chest controls to depressurize the suit. Its fabric limped. He snatched the helmet release open and pulled it away.

"Jesus, no! No!"

Her head flopped loosely, like a ball balanced on a stick. Bubbles of yellow emesis foamed from her mouth and clung to her cheeks. Her eyelids drooped half closed, showing only crescents of white.

He jammed his fingers into her mouth to clear the fluid, then leaned closely to listen for breathing.

Nothing.

His fingers sampled her carotid artery for a pulse, but the pounding of his own heart washed out any sensation of hers. Pushing up her right eyelid, he stared into green glass — not a flicker of animation.

"No!"

He would *pound* life back into her. He tore away the communications headset and jerked off the gloves, ignoring the brutalized flesh of her hands. The pants were stripped and her body pulled from the torso. Only the liquid cooling garment remained to cover her, and he slashed its zipper down and pulled it roughly from her shoulders and arms. Her breasts bobbed free, each undercut with oozing purple bruises.

"Houston! I've got to do CPR! What locker are the harnesses in?!"

The flight surgeon answered, "They're in locker MF41K. What's her condition?"

"She's not breathing! She's sheet white and not breathing!" Pettigrew released the microphone. There was no time for discussion. He was at the locker, rifling its drawers.

"You said she's *white?* Check for cyanosis! Check her fingernails! Are they blue? If she's in cardiac arrest, her extremities will be cyanic... blue colored. I think she may be in shock. If so, her respiration may be so shallow and her pulse so weak you'll have a difficult time sensing it. Check her for shock before you start CPR. You may be treating the wrong thing!"

The caution slapped Pettigrew. Could he be mistaken? He released the drawer and turned back, batting pieces of the suit out of the way to get to her. At the sight of lily-white fingernails, hope returned to his soul. Wrapping his arms around her back, he crushed his ear to her breast and concentrated through the thudding of his own heart.

Yes! Yes!

A weak, birdlike flutter and a rapid, shallow respiration signaled life.

"Houston, she's alive! I can hear her pulse! She's breathing!"

"What's her pulse?"

"I don't know... fast, weak!"

"She's in shock, Bob! Get an IV going! Don't give her anything by mouth. As soon as you're done, get a blood pressure cuff on her and call those numbers to me."

Pettigrew acknowledged the instructions and began a ransack of the kit. He located the IV fluid bag, inserted its needle into Anna's arm, and clamped the bag to force its contents into her body. Two minutes later he had a blood pressure reading. "Houston, I've got the IV going. Her blood pressure is hard to measure, but I'm seeing about seventy over forty."

"Bob, that's dangerously low!"

"Then fix her! This fuckin' bag is full of shit! What else can I give her?!" He demanded a miracle.

"Nothing now. We're just going to have to observe her for a while. Keep the IV going and take her blood pressure every fifteen minutes. Keep her warm."

The words "dangerously low" pushed him into new excesses of activity. He stripped her of the remainder of the LCVG and ripped off her urine collection diaper. Rub burns on the insides of her thighs were angry red and covered with droplets of urine. He wiped her dry.

His sleeping bag was still in place on the mid-deck wall, and it took only a moment to unclip it, push her inside, and tow her to the flight deck. Heat from the instrument panels and sunlight through the windows always kept the cockpit warmer than the mid-deck. He tethered her beneath the overhead windows, then climbed in the bag to add his own body heat. Thanksgivings for her rescue were sobbed into her neck.

❖

Wednesday, 23 November
Freedom

In the last seconds of their final burn, both men thought they would die, but not at the hand of the Soviets. *Freedom* — down to her final two stages — abused them with g-forces that now weighted their bodies to half a ton.

The propellant valves slammed shut and returned them to weight-lessness. Mark immediately checked the navigation display. Striegel's machine had done it! They were there! At geosync! Twenty-two thou-sand miles above the earth!

With the exception of Darling, no man had been where he was now. His skin tingled. His heart bounded. They would be the first and probably the last humans to see the world from such a vantage — not as a marble like the *Apollo* astronauts had seen, but as the fixed globe the authors of Genesis had envisioned. That an enemy might be searching and schem-ing to kill him was, for these few seconds, of no consequence. *Higher! Farther into the sky! Deeper into the black!* The call had beckoned him for a lifetime, and he was there!

He watched the earth. It was still in eclipse, a darkened disk ringed with an airglow halo the diameter of thirty-five full moons. The north and south polar regions were necklaced in the hazy green of an auroral storm, while the tropics were sequined in the glitter of a thousand lightning flashes. Glancing lunar light sheened the Pacific Ocean like a moonlit lake. *The entire Pacific Ocean reduced to a lake!*

Minutes passed, and the sun rose to trace the earth from pole to pole with the purity of prism-split color. The rainbow was thin — at this distance almost a pencil line. It disappeared in the star's blinding resurrection, and mother earth took the form of an enormous crescent moon. He could see only the extreme eastern Atlantic as a white sliver. The continents beneath him, North and South America, were still in darkness and would be for five more hours. As if he were standing on a mountaintop, the sun had risen on him before those in the valley.

With the dawn, he brought his attention forward. Another star had arisen in the heavens — the *KOSMOS* — gleaming white in his face, shaming all others in its morning-star brilliance.

"Range?" He queried Darling, who had activated the laser range finder.

"Thirty-seven miles. Closing at one-o-four point seven."

To minimize their lighted exposure, they would cover these final miles in a sprint, reaching zero velocity in a hover over the space-facing side of the machine.

Mark began braking, cursing the snowstorm of ice particles the jet firings produced. He could imagine how their approach must look to a

KOSMOS sensor searching in the visible light spectrum — like he had brought along a rock band laser show.

At twenty-one miles the FUEL LOW caution light illuminated — a glowing amber scream. His heart rate soared. The light was early, indicating fuel consumption had been higher than expected. His eyes fell on the red ABORT light — the next and last warning they would get. When it illuminated, the rendezvous would have to be terminated and the return to *Atlantis* immediately initiated.

The distance closed to ten miles… five… two. Except for technical exchanges, the intercom was mute, the silence no longer a quirk of personalities, but rather induced by the shock of the *KOSMOS*'s immensity. It reduced *Freedom* to a mere fly. It had a cruciform shape with a central box beam that measured at least two football fields in length and thirty feet on a side. The northern end of the truss bristled with an assortment of antennas — dipoles, large mesh dishes, helix spirals, and microwave reflectors. The southern end was ringed in white spheres, each as big as a house. The crossbar of the cruciform was seen to be rectangular panels extending for a hundred and fifty feet on either side of the center structure. They were acres in size.

At five hundred feet, they entered a hover, and Mark began to uncoil. From their topside vantage, there was nothing to suggest the *KOSMOS* was anything more than the world's tallest TV tower. He pulsed the THC to begin a drift that would take them below the machine and give them a view of its earth-facing side.

"See anything, Frank? It looks clean to me." The FUEL LOW light was hurrying him for the confirmation.

Darling had unstowed a camera and was busy with photos. "The north end must be a communication relay. But the south end? What are those spheres? They resemble pressure vessels."

"Probably fuel storage. Something this big would need some significant fuel reserves to maintain position."

In the interest of fuel conservation, he accepted the trajectory of their glide. They would pass down the west side, just aft of the point where the wing joined the main body. *Freedom* was pointed north, and after they examined the belly in that direction he would flip the vehicle for a southern view.

"There's not a solar cell anywhere on these things." Mark was baffled. Up close, the machine's wings were vast, silvered sheets. Their function suddenly struck him. "They're radiators. Just like we have on the inside surface of the shuttle payload bay doors… for cooling. So what are they using as a power source?"

Darling offered an opinion. "Nuclear power."

"A nuke?" It was the obvious answer. The spacecraft was not solar powered, and chemical batteries were out of the question for a machine that was clearly designed for decades of operation.

"Mark, the communication system on the northern end would not need the wattage of a nuclear generator. The power would be wasted."

Even without the comment, Mark's doubts had resurfaced. The *KOSMOS* was overbuilt and overpowered. Why? For a rail gun? That would certainly need a large power source. But where was it?

It wasn't on the northern third of the belly. *Freedom's* drift had finally brought them a view of that. It held only three large, cylindrical modules. The two most northern ones were hung parallel, like enormous D-cell batteries. Directly below the wing attachment was the third cylinder.

"That is the reactor vessel."

Mark agreed and wondered if they were already dead by radiation exposure.

"You have any idea what those other two are?"

"No." Darling was busy with more photographs. "They do not appear to be associated with the reactor or the antenna assembly."

"Well, there sure as hell isn't a rail gun here. I'm going to flip around and see what's to the south." He pulsed the RHC to begin the turnaround. "We need to get out of here as fast as possible. The radiation could be killing us."

"There is no danger. The reactor is shielded."

"What?"

"The containment vessel is too large for only a reactor. It is shielded."

"That doesn't make any sense. Why shield a reactor up here?"

The question was unanswered. As he touched the RHC to slow their rotation, the ABORT light illuminated. He was still staring at that when the southern portion of the *KOSMOS* belly came into view.

"Mark! Up! Up! Get us up!" It was the first time he had heard Darling scream.

CHAPTER 16

Killingsworth imagined the scene on the other end of the phone —
in the National Security Council chambers. It was probably similar to
what he was seeing in Mission Control. Men could do nothing further.
They waited at their consoles. Some had their heads bowed — in fatigue
or prayer, he could not tell. Others crushed cigarettes into overflowing
ashtrays while simultaneously reaching for more tobacco.

"Mr. President, they are now indistinguishable from the *KOSMOS*.
The NORAD radar cannot separately resolve the two objects."

"How close is that?"

"I'm told they must be within a mile."

"A mile? Shouldn't we have heard something? Surely they should be
able to see if it's a weapon. Could something have happened?" The
frustration of the wait, of having the limits of technology reduce him to
a powerless observer, tainted the president's voice.

"I'm sorry, Mr. President, but we are totally blind. All we can do is
wait for the call. I'm assured, though, that up to the moment we lost radar
contact, Colonel O'Malley and his machine had to have been fully
functional. The rendezvous could not have proceeded to that point if it
had not been so."

"Yea, which I guess should give us a warm feeling we have just been
made idiots. The damn thing is harmless. God, if this ever gets public, the
press will eat me alive. A couple of billion dollars down the drain. Not
to mention the risk we took of provoking the Soviets... *or* the risk to

O'Malley and Darling."

"Regardless of the outcome of the mission, you did what was in the best interest of the country, Mr. President. You cannot be criticized for that." Even as he was saying it, Killingsworth knew better. The press and political opposition would crucify his friend when the story leaked, as he was sure it ultimately would.

"Thanks, Hobie. You're a loyal deputy... and a lousy liar."

The two men fell into the silence of their respective companies. Killingsworth pulled his tie loose and unbuttoned the collar of his shirt. He laced his hands over his paunch, taking on the appearance of an unblinking stone Buddha. His eyes dwelled on the speaker from which O'Malley's call would come. In spite of the political embarrassment it would mean for the president, he prayed that the call would be *mirage,* the code for a historic folly — a benign *KOSMOS*. He knew it was the president's prayer also.

The wait lengthened. Coffee cups were filled, emptied, and refilled again. Men walked briskly from the room to relieve neglected bladders. The pall of tobacco smoke grew heavier. The minutes dragged.

"Flight... INCO... I have a carrier. No modulation."

Killingsworth did not understand the call to the flight director from the communications officer but knew by the reaction of the control center it had to be significant. Several men jumped from their seats to look at the position occupied by the INCO.

"How is it?" The presence of the carrier wave indicated that *Freedom's* transmitter had been turned on. The modulation — O'Malley's voice — had to be imminent.

"Signal strength is good, Flight."

Killingsworth had just opened his mouth to request a translation of the technical jargon when he heard Mark's voice.

"Houston... *Freedom!* High ground! High ground! Houston... *Freedom!* Repeating! High ground! High ground! High ground!"

Oh God, no! The fat man had been unprepared for it. Even in his most despairing moments, there had always been that glimmer of hope they had imagined a threat where none existed. Now O'Malley's words — the code for a weapons platform — had crushed out that light. The world was changed. America was naked, her shield of missiles an impotent facade.

He leaned to the microphone. "Mr. President?"

"I'm here, Hobie. Any news?"

"Yes, Mr. President. Colonel O'Malley has called from the *KOSMOS*. I regret..." He choked on the words. "...I regret to tell you he has found it to be a hostile installation."

For several seconds the line was silent. Killingsworth pitied his friend — at the moment, the loneliest man in the world.

"Hobie, I've been praying it wouldn't come to this. Goddamnit! I've been praying! We believed those people... the promises, the treaties! *I* believed them!" The voice was simultaneously sad and bitterly angry. "I didn't want this, Hobie! Goddamn those people to hell! Goddamn them to hell's fire! Tell O'Malley to destroy the goddamn thing!"

❖

Wednesday, 23 November
Freedom

Mark snapped his head to see what had panicked Darling. "Oh, Jesus!" Thoughts of fuel wastage were obliterated. He banged the THC upward while simultaneously making his *high ground* call. A two-hundred-foot-long rail, rooted at the midpoint of the truss, extended straight earthward. Their approach from above had been all too effective. The center beam and the massive radiator panels had blocked the stinger from view. But it was not the weapon that had driven him to forget their fuel state. The rail was pointed away. Rather, it was a robotic arm, similar to the shuttle's, that was in motion and swinging dangerously close to *Freedom*. The thin skin of her fuel tanks was as fragile as a soap bubble and perilously vulnerable to puncture. The arm missed them by inches.

Mark stabilized in the protection offered by the center beam and wondered if the arm could have yet killed them. It would just take a while to find out — when they ran out of gas before reaching *Atlantis*.

Darling added a new worry. "Could the robot arm have cameras? The ground might have seen us."

"I hadn't even thought about that! You're right! We use cameras. They must also." Was an alert already going out? He cursed himself for not having foreseen the possibility of robotic devices — and their cameras. How else could the Soviets have assembled and maintained the weapon?

"*Freedom*... Houston. Execute Armageddon. Repeat. Execute Armageddon."

"Roger, Houston. Copy Armageddon." It was the code directing them to proceed with the destruction of the machine.

Mark considered docking where they were but then dismissed the idea. To do so would mean a hundred-foot translation back and forth from the gun. That would take too much time, and every minute they were crawling around was an opportunity for some camera to see them. He would move south and dock directly over the root of the weapon.

A tap of the THC started movement and made him wince — another eight pounds of fuel swallowed by the thrusters.

"Get ready to grapple."

He steadied *Freedom* near a piece of the truss, and the iceman maneuvered a ten-foot probe toward it. At its end was a clawlike hand he closed around the metal. They were finally docked to the *KOSMOS* and *Freedom's* propulsion system could be powered down. Only time would tell if they had waited too long and flown themselves into a suicide.

"Check your tether." Mark gave the caution as Darling reached for the handle to separate from the cockpit.

"I have." He floated from the cockpit and went immediately to the craft's chin-mounted equipment bay.

Mark checked his own anchor, a reel attached to *Freedom's* side. He had no intention of ever separating from his ticket home. Then he released his EMU from the cockpit and dismounted to the left. After twenty-four hours of hanging on a high-tech clothes peg, the feeling of mobility was nearly orgasmic.

He paused to survey their prize. Massive, he decided, was hardly an adequate adjective. It was a space battleship, a thing of science fiction. The central beam stretched north and south, its edges converging in both directions like rail lines toward a horizon. At opposite ends were the antenna farm and the ring of spherical tanks — areas they would have no time to investigate. The earth-facing side of the machine was the target. In their very brief glimpse of it, they had seen a miniature city of boxes gathered near the base of the rail gun — no doubt its vital organs.

Darling finished tethering an electric saw, a drill, and several other tools to his waist and chest, taking on the appearance of a spacesuited lumberjack. He moved aside to allow Mark to retrieve the detonating cord and timer.

"Let's go."

"Watch out for cameras," the iceman cautioned.

Armageddon began.

❖

Wednesday, 23 November
Soviet Embassy, Washington, D.C.

"I can't wait any longer. Send my driver to the front. Notify Moscow I am proceeding with the alternate plan." Foreign Minister Skripko punched off the intercom, rose from his desk, and began to hurriedly stuff his briefcase with papers. He allowed one interruption to check his watch — 6:10 P.M. The pre-holiday traffic would be thick and slowed even further by a wet snow that had begun to fall. He cursed the delay in the telex, wondering what had gone wrong. He found it impossible to believe Hashemi had double-crossed them.

But he had no time to dwell on what contingencies might have developed. In fifty minutes he had an appointment with the president of the United States. He could hardly go into his office and talk about the weather, as unusual as it was. The documents in his briefcase — a dressed-up version of last year's tome on eradicating short-range missiles — would fill the time.

He walked to his washroom and paused for a moment to check his appearance. Satisfied, he exited the office and met his entourage in the foyer. An aide offered him his hat and coat and ushered him toward an idling limo.

Damn the stars! More delay on the roads! The snow had become heavier.

"Comrade Minister!" The shout from his personal secretary stopped him from entering the auto. "The telex just arrived."

He accepted it and read the single line, "Hashemi has issued invitation. Proceed with Iranian Initiative. Stop." The day had turned beautiful after all.

He unzipped his briefcase and handed over all but one piece of paper to the courier. It was the only page he would need.

❖

Wednesday, 23 November
The White House

"He's here, Hobie. The bastard's late." The president watched from his office as the limo, with its twin red flags fluttering from fenders, pulled to a stop. He had left the room microphones hot so Killingsworth, in Houston, and the nearby Security Council could listen to the conversation.

The fat man sensed the president's fiery Texas temper rising to the fore. "Mr. President, I urge restraint. A cool head will be needed in this meeting."

"Don't worry, Hobie. I'll be *diplomatic*. I'm going to give this Russian bear a mile of rope to hang himself and then I'm going to enjoy every minute of watching him swing… *diplomatically* of course."

A minute later his secretary announced the visitor, and a relaxed, smiling President Corbin rose to greet him. Although four years of postgraduate study in the United States had given Skripko an exceptional mastery of the English language, he entered with his interpreter. It was a tactic he felt unnerved his opposition and gave him an edge in negotiations. He could understand them directly, while they had the distraction of an interpreter to contend with.

"Dmitriy, good evening! Please come in. Have a seat."

"I apologize for being late, Mr. President. This weather." The interpreter droned the excuse.

"Yes, it is getting bad out there… more like Moscow than Washington." A laugh. "And this city is never prepared for it. I think they only have one snowplow." The president motioned to a tray. "Tea? Coffee?"

"Yes, thank you." Skripko accepted tea.

During the beverage preparation, the president found himself slipping back into a scowl. The Russian interpreter, a weasel-faced man with slick dark hair, was staring at him — a sponge, soaking up every nuance of body language. Corbin reached into his reserves of patience to renew his camouflage. "The apple pie is fresh. Help yourself." He indicated a second tray. "My wife just baked it. It's an old Texas cowhand recipe, though I suspect the cowhands used beans instead of apples." More laughter.

"Thank you, Mr. President." Skripko took a slice and tasted it. "Delicious! Please tell Mrs. Corbin it is the best I've ever had."

"I'll do that. In fact, I'll make certain you don't leave Washington without the recipe… for Mrs. Skripko."

"I would like that. My wife is also quite an accomplished baker. The next time I visit Washington, I will have my embassy cook prepare some favorite Russian pastries from her recipes and bring some to the White House."

"I'll look forward to it." The president hastened to business. "In fact, maybe we can share some of your wife's handiwork when we toast the finalization of a new arms-control pact." He nodded at the foreign minister's briefcase. "If this one's as *fair* and *verifiable* as has been hinted, I imagine it will win easy approval in the Senate." He placed just the right amount of emphasis on the perennial stumbling blocks to agreement.

Skripko leaned forward to replace his cup, then straightened in his chair. "I can assure you, Mr. President our proposal is... *was*... absolutely fair and verifiable."

The president raised his eyebrows to fake the surprise he didn't feel. The man before him was changing like a werewolf — the tone, the emphasis on past tense, the face. There would be nothing more about grandma's cooking.

"The Soviet people are weary of arms expenditures, and Chairman Belidov has been trying mightily to reduce the burden."

"No more than I." The president tuned his voice from *cordial* to *concerned* to match the chill he was sensing.

"Yes, until recently, we believed there was a real partnership between our nations on limiting our arsenals."

"Dmitriy, pardon me for saying so, but I detect a definite posturing here. You are speaking in the past tense, as if something has changed. Could perhaps your translator be misinterpreting your comments?"

The weasel stiffened at the implication of incompetence and paused a moment before making the interpretation. Skripko snapped a curt order to the man, who then rose and turned for the door.

The president was shocked. The man was going sans translator.

"My interpreter has not misconstrued my words, Mr. President." The voice chilled further. "I have been speaking in the past tense because things have changed."

"Changed?"

"Yes. Dangerously so. Until mere hours ago, my mission had been to bring you the latest of Chairman Belidov's disarmament initiatives. But that is now impossible."

"What?! Why? There has been no change of policy in my administration. We welcome any genuine offer of disarmament."

"Mr. President, as you are no doubt aware, earlier today, the Iranian leadership was decimated in a car-bomb attack."

He had been briefed on the slaughter hours ago, but the CIA had seen no Soviet involvement. There were too many other more likely suspects — the Iraqis, the Kuwaitis, the Saudis. Even various Iranian factions could have been involved.

The Russian's voice inched lower on the diplomatic thermometer. "My intelligence sources have informed me the attack was the work of the CIA... a prelude to an American-sponsored invasion, another Bay of Pigs intervention to forcibly install a pro-Western government. I am here to condemn, in the strongest possible manner, your dangerously provocative activities. Iran shares a fourteen-hundred-kilometer border with the Soviet state. Already you have effectively annexed her neighbor, Afghanistan, with your support of Moslem fanatics. The addition of Iran to your ledger would mean the dagger of Islamic extremism would be aimed at the Soviet belly from the Black Sea to China. You wish to inflame ethnic unrest among Soviet Moslems. We cannot allow that. We will *not* allow it."

It was no longer necessary for the president to pretend surprise. Skripko's accusations were explosive. But where was the *KOSMOS* connection? The president saw none.

He bolted from his seat. "That's crazy! Insane! This country had nothing to do with that car-bomb attack! Nothing! Invasion? That's idiocy! The Iranians are seeing ghosts behind every sand dune! Where are our troops if we are planning such an action?"

"The Iraqis and Saudis would be happy to be your surrogates." The foreign minister rose to face his target. "And idiocy, Mr. President? Ghosts? America's involvement in that sad country has been all too real. Your first efforts at imperialism failed when you tried to prop up the corrupt throne of the shah. Then, your allies were major supporters of Iraq when it attempted to brutalize the country. Ghosts, Mr. President? It was not ghosts that shot down an Iranian airliner. Or spirits that attacked Iranian oil platforms and ships. Or phantom bombs that fell from American war planes onto Iranian soil only weeks ago. And are those merely *visions* of American warships that continuously fill the Persian Gulf?"

"Mr. Skripko, you know as well as I, the provocation for our attacks on Iranian military installations was Teheran-sanctioned terrorism against American citizens. Our actions were strictly retaliatory in nature. We hold no designs on Iran and had nothing whatever to do with the Teheran bombing. I request you immediately relay that message to Chairman Belidov."

"There's more, Mr. President." Skripko's voice was now that of a Perry Mason offering incontrovertible proof of guilt. "One of the car bombers has been captured. He has confessed to being an Iraqi agent, trained and equipped by the CIA. Articles on his person — instructions, routes of escape, money, bombing paraphernalia, maps — support the confession."

"Mr. Skripko, I reject your allegations and will continue to do so. And I suggest you tell your KGB friends they should improve their intelligence collection efforts. They've been duped."

"I think, Mr. President, our intelligence service has performed admirably. Your plot has failed. Only an hour ago, the heir to power, Ayatollah Hashemi, requested Soviet military assistance in countering the impending invasion. Tomorrow, Soviet naval forces will be welcomed into Iranian ports."

It was a thunderbolt that brought instant enlightenment to the president. The Soviets were behind the assassinations. They had a puppet in Teheran. They had created a client state that would dominate America's oil jugular.

The president seethed. "I know flimflam when I hear it, Mr. Skripko. And that's what I'm hearing right now. Tell Chairman Belidov I consider the invitation from this Iranian ayatollah prima facie evidence that Soviet forces were responsible for the car bombing. Tell him the strategic interests of this country in that region will be defended per the Carter Doctrine of 1980. Tell him I will consider a Soviet presence in Iran, invited or not, an invasion of that country and will respond as if American soil itself were being violated. Tell him, Mr. Skripko, if a single Soviet ship enters Iranian territorial waters, it will be fired upon by American forces. Tell him I'll see him in hell before I stand by and preside over the strangulation of this country!"

The president maintained a threatening pose. For a moment, Skripko mirrored it, then broke into a smile. He turned for his briefcase. "I will deliver your messages, Mr. President, but I believe Chairman Belidov will ignore your threats."

"Then he does so at his, and his country's, peril."

Skripko unzipped his case and pulled out a single page of paper. "I think not, Mr. President. Please, look over this list. I think you will find it most interesting."

The president angrily grabbed the document. "What the hell is it?" His display of surprise was Oscar winning. The *KOSMOS* card was finally being played. On the paper was a list of the satellites that had been inexplicably lost.

"What the hell is this?" He repeated the question, brandishing the page in the foreign minister's face.

"That, Mr. President, is the demise of America as a superpower… and why your threats of moments ago are meaningless rantings. There are eleven American spacecraft listed on that paper. When you check with your experts, you will find each suffered catastrophic failures at the exact times listed. However, Mr. President, they really were not failures at all. Those eleven satellites were victims of a Soviet antiballistic missile killer… a Star Wars missile killer. Your nuclear missile force is now impotent."

"Do you expect me to believe this… this… garbage?" The president crushed the page and hurled it into a wastebasket. "You people can't even make a decent refrigerator! Do you expect me to believe you've ringed your country with laser death rays?" He added the latter sentence to fake his ignorance of a space-based killer.

"No, Mr. President, I don't expect you to believe my claim. It is for this reason the Soviet people — the people incapable of building a refrigerator, as you say — will demonstrate to you just how effective their missile killer actually is. Tomorrow, at exactly 1:00 P.M. Washington time, one hundred of your spacecraft will be destroyed in a five-minute period."

One hundred! In five minutes! The president's face was transfigured. It blanched and sagged in genuine horror at the capability represented by the numbers. Only the knowledge that O'Malley was, at that very moment, stringing explosives to destroy the threat, saved him from collapse.

Skripko relished his antagonist's defeat. Kobozev had been right about the shock effect. He was seeing it now. The man was white, choking on his own threats. "So you see, Mr. President, given the inadequacies of your strategic attack systems, you would do well not to threaten Soviet forces. Soviet ships will enter Iranian waters tomorrow, shortly after you are *convinced* by our demonstration."

The president did not answer.

"I will be at the embassy awaiting your pledge of noninterference. Good day, Mr. President." The man turned and exited.

When he was out of earshot, the president detonated. "Bastards! Lying, cheating, murdering bastards!" He slammed his palm on his desk. "You heard, Hobie?"

"Yes, Mr. President, I heard."

The president circled his desk, gesturing madly with his hands, slamming his swivel chair out of the way. "To imagine barbarians like that coming into this office and threatening me... this country! Blackmailing us?! Well, Mr. Skripko can wait until hell freezes over and he's not going to get that call... Hobie, how soon before O'Malley finishes blowing up Belidov's little toy?"

"That's difficult to say, Mr. President, because we don't know how long it will take them to strip the device of important equipment. Several more hours is likely."

"That's still well before their deadline. I want to know the second after O'Malley calls. Richard, are you on?"

General Richard Bachman, chairman of the Joint Chiefs of Staff, answered from the Security Council chambers. "I'm listening, Mr. President."

"I'll be down there in a little while... after I bring the appropriate members of Congress in on this. In the meantime, though, I want you to immediately order our forces in the Persian Gulf to blockade all Iranian ports to Soviet ships. Warnings should be given first. If those are ignored, I authorize the use of conventional weapons. Have your commanders fire across their bows. If they ignore that... sink the bastards. Reinforce our forces as quickly as possible. I want you to put everything you can in the Gulf. When O'Malley finishes with this *KOSMOS* thing, I want Belidov to feel like he's standing naked in front of a firing squad... exactly the way he thinks I'm feeling right now."

❖

Wednesday, 23 November
Moscow

A continent away, Chairman Belidov had slipped into a terminal coma knowing nothing of Red Sky's readiness, of the Iranian Initiative, of Skripko's White House meeting. At his bedside, Mikhail Sorokin meditated on the new Soviet order of reconciliation and democracy he would invoke upon his ascension to power. He would rescue his nation from the real enemy of the Soviet people — communism.

Wednesday, 23 November
Mission Control

An hour later, Killingsworth took the call from Mason. He had been maintaining a close, personal contact with the genius from the very beginning of the crisis. "Hello, Lieutenant."

"Sir, we're seeing fragmentation of the *KOSMOS*! They've done it!"

"What?!"

"Yes, sir... three pieces! The radar data is being transmitted to Mission Control right now. You should have it momentarily."

The fat man heard an eruption of voices on the flight director's communication loop. The data had arrived.

"Are you sure, Lieutenant? The *KOSMOS* has been destroyed?"

"Yes, sir. I mean, if it's in three pieces, it's sure as heck a kill. And there might be more pieces we can't see yet. Those three are probably the first ones to get far enough scattered to be discerned individually. We're checking right now to see if the *KOSMOS* comm system is still on the air. That'll be another signature of a kill."

"But why didn't Colonel O'Malley call? That was the plan."

"Don't know, sir. Maybe he's just too busy." Background cheering appended the sentence.

"What was that?"

"Sorry about that, sir. Another piece of the *KOSMOS* just came into view and everyone in the room is yelling their heads off. It's like watching one of those flicks of a fighter shooting down a bomber... pieces flying everywhere! Colonel O'Malley got himself a kill!"

The comment fell into the sinking pit that used to be the fat man's stomach. Something was wrong. "Is one of the objects the *Freedom*?"

"It's difficult to say just yet, sir. We're in the process of sizing each

of them right now. It'll take a few minutes. But I suspect one of them is
the *Freedom*."

The confidence did nothing to allay Killingsworth's concern about
O'Malley's silence.

"Thank you, Lieutenant. Call me as soon as you have more information."

"Willco, sir." An ebullient giggle followed. "God, I'll bet there're
some long faces in Moscow right now! We really stuck it to them!"

"Yes, I'm sure there are. Good-bye." Killingsworth punched off the
speaker. *Why didn't O'Malley call?*

The flight director came to him, and he could see his own worry
mirrored in the man's eyes. "Mr. Killingsworth, NORAD shows *KOSMOS*
fragmentation."

"Yes, I was just talking to them. Why didn't O'Malley call before the
destruction was initiated? That was the plan. They were to set the
explosives, fly away, then call. And if the *KOSMOS* destruction is
complete, why doesn't he call now?"

"I don't know. They could be having comm problems."

Killingsworth wanted to grab at that straw — an equipment malfunction, nothing more. He drummed his fingers on the desk. It was all so
maddening. They were guessing. Radar data. Radio malfunctions. The
president needed facts. A war loomed.

"Order Colonel O'Malley to break radio silence and to report their
status."

The flight director nodded to the capcomm to make the transmission.
"*Freedom*... Houston. Requesting status check. Over."

Killingsworth became transfixed by the flashing digits of the mission
clock. Thirty seconds passed. A minute. Mission Control was again a
tomb. *Please. Please answer!*

Silence.

Another call was transmitted. Another silence followed.

What's wrong?! Why doesn't he answer?!

The NORAD call light illuminated, and Killingsworth jumped in his
seat to stab it. "Yes, Lieutenant, do you have any news?" The encryption
sync was still in progress. He had forgotten to wait. "Damn!"

"Mr. Killingsworth?"

"Yes. Do you have any news?"

"Sir, there's something wrong. It doesn't appear the *KOSMOS* has fragmented."

"What? But you said there were pieces!"

"Yes, sir, that's what I said. And there are pieces. It's just that... well... we've sized the pieces and the largest is still *KOSMOS*-size. In fact it *is* the *KOSMOS*. We're sure of it. Its comm relay package is still on the air."

"Then what... how...?"

"Sir, one of the other objects is *sixty feet long.*" Mason paused, as if the number itself was enough to finish the explanation and save him from the sickening details. But the fat man remained baffled.

"I don't understand, Lieutenant. Sixty feet?"

"Sir, *Freedom* is sixty feet long."

At the words, Killingsworth spiraled into hell.

"And our data indicates the object is propulsive. I mean, it looks like it's thrusting in a random, tumbling manner. That's what a pressure vessel would do in a vacuum. If *Freedom* sustained an impact, its tanks would rupture and it would tumble like that."

Now it was clear to the fat man. Sometime in the last mile of their approach, the *KOSMOS* had fired on O'Malley and Darling. *Freedom* had been hit. Maybe it had been a trap from the beginning. Maybe, he thought, the Soviets had watched until *Freedom* was farthest from safety before firing on her. And now, two men were dead. The mission had failed. The country was doomed.

"Sir, the other objects... One is the same size as a decoy. They must have fired it at the last moment hoping to draw off the attack."

God, why couldn't it have worked? Why?!

"And the other object?" Killingsworth's falsetto voice was higher yet in his grief.

"Sir, it's six feet long... the size of a man's body."

❖

"You're sure, Hobie? There can be no mistake?" The president's voice was pleading.

"I'm sure, Mr. President. They are dead." Killingsworth spared the man the other possibility, that O'Malley and Darling were in the agony of a slow death. At least one body was drifting free. It was impossible to know if it was lifeless, but he prayed that it was. He was faint at the

thought of the twin tortures of slow suffocation and falling into blackness... forever. "We have repeatedly called for over an hour and there has
been no answer. And NORAD is certain about the identity of the objects.
They are tracking *Freedom's* wreckage, one of her decoy balloons, and
a body-sized object."

"But how can they be *sure*? Maybe O'Malley is dead, but couldn't he
have destroyed the *KOSMOS* first? Maybe the explosives malfunctioned
and the thing blew up early and got him too. I mean, if there are pieces
up there, it's possible. Isn't it?"

The fat man excused the president's seeming insensitivity to Mark's
and Darling's deaths. He was responsible for a nation of millions. "No,
Mr. President. The *KOSMOS* was not damaged. The communication
relay function of the machine is still operating."

"But the Soviets have said nothing to us about the assault! Why isn't
Belidov on the phone right now accusing us of some goddamn act of
aggression?"

"I don't know, Mr. President. That makes no sense to me, either.
Perhaps they hope their silence will further distract you from terrestrial
events."

"Oh God, Hobie, Hobie, Hobie." The words came on a mournful
sigh. "What's going to happen to us? What's going to happen to the
country? We'll never be able to successfully attack that thing. Belidov is
going to use Iran as a valve on our oil. The Soviets won't have to fire a
shot to bring us to our knees."

Killingsworth had no answer for his friend. He could only envision
the same black future. America could try to make up the massive energy
shortfalls with nuclear energy, but that would take years. Decades
maybe. In the meantime, the havoc to the economy would be instantaneous — a deep recession certainly. A depression, probably. At the news
the stock market would drop a thousand points. Economic power was
real power, and without Middle East oil, America was anemic. The
Soviets, he thought, had quite literally won World War III by firing a
single shot into O'Malley's rocket.

He left the subject of the *KOSMOS* catastrophe. The president would
soon come to grips with it and make his plan. Now there was another
matter of great urgency. "Mr. President, with your permission, I am
going to order the shuttle's immediate return to earth. The Soviets could

be preparing to attack it at any moment. They could even now justify such an attack as self-defense, considering our assault originated from *Atlantis*."

"Yes, of course. Order it down. The mission has failed. We don't need more dead."

Killingsworth had never witnessed a despair as abysmal as the president's. The man could barely whisper the order.

Wednesday, 23 November
Atlantis

Pettigrew adjusted the clamp that squeezed the IV fluid bag. Without gravity, pressure was the only way to transfer the contents to the vein.

Anna remained unconscious, but that was due to the tranquilizer the flight surgeon had prescribed after her blood pressure had recovered. By all indications, she was out of danger. Her pulse was strong, her color good. She would sleep for several more hours.

Pettigrew's spirits were soaring. Not only was the woman safe, but Mission Control's last report on Mark and Darling had indicated they were safely aboard the *KOSMOS* and were preparing to destroy it.

It hadn't surprised him to hear the *KOSMOS* was a weapon. Only fools would have put faith in Soviet promises to not militarize space. He had come to learn, though, there were plenty of those around in the form of politicians and their advisors. Coddled in ivy-covered universities, insulated from reality, they had listened to bearded, pipe-smoking, New England–accented professors tell them how they could bring world peace armed with nothing more than a law degree and a Senate seat. Blind men teaching others to be blind. The Soviets were the enemy and you never trusted the enemy. To Pettigrew it was as plain and simple as that — a thesis on international relations in a sentence.

The IV finally emptied, and he unzipped the sleep restraint to remove the needle. The work brought Anna's minced hands into view, and he was suddenly alert to the need to treat her wounds — and to clean her. Dried vomit crusted her cheek and matted her hair.

He glided to the mid-deck to gather a water container, washcloth, and the antiseptic ointment and bandages of the medical kit. After dressing her hands and elbows, he pulled the sleep restraint zipper lower to reveal the oozing cuts beneath her breasts. Suddenly the cabin was warmer and his mouth drier. Over the past hours, the threat to her life had made him senseless to her sex. But that threat was now past, and he was suddenly and acutely aware of all that was female hovering next to him.

He momentarily considered not even treating the injury, but a festering, yellowish film made it obvious treatment was necessary. He narrowed his vision to the wounds and began by cleaning the flesh with the damp cloth. The resulting chill unfurled her nipples into pink blossoms, a change that was impossible to miss. He gulped audibly and hurried with the dressing.

He continued lower to clean and bandage the urine-contaminated leg injuries, wishing again he could have somehow watched through a straw to do the work. No matter how hard he tried, the view of the blond pubic curls and the thin line of the cleavage they covered found a place in his brain. He was bomb-squad careful not to touch any more of her than was necessary.

When he finished, he dressed her in a clean T-shirt and shorts, then turned to another cleanup — his own. He was filthy and reeked of vomit and sweat. His hair was oily, and a coarse, two-day beard added to his grimy sense of hygienic neglect.

He stripped naked and drifted to the toilet to urinate, holding the vacuum-cleaner-type tube near his penis to collect the void. Just as he had been told by veterans, the surface tension of the fluid produced a significant last drop. In an instinctive male reaction, he tried to flick the yellow bubble free, but the motion only caused it to elongate like a faucet drip, then rebound into a love affair with his crown. He grabbed a tissue and blotted the fluid, thinking how embarrassingly feminine it felt to do so. *Wiping after pissing! I'll never admit it!*

After a washcloth bath and shave, he returned to the flight deck and resumed his vigil over Anna. He noticed her portable tape player velcroed in a ceiling corner. He grabbed it, popped the tape free and read the titles. It was a compilation of classics, the first title reading *Johann Pachelbel — Canon and Gigue in D major. Pachelbel* could have been a French wine, so illiterate was he in the music of the masters, but the word *Canon* did remind him that Anna had been particularly poetic about that arrangement when they had talked on the dock.

He inserted the tape and turned it on, then darkened the cabin so as to better watch an approaching sunrise. This would be his twentieth orbit dawn, but it was the first he could really enjoy. The sickness, worry about

Mark and Darling, Anna's near death — all of it had made it impossible to appreciate the earlier displays of grandeur.

Now the sable blackness swallowed him. The windows, walls, ceiling — *Atlantis* — disappeared. He was surrounded with the purity of the infinite; overcome with a sense of detachment from the machine, from any bond with earth. Stars fogged the heavens, bright and dim, colored in white and orange and yellow and red and blue. The far-distant galaxies, with their innumerable suns, appeared as faint, tenuous wisps, their light muted to a milky mist by the trillions of miles.

Then the first notes of *Pachelbel's Canon* jerked him into church — into the most sacred sanctuary of flight. A high mass was being sung in harpsichord and violin, and his mind's voice stilled in reverent silence. The combined beauty of sound and sight was very nearly fearful — a pleasure so intoxicating, an orgasm so rich and enduring, it must be forbidden to mortals.

He pulled himself cheek to cheek with Anna and stared straight eastward into the cathedral, falling into the black, appreciating for the first time the rush of its totality, its eternity.

And the music! The music! Surely, he thought, Pachelbel must have lived this moment, seen these sights. What else could have inspired him? There was no earthly beauty, no veil of waterfall, no mountain or glade that could have prompted him to this genius. Space, weightlessness, *flight* was created by his sound, by the music of these violins. It cradled him, carried him, propelled him through the abyss.

Then the colors came, commanded by the magical violins. The first brush of indigo, the first displacement of absolute black, was called with a slow solemnity that befitted the unveiling of creation. Thousands of hours of flight had exposed him to beauty that would fill his soul and give him wing beyond that of the machines that had enveloped him, but never, *never*, had he witnessed beauty as he now beheld it.

Blues, in shades from royal to the palest turquoise, shrugged the indigo upward. The violins danced gayer and the lighter colors came, pinks and yellows only God and spacefarers had ever seen. The arc grew broader and more strings joined to herald the blossom of reds — of scarlet and ruby.

Pettigrew was drunk with the view. The colors were at peak, the music at crescendo, and he wanted both to remain fixed, the moment to never end. If there was such a thing as an infinite, happy afterlife, he envisioned it would be this second, this heartbeat, lived forever.

As the sun breached and he closed his eyes to its fierce white, his thoughts returned to the woman next to him. Had she heard him on the radio? Had she understood his fear, his love? Could he yet have her?

The worry could not keep him from sleep. That had been abused for seventy-two hours and would wait no longer. The cool of the cabin fan, the warmth of the sun, the music, the scent and softness of Anna's skin against his face — all of it summoned sleep.

"*Atlantis*... Houston." He jerked awake at the Capcomm's call.

"Go ahead, Houston."

"Bob, Mr. Killingsworth wants to talk with you."

"Put him on."

In Mission Control, the fat man wiped a handkerchief across his eyes. He had always cried easily in movies and opera for lost love or for a hero's death. Now, heroes had died and he cried. He depressed his microphone button and waited for the right words to come.

"Colonel... There's been a problem."

At the word, Pettigrew went rigid. *Atlantis* was functioning flawlessly. *She* couldn't be the problem. Anna was fine. It had to be — "Mark? Darling?"

"I'm sorry, Colonel. They're gone... dead."

The marine listened as Killingsworth struggled to finish the story. Mark had been a brother. More, really. He had been a member of the *brotherhood*. Pettigrew had loved him as much as any man could love another man.

He spiraled into hell's despair.

Killingsworth finished. "And so, Colonel, you must immediately come back to earth. The Soviets will kill you, too."

"No." His single word was spoken calmly, evenly.

"Yes, Colonel, of course you're correct... It's been explained to me. You just can't come back *immediately*. That was my sense of urgency spilling over. I understand your next deorbit opportunity isn't for two hours. Although that is a very dangerous exposure to Soviet attack, we can do nothing to shorten it. You can come back then."

"No, Mr. Killingsworth, I won't."

"What? You must!"

"Listen up, Mr. Killingsworth! I'm not coming back! I'm not going to leave Mark!"

At the statement, the fat man feared the marine had gone insane. "O'Malley is *dead*! You can do nothing for him by staying. The Soviets have killed two men already. They will…"

"Goddamn you! I don't leave a wingman!"

"But, they're dead!"

"You don't know that!"

"Colonel, we know…"

"Shut the fuck up! You don't know jack shit! A bunch of blips on some screen! Mark and Darling left with four days of oxygen! When that's gone, *then* we'll know they're dead! Until then you're guessing! I'm staying!"

"Colonel, please. I've got enough blood on my hands. Colonel O'Malley and Frank Darling are *dead*. We've seen *Freedom* spinning away. We've called repeatedly and there's no answer. The destruction of the *KOSMOS* should have been completed hours ago, but it's still intact. The evidence is irrefutable. They are *dead*!"

"I'm not leaving them! Not until their oxygen is gone!"

"Colonel, think of Lieutenant Rowe! If you don't care for your own life, think of hers."

"She's a pilot. She'd do the same thing."

"Colonel…"

"Go fuck yourself, Mr. Killingsworth! I'm not leaving!"

Wednesday, 23 November
Approaching Moffet Naval Air Station

Sitting alone in the rear of a presidential jet, Killingsworth watched the lights of San Jose, California, pass under the wing. They revealed a city alive with the preholiday rush. Crawling white dots of auto headlights mingled with the sodium yellow of the streetlights to form a crazy kaleidoscopic grid. People in the pursuit of happiness, he thought — every American's birthright for more than two centuries. But now, a birthright that was in grave danger. What would these same highways look like next Thanksgiving, he wondered? Deserted, ghostly channels of commerce of a waning civilization? The citizens who now hurried to their parties and dinners and theaters would be — where? Quietly huddled in their homes remembering last year's — *this year's* — gaiety? As their grandparents had done throughout World War II, would they be rallied around the radio listening to their president ask for greater and greater economic sacrifices? Would that request be met with the same patriotic fervor of the war years? Could the crisis fuse the nation in a common goal — to preserve America as the light of freedom? He had darker thoughts — of a nation sundered along economic and racial seams, of class struggles, of the fragile fabric of democracy unraveling, of these same rushing citizens marching in the streets, rioting, demanding what they could never again have — the careless pursuit of happiness.

"*Freedom...* Houston. Can you read us?"

Silence.

The aircraft's sophisticated communications system allowed him to monitor Mission Control's call. It was the only sound he had heard for the past three hours — a skipping record, repeating every five minutes. They were calls to the dead.

The lights began to blur. Tears were coming, and he quickly squeezed them away, wiping the wet from his cheeks. He could not release himself to the grief he felt. He had to remain composed. Judy had to be told. The crisis atmosphere at the White House would soon spill into the press. When that happened, it would not take long before some sleuth uncovered news of Mark's and Darling's deaths.

Of all the important missions he had ever undertaken, this was the first he felt incapable of performing. He was too vulnerable, too feminine in his ability to deal with such grief. He was likely to give into his own emotions and crumble into sobs when he confronted her. He rehearsed a speech in his mind. He would tell her of her husband's great sacrifice for his country, that he had died a hero, that he would not be forgotten — the spontaneous eulogy that death messengers delivered in Hollywood films and that somehow always seemed to make a difference to the widow.

Forty minutes later, he was still rehearsing the speech when he pulled to a stop in front of Peggy's house. Lights were on in the windows. Somebody was home. But the speech left him, erased in the panic of seeing the door he would have to confront. For minutes, he waited in the car merely to delay the pain, to give an unsuspecting woman a few more heartbeats of life. Then, one of the lights was switched off. Was Judy preparing to leave? He could wait no longer.

He climbed from the auto and walked the brick pathway. At the door, he hesitated, begged God for strength and inspiration, then pressed the doorbell.

Inside, Judy was preparing a pumpkin pie. Neighbors were coming over tomorrow and Peggy had run to the store for a forgotten item.

"Just a minute!"

The open house and its attendant preparations had been Peggy's idea to distract her guest from the incapacitating terror of "the feeling." And it had worked. In her hurried walk to the front door, Judy wasn't thinking of death. She was wondering how they could ever store all the desserts.

"Sorry, I..." She stopped. *No! No! No!* She knew instantly. The strange little fat man whom she had met in Houston did not have to say a word. She knew. Mark was gone. It was so different than she had imagined on countless other times — being told this way. There was no blue air force car parked in the street, no uniformed wing commander, no somber chaplin. That was the way it was supposed to be. Not a little fat man with miserably sad eyes standing in a coat and tie. But she knew. Without a word, she knew. Mark was gone.

"Mrs. O'Malley, I'm Hobart Killingsworth. We met..."

"He's dead. Isn't he? Mark's dead?" It seemed to her someone else had spoken. The question was delivered softly, calmly. It could not be her speaking. Some other being was using her faculty of speech. The real Judy O'Malley was standing in a mute trance.

Killingsworth struggled to keep from looking away. The elemental fear she displayed should not be seen by anyone. She should be hooded, like the condemned at the gallows. At first, all he could do was nod to her question, but then managed the words. "Yes. I deeply regret to tell you, your husband has perished in the service of his country. He was a superb pilot, Mrs. O'Malley, a brilliant astronaut. There were things... circumstances beyond his control. Please, may I come in? You should sit."

Judy's complexion was chalk, and he feared she might faint. Without waiting for an invitation, he stepped inside, took her by the arm, and brought her to the sofa. He cursed his oversight of not bringing a NASA doctor to administer to her. If she needed help, a civilian doctor would ask too many questions.

"Is there someone home I can call for you?"

She sat and stared dumbly ahead, unaware of how she had even moved from the door. "Peggy will be back in a few minutes." The other being answered, while the real Judy O'Malley was being overcome with a vision of the first time she had ever made love to Mark. She had not willfully called the scene into her brain. It had spontaneously arisen, a crystal-clear memory across a quarter century of time. It was incredible such thoughts came to her now, and she wondered if death always did that — cruelly teased a person with life's most joyous memory.

It was the evening at the windmill, her first time with Mark. Regardless of what the conventions of man said, *that* was her wedding day. She wore a veil of indigo twilight and was anointed with the evergreen perfume of the desert. The drums of a mountain thunderstorm filled the cathedral with its bass song. God watched as the only guest — watched the pristine purity of a woman's love of man. It was her supreme moment of joy. She had captured the man who would love her and give her children and stay with her forever. And now, she saw that marriage in her supreme moment of despair. In the same heartbeat, she could see it, feel it — the joy and the despair. Of an entire life, only the beginning and the end were visible, nothing in between. She could see herself touching Mark's shivering body, see his boyish face in the glow of the campfire, feel his hands awkwardly exploring her breasts. And, simultaneously, she could see the little fat man at the door. Life and death together.

"Where have you taken his body?"

"Mrs. O'Malley." Killingsworth had taken a seat next to her and now removed his handkerchief to dab at his own eyes. "I'm so very sorry to have to tell you this. There are no remains. The accident... it occurred in space."

No remains. She thought how the sky had finally won — taken him completely. Not a trace had been left for her to share. Even the earth had been cheated of its dust. There would be no grave for her to weep over, no parcel of earth to feel close to. He was gone. Completely. Forever. Her soul shrieked its agony.

"Is there something I can get you? A glass of water perhaps?"

She was crying now, great rivulets of tears flowing from her cheeks and wetting her apron. Killingsworth put his arm around her.

"I would like to be alone, Mr. Killingsworth." The request was not an order, just a statement.

Killingsworth worried. She was clearly in need of emotional support. "Mrs. O'Malley, I really don't think it would be wise to leave you alone just yet. I would like to remain at least until your friend returns."

Judy craved solitude. Peggy would soon come home and console her, and she needed that. But afterwards she wanted to be alone. Afterwards, she wanted to be with Mark. She wanted to be alone in the desert and touch the earth where they had coupled and watch the sky and... remember. It was a ridiculous thought, she realized. Even if she could get to New Mexico, she had long forgotten the route she and Mark had taken to that sacred site. But the need remained, as intense and powerful as any she had ever known. She had to be alone.

"You're welcome to stay, Mr. Killingsworth, until Peggy returns. Then I would like to be taken to the beach house." The idea had rushed upon her. His spirit would be there — close to his mistress. It would always be there.

Killingsworth did not understand. "I beg your pardon? The beach house?"

"Yes. The astronaut beach house at Cape Kennedy. I want to be alone." Now that she knew of a place, there was urgency in her words.

Killingsworth saw the request as a godsend. He knew of the facility, having been entertained there during one of his visits. Guarded, isolated — it was the perfect place to hide Judy and her children from potential press leaks while plans were made on breaking the news. "I think the beach house would be an excellent retreat for you and your children. I have an aircraft waiting at the naval air station and will fly you there tonight. En route we can pick up your children."

"I hope you can understand, Mr. Killingsworth, but I would like to be alone at the beach for a while... before I tell my children."

Killingsworth could appreciate her need to prepare herself, but the delay could be risky. "Yes, of course. I can arrange for them to be picked up later." And, he thought, he could order guards to discreetly protect them in the meantime — in case there was a leak.

CHAPTER 17

Thursday, 24 November
KOSMOS

A thump sounded through the module, and Mark jerked his attention to the window. He wished he had not. The lanyard of the frozen corpse had tangled in the *KOSMOS* structure, and the mess that, only hours ago, had been a human being now slowly yo-yoed back and forth along the length of the tether. With no other forces to dampen it, the motion would remain for days. And with no mechanism for decay, the body would remain uncorrupted gore for millennia.

He gagged. The body had floated face into the window, the mouth fixed grotesquely open as if screaming for help. The expression was not too unlike what he had seen seconds before the man's visor had fractured — eyes bugged in fear, a tongue displaced in a silent shriek. But the explosive decompression had added its ghoulish effects. The eight pounds per square inch of pressurized oxygen that had filled the lungs had turned those organs virtually inside out. Even now, hours after death, residual tissue pressure still jetted frozen shards of bloody mass from the mouth and nostrils. As did all ice particles, these caught the sun and glistened beautifully, like a ruby-tinted fireworks fountain.

But the eyes were the worst. There had been no body orifice to relieve the cranial pressure and the vacuum had sucked them from their sockets until the white had assumed golf-ball dimensions. The demonic mime was accentuated by the man's arms and hands, which had been rigidized in a last-second protective reach for his face.

Mark trembled with the memory of how the man had gotten there, of how very close it had come to being his flesh rebounding from the window.

The shadow fell across his arm. "Are you already done, Frank?" He did not look up from his work.

"No. I have drilled out two of eight fasteners. It will take time." The iceman had moved his tether from *Freedom* and was now anchored to the *KOSMOS* belly.

"What's the robot arm doing?"

"It is stationary. I will stay on the north face of this box to avoid detection." He had found a large electronics module connected to the gun by a skein of cabling. Lettering indicated it was a *magnetic field control assembly*. It was one of three devices he intended to strip.

Mark considered the robot's inactivity as proof its cameras had not seen them. But his worry about the machine had made him oblivious to the discrepancy — the shadow could not be Darling's. The man was on the underside of the truss. He was on top.

Another movement of the shadow teased his subconscious. "Frank?" He rolled to look. "Oh Jesus! Frank!"

The screwdriver arced toward him, and in his frozen surprise, all he could do was watch it rip into the right forearm of his suit. The blade cut into the thermal covering and the tear began. Strings of broken fabric and multilayered insulation expanded into a four-inch slash as the instrument was raked along the arm. The underlying pressure bladder herniated outward into a yellow balloon. At any instant, he expected it would rupture, and nature, in its abhorrence of a vacuum, would explode his body.

But his turning motion to investigate the shadow had been just sufficient to throw off the attacker's aim. The tool slipped along the neoprene blister, merely creasing it.

It's manned! The KOSMOS is manned! The red banner of Lenin's revolution, embossed on the shoulder of the cosmonaut's suit, came into view as the man repositioned his body for another attack.

Mark cursed his stupidity. Since man had first hurled a spear, there had never been a weapons system that didn't need his dexterity and reasoning abilities to maintain. In a heartbeat, it all made sense to him — the steady traffic to geosync, the shielding of the reactor, the strange cylindrical modules he had seen on the belly of the machine. Men needed supplies. Men needed transportation. Men had to be guarded from radiation. Men needed a place to live.

How many? There were at least two. Darling's screams told him that. The iceman was out of view but obviously engaged in his own struggle.

The attack was less than five seconds old when the weapon came arcing down in a second stab. Instinctively, Mark reacted to protect his body with his hands, realizing too late it was a reckless maneuver. His torso was shielded by the suit controls. It was his arms and legs that were vulnerable. The blade ripped into the suit just forward of his elbow and was immediately jerked upward for another attempt. The attacker had excellent body position, holding himself with his right hand while savagely pounding downward with his left. Mark rolled to avoid the third blow. The blade missed his shoulder, incising a long curve across his visor and knocking one of his helmet lights free. It spun into a hover a yard away, the beam strobing the fight scene like a police-car beacon.

What would happen now, he wondered? The cosmonaut's mouth was moving in shouts — inaudible because of their incompatible radio frequencies — but certainly being heard in Moscow. They had been caught attacking a manned Soviet asset. Would the Russians use it as an excuse to mobilize for a terrestrial war? It was a brief wonder. His war had already begun.

Flight was his only defense, and he flailed his right arm in a search for his waist tether. Its other end was attached to *Freedom,* and he intended to pull himself to it and release the machine from the *KOSMOS.* The cosmonaut could not follow, and he would be free to fly around the truss and rescue Darling. After that, he had no idea how they could dodge the twenty-thousand-mile reach of the rail gun, but for now they were dead men if they didn't get off the platform.

Another stab crashed into his visor, the attacker now thinking he would be more successful in breaching the plastic.

Mark finally found the tether, and a sharp pull snatched him clear. But it was a temporary sanctuary. In his tumble he caught sight of his pursuer, now in a hand-over-hand sprint along the truss, his own safety line unwinding behind. The man had taken aim on *Freedom* and was rushing to it, intent on releasing the American's anchor and burying him in the black.

Mark reefed in his line and hurtled toward *Freedom*, not caring he was doing so at bone-breaking speed. He had to beat the Soviet — and did. The impact on the side of *Freedom's* cockpit smashed his chin against the neck ring and opened a two-inch cut. Droplets of blood bubbled free and began to stick on the inside of the plastic, threatening him further with their obstruction.

"Frank! How many are on you?!" He madly fumbled with *Freedom's* release mechanism.

Silence.

"Frank! I've got one here! I'm going to try to get to you in *Freedom!* When you see me, jettison your lanyard and push off the platform! I'll catch you!" The airwaves remained silent.

He cursed the latch. Its manipulation required a restrained body position, something he didn't have.

Then, the blunt pressure of the screwdriver blade slammed squarely into the back of his right calf. The cosmonaut was on him again. His panic intensified, totally stealing any remaining dexterity from his fingers. He thrashed his legs. Another strike. Another. A puncture was imminent, and he finally faced the reality he could not escape. He had to defend himself and yanked his body to the toolbox to find a weapon. There was no time for a selection, and he seized the first item he touched — a large wrench. He unsnapped its tether, then whirled to confront the enemy. For a second, it seemed an almost hilarious nightmare to him — that in an era of lasers and rail guns and nuclear weapons, the first space combat was being waged with a wrench and screwdriver.

The cosmonaut was unrelenting. A direct hit excavated a large crater in the center of Mark's visor and jarred loose the remaining helmet light. Both men separated from the platform, and the unwinding, silvery lines of their tethers gave them the appearance of combatant spiders.

Their unrestrained attempts to stab and hammer each other were totally ineffective, but luck came to the cosmonaut first. Their trajectory brought them near *Freedom's* aft fuselage, and he reached out, seized a handrail, and pinned Mark's back to the side of the machine.

The blade arced straight between his eyes, and in an effort to avoid it, he smashed his head on the inside of the helmet like some demented asylum inmate. But a loud thud signaled impact and another crater was excavated.

When he saw the success of his effort, the cosmonaut's motion became machinelike. Arm up. Arm down. Arm up. Arm down. He worked furiously, as if he was attacking a block of ice with a pick, concentrating on the same spot, managing to achieve deeper and deeper penetrations with each blow. A mist of plastic debris rose from the impacts. Mark howled his terror and continued a futile struggle to get from underneath the blade. His left arm shot outward in blind gropes for a handhold.

Arm up. Arm down. Arm up. Arm down. The crater widened and deepened.

As the cosmonaut cocked his arm rearward, Mark's fingers finally curled under an adjacent handrail. He pulled as hard as possible.

This time, the plunge of the screwdriver blade was unimpeded. Mark had jerked himself clear. The tool punctured *Freedom's* paper-thin steel, and the explosive energy of four hundred pounds per square inch of tank pressure found the outlet. Like a rifle shot, the screwdriver exploded backward, smashing squarely into the cosmonaut's faceplate. What he had labored for the previous minute to do to Mark's visor, the tank penetration did instantaneously to his. The plastic fractured at the impact, but not catastrophically so — just a hairline crack that began to slowly migrate. The man screamed, and his hands came to his face in a ridiculous attempt to seal the breach. He would have had as much success sealing a crack in Hoover Dam.

Mark's desperation pull had turned him away from the enemy, and he was unaware of the fatal stab. He only knew he was momentarily free of the blade and had another chance to defend himself. He whirled with his wrench at the ready, expecting to see the cosmonaut pressing the attack, but instead the man was fleeing, pulling himself along his tether back to the *KOSMOS*.

Mark didn't waste any time wondering about the reason for his retreat. He now had a chance to get back to the cockpit, disconnect *Freedom,* and search for Darling.

As his head came down to follow the handrails, he saw it — a thin geyser of ice particles spewing from the tank. *Jesus! He stabbed into the tank! He punctured the tank! We're dead!*

Freedom was bleeding to death, and there was absolutely nothing he could do to stop the hemorrhage. They were stranded. Lost. Dead.

The leak worsened. He could see cracks propagating away from the puncture, and the metal began to rip like cloth. Wrinkles waved through fatigued steel. Welds popped. Whole sections crumpled like wadded paper. The entire machine was dependent upon pressure for structural integrity, and that pressure was rushing into vacuum. *Freedom* was self-destructing.

Like a man trying to run from an earthquake, Mark released the wrench and shot forward along the handrails, suddenly overwhelmed by a single thought. He was tied to the dying beast! It would kill him, too. It was a choice of death now or later, and later looked infinitely better.

Three seconds into the sprint, his fears were realized. The tank failed catastrophically, and the geyser silently exploded into a volcano. An enormous column of glittering liquid hydrogen crystals rose from the wound. On the part of the cloud that sprayed down-sun, a black shadow of the entire *KOSMOS* momentarily appeared and rushed away with the hundreds-of-feet-per-second velocity of the effluent. Errant tracers of the ice ricocheted madly from pieces of the *KOSMOS* and gave Mark the illusion he was trapped in an infantry firefight. But he did not let the stunning visual effects distract him from his escape. Already he could feel the machine bending from the jetlike thrust of the vent, and he watched forward to see the claw failing. Bolts yielded and popped free.

The last two rungs of *Freedom's* handrails shot past, and he impacted the truss. At the same moment, the steel of the claw gave way and *Freedom* became a loose cannon, wobbling drunkenly like an off-balance top and spooling Mark's tether. He was seconds from being pulled away, lashed to *Freedom* as Captain Ahab had been lashed to Moby Dick and headed for an abyss just as deadly. His hand reflexed downward and jettisoned his waist attachment just as *Freedom* sucked up the last of the line and snatched the clip away. He was free — of *everything*. Now, only his hands would keep him on the truss.

Fifty feet away he could see his attacker. The man had stopped and seemed to be preoccupied with his suit controls. Mark moved closer, considering him at the moment to be less of a threat than the out-of-control *Freedom*.

In his translation, a metallic twang waved through the truss and he turned to look. *Freedom* had tumbled into the frame of the *KOSMOS*, and the impact had smashed the decoy housing, somehow firing the remaining missile. The machine's oxidizer tank also ruptured, and a new geyser — this time of liquid oxygen crystals — plumed from the opening and provided another source of thrust. The wounded behemoth began to pinwheel away, tumbling as insanely and soundlessly as one of the tiny ice crystals that streamed in its wake. Striegel's beautiful rocket had been reduced to a deflating, twisted hulk — a space *Hindenburg*.

The cosmonaut turned toward him, and the prayers of the condemned rose from Mark's soul. He was going to die. *A. Volkov* was going to kill him. The enemy's name tag was prominent on the suit chest.

Mark looped his left wrist tether around a piece of the truss and clipped it closed. He would fight to the death one-handed, like an Indian staked to the ground.

But as the man came closer, he saw he was not under attack. The screwdriver still floated uselessly on its tether, and behind the acrylic of the visor, he could see a face mad with terror — the reason now obvious. The crack had widened to nearly bisect the visor. Mark finally understood. Somehow, *Freedom's* destruction had caused the damage. The Soviet had been trying to get back to his airlock when it had become apparent he would never make it. In the madness of that realization, his primordial fear response had turned him to the nearest human — his enemy — for salvation.

But Mark could do nothing. The man was screaming a silent shriek and hysterically clawing at the plastic when the fracture lengthened a final, deadly inch. The helmet exploded outward into Mark's chest. He startled and jerked his head away, and when he next looked back, the cosmonaut's eyes bulged enormous, his bottom jaw shivered in spasms, his mouth frothed with red ice. A piece of his lung exploded from the orifice, froze instantly, and smashed into Mark's own visor, creating a pink snowstorm. His death mimicked *Freedom's*. Like the crumpled machine, A. Volkov's body began a slow, silent, end-over-end tumble, propelled by the red effluent of escaping gases. Legs and arms and fingers shivered as last, confused neurons pulsed from the dying brain. The mess arced around the edge of the truss and out of sight.

Mark snapped from the horror and jerked his head in a search for other attackers, but there were none. It was a lull that allowed him to make a plan. He would locate the dead Soviet's anchor point, pull the body back, and steal its tether and screwdriver. He was going to die — there was no doubt in his mind about that outcome — but at least he could die fighting and possibly even take another attacker with him. And he still had the explosives tethered to his hip. If he could elude the cosmonauts for thirty minutes, he could rig the cord and commit a suicide that would kill the entire spacecraft. But first, he had to find Darling. If the man was alive, they could survive longer as a team and have a better chance of setting the explosives.

He came to the edge of the truss and looked over. Nothing was visible but the immense, blue circle of the earth. He continued lower, around the side of the box beam and to the belly of the machine. The cosmonaut's body returned into view — a vile Peter Pan lazily circling on the end of its tether and spewing a wake of red glitter from the mouth. Also visible was the chaos of boxes and plumbing and cabling that formed the root of the rail gun. And near those, he saw Darling.

The iceman was alive, locked in his own combat with another cosmonaut. It was immediately apparent why he had not answered any of Mark's calls — his radio was damaged. Large sections of white fabric insulation were torn away from his backpack. A twisted piece of aluminum flopped loosely from the same area, as did a frayed edge of torn fiberglass and the radio antenna that had been a part of it. The mechanism for such extensive damage was in the cosmonaut's right hand — a space station maintenance power tool. It extended the man's reach and was tipped with an electric jaw. He launched forward, but Darling parried the thrust with his own tool — an electric hacksaw. Mark watched the duel, powerless to do anything to affect the outcome.

The fight remained neutral through two more Soviet attacks, but on the third, the clash of machinery loosened Darling's grip on his weapon. The cosmonaut rushed to take advantage of the opening. He stabbed the jaws into the American's thigh, then squeezed the trigger that commanded "close and rotate." The bite was deep, and a wad of material ripped away as a ragged clump.

Darling's reaction left no doubt that his suit bladder had been breached. His attention was instantly at his instruments to assess the damage, and the numbers announced it would be a fatal hemorrhage. Already the emergency oxygen supply had automatically activated to make up the loss, but that would be gone in minutes. His options were to die alone or in the company of the enemy. It was an easy choice, made even more so by the overconfident cosmonaut who was now moving inward to finish his cripple.

The iceman kamikazed his body into a head-on collision, stunning the Soviet and sending both of them hurling off the *KOSMOS* in a tangle of tethers and flailing arms. In the tumble, Darling found the handgrip of his still-tethered saw, squeezed the trigger, and made a violent upward slash.

The cosmonaut had been concentrating on his tool controls and had failed to see his victim rearm. He thought himself lucky when the blade missed his suit, and he hurried to separate himself from further danger by shoving hard against Darling's chest. The men somersaulted apart.

There was no reason to pursue the American, he thought. Instead, he would pull himself back to the truss and watch the man die from a safe distance. It could not take long and then he would search for Volkov's killer. He grabbed his tether and pulled for the spacecraft, but there was no answering tug. Just the frayed end of the severed steel rope — his lifeline to the *KOSMOS* — came coiling into view. The American's tool had missed his suit, but not the tether. He had been cut free.

Darling could not hear the screams, but the man's panic was clearly visible. He was a drowning victim, his arms and legs scissoring insanely in an effort to propel himself to the *KOSMOS* island. A piece of the truss passed within inches of his fingers, and his struggle took on a new ferocity to close the gap. But the motion was as wasted as the leg kicks of a lynching victim. In a zero-gravity vacuum, the three-inch gap at his outstretched fingers was as unspanable as three miles.

The iceman spotted Mark and the two men crawled to a meeting. Mark immediately snapped his left wrist tether to Darling's right. It was a cumbersome anchor, but at least it would save him from joining the company of the thrashing man drifting slowly into death.

"Move!"

Mark didn't wait for comprehension. The iceman's suit damage was obvious. He would be dead in minutes. Mark jerked him forward, and they fell into the spastic movement of manacled prisoners in headlong flight. Seconds later they were at the fifteen-foot-diameter domes of the twin modules. He was certain they were the cosmonaut living quarters and an oasis of pressurized air existed on the opposite end — an airlock.

They flew down the length of the tubes and found the chamber — a large, green sphere that looked more like a bathysphere than a thing of space. Lights illuminated its interior, and Mark could see the inner airlock door in its depths. A warm, inviting glow shone from a small window in its center. It was light from a home the owners would never see again.

They entered the alien vessel. The outer-hatch articulation was trivial and Darling cranked it tight, then joined Mark in a frantic search for the controls to repressurize it. Mark flew across the panels of Cyrillic-labeled switches and valves making blind guesses — open, closed, on, off, clockwise, counterclockwise. But the only response was the cycle of various lights.

Then they heard it. A hiss. Air was flowing into the chamber. Air! He had stumbled onto the correct valve arrangement. The volume had already filled enough for sound conduction.

But the reprieve was short. The quiet returned and their suit instruments showed a rapid decrement to vacuum.

It was Darling who first noticed the cause and pulled Mark to the inner-hatch window. The panicked face of a third Soviet floated not more than a foot away, peering into the chamber at the invaders. The man had overridden the airlock repressurization.

"Goddamn you!" Mark whirled to Darling, unfastened the electric drill from his tool caddie, and brought the diamond-tipped blade to the glass. It bit into the crystal and raised the first flecks of debris. No radios or translators were needed to convey his message to the cosmonaut — *You will die, too.* The drill was as good as a pistol pointed at his brain — a mechanism for decompressing the *KOSMOS* and killing everyone inside.

The bit penetrated the first layer of the multipaned glass and cut into the face of the second. The cosmonaut's mouth formed silent shrieks for Mark to stop.

"Give us air! Goddamn you! Air!"

More glass fragments floated from the tip of the slowly turning blade and intensified the Soviet's horror. The invaders were mad! They were going to kill him! He fled to a control panel and began a furious manipulation of valves.

The airlock pressure increased. Two psi. Four. Eight. Darling was out of danger. The numbers stopped on fourteen-point-seven-pounds per square inch — a sea-level atmosphere. Both men immediately jettisoned their gloves and helmets.

The iceman seized Mark's shoulder. "Leave me!"

"What?!"

"I cannot go back with my suit damaged. I will stay with the *KOSMOS*. Leave the explosives. You take *Freedom* and deorbit to *Atlantis*. Maybe the ground can send something up to get me. If not, I can destroy…"

"There is no *Freedom*. The cosmonaut stabbed a screwdriver into it. The tank ruptured. It's gone."

"Gone?"

"Yea. We're stranded. Now help me out of this thing… quick! That son of a bitch might try venting this airlock again."

Darling opened Mark's waist ring and he struggled from the torso, then quickly wiggled out of the pants. He helped Darling undress.

"I only see the one, but there may be more." Mark peered into the module, moving his head to different angles to see around the damage of the drill. The cosmonaut now floated at the far end of the sixty-foot tube, brandishing a long-handled flashlight as a club — another space weapon the science fiction writers had missed. "Grab something for a weapon. We've got another fight."

Darling seized a crowbar from the tool caddie, while Mark armed himself with the largest screwdriver he could find. He holstered it through a piece of his cooling garment, then unlocked the hatch and pushed it inward.

Immediately, the smells of confined human habitation came to him — the stale odor of unwashed bodies and food. There were also the familiar sounds of a spaceship — the steady hum of cooling fans. But that was barely audible over another noise — the sobs and cries and screams of a man. It was a Russian voice, but not that of the cosmonaut facing him. That man remained silent and postured for self-defense. The voice was coming from a radio speaker.

"What's that?"

"It is the cosmonaut I cut loose. He wants to be rescued." There wasn't a trace of human care in Darling's comment.

Mark was nauseated. There was now a voice to go with the face of death. There was no hope of rescuing the man.

He pushed slowly into the volume, careful to investigate the ceiling above the airlock hatch for an ambush. There was no one. Darling followed, and the two men grabbed handholds to face their latest enemy.

The man was small — no bigger than Mark himself — with thinning hair, a several-day-old white beard, bifocal glasses, and a tube of flab bulging his tan jump suit. And he was old, probably in his mid-fifties, was Mark's guess. A name tag read "V. Maksimov."

Without the encumbrance of the spacesuit, size and youthful strength would be the winner in this fight, and Mark was glad for Darling's imposing frame. The iceman radiated the cool confidence of an intercity gang leader, an expression not missed by the cosmonaut. His eyes darted nervously over the American giant — a nervousness that intensified when the iceman spoke in Russian.

"What did you tell him?"

"I will kill him."

"We're not killing anybody unless we have to. And this guy is no fighter. He's ready to wet his pants. Tell him if he drops that light, we won't hurt him. And let's start closing on him while you talk. I don't want him to find his balls and try a suicide. Those controls next to him could do anything."

While handling the screwdriver, Mark guided himself around a chair anchored in front of a bank of computer screens and came within six feet of the man. Darling demanded surrender, but the Soviet answered angrily and gestured with the flashlight.

"He does not believe us. We have already killed the others, he says." Another burst of screams from his dying comrade emphasized that fact.

"Self-defense... tell him that. And I'll stay to his right. You take his left."

Darling offered the self-defense excuse while they made the split. The cosmonaut shouted and took an ineffectual swipe at Mark before floating a yard backward into a corner.

"Let's go!"

It was no fight. Mark's shout drew another swing of the flashlight, which Darling countered with a vicious stroke of his own. The steel bar narrowly missed shattering bone and instead fell on the light. That exploded in a shower of plastic splinters before ripping loose from the cosmonaut's hand. Then, with a skill and swiftness that had "professional" written all over it, Darling was behind the man and pulling the tool into his neck in a strangulation lock. Sickening, guttural noises came from his throat to form a stereo horror with the shrieks from the speaker. The Soviet released his handhold to fight the choke, and both men spun into the center of the module.

"Hold him in that chair!" Mark grabbed Darling to stabilize and guide him so the cosmonaut's body was over the seat. A lap belt floated from its sides, and he snapped it around the prisoner's waist. It was hardly a jail, but at least it gave Darling an anchor. The iceman moved behind the seat, clasping it with his knees and keeping the crowbar jammed into the cosmonaut's throat.

Mark searched the cabin for something to serve as a rope and was gratified to find the Soviets had discovered the same space flight essential as had the Americans — duct tape. A three-inch-wide roll of it was stuck to the *KOSMOS* wall.

"Frank! Jesus, you've killed him!" When he next turned back, the cosmonaut's tongue was disgorged, his eyes bulged, his face purpled in asphyxiation. The iceman maintained his choke hold, his own face reddened with the exertion of his effort.

"Frank! Let go! Goddamnit, we need him!"

"He is not dead. He has been without oxygen for only thirty seconds." Mark was stunned at the matter-of-fact reply. In his entire military career, he had never met a man who appeared so indifferent to the excesses of combat.

"And now he will not resist when we tie him." Darling released the bar and steadied himself over his victim, whose starving brain now commanded great, heaving breaths.

The iceman was correct — there was no resistance as they taped his arms and legs to the chair. The man was a defeated, wheezing hulk.

"Ask him if he's alone and where this leads." Mark pointed to the entrance of a darkened tunnel near where the cosmonaut had made his last stand. "And find out how to turn off that speaker." Darling seemed unaffected by it, but the childlike pleading was torturing Mark.

The iceman translated and the cosmonaut motioned sullenly with his head. Mark followed the nod, grabbed a switch, and flipped it. A welcome silence followed.

The man balked at providing more information, but Darling brought the crowbar to his throat and he immediately found his tongue. "The tunnel leads to their habitability module. This is the control module. He says they were a three-man crew, but others are on the way to rescue him. We should surrender to him, he says, and he will ensure our safety."

"Yea, I'll bet. And I believe in the tooth fairy." Mark had no doubt that others were on the way. Time and again, in crisis situations, the Soviets had demonstrated their ability to mount ambitious space missions on extremely short notice. They had launched a reconnaissance satellite every day during the Falkland and Israeli-Arab wars, and they would certainly work even greater miracles to retake their space flagship.

He looked from a large, floor-mounted window that held a view of earth, thinking bitterly of how long it would take his own country's anemic space forces to respond — months if they were lucky. And that assumed they could be alerted. Their sole source of communication with the ground had been lost with *Freedom*. The suit radio transmitters could not reach earth.

"I'm going to search the rest of this thing. Stay here and watch him. Close the hatch after I'm in this tunnel and jam the handle with something. Don't open it unless you see my face in the window."

Mark floated to the airlock to retrieve a light from Darling's helmet, then took the crowbar as a weapon. He glided into the tunnel, and Darling closed the hatch.

The tunnel was not long — only about six feet — and exited into a ball-shaped node that connected to another tunnel at right angles. He carefully swept the beam through both volumes. They were empty. Floating the fifteen-foot length of the second tube, he entered another node and adjoining tunnel. The course was a square U-turn that had brought him across the end of the two modules and turned him into the living quarters. It was vacant.

The module was dimensionally a twin of the other — sixty feet long by fifteen feet in diameter — but contained less of the complex computer equipment and displays he had seen next door. An exercise bicycle was bolted to the ceiling, and a food-preparation center occupied a piece of wall. An open folding curtain revealed the white plastic of a toilet seat and the multifarious plumbing that was part of a zero-g waste-collection system. Storage lockers checkered the floor, and there was a niche for a small library of books. In several places, large color posters of earth scenes were taped as decorations — scenes of mountains and forests and streams, and of women in various nude poses. The entire layout suggested long-term, male habitation.

But the furnishings that most held his eye were the six coffin-size berths aligned vertically on one wall. Each had a sliding privacy door. They were all open and all empty, but their number suggested the possibility of more men. It was a possibility that prompted him to wipe the sweat from his palm for a better grip on the tool. At the far end of the tube there was yet another darkened cavity that could be an ambush site. He floated to the entrance, probed it with the light, and found the cramped complexity of a spaceship cockpit — the earth-return module. Three couches faced a panel filled with dials and switches. For the moment, his only interest was that it was empty. Their prisoner had told the truth. He was the lone *KOSMOS* survivor.

Back in the control module, he explained his findings to Darling. "He's alone. There's some type of earth-return capsule docked at the north end of the tube, and I'll bet every one of these nodes can handle another capsule. I'd give us three days before we have armed company."

They were interrupted by the sound of a scrolling printer. A teletype machine was receiving a message. The cosmonaut snapped his head to the noise, and a new wave of panic appeared in his eyes.

"Our friend is worried. See if you can translate that."

Darling floated to the machine and began to read.

"What is it?"

For an instant, the iceman was too stunned to answer.

"What is it?" Mark repeated his question.

"They do not know we are here!"

"What?! The Soviets?!"

"Yes! Moscow does not know we are here!"

"That's impossible! They have to know! These guys had to have told them!"

"But this is a list of targets! Look. Look at this! See this table?" He pointed to the headings. "This says 'Red Sky Demonstration Targets,' and here, 'Engagement Times.' I am not sure of these titles." He indicated other columns. "They are technical acronyms or abbreviations, maybe information they load into the computer for gun control. But there is not a word in here to indicate anything other than an operationally ready *KOSMOS*!"

Business as usual? Mark could not believe it. How could Moscow not know?

The printer stopped and a tone sounded. Darling read the last entry.

"They ask for message acknowledgment."

"Jesus!" Mark rocketed to the cosmonaut and began to untape him from the seat. "Tell this son of a bitch to do it! I don't care what it takes, but get him to acknowledge the message! We'll figure out later what the fuck is going on... how we've stayed hidden... but for now, get him to acknowledge that message!"

Darling seized the man and shouted the order, but he refused to cooperate. "Others will come and rescue me! You will be spared if..." The iceman calmly backhanded the speech to an abrupt end. Blood percolated from the Soviet's nose and floated around his head as ruby planets.

The printer scrolled another line, identical to the last. A tone repeated.

"Make the acknowledgment or you will die."

"By the articles of the Geneva Convention, I do not have..."

Another vicious backhand atomized the module atmosphere with more droplets of blood. Mark watched the terror building in the prisoner's eyes. He was awakening to his interrogator's latent, deadly violence — to an expression that projected *enjoyment*.

Another tone requested acknowledgment.

"Listen, you fucker!" Mark shoved Darling aside, grabbed the cosmonaut, and screamed in his face. "Answer it or I'll personally put you in that airlock and depressurize it and cheer when your fuckin' eyes explode! Tell him, Frank!"

Darling did, and added his own encouragement. He reached to the speaker switch and flipped it on to return the hideous pleas of the drifting cosmonaut. Then he clamped the back of his subject's neck and smashed his face into the floor window and into an eye-to-eye stare with the frozen corpse.

"Meet death." He paused for several seconds, then turned the man's face to the printer. "Meet life." The iceman's calmness, his economy of words, was far more terrifying than Mark's hysteria. There was no longer any doubt in the cosmonaut's mind, Darling would actually prefer him to resist or attempt to signal a warning. The American wanted to kill.

The iceman returned him to the window and waited for a fresh burst of radio pleas to end. "Remember… death." He whispered the threat as a man might whisper an endearment in his lover's ear. "Choose." He released the prisoner.

It was suddenly an easy choice. Wiping the blood from his face, he drifted to the printer and typed the acknowledgment the ground expected. Darling stayed next to him, watching for the slightest display of heroism. There was none. Moscow ended the transaction with more text, which Darling read. "Comrade Kobozev sends his greetings and wishes the Red Sky cosmonauts good hunting."

"Comrade Kobozev is going to be disappointed. Get him in the chair and let's get some more answers."

After retaping him, Mark began. "Who are you? What is your job on this thing?"

The cosmonaut hesitated for a moment, entertaining thoughts of resistance, but another glance at Darling ended the consideration. His answers flowed through the iceman. "I am the Chief Scientist Doctor Maksimov. I am here to oversee the operation of the rail gun."

That was easy for Mark to believe. The man looked like he belonged in a lab.

"The others?"

"You have murdered pilot Volkov. Commander Abramov is adrift."

"What were they doing outside?"

"Correcting a malfunction with a backup current limiting device. We had just finished installing a replacement unit with the aid of the robot arm when we sighted you."

"How is it that Moscow doesn't know we're up here?"

Answers to the past questions revealed little. The answer to this one would help the Americans. He paused, looking nervously from man to man. Darling grabbed him by the throat and squeezed a reminder of his earlier strangulation. "We use a laser communications system that requires a relay to contact Moscow." That much was obvious to Mark. None of the Soviet landmass was visible from the window, so none could be in direct contact by a beam of laser light. "Normally we use *Molityna East* as a relay, a stationary satellite over the Indian Ocean, but several days ago it malfunctioned. We have been forced to use *KOSMOS 1842* as a backup. It was never intended for this purpose and is in a highly elliptical orbit."

He continued, but Mark did not need the further explanation. An elliptically orbiting satellite would only be in view for portions of the day. It had been eclipsed by the earth when he and Darling were discovered. There had been no way to contact Moscow. They had been saved by the idiosyncrasies of a machine, by the unpredictable insanity of a chip of silicon in the *Molityna East* spacecraft.

"Do you have a UHF radio?" It was a standard medium of aircraft voice communication. The shuttle had one, and Houston monitored it through sites around the world. If the *KOSMOS* was UHF-equipped, there was a chance they could tune into Mission Control.

"No."

"Don't lie to me!" Mark surprised himself by slapping his prisoner. Fatigue and desperation had pushed him beyond care that he was beating a defenseless, portly, middle-aged man.

"No! I am not lying! Secrecy was essential to the success of our mission. We could not dare to communicate through a radio, even encrypted radio. The very existence of such communication would reveal our presence."

Mark accepted the answer. It made sense. A laser communication link was highly directional. U.S.-based monitors could have never intercepted it. The spillover of a traditional radio link would have been easily detected.

"What about the return-vehicle comm system? What frequency does it operate on?"

"It is S-band at twenty-two hundred megahertz."

That, too, was incompatible with the NASA and air force links. There would be no communication with Houston.

"What are your duties on the earth-return vehicle?"

"Engineer. I operate the electrical, environmental, navigation, communications, and the other systems."

"Navigation? Are there deorbit targets loaded onboard?"

"No. Moscow provides those in the last hour before return."

Just like the shuttle, Mark thought. They would want the freshest vector before reentry. To attempt a return with anything else would be fatal.

"Could you pilot the return vehicle?"

"No. I am a scientist, not a pilot."

He was the analog of an American mission specialist astronaut, capable of everything but actually flying the vehicle.

"What is Red Sky?"

Dr. Maksimov continued to tell of the Soviet plan.

Maksimov's story had ended two hours ago. Now, except for the cyclic thump of the cosmonaut's body against the window, the module was quiet. Mark had taken the first watch and ordered Darling to sleep. The prisoner remained taped to his chair. Over the hours, his expression had slowly returned to one of defiance. And Mark could understand why. The man sensed his rescue was only a matter of time.

They were hopelessly stranded. There was no possibility of communication with the ground. The return vehicle, with no deorbit targets and no pilots to fly it, was as useless as *Freedom*. At nineteen hundred hours Greenwich Mean Time — in thirteen hours — the Red Sky attacks were to begin. Moscow would scream for answers when they didn't. *What then,* Mark wondered. *The Soviets would be coming for us, that's what.* And what could he do when that happened? Surrender? The only other alternative was to destroy the platform and commit suicide in the process. Like a defender at the Alamo, he was faced with a line in the sand. He could remain behind it and save his life by surrendering, or he could step across it and into the grave of a heroic last stand. In his career, he had imagined an airborne death in many forms, but never like this, never from a considered act of self-destruction.

The tethered cosmonaut's body continued its drunken sail. The other cosmonaut had drifted four hundred feet away — not yet far enough to hide the fact he was a live, kicking human being. *Freedom* was a distant geysering pinwheel, and the remnants of its destruction were visible everywhere — ice particles, shards of metal, the bright star of the errant decoy. As countless veterans before him, Mark stared into the silent, chaotic aftermath of a first battlefield and wondered what titanic forces had been unleashed.

CHAPTER 18

Thursday, 24 November
Atlantis

As her eyes flickered open and she was blinded by the sun, Anna's first thought was she was dead. She recalled that death — the pain in her hands, the distraction of extreme thirst, the mistake with the tether, floating free, seeing *Atlantis's* lights slowly moving away. She remembered screaming and beating at the vacuum with her arms, trying to swim to *Atlantis*, and the overwhelming fear of death, the panic, the vomiting. The emesis had fouled the suit oxygen system, and the machine had begun to sing its own alarms of death. She had choked on the fluid at her face. An incapacitating shock had claimed her. And she had died.

But the dreamy illusion ended as *Atlantis* streaked into eclipse. Her eyes opened to the fading colors of sunset, and her other senses followed with their messages of reality. She could hear the rush of air from the cabin-fan outlets, feel the throbbing pain in her fingers and breasts, taste the metallic dryness in her mouth. And there was more — the bandages on her wounds, the sleep restraint around her. This was not death.

Now she tried to recapture the missing hours — or were they days? She had no idea. How did she get into the cabin? There were fragments of memories of struggling with the airlock hatch, of Pettigrew shouting at her, but no certain recollections. There were also other memories — of Pettigrew calling, of a woman being mentioned. Kathy? Carol? No, it had been Karen, she remembered. But what was the message? She could not recall. The events had been hopelessly scrambled by the suffocating panic.

Pettigrew! Her hands jerked to her body and felt the clothes, the bandages. *On my breasts! My thighs! He saw me! He touched me!* She felt dirty, violated.

She rolled her head to search the cabin. Only the green glow from a single computer screen provided illumination, but it was enough to see the outline of the pilot's body around his seat.

"Bob?"

There was no answer and she floated to his side. A lap belt held him and he was zero-gravity flaccid, his arms floating in front of his face as if they had been bizarrely splinted. But he was not asleep. His eyes were open and staring blankly into the computer screen. Its light was mirrored in his pupils and gave him an alien appearance.

"Bob?" Still there was no response. "Bob? Are you okay?"

She followed his line of sight to the screen to see what had so captured him. A routine status message was flashing on the fault line. It was certainly nothing to explain the look on his face — absolute despair. She punched off the message.

"Bob, what's..."

"Mark and Darling are missing and presumed dead."

"Oh, God! No!" The same blade that had pierced him now twisted in her breast.

"Killingsworth called. They made it to the vicinity of the *KOSMOS* and confirmed it was a rail-gun platform, but that was the last word from them. Then NORAD saw *Freedom* tumbling away, out of control. The *KOSMOS* is still in one piece. Mark hasn't answered Houston's calls, and a body-sized object was seen by air force radar."

The story refreshed the terror she had just lived — the fall, the waiting to die, to suffocate, the screams, the kicking and clawing at nothing. She prayed it was not so, that the men were somehow safe — or, if not, they had been mercifully taken.

Pettigrew continued. "Killingsworth wants us to come home. The Soviets have given the president an ultimatum. In seven hours they are going to fire on our satellite fleet to convince him of the lethality of the goddamn thing. Killingsworth thinks we're a target."

"What?! Deorbit?! No! We can't leave them!" Her eyes returned to the computer, afraid Pettigrew had already begun entry preparations. She was prepared to break his arms if he had. "They might have made a mistake! Maybe their radio has failed! They could still be alive! We can't leave them!"

As miserable as he felt, the vehemence of her answer, her willingness to put her life on the line for a fellow pilot, filled him with an intense sense of camaraderie, of intimate oneness. He had known she would be this way.

"I told him the same thing. We're not going back until their oxygen is known to be depleted. That's the only real measure of their lives."

At that reassurance, Anna backed away. She retreated to the left seat to confront her own mountain of grief. She had been close to Mark. Not as close as she knew Pettigrew had been. No woman could share that male bond of friendship. But she suffered identically.

Prayers came for the missing men, for Judy, for the nation. *The nation.* What would happen to it, she wondered? How could it survive?

❖

Thursday, 24 November
The White House

The president signaled for the Security Council briefing to begin. He was anxious for an update after having been gone for two hours to make calls to London, Paris, Bonn, and Tokyo. Inside, he raged at some of the hedging he had already heard in those conversations:

No, Mister President, France will not authorize the use of its air or naval facilities for the purposes of deploying American forces to the Persian Gulf.

Mister President, please understand our position. Japan gets virtually ALL of its oil from the Middle East. It is critical that nothing be done to interrupt that supply.

We feel, Mister President, that it would not be in West Germany's best interest to move to a higher alert status at this time.

It was already starting, he thought — the disintegration of the Western Alliance. Their economies were lubricated by Middle Eastern oil, and just the hint of an interruption was enough to send the politicians into panicked reappraisals of long-standing treaties and military agreements.

General Bachman moved to the wall map and began his briefing. "We have identified the Soviet naval forces converging on the Persian Gulf. Those are the aircraft carrier *Kiev* battle group, consisting of that ship plus the guided-missile cruisers *Kirov* and *Frunze*, four guided-missile destroyers, and probably a screen of *Oscar* and *Mike*-class attack submarines. That battle group had been on routine maneuvers in the northwest Indian Ocean until the ultimatum was delivered. At that time, it altered heading for the Gulf of Oman. Also, two destroyers, which were already in the Persian Gulf, are now steaming south for the Straits of Hormuz. It appears the Soviets intend to enter Iranian territorial waters in the vicinity of the naval base at Bandar Abbas. That is the choke point for all Persian Gulf traffic."

"When will they reach that objective?"

"The *Kiev* group has cut its speed so arrival will occur nearly coincident with the *KOSMOS* demonstration. The two other ships are running at flank speed and should make a rendezvous with the battle group about an hour later."

"And tell me again what we have to face their navy?"

The chief of naval operations took the question and rose to point at blue-colored ship symbols on the map. "Mr. President, we have the guided-missile cruiser *Alabama*, two destroyers, a mine sweeper, and an unarmed oiler."

"Your assessment, Admiral, of the results of a conventional engagement between those opposing forces?"

The officer shook his head. "Not good, sir. Not good at all. The *Alabama* and the destroyers are armed with anti-ship cruise missiles, as are the Soviet ships. But the Soviets have a full contingent of attack aircraft aboard the *Kiev* that we could not counter. Our losses would be heavy, perhaps even total. The enemy would certainly take some hits, but there is no doubt they would run us over. Of course, that situation will change in a few days when the aircraft carrier *Kennedy* and her battle group gets on station."

A few days might as well be a few months, the president thought. He had only hours to work with. The Soviets could not have planned a better Pearl Harbor.

"So... we keep coming back to the same bottom line. We have a nuclear-missile strike force as useless as a slingshot and a pitifully weak conventional force in the Gulf."

"Mr. President, I would not write off the deterrence of our missiles." General Bachman spoke. "Even with the successful demonstration of the destruction of our satellites, we don't know that a significant number of our missile warheads wouldn't get through."

"General, would you be willing to bet this country on that? How do we know there aren't three or four or *ten* of those goddamn rail guns up there? Maybe they could shoot down everything we could throw at them… four times over."

"Of course, we can't positively know, but…"

"Goddamnit, Dick!" The president was not finished. "How many times did you, yourself, defend Star Wars in Congress on the basis that even a *limited* system would call into doubt an enemy's missile force? Well, you were damned right about that! They've got at *least* a limited system, and I sure as hell doubt *my* missile force!"

The officer nodded. It had been that way through the night — the military brass struggling to accept the reality of the amputation of two legs of the nuclear triad.

"Mr. President." Air force Chief of Staff, General Ron Lawson, the most outspoken of the hawks, claimed the floor. "We do have another option. Launch our strategic bombers. Those would be invulnerable to any space-based weapon."

"Ron, those bombers of yours are vulnerable to Soviet air defenses. I know it and the Soviets know it. And *you* know it! You've said as much in your frequent testimony to Congress to get funds for improvements in their penetration capabilities."

"But *some* would get through, Mr. President! And Belidov might have second thoughts when his radar reports a wave of four hundred B-52's and FB-111's coming over the pole for him."

"And what do I do, Ron, when he reciprocates? When I see a couple hundred bombers coming over the pole at *me*? Or worse, when I see a couple *thousand* warheads headed toward me because he's panicked and pulled his nuclear trigger!"

"Mr. President." Senator Bowen joined the conversation. He was among three key members of Congress invited to share in the crisis management. "We should not give in to… to rampant militarism and have this thing get out of control." He glanced at General Lawson, who bristled at the innuendo of recklessness. "The Soviets have made a threat. We should match that threat identically. Escalate as they escalate. That type of restraint has served us well in past crises."

The president wanted to snap at the man's idiocy but checked himself. "Tom, we've considered that, but a game of escalation only works when both sides have the same toys. Otherwise you can get into some complex and very dangerous equivalency situations. What is the equivalent worth of one hundred military satellites? Is it one Soviet ship? A squadron of their planes? A battalion of their men? A grain embargo?"

"No, of course not. We attack their satellite fleet as they attack ours."

"How, Senator?" It was General Lawson's challenge.

"With those missiles of yours, General."

"Senator, I believe it was your peers who terminated our ASAT program. As a result, we have exactly *four* rounds that have been sitting in storage for ten years. I doubt any of them would work."

The president interrupted the confrontation. "What is being done to protect the satellites, Ron?"

"Sir, there is little that can be done. We are changing the orbits of those that have the fuel to do so, but how effective that will be is anybody's guess. We don't have any idea of how the rail-gun projectile is guided."

"What about the space shuttle and her crew?" The president admired Pettigrew's guts and loyalty and was glad the man had stayed in orbit. Killingsworth's call that the marine had mutinied with a cry of "go fuck yourself" had been a tonic. It was what he had wanted to say to Foreign Minister Skripko, and Pettigrew had done it for him by not running. In spite of his gloom, he was tickled with the thought that the marine's message might live in the annals of American battle cries: "Remember the Maine" at San Juan Hill; "Nuts" at the Battle of the Bulge; "Go fuck yourself" at the first battle for space.

"Again, sir, there is little that can be done. Her crew refuses to use fuel for orbit changes. They want to save it in case O'Malley is alive and makes it back to low earth orbit. They would then need it for the rendezvous."

"Has anyone's opinion changed on the debris that has been sighted?"

"No, sir. My people in NORAD are more certain than ever, they are tracking the wreckage of *Freedom*."

"Then why haven't the Soviets said something about that attack?"

Fifteen blank faces stared back. It was a question that had been asked repeatedly through the night and it still lay unanswered. At every summons to a phone, the president had expected news of a righteous Soviet protest against O'Malley's assault. But it had never come. *Why?* The silence made no sense. Why weren't they crowing the mission failure was proof of the invincibility of the platform? The more he considered it, the more baffled he was.

He left the question. "Dick, I want you to continue to move everything you can into the Gulf. And go to a higher alert status with our strategic missile forces. Our silos may be just holes in the ground, but I will concede to you — we should capitalize on whatever deterrence they do represent. Be obvious. Make sure the Soviets know. I don't want them guessing about what we're doing. We're walking the razor's edge of a nuclear apocalypse here and I don't want any misunderstandings. As for our bombers... arm them and disperse them. Put some on airborne alert over U.S. territory. Again, be obvious."

"Yes, sir."

"Ron, dust off those anti-satellite missiles of yours and be ready to engage four of their satellites after ours are hit. It'll just be a pinprick to them, but it's something.

"Admiral, I want your forces to hold their blocking positions between Iranian territorial waters and the Soviet forces."

The chief of naval operations nodded.

Then the president fell silent and swiveled his chair to watch the sunrise from an east window. The horizon was pink with the promise of a glorious Thanksgiving Day. The new-fallen snow blanketed the ground and gave a post-card-perfect sense of tranquillity to the scene. It was a sight totally incongruous to the black mood of the room. He stared at the beauty for long moments, so long that some wondered if he had nodded off. But he was awake, struggling with the monstrous decision — to stand or run?

❖

Thursday, 24 November
KOSMOS

It was an uncomfortable feeling to wear a dying man's clothes, but Mark had no choice. The struggle on the platform had opened a small leak in his UCD bladder and urine had wetted the cooling garment. The mess had sent him on a search of the *KOSMOS* lockers where he found S. Abramov's tan coveralls.

Except for the drone of the cooling fans and the rhythmic drumming of a pump somewhere in the bowels of the machine, the *KOSMOS* was quiet. Darling remained asleep, floating from a ceiling tether he had attached to his waist. His torso and limbs were bent as if he were riding an invisible motorcycle — the pose of zero-gravity sleep. The cosmonaut was a sullen wreck, with one eye swollen closed and bruises beginning to darken his throat. He was virtually mummified in the duct tape, relieving Mark of any worry he could escape to call Moscow.

Mark distracted himself from his own nearly overpowering need for sleep by examining the module in greater detail. The cylinder was primitive. There was no finishing veneer as on the shuttle, and a spaghetti of wires and plumbing crisscrossed bare metal. Like the airlock, the volume had the look of a submarine, not a spacecraft. The curved walls were intermittently ribbed with hoops of reinforcing steel. These were attached with large, round-headed rivets installed in seemingly careless patterns. It was a minimum-wage, boiler-works form of metalworking — crude, cheap, but functional.

But if the basic module seemed to be the work of a third-world shipyard, its contents were not. At the rail-gun control station, the unknowing betrayal of western merchants was seen in the logos of major American and Japanese computer companies. He wondered how much of the equipment outside was similarly marked or of direct western lineage. It was the communist prophecy fulfilled — that capitalistic democracies would sell the very rope needed for their hanging.

He checked the clock and floated to Darling. "Frank… Frank, wake up."

The iceman startled. His eyes took in Mark's new wardrobe and he had a short-lived panic the cosmonaut had escaped.

"Everything's all right. I needed some clean clothes. I brought you one of Volkov's flight suits." He nodded toward the garment wedged under a cable. "He was the biggest of the three. You may want to try it on… and stand watch for me. I'm going to have another look at the *Soyuz*."

The iceman nodded.

"And keep looking through these documents and see if you can find any information on deorbit targets. Call me if anything comes through on the teleprinter."

The silent man nodded again.

Mark grabbed a flashlight, then glided through the tunneling and into the habitability module. He went immediately to the earth-return vehicle. Their prisoner had identified the machine as a *Soyuz* capsule — the 1970s-era workhorse of the Soviet manned program.

By the arrangement of instruments and controls, it was obvious the left position was the commander's, and Mark buckled himself into that couch. His hands came to the knobbed controls of the THC and RHC, and the touch of their cold plastic quickened his pulse and warmed his soul. He was once again in a cockpit — primitive and alien, but a cockpit nevertheless.

If only he had some deorbit burn targets, he thought. It was a machine that could return three men to earth. Anywhere on earth, he reminded himself. The *Soyuz* was an antique of the space age, hardly more than a sophisticated cannonball. It did not need a fifteen-thousand-foot runway and good weather and adequate lighting to make a landing — all requirements for a shuttle landing. It was a reentry capsule with an ablative heat shield and parachutes — the old "Spam-in-the-can" design monkeys had first certified as safe for man and the early test pilots had so vilified. Mark had even done so himself and on countless occasions had thanked God he had been born late enough to avoid such a denigrating experience. Now he begged God to allow him to pilot a Spam can to earth — a Soviet Spam can — one that was better in design than its pre-shuttle American counterparts because it could land *anywhere*. The old American space dinosaurs had only been capable of surviving water landings. The *Soyuz* had the added feature of touchdown braking rockets that fired at the last second to make a land impact survivable.

It would be a simple flight home, he thought. Perform a plane-change burn to tilt the orbit to track across the continental United States and then a second burn to drop out of orbit. They would have to jettison the propulsion module before reentry, but the surviving cosmonaut would know how to do that.

But it was merely a flight of fantasy without burn targets. The plane change could be done safely by the seat of the pants — put the nose on the North Star and fire the maneuvering engines. But it would be suicide to try to "John Wayne" a deorbit burn. They would have to hit an extremely narrow entry corridor to survive — thread a needle from twenty-two thousand miles. An overburn would result in too steep an impact on the atmosphere, which would either incinerate them or crush them to grease spots by the enormous g-forces of the braking action. Too shallow an entry could skip them off the atmosphere and into an orbit from which a return would be impossible.

Mark was sure the cosmonaut was not lying — he did not have the targets. And he was sure Darling's search of the checklists would be futile. Autonomy of any type was an anathema to the Soviet system, a system founded on the belief the individual could never be trusted — not on earth, not at geosync. To find Moscow had given the *KOSMOS's* crewmen the means of calculating their own deorbit targets would have been as astonishing as finding they had given their citizens the right to keep and bear arms.

Certain he was wasting his time, he slipped from the harness and began his exit, but the view from the port window stopped him. It was the view that he had, for so long, begged God to give him. It was there, beyond the glass, beyond the gore of the battleground — Earth. A blue-white marble, the moon walkers had called it. He saw it as a blue-white basketball, dominated by the immensity of the Pacific Ocean. That mass extended from pole to pole and wrapped out of sight around the western rim. Vast frozen plates of it reached around the ends of the hemisphere. The landmasses appeared as an insignificant afterthought of a God of water and ice. The entire North American continent was reduced to a brown, barren island, with only the most colossal of its features visible — the dark cavities that were the great lakes, the peninsulas of Florida and Baja, the gnarled spine of the Rockies. The great rivers — the Mississippi, the Colorado, and the Rio Grande — were diminished from view. So, too, was that most titanic of world wonders, the Grand Canyon. The South American continent was even less impressive. Clouds covered the Brazilian bulge, and the mighty Andes were seen as a thin gray rill. On both continents, man and all forms of his celebrated genius — cities, pyramids, cathedrals — were gone... nothing.

Then his eyes came to the California coast, to where he knew Judy waited. *What has Killingsworth told her? NORAD has to have seen Freedom. What would they think? That I'm on it? That I'm dead? Is that what he's told her? God, how will she handle that?*

He tried to make the impossible transformation from man to woman, to imagine what it would be like to be a wife, to be Judy and be told that *he* was dead. He could see the grief, the tears, but not beyond. That a bond of love to another human could be so intense, so total as to be a bond to life itself, was a concept that overwhelmed his simple emotional being. He had never needed anyone as a fundamental reason for existence. How could Judy — or any man or woman for that matter — be so dependent? The pilots with whom he had flown, had not. Oh, a rare few could cry over a friend's death, but they would quickly recover. Nobody really *needed* anybody. Life went on.

He buried the thoughts and returned to the control module to find Darling engrossed in a library of technical documents.

"Anything?"

"Nothing on burn targets. You are certain the *Soyuz* cannot be used without them?"

"It would be suicide."

❖

Thursday, 24 November
Atlantis

Anna was fixated on the slow rotation of the three-axis ball. It was nearly identical to an aircraft attitude indicator, inscribed with vertical and horizontal markings like lines of longitude and latitude on a globe. One hemisphere was painted a light gray to denote sky, the other black for earth. Outside, the real sky and earth had both disappeared in *Atlantis's* thirty-second eclipse. Only an occasional flash of lightning or the yellow smudge of a city's lights hinted at a nearby planet.

She interpreted their attitude from the sphere — nose to earth, tail to the *KOSMOS*. The autopilot was holding the track.

At the time of the demonstration — six hours away — they would definitely be in the *KOSMOS's* line of sight. Coincidence? No one believed it, and Mission Control had suggested the tail-up countermeasure, feeble that it was. The end-on attitude presented a smaller target, kept the cockpit shielded, and gave them the steel of the engine bells for protection.

Anna watched the ball, wondering if the attitude would save them. Perhaps they could take a single hit and still be okay. But nobody had any idea what the *KOSMOS* might throw at them. One small slug? An explosive warhead? A spray of steel? If they were a target at all, surely they would be the primary target. She envisioned five, ten, a *hundred* projectiles streaking at them. *Atlantis* would never survive.

The thought shivered her with a new type of fear — fear of a predator. Always before, it had been the threat of the machines themselves, the threat of her own mistakes in controlling them, that had been a latent horror. Now she had entered that exclusively male domain — *combat*. A living, thinking enemy was plotting to kill her.

Her mouth was sand, and she pulled a drink container from its velcro, sucking down several swallows of iodine-tainted water.

The waiting was the torture. She had time to think, to *feel* what every warrior of every age had felt — the sweat, the cotton mouth, the pounding heart, nerves singing in high tension, an entire body hypersensitized by adrenaline. And, like them, she had time to wonder about her loved ones. There were not many — her aged aunt and uncle, and Richard. She wondered how he would take the news of her death. Bitterly, she was certain.

She tried to think of others — men or women — to whom she was exceptionally close and who would shed tears over her grave. But none came to mind. It was so strange, she thought, that her pursuit of a dream in a male-dominated profession had alienated her from both sexes. Other women had never seen it as a dream quest, never known the enchantment of dancing in the sky. To the militant ones, she was nothing more than a battle cry, a victory flag flying over another conquered male bastion. To the traditionalists, she was a hormonal aberration. Even the other women of the astronaut office, all scientists and engineers, were cold to her. Her dream was different than theirs. She was different.

And to the men? To some, she was just a number in the affirmative action quota, a woman stealing a man's job just to prove a point. Some saw her wings as a threat to their egos. To others, she was a pseudo man, a ball-less wonder, a freak as original as those headlined in the supermarket tabloids.

For three men in her life she had been sexual entertainment. None, other than Richard, had really loved her. None had ever wanted to know her, to share in her dreams.

Pettigrew had. The aside was from the other being. She reminded Anna of the magic night on the dock, of looking at the same stars that now flecked the windows and knowing the man at her side saw them as she saw them — *dreamed* them as she *dreamed* them. The other being reminded her of the day in the air when they had mated in their machines and danced on billowing threads of contrails.

But Anna was quick to also remember his lies.

She looked across the front cockpit to the marine. He was asleep and she was thankful. Sleep — his or hers — was an escape from having to face him.

An hour later, a flash of light brought Pettigrew awake. It was not lightning this time. A cosmic ray had passed through his eye and scintillated the optic nerve. He damned the interruption.

He also damned his body. Another powerful and useless erection bulged the crotch of his shorts. It stood to laugh at him, to remind him.

He remembered uttering the same curses for the same reason when he had been a POW. Lying in filth and vermin on a bamboo mat in a stinking Asian prison, he had awakened to the mocking laugh of stiffened flesh. Full and useless it had stood — a reminder of sweet Karen, of every second of their lovemaking, of the infinity of seconds that remained before he could again sleep with her. It had been a torture beyond any his diabolical captors had been capable of. Why couldn't it be like the rest of his body, he had often asked. Why didn't it shrivel and atrophy as his malnourished arms and legs had? But it had not. And neither did it now.

The thoughts that had been with him before he had fallen asleep came back. If he survived the mission, he would leave NASA. The marines had compensated their repatriated POWs with a promise of exceptional treatment for the remainder of their careers. He would ask for a flying assignment — anywhere. It did not matter, as long as it took him far, far from Houston... far, far from Anna.

Mark's death — and deep down he believed his friend was dead — made him see clearly again that love was inseparable from pain. To get close to anyone would always expose the heart to loss. And it was a message repeated by Anna's actions. Since her recovery, she had said nothing of his radioed message. Perhaps she had not heard it. Perhaps she had heard it as another lie. But it no longer mattered to him. The cost of love was too high. It was better to walk the earth alone than suffer the torture of getting close to a woman and then losing her.

Thursday, 24 November
KOSMOS

Mark awoke to the unmistakable sounds of earth — the peal of distant thunder, the soft patter of rain, the hiss of wind through pine. In the first instant of consciousness, he thought he *was* on earth. The flight to the *KOSMOS*, *Freedom's* destruction, the desperation of their situation — all of it had been nothing but a terrestrial nightmare. Then his eyes opened, and the cluttered cylinder of the control module brought him back to reality.

"What's that sound?"

Darling looked up from a document. "One of the recordings I found. They have others… children laughing, city traffic, birds singing, soothing poetry narrated by a woman. Also, the love moans of a woman."

"What? A woman?"

"They are for crew morale."

It made sense. The recordings, like the posters he had seen in the habitability module, were some Soviet psychiatrist's attempt to lift the spirits of men who endured lengthy isolation from mother earth's sensorial pleasures.

Mark checked his watch and floated to the window. The view confirmed the clock. Dawn was chasing the terminator from the eastern seaboard of North America. Thanksgiving Day. It would be a beautiful one for the northern and central states. The skies from Savannah to Bangor were clear. But Florida was threatened by a low-pressure system. He could see the counterclockwise swirl of clouds reaching inland. To the extreme north and south, he could see the finishing acts of earth's nocturnal glories. Undulating snakes of green-purple belted the magnetic poles — auroral storms. The northern tumult was the brightest, and great massifs of arctic ice were illuminated under a rain of electrically charged particles that had been thrown from the surface of the sun. As always, lightning flecked the tropics from Capricorn to Cancer. It was a sight that made him wonder why anyone would ever need recordings of birds or moaning women to be entertained.

"Have you given him anything to eat and drink?" Mark nodded toward the cosmonaut.

"I have. And I took him to the toilet. I have also remembered who he is… Chief Scientist, Professor Viktor Maksimov, a past winner of the

Nobel prize in physics. His specialty is superconductivity, which I am certain is at the heart of this machine. We have captured the father of Red Sky."

The irony struck Mark. The smartest man of the century was theirs, but even *he* could not conjure up the handful of numbers — the deorbit targets — needed to save their lives.

He glanced back at the window and watched what he knew would be the last geosynchronous sunrise he would ever see — probably the last sunrise of his life. Time was running out. In five hours, the demonstration had to fail. And it had to fail *spectacularly*, a public death that would leave no doubt in the minds of the Soviets and the Americans that Maksimov's genius had been taken out of the war-fighting equations of both nations. To risk any delay, to succumb to his fears and merely let the time expire with the *KOSMOS* still intact in the hope something — *anything* — would develop to save them, would be to risk the country, perhaps the world. Decisions were being made by the forces of good and evil on the assumption a rail gun commanded the high ground, that the precarious balance of nuclear terror had been irrevocably altered. The decision makers had to know the world was unchanged. They had to see the *KOSMOS* reduced to a grand folly.

"I'm going back to the *Soyuz*."

In a minute he was again under the harness, his hands caressing the controls. He rocked the RHC between its roll stops, listening to the soft *tick, tick, tick* as microswitches closed and opened, imagining the response of the vehicle to the thruster firings each of those switch closures would command.

He had made the decision before fatigue had overpowered him. Really, there was no other choice. Slim as it was, their only hope was in this machine. They would fly it home. Or rather, he told himself, *attempt* to fly it home. In the end, he suspected he would merely be trading coffins — the *Soyuz* for the *KOSMOS*. But if he was going to die by his own hand, it would be like this — strapped in a cockpit, flying a machine — not as a passenger in a *KOSMOS* tube counting the seconds until he was transformed into vacuum-boiled gore. He returned to the computations of escape that had been interrupted by sleep.

Their orbit speed was six thousand miles per hour. If he burned due north or south for an identical speed, it would tilt the orbit exactly forty-five degrees. The *Soyuz* would then be in a new orbit that passed over all of the United States landmass below forty-five degrees of latitude. He would avoid the considerable dangers of a direct deorbit by next moving into a lower orbit, as they had planned to do with *Freedom*. After two months of simulations, he had her braking burn velocities committed to memory. If he made it to that point, there would be no more estimates, just guesses, because *Freedom* had never had targets beyond that orbit. *Atlantis* would have been the ticket home from there. He did not even consider the possibility of a shuttle-*Soyuz* rendezvous. It would take an incredible miracle to put them in an orbit Pettigrew and Anna could reach, and even if that were granted, only one person would be able to make the transfer to the shuttle. They had only one EMU.

He surveyed the instruments carefully. There was nothing that looked like a velocity indicator, so the burns would have to be done on time. He would use Newton's most famous of equations, that force was equal to mass times acceleration — F=MA — to solve the conversion to speed. Their prisoner would know the weight and thrust of the *Soyuz* — mass and force. He would use the numbers to solve for the unknown — acceleration. From that, he could estimate the time required for any burn to achieve any velocity. It would be a crude estimate, probably a deadly one, but it was all he could do.

He returned to the control module to explain the plan to Darling. They would set the explosives, then leave in the *Soyuz*.

"Frank. We're leaving."

Darling listened as Mark sketched his plan on a tablet. It took only a minute.

"So, all I need to know is the weight of the *Soyuz* and the thrust of its engines."

"What do we do if we make it into a lower orbit?"

"The only thing we can do… take a guess on the time and duration and attitude for a reentry burn and then pray. I'll err on the steep side for duration. I don't want to skip off the atmosphere and get stranded. I'd rather take my chances with the alternatives… burn up or have the *Soyuz* come apart due to the g-forces. There's also the possibility of ending up in the Soviet Union. We'll pass over all of it below forty-five degrees of latitude. Another, more likely possibility, is we'll land in the ocean and die out there. There won't be anybody looking for us, and I doubt the module carries more than a day or two of survival rations."

"It is better than staying. I am ready."

"Good. Tell this guy what we're going to do, that we'll need his help."

Darling made the translation, the cosmonaut's face blanching with a new attack of terror.

"Nyet! It's insanity! You are mad! We cannot return without Moscow's assistance! We will die! Nyet! Nyet!"

It did not take the iceman's translation for Mark to understand what was happening. He pushed to the airlock and retrieved the demolition cord and timer assembly. "Translate, Frank! I'm blowing this fuckin' platform to hell! See this?! See?!" He brandished the device in the man's face. "This is a linear-shaped charge. When it explodes, it forms a wave of white hot gas that will cut through these walls in a heartbeat. Now, if you're the smartest goddamn man in the world, you can take a guess on what that's going to do to you!" In his rage, Mark was running away from the translation and paused for Darling to catch up.

"Now, what's it going to be? Stay on this goddam platform and die, or come with us on the *Soyuz* and maybe... just maybe... we can make it home!"

"Nyet! Nyet! Nyet! You cannot return! We will die! You must surrender! I will ensure you are returned to America!"

"I will make him tell us." The iceman grabbed the crowbar.

For the first time, Mark doubted Darling's powers of intimidation. It was not patriotic fervor steeling Professor Maksimov's spine. It was gut fear of the risk they would face in the deorbit.

"Forget it, Frank. He's more scared of trying to deorbit without burn targets than he is of us." Smart guy, was Mark's additional thought. "I'm going to show him he has no choice."

He set the demolition timer and activated its countdown. "Tell him I've set this to the Red Sky demonstration time. We can't risk letting this thing remain intact any longer than that. When it reaches zero, he's dead."

Maksimov listened to the translation and watched the vanishing digits. His bottom lip quivered. His throat bobbed in deep swallows. Finally, he made his decision.

"Nyet!"

"We're wasting our time. I'm going outside to set the charge. If the bastard wants to join Lenin in the great worker's paradise beyond, I'll help him."

He pushed to the airlock and began to dress in the EMU.

❖

Thursday, 24 November
Beach House

"Mrs. O'Malley, there's a storm coming."

"We're going to have to leave?" There was a touch of panic in Judy's voice. There was nowhere else she wanted to be. Here, she could feel Mark's presence.

"No, the security police came by and said we'd be okay. The tides won't be above the dune line. But I really think it would be better for you to stay inside."

"I'll be okay."

Since her 3:00 A.M. arrival, Judy had spent little time in the house, preferring the solitude of the beach instead. She had only come inside to use the toilet and was now preparing to leave again. A matronly air force nurse, recruited as a guardian from nearby Patrick Air Force Base, tried to convince her otherwise.

"Would you stay just a moment to have some coffee? It'll warm you up." The woman held her patient's hands.

"Maybe later."

"Are you sure you're okay? I really think sleep would be better therapy than the beach. The doctor left me some sleeping pills, or I can give you something stronger… an injection. Or maybe you'd like me to call the doctor back?" Nurse Infield had been told enough of the story to appreciate Judy's heartache — that her husband, an astronaut, had died during a classified operation.

"No, Trudy, I don't want to go to sleep. Not yet."

The grief response frustrated the major. She appreciated the need for solitude, but hours of it on a windswept Florida beach seemed excessively morbid and unhealthy.

"Well, at least wear this extra sweater."

Judy accepted it, pulled on her own coat, and departed.

As her figure faded to a dot on the northern dunes, the major sipped her coffee and wondered why the woman always walked north. There was plenty of solitude directly in front of the house, and the walk into the wind had to be miserable.

Bed is where she should be. But that would come, her nursing experience told her. Nature would take care of things. The woman was so obviously exhausted that, like it or not, sleep would soon force her inside.

❖

Thursday, 24 November
KOSMOS

Mark double-checked the tether he had scavenged from Darling's suit and then raised his body from the airlock. There was still a swarm of ice particles flashing around the structure, and some soundlessly touched his suit and assumed new directions. He had also taken Darling's helmet to replace his own — the pieces were interchangeable — and was now looking through pristine acrylic. Overhead, the sunlit labyrinth of the central truss was blinding white against the abysmal black, and he pulled his gold visor into place to shield his eyes.

His plan was simple — to gird the entire *KOSMOS* structure, including both modules, with the demolition line. He would trace a figure-8 with the charge, the top circle of the 8 being the truss assembly, the bottom circle being the twin cylinders. The placement would ensure the machine would be cut in two and both volumes ruptured. The gymnastics to lay the charge would also wrap his tether in the same loops, but that was of no concern. This was the last time it would ever be used.

He began the weave at the control-module window and thirty minutes later ended it at the same spot. He wanted to be certain Professor Maksimov had a good view of the countdown digits. When they reached zero, the cord would blossom into a ten-thousand-degree torus of gas, and anyone remaining on the platform would join A. Volkov — whose body remained entangled near the window — as incorruptible slop. There could be no greater incentive for cooperation, Mark thought, than for Maksimov to take in the view.

He lifted the cover to the arming switch, flipped it to on, and raced his oxygen supply to the airlock. As he reentered the control module, the red numbers of the timer were toggling through one hour and fifty-two minutes.

CHAPTER 19

Thursday, 24 November
KOSMOS

Maksimov's arms and legs were still bound with tape, but Darling had removed him from the chair and used checklist tethers to suspend him over the window, ensuring he had a constant view of the time remaining in his life — and how he would look in death. It was an effective terror tactic. His unblackened eye maintained a constant, fearful sweep between the detonator and the airlock.

Mark hovered near him, away from the airlock and any suggestion he was entertaining thoughts of entering it. Unless Maksimov helped them, they would die when the numbers touched zero.

Behind him, Darling acted the optimist, busying himself by plundering the *KOSMOS* of folders of message hard copy, checklists, video cassettes, audio tapes, manuals, and code books. He had even stripped some electronic boxes he suspected were decryption devices. All were stamped "RED SKY / MOST SECRET" and he intended to return the package to earth. An intelligence treasure was how he had described it, but with each twinkle of the digits, Mark morbidly considered it would be as much a treasure to the CIA as sunken New World gold had been to the Spanish crown — acquired but never delivered.

"Toilet." Professor Maksimov spoke the single word.

"He wants to use the toilet."

"Tell him he can piss in his pants. The wet won't bother him when he's dead."

A greater degree of pain contorted the prisoner's face.

The hour digit blanked as the countdown reached 59:59. Maksimov's respiration soared. His face reddened with a spike in blood pressure. Still, he tenaciously clung to the hope the American would go outside and disarm the explosives.

"Translate for me, Frank, and stay with my tone of voice. Don't threaten unless I do." He moved to confront Maksimov face on.

"Doctor." The Soviet startled at the polite address. It was the first time the Americans had said anything to him without the venom of cobras. "You have many years of life ahead. You have a great mind. You have won a Nobel prize. I am told you are a modern-day Einstein. Think of what you could accomplish in the freedoms of America. Great, great things! The best laboratories. The best libraries. The best assistants. My country can ensure your safety. We have done it for other of your countrymen." Mark had no idea if the claim was correct, but vanishing time made him innovative.

"Think, Doctor! Think! Your leaders know nothing of our presence of our presence on the *KOSMOS!* Nothing! The *KOSMOS* will be destroyed! They will assume a malfunction! They will assume you and the others were lost. You can literally be born again. You can assume a new identity. A new life! You will have wealth beyond your wildest dreams. If you want your family with you, we can get them out of the Soviet Union. We have also done that for other of your countrymen." Another expediency. "If you are tired of your wife, you can have another. Perhaps a younger, more beautiful woman.

"But you must cooperate! If you do not, in fifty-eight minutes you will die. And think of that death. Look at your friend's face! When the explosives fire, it will be *your* face! It will be your lungs ruptured and filling your mouth! Your eyes bulging from their sockets! Your blood boiling in your veins! Our only hope is to escape in the *Soyuz*. I can pilot it, but I need your help."

The cosmonaut looked past Mark at the unmentioned alternative — the airlock. The American could turn off the detonator and surrender to him.

"Think, Doctor! Think of your new life! Think of death!" Mark ended the speech. Sex, money, fame, life — there was nothing else to promise.

Seconds passed. A drumming blue vein at his temple revealed Maksimov's cardiac panic. The cyclopean eye touched on Mark, on

Darling, on the detonator, and then on the airlock. Finally, the answer came. "Nyet! We will die in the *Soyuz*. You must stop the detonator!" His screams were accompanied by a violent and useless struggle against the bonds of tape and tether. The digital death dance and Mark's macabre description had pushed him over the edge. "The detonator! You must stop the detonator!"

Mark's panic was hardly less. "Help us! Tell me the weight and thrust! Help us! It is too late to stop the detonator! The *KOSMOS* is going to be our coffin!" He held onto Maksimov's coveralls, pulling face to face, matching scream for scream.

The Soviet continued his rocking, twisting mania, his eyes never leaving the airlock — the gateway to life.

"Help us! Goddamn you… Help…" Mark stopped. His own eyes suddenly bulged in a fixation on the chamber. Maksimov's screams died. The module fell still. Mark released the cosmonaut and hurled toward the opening.

"Yes! Yes!" Maksimov howled. He had won. The American was racing to turn off the detonator. "Yes! We will be rescued! Moscow will come for us! I will ensure your safety!"

Darling's shouts mixed with the Soviet's celebration. "No, Mark! He is weak! He will help us!"

Mark shoved him aside, grabbed the EMU pants, and rocketed back to Maksimov. The light of victory twinkled in the open eye. But it was a light quickly extinguished.

"No! No! Don't! You are mad!"

The scream would have been no less animal if the instrument had been rammed into the man's gut. But the scissors Mark wielded penetrated only the neoprene of the suit. In one stab, then another, and another, he ensured total penetration, total destruction. Their only means of EVA was gone.

Maksimov's shrieks rose louder. The Americans were psychopaths. They had sealed their deaths. His death. The *KOSMOS* was a tomb. The *Soyuz* would become one.

"You have killed us! Release me! There is no time! We must hurry!"

"The *Soyuz*? You will help us fly it?"

"Da! Da! Release me!"

Thursday, 24 November
The White House

Foreign Minister Skripko and his weasel-faced interpreter were ushered into the Oval Office. The former wore a diplomatically correct smile.

"Good afternoon, Mr. President." Extending his hand, Skripko took two steps toward the seated executive. But there was no reciprocal greeting. President Corbin remained in his chair and pierced his visitor with a loathing glare. Killingsworth cringed at the affront. The president was allowing himself to be victimized by the animal passions of his Wild West forebears. Individuals could indulge themselves in the insanity of hate. Nations could not. And now, two nations faced each other in the form of these men. The fat man prayed the president would remember that and stick to the game plan he had drafted while cool of head.

Skripko's arm dropped to his side. His smile slowly melted and his look became one of indignation. The interpreter attempted to save his superior some face by escorting him to an empty chair.

The president picked up the stereo remote control and punched down the volume to the album of classic western movie themes that was playing. The haunting, evil whistle from "The Good, The Bad And The Ugly" diminished into the background. The fat man wished it was "The Sound of Music." The room did not need an aural reinforcement to the gunfighter mood already chilling it.

"Mr. Skripko…" The president finally leaned forward to play his bluff. The Soviets were holding all the aces, but he would raise the ante to the limit before throwing in his hand. "…Cut the crap."

The interpreter hesitated on the word 'crap' and the president taunted him. "Crap. C—R—A—P. If it doesn't translate and Mr. Skripko continues with the ridiculous charade he doesn't understand me directly, then try 'bullshit.' Maybe that's in your goddamn dictionary. B—U—L—"

"I can make the translation, Mr. President." The man strained to remain a neutral mouthpiece.

"Good, then I will continue. Your nation was behind the Teheran bombing and is intending to take Iran into the Soviet sphere of influence. Besides being guilty of the assassination of a head of state, you are violating the Carter Doctrine of 1980. In case you don't recall, Mr.

Skripko, that doctrine specifies the United States will defend its interests in the Persian Gulf as we would defend the United States itself. Nothing has changed from what I told you yesterday. I intend to enforce the Carter Doctrine. Any Soviet ship that attempts to occupy Iranian harbors will be fired upon by American forces."

Skripko batted away the threat as if it were merely an annoying insect. "Mr. President, it is ten minutes of one. I suggest we wait until after the hour to discuss this issue. As I told you yesterday, you will then see the situation in an entirely different light."

"Are you still under the delusion your country has an effective missile defense system?"

Skripko laughed. "Delusion, Mr. President? If I may suggest, *you* should cut the crap." The interpreter enjoyed throwing the word back into the president's face. "I'm certain General Bachman has told you American satellite losses to date were real enough." He glanced at the general, who sat near Killingsworth.

"Those *losses* were all explainable as equipment malfunctions."

"And I suppose you will tell me, after one o'clock, equipment failure was responsible for the nearly simultaneous failure of one hundred of your machines?"

The president could not answer. It was the last ante and all his chips were on the table.

❖

Thursday, 24 November
KOSMOS

"Move!" Mark ripped the tape from Maksimov and shoved him toward the tunnel. Other than keeping him from the radios, there was no longer any need to guard him. Death was the most vigilant of sentries and it stood watch outside the window, winking eyes that read 53:02.

"Frank, let's go!"

Darling grabbed his bag of treasure and followed the cosmonaut. Mark floated on his heels, pausing for just a moment at the tunnel entrance for a last look at the control module — the genius of socialist man. Humming, whirring, flashing robots continued their myriad duties, unmindful another silicon brother counted downward to their deaths. He ducked into the tunnel and fled to the *Soyuz*.

"He says you should take the left position." Darling spoke. "His position is as flight engineer… the starboard seat. I will be in the center."

The cosmonaut was already in his couch, paging through a checklist and flipping switches that were bringing the machine to life.

"Get in," Mark ordered the iceman, then swung himself into the capsule. In his earlier visits, the module had seemed roomy. Now, with three bodies inside, it was uncomfortably cramped.

The first delay to eat minutes from the clock was the hatch closure. Its articulation was more complicated than that of the airlock, and after four fruitless minutes, Mark had to solicit Maksimov's help. With the time-consuming overhead of Darling's translations, it required an additional three minutes for the men to secure the seal.

The second interruption came when the Soviet attempted to don a headset. Mark ripped it out of his hands and passed it to Darling.

"Tell him we don't need radios. All I want him to do is make the RHC and THC hot and I'll fly it. As soon as we get safely away from the KOSMOS, I'll also want the weight and thrust numbers to calculate the burn times."

Maksimov did not argue the issue of the radios. There was no time. He would find some other way to contact Moscow. If they could get into a low orbit, rescue from these madmen might still be possible.

The globe of the attitude indicator was slowly erected by spinning gyros. Other instruments shivered awake, their needles steadying on pressures, temperatures, and voltages. The language barrier was an excruciating source of delay, and by the time Maksimov had given Mark a cursory explanation of the commander's controls, only twelve minutes remained until detonation.

"Your controllers are on! Pull that to release us!" The cosmonaut jabbed a finger at a yellow-striped handle and Mark jerked upward on it. A loud thump sounded, and the Soyuz wallowed loosely in the KOSMOS docking collar. They were finally free of the ticking bomb, but it remained a gun at their heads. Flying debris could puncture the Soyuz tanks and turn them into another Freedom.

The familiar sound of thrusters booming and a swirl of ice crystals outside the windows answered Mark's first pull on the THC. He glanced through the periscope and watched the docking target shrink.

"Faster! Faster!"

He resisted the impulse to give into Maksimov's panic. The Soyuz's fuel reserves would be no better than *Freedom's* had been — nil. Excessive waste now would kill them later. He indulged in only two more pulls on the hand controller to speed their retreat.

"We will be too close! You must accelerate!"

Mark was preparing to explain his actions when another thump shook the machine. It was unmistakably different than the noise of the thruster firings, and all three men stopped their shouting and stared in a listening wonder. A weaker, periodic hammering followed. Darling questioned the cosmonaut with a glance.

"I have never heard this sound."

And it was eerily alien to any spacecraft sound Mark had ever heard. The shuttle, the *KOSMOS*, and, until a moment ago, the *Soyuz* had all had similar respirations — the soft whoosh of cooling fans, the whir of gyros, the faint clicking of gears within analog instruments. This sound was none of those.

A slow roll had developed, and Mark tapped the RHC to correct it. It was another indication the machine was betraying them.

"Frank, tell him there's something wrong in the control system. At that first thump our attitude began to deviate. Find out if any of these lights or meters identify a problem with the RCS system... a tank leak maybe. That would explain the drift in attitude."

The cosmonaut scanned the meager instruments. "All is normal."

The noise on the hull became louder, its epicenter moving forward along the length of the fifty-foot propulsion module and onto the return capsule. Huge eyes followed it to a stop over their heads.

"Ahhhhhhhhhh!" The scream was international. The hatch handle was turning. The shock immobilized all three men, and they could only stare stupidly as the wheel rotated. The locking mechanism prevented it from moving more than a few degrees. At the stop, the motion was reversed and tried again — over and over, a desperate, futile banging of steel into steel.

"Jesus!"

It was Mark's exclamation as the tortured face of S. Abramov came into the starboard window. The initial thump and attitude deviation had been his landing on the *Soyuz*. In their slow glide from the *KOSMOS*, the *Soyuz* had passed within reach of the drifting cosmonaut and he had grabbed one of its handholds, then moved forward to the capsule, trying to alert its occupants by hammering his fist against the hull. Now he pressed his helmet against the island and pleaded, his voice conducted through the acrylic and steel and coming to their ears as the faintest of whispers.

"Help me! Please help me! Don't leave me! Please!"

There was no possibility of rescue. The *Soyuz* had no airlock.

The begging life beyond the glass brought Mark's stomach to the back of his throat. He had assumed the man had died hours ago, but the Soviet suits were obviously longer-lived than NASA's. He grabbed the THC. Regardless of the cost in fuel, he would do what had to be done.

The boom of thrusters shuddered the *Soyuz* rearward. Another boom immediately braked the motion. Abramov's mouth formed shrieks only God could hear. His only anchor was his hand, and his body waved around it like a pennant in a windstorm, until inertia broke his grip. He was retossed into his infinite tomb. Another control input sped them away, and the cosmonaut diminished in size — kicking, crawling, screaming like a man hurled from a skyscraper.

The extended silence that followed was finally broken by the iceman. "Mark, there is only a minute remaining before the explosives fire."

Mark struggled to put aside the horror. The mission was still unfinished. The destruction of the *KOSMOS* had to be confirmed.

"Yea. I'll yaw us over for a better view." He twisted the RHC and steadied the port window on the battle star, now floating a quarter mile distant. They were looking upward into its belly, into the glowing yellow eyes of the module windows.

Darling counted its final seconds of life. "Three, two, one."

A white flash completed the cadence. In the moments immediately following, the structure seemed to remain whole, and Mark feared the explosives had not been enough. But the worry was groundless. Very slowly, the *KOSMOS* began its death dance. A shower of debris marked the rupture of the control and habitability modules. Clothes, food, tools, cameras, pressure suits, helmets, all manner of items unrestrained were sucked into the vacuum. Under the propulsive effect of that decompression, the broken truss folded together like a snapped pencil. Cryogenic storage vessels were breached, and the thrust of their escaping gases wrenched them from their mounts. Like balloons released into chaotic, unguided flight, the dewars darted crazily among the larger mess, trailing comet tails of glittering ice. One impacted directly on the antenna farm, raising a mist of additional debris. Increasing g-loads from the end-over-end tumble of the main beam ripped the radiators loose. The cantilevered rail gun suffered the same fate, waving in divergent oscillations until it was uprooted from its truss attachment and left spinning by itself.

Mark watched in a thankful silence. His mission was now complete. Earth men would soon know the balance of nuclear terror was intact. It only remained for him to save himself and the others. Mission impossible, he thought.

Using pencil and paper, he consulted with Maksimov in the universal language of mathematics. The genius agreed with his estimated burn time for an orbit plane change of forty-five degrees. Actually, it was a plan Maksimov silently cheered. They would pass over Mother Russia, enhancing the probability he could contact Moscow and be rescued.

Referring to the attitude ball, Mark steered the *Soyuz*'s nose to the north, then double-checked that Polaris was visible in the periscope. It was — centered on the cross hairs. Maksimov armed the maneuvering engines, Mark depressed the THC, and a welcome crush of acceleration followed. But the g-forces were light enough for him to roll his head and watch from the window as the remains of the new-age weapon shrank to a hazy globular galaxy. He said a prayer for the two stars within it that were human, knowing that, after all, they had been like him — warriors doing the bidding of their chiefs.

❖

Thursday, 24 November
The White House

An instrumental of the "Magnificent Seven" ended, leaving only the ponderous tick of a Danish grandfather clock — a gift from that nation's queen — to amplify the stillness. It was one minute past 1 P.M., and the men waited for the phone call from NORAD that would tell of the satellite destruction. The president sat in his chair, his gaze on a flicker of flame in the fireplace. General Bachman paced quietly in front of the hearth. The two Soviets remained seated, Skripko holding a confident smile.

Killingsworth sat on the sofa and struggled through a quagmire of black thoughts. What would happen to the nation? To the world? To Judy O'Malley? To the president? He sequentially prayed for each until the entreaties were for those already dead — the men of *Freedom*. Finally, they were for Pettigrew and Anna. Or were they, too, dead? Would he have to go to other doors and knock as a messenger of death? He despaired that he would.

The phone rang and all five men drew upright. The president leveled a stare of base hate at the Soviet delegation, then lifted the receiver.

"Yes?" The question was barely audible. "Put him through." For fifteen seconds he said nothing else. But Killingsworth did not need words to know the worst had happened, that the attack had been successful and that it had included *Atlantis*. Pettigrew and Anna were dead. The president's stunned expression revealed it.

"You're certain?! Absolutely certain?!"

The incredulous tone buoyed Skripko. He had feared a small percentage of Red Sky misses might embolden the president into further saber rattling, but from his look, the attack must have been devastating.

The president cradled the phone and paused, touching each man in the room with his eyes. Finally, he spoke. "Mr. Skripko, that was NORAD." The interpreter began to pace him. "*KOSMOS 2069* has blown up. I believe that was your *death ray.*"

The interpreter choked on the translation.

Killingsworth and General Bachman were cast as still as the Remington brass on the mantel. Both wondered if the president had lost his faculties. What could he possibly gain with such a fiction?

Skripko's first reaction was a slight panic, not because he believed for a second that Red Sky had failed, but because the Americans had traced it to the *KOSMOS* platform. How had they found out? But the announcement the machine had exploded? That was a grand bluff. He waved his underling silent and switched to English. "Mr. President, it is time again to cut the crap. My congratulations you have so quickly identified Red Sky, but… exploded? Please, do not continue this farce. I can even see from the faces of your associates, Mr. Killingsworth and General Bachman, you are not believed."

He was correct.

The president calmly replied. "Mr. Skripko, your ray gun is in pieces. I suggest you phone home. My secretary can get you a line."

The challenge was so confidently delivered that, for the first time, Killingsworth began to believe it. *In pieces? But How?!*

Skripko noticed the fat man's genuine transition from despair to hope. His eyes darted to General Bachman to see a similar phoenix rising from the ashes. These were not acts. These men actually believed the president. *And the president!* His body language said volumes more than his tongue. In seconds, he had changed from a beaten, defensive man into a panther ready to leap.

The foreign minister's smile began to fail. Something was wrong. He whispered in his interpreter's ear, and the man jumped from his chair and exited the room on a mission to phone Moscow.

"We will expose your hoax." With tone and expression, Skripko tried to recapture the initiative but failed. The subtle pull of muscles around his eyes spelled *fear*.

The president said nothing more, and the room was returned to the clock and the music. Killingsworth and Bachman were ready to explode with questions but followed their boss's lead and maintained their silence.

A minute ticked by, then another and another. Skripko's blink rate trebled.

"Have you ever seen the movie *High Noon*, Mr. Skripko?" The president avenged himself with the psychological warfare. He would torture this man as he had been tortured. The question was so frivolous, so inappropriate for their circumstance, it could only come from someone occupying a position of diplomatic and military strength.

"Movie?" The question rattled Skripko. His blurted answer was another indication of his eroding confidence.

"Yes. A great American western classic."

"No, Mr. President, I have not seen it." He recovered and forced a calm to his voice. It was blatantly counterfeit.

"Pity. Its theme music is so beautiful. And the lyrics… You should listen to them."

Killingsworth and Bachman exchanged bewildered glances. Skripko saw and was further confused by their confusion. *What was said in that telephone call?!*

President Corbin toyed with his mouse. He facilitated the lesson on *High Noon* by grabbing the stereo remote control and punching up the volume. The music rose to fill the room, the words conjuring up images of Gary Cooper facing down a killer.

I do not know what fate awaits me.
I only know I must be brave.

The president stared straight into his enemy, his face hardening to unflinching steel. Killingsworth watched the transformation. Word by word it occurred, until, he thought, even Gary Cooper would have run screaming from this man.

For I must face a man who hates me.
Or lie a coward. A craven coward.
Or lie a coward in my grave.

Skripko, too, watched the metamorphosis and cowered under its arctic malice. This was not how it was supposed to be! *What has Lushev learned! Where is he?!* He damned the delay, cursed the music. His eyes flashed to the clock. The president skewered him with another volume increase. The words now being hurled from the speakers taunted his sudden fixation with time.

Look at that big hand move along. Nearin' high noon.

Finally, the door flew open and the interpreter rushed in. What little confidence remaining in Skripko's soul was instantly vaporized by the man's urgent visage. The foreign minister sprang from his seat and met the messenger in a midroom huddle.

The president muted the stereo. He wanted Skripko to clearly hear from his own side what NORAD had told him.

The man received the news and was overwhelmed by the implications of the disaster. *Failed! Exploded! The initiative has failed! Sorokin will uncover the conspiracy! We are dead! I must get to the embassy! I must speak with Kobozev!* He hurried to the door.

The president stopped him. "Before you leave, Mr. Skripko, there is something else I want you to hear."

The minister turned and pretended sudden ignorance of the English language. It was an old ploy to dodge an uncomfortable situation.

"You can talk in goddamn Russian if you want, but be certain you listen in English. General Bachman?"

"Yes, sir?"

"I want you to use our remaining anti-satellite missiles to shoot down Soviet spacecraft."

"Yes, sir."

"And scramble your SAC bombers. I want them holding at their call-back lines. If any Soviet ship attempts to enter Iranian territorial waters, I will release them to their targets."

"Yes, Mr. President."

"And inform the naval units in the Persian Gulf to fire on any Soviet ship that might make such an attempt."

"Mr. President, I protest! These are acts of war!"

"War, Mr. Skripko? And what were your unprovoked attacks on American spacecraft, if not such acts? As it is, you have murdered two American astronauts! Is that not war?!"

Skripko's eyes widened at the accusation. *Astronauts? Dead?* Moscow's message had been *no* targets had been engaged, the machine had exploded. How could astronauts have been killed? But there was no time for speculation. The president continued his diatribe, moving from around his desk and into the minister's face.

"You and your criminal nation have started a war, and it will end only when your naval forces are ordered out of the Persian Gulf! Do not attempt an occupation of Iran, or the Soviet Union will be attacked! Do I make myself clear, Mr. Skripko?!"

The foreign minister hesitated, reading the eyes of the enemy, hoping to see signs of rhetoric but seeing nothing but a total resolve to back up the words. "Perfectly clear, Mr. President."

"Good. Then we can end this meeting."

Like a chameleon, the president changed. He extended his hand and mimicked Skripko's entry smile of thirty minutes earlier — the smile of correct diplomacy. The minister gaped incredulously at the palm and the defiant sarcasm it represented. He refused it, turned his back, and fled the room.

❖

Thursday, 24 November
Red Sky Control Room

Hysteria such as Yazov's was seldom seen beyond the asylum walls. Word of the disaster had sent him over the edge. He was fearless with fear, defying the ghost of Stalin that sat the width of the table from him. "I warned you! I warned all of you! It was insanity! From the very beginning it was insanity! We are dead men!" He belched sourly.

"Idiot! Shut up!" Kobozev slammed his fist on the table. "We must think!"

Yazov did not stop. "American bombers are being launched at the motherland! Sorokin will discover our plot. No! Not *our* plot! *Your* plot!" He whirled to accuse each of the others. "I was never a willing partner to this… this… madness! Never! I am innocent of treason! Innocent!" His facial tic was now so continuous it virtually blinded him in one eye.

Kobozev wished for a weapon, wished they were at the hunting lodge. He would put a bullet into the swine's brain.

"Ha!" Yazov spit the derisive laugh in their faces. "You think you can hide this conspiracy from Sorokin? You have brought the motherland within hours of nuclear destruction! The gods alone know what disastrous fallout there will be to Soviet-American relations because of this folly! America will build its own Red Sky… one that works! It will be *our* missiles that will be useless! You have reduced this nation to a third-world military power! You think Sorokin will never know!? Some of our satellites are to be shot down! Can you hide that!? Can you hide Red Sky's destruction!? Belidov is in his last hours of life! Sorokin will be chairman! He will know everything! Then he will charge us with high treason!"

Yazov frothed like a lunatic, but there was nothing of an idiot in his words. He had summarized their position exactly. The Iranian Initiative was to have been a bloodless *fait accompli*. The Americans were to have meekly surrendered their superpower status. It was to have been the grandest of all prizes, laid before the Politburo and ensuring Kobozev's ascension to power. Now it was a treasonous mess of monumental proportions — treason that could not be hidden for long and for which Soviet justice specified a bullet.

How long could it be hidden, Kobozev pondered. Hours? No, their secret would be safe for longer. If Sorokin suspected anything, he would first go to the KGB and Ryabinin could then sound the alarm. They would have a day before the conspiracy would be uncovered.

He ignored the arguments and counterarguments detonating around him like so many bombs. Blame-laying, accusing, protesting fools, they were. Even in this dark hour, he wanted to laugh. The wolves were devouring each other, and he watched the slashing pack while willing himself calm. Fear was the greatest enemy. It had already taken Yazov. The pig was incapable of rational thought, and he would die as a result. Of that, Kobozev was certain. The others were close to following him. There was ample time to plot a salvation, and he would do so. Of course it would be *his* salvation. The lifeboat he had in mind had room for only one.

"Silence!" His shout quieted the others. "There is still time to arrange an escape. Your insanity will only succeed in consuming that time." Ryabinin and Zhilin moved from each other's throats. As he had intended, the straw of hope ensnared them.

"Musa... order our forces away from the Persian Gulf. That will end the Americans' response. Skripko will ensure that message traffic from Washington does not reach Sorokin. We will meet at the hunting lodge tomorrow at 3 P.M. Musa, arrange to have a helicopter pick us up there at 4 P.M. We will take it to a military field of your choice where you are to position air transportation for us. We will flee the country. Comrade Yazov, you will arrange to have a sufficient wealth of hard currency deposited in worldwide accounts for us... that is, if you and Mrs. Yazov have not totally plundered the treasury."

Yazov ignored the accusation. "And where are we to go, *Comrade Leader...*" he sneered the address, "...that the KGB dogs Ryabinin leaves behind won't find us?"

"A host of Nazis disappeared after the great patriotic war and better hounds with greater motivation never found them. It is possible. Particularly with large sums of money, anything is possible. But we cannot remain here to discuss it. Belidov could die at any moment, and Sorokin might convene an emergency meeting of the Politburo. He will waste no time in seizing power. We must return to Moscow. We will consider a destination tomorrow at the lodge."

"What of Skripko?"

"Comrade Skripko will be arriving later today and I will notify him of our plan. We will meet at the lodge at 3 P.M." He encouraged the lambs to the slaughter.

"And Comrade Yazov, remember your loyalties. Betray us and I will kill you." Kobozev knew he could no longer be subtle with the coward.

The economics minister had no plans for betrayal. He had no hope. "You have already killed me... and yourself."

The answer prompted Kobozev into another enjoyable vision of the man's face in his rifle sights, but General Chernavin came to the door and interrupted it.

"Comrades, I must speak with you. It is urgent."

Kobozev coiled in his seat like a snake. Chernavin was another to be eliminated. He had directed the Red Sky program. He had certified its readiness. He had lied — lies that had destroyed Kobozev's grand vision of absolute power.

"What is it?!"

"Comrades, the Cuba tracking site has reported the Red Sky return vehicle is deorbiting."

Zhilin sprang to his feet. "What?! The crew survived?! But you said there was no answer to our calls!"

"We have still not established radio contact. We are receiving the radar tracking transponder only. It is being turned on and off in a Morse signal... two words." The general hesitated, frightened of the new Kobozev fury the news would certainly provoke.

"Yes?" Zhilin prompted him.

"*Maksimov.* One of the words is *Maksimov,* a Red Sky crew member."

"And the other?"

"*Americans.*"

The announcement stilled the room. Brains slowly comprehended. Eyes grew huge.

"No. No! It is not possible!" Zhilin went white.

"But... how? How could they?" Ryabinin's cigarette fell from his fingers.

"Americans?! Americans?! You fools! You bastard idiots!" Kobozev savaged them. "It was the Americans! They knew! All along they knew! They destroyed Red Sky! The machine would have worked! The power! The power! Gone! Gone because of your idiocy!"

The outburst prompted Yazov into a laugh — a high, shrieking, hyena laugh. A madman's laugh.

"Shut up!" Kobozev smashed a palm across his face. Yazov howled louder.

"Zhilin!" Kobozev whirled to the defense minister. "Do you have the capability of shooting down the Red Sky capsule?"

"What?!" General Chernavin rushed to protest. "Shoot it down?! There is at least one of our own men aboard?!"

"General, you will be silent! I did not ask for your opinion! Zhilin, can you shoot it down?"

"If it arrives in low orbit, yes. We have the older anti-satellite rockets. But…"

"Then kill it! Kill it! They have destroyed me and I will destroy them!"

❖

Thursday, 24 November
Cheyenne Mountain

Lieutenant Mason sat at his console and watched the mosaic of ruin being painted by the Cray computer. Tracks of phosphor slowly diverged, each line representing a piece of the *KOSMOS*. There were now hundreds of them — an unintelligible web of lines and curves.

"Any ideas yet, Mike?" Lieutenant Haswell pulled a chair to his friend's side and took a seat.

"Huh? Ideas about what?"

"What caused that fucker to blow?"

"No. Not a clue. It sure is strange though. If it had occurred earlier, I would have bet my bars O'Malley had somehow planted those explosives before he was killed. But with the breakup being almost coincidental with the demonstration time…" He shook his head. "I don't know. Seems to point to some type of catastrophic systems failure."

"Well, whatever it was, I'm glad it's over. The commies are running away from Iran likes it's radioactive. Maybe we can get back to twelve-hour days instead of sixteen."

"Yea." The tone of Mason's answer said he didn't have any idea what he was agreeing with. He was too preoccupied with the screen to listen. "Blaine, what do you suppose this is?" He pointed to a graceful curve that had rapidly outpaced the other lines and was nearing the edge of the screen. He had watched it for the last half hour, his curiosity growing with each update of radar data.

"What do you mean? It's just another piece of the *KOSMOS*."

"Yea, I'm sure it is, but look at how rapidly it's diverging from the other pieces." As he spoke, he touched it with his light-pen, then typed a request for its orbit parameters. WAIT flashed on the message line.

"It must have just picked up a bigger delta-V in the breakup." Haswell offered his opinion.

"That much of an orbit change represents *a lot* of delta-V. I wouldn't think an explosion could spit something that far away."

"Well, now that you mention it, it does look different. Maybe…"

"Jesus!" Mason interrupted. The computer was answering his request. "It's moved to an inclination of forty-two degrees!" He snatched the phone from its cradle.

"Who are you calling?"

"Major Jake. I want him to take a look at this. Maybe we can get some resources dedicated to tracking it. We're going to lose it pretty soon."

Five minutes later, Major Jacobson was standing by the two men, shaking his head. "I don't know, Mike. I'll grant you that it's odd, but… so what?"

"Sir, it's more than odd. To get into that orbit required a huge delta-V! It's got to be propulsive!"

"Maybe it is. Maybe it's an errant round from the rail gun. Maybe as the thing was coming apart, a missile got squeezed off that ended up at a forty-two-degree inclination."

"But, sir…"

"Mike, if we had the resources available, I'd push your request up the line. It would be interesting to see what that piece really is. But every radar we have is being dedicated to the TAC turkey shoot. The president wants four Soviet birds splashed. Chasing a piece of the dead *KOSMOS* is a very low priority. After that ASAT work is done, sure. I'll make your request. If we could identify it as one of the rail-gun rounds, maybe the foreign-technology people could learn something from the data."

Mason accepted the plan. It made sense. Anything in a twenty-two thousand mile, forty-two degree inclined orbit was of low priority interest. It would only be around for the next couple thousand years.

❖

Thursday, 24 November
Soyuz

Like a stone dropped into a twenty-two-thousand mile deep well, the *Soyuz* fell toward perigee — the low point of her orbit. The machine was in umbra — eclipsed from the sun — and the men waited for sunrise to determine their fate. It was all they could do. The machine had no instruments to measure their orbit. That was a ground control function.

After the plane-change firing sped them from the *KOSMOS*, Mark had immediately made the perigee-adjust burn. Normally there would have been a wait of hours between such multiple maneuvers as ground radar precisely measured the effects of the first burn and refined the targets for the second. But for this return there was no reason to wait. They were an autonomous speck in a blind, silent fall. No one would watch them. No one would call. If the burn had been good, the sun would rise to reveal an earth approximately two hundred miles distant. If it had been bad, there would be no sunrise — ever.

The cosmonaut checked his watch. "It is time again. I must adjust the helium regulator."

Darling made the translation and Mark nodded an approval. When it came to the care and feeding of any of the *Soyuz* systems, he was completely dependent upon the Soviet's expertise.

Maksimov turned to the switches. Shortly after the first burn, he had convinced the Americans there was a problem with the helium regulator that pressurized the propellant tanks. It would require adjustments every fifteen minutes. But the switches he modulated were unrelated to the propulsion system. Instead, his toggling was pulsing the radar tracking beacon in a Morse code, alternating with his name and the word *Americans*. He prayed on his mother's soul that somewhere in the worldwide Soviet tracking network the words would be heard. If so, he was certain the message would be understood — that Americans had destroyed the *KOSMOS* and kidnapped him. Moscow would never allow the latter. He was the genius of the modern age, the father of Red Sky, the prelate of superconductivity. The Americans could never be allowed to steal him. Moscow would rescue him. An airlock-equipped *Soyuz* would be sent, and, when he saw it, he knew how to stop the Americans from doing anything to prevent its docking.

The switching was slow, crude work. To ensure it did not sound too much like code tapping, he had to interrupt each letter with a pretended, perplexed survey of a meter or dial or checklist.

He ended the trick and silence reclaimed the capsule. Mark floated a pen in front of his face and watched it with the intensity of a hypnosis subject staring at a swinging bauble. Maksimov and Darling joined him in the séance. They understood its purpose. If they had miscalculated the duration of the perigee-adjust burn and were falling too steeply, the instrument would prophesy their deaths. It would begin a slow downward drift as the far, faint reaches of the atmosphere began to brake the craft. They would then have twenty minutes to anticipate what several-thousand-degree heat would feel like on their flesh. For now, though, the pen hovered where he had released it — a vote for life.

It was ten minutes later when Maksimov saw it from his window — an indigo arc tracing the earth's horizon, the opening act of sunrise. He screeched his joy. Mark loosened his harness and leaned to see. He had seen this same glory countless times from the shuttle — a near-earth sunrise! The blooming colors were not defining a disk, not even a hemisphere or a quarter circle, just a mere portion of one.

The star rose higher and another featureless ocean, this one of blue, replaced the one of black. They were literally lost over one of earth's seas. But Mark did not care. Eventually they would pass over land, and when they did, he would know into what orbit the first burn had tilted them. With that information, he could guess on the point for the final deorbit burn. Orbital mechanics said they would have to pass that magic point sometime in the next twenty-four hours.

For the moment, though, all that mattered was their ellipse had not intercepted the earth's atmosphere. His eyes drank in the details of the pointillistic panorama of clouds that dotted the unknown sea. He could see billows and turrets and bulges and shadows, all minutiae indicating they were within two hundred miles of the planet. For the first time since plotting the escape, Mark was euphoric with the thought it would actually succeed, that he would really bring them home.

He retightened his harness and shouted orders to Maksimov to arm the engines for the apogee-adjust burn. He would be fearless in this firing. It would be an exact duplicate of the perigee adjust, shrinking the outer tip of their ellipse to match this low point, to make a near-earth circle. After that, they would be one final burn from home.

CHAPTER 20

Thursday, 24 November
Atlantis

Anna and Pettigrew watched the mass of clouds that was keeping them in orbit — a wet, North Pacific cold front had stalled over the high deserts of Southern California. The normally dry lake of Edwards Air Force Base was under several inches of water.

"Bob, we're going to have to keep you up for at least another day. The weather is just too unstable to take the chance. The Edwards' forecast is for heavy rain with a possibility of hail and moderate icing. Florida will be no-go until that tropical storm is past… probably another forty-eight hours."

For all the violence a space shuttle endured during launch and entry, she was perilously vulnerable to the hammer of Thor — the weather. Precipitation would ravage her fragile silica heat tiles.

"Okay. We'll wait." Pettigrew was now completely passionless on the subject of their return. He would follow Mission Control's orders. The *KOSMOS* destruction had eliminated both fear and hope — fear that *Atlantis* would be fired upon and hope that *Freedom* was docked to the platform and would yet bring Mark and Darling back.

He reattached the microphone to a piece of velcro and returned to the solitude of the black. Anna did likewise. It had been this way for hours. Not a word had been exchanged, as they each had struggled to find reason in the madness of fate. As always, it had been a futile struggle. How could reason be divined from the waste of two lives? The *KOSMOS* had self-destructed. The joker of fate had laughed in their faces. The nation could have done nothing and the world would still be unchanged. Two lives gone for nothing.

Atlantis streaked soundlessly eastward. The sun rose, shone for forty-five minutes, set, and reappeared forty-five minutes later. Orbit after orbit, the glories of the planet passed unappreciated by the man and woman who watched.

When breaks occurred in Anna's grief, she thought of the future. She would marry Richard. She did not even try to rationalize the act as anything other than what it was — an escape. An escape from her sex, an escape from the womanly whispers that said it was possible to love and not be hurt. A loveless marriage to Richard would be the perfect escape.

❖

Friday, 25 November
Kennedy Space Center, Florida

The approaching squall line had turned the horizon black, but Judy was oblivious to the threat. She stood over the spot where they had coupled those many weeks earlier. Or rather, she convinced herself this was the place. Any sane person would have argued that identifying the exact point along a stretch of sand was impossible. The wind and sea had long since erased the evidence — the form of Mark's back, the shallow depressions made by her knees as she had straddled him, the fists of sand his hands had squeezed at the moment of climax. The signatures were all gone. Where human throats had once uttered the cries of loving sex, only the wind now screamed. Tufts of sea oats broomed the sand where, a lifetime ago, the seed of man had seeped from woman and glistened. All was gone, taken by the giver of life — the sea. It had renewed the earth and stolen all traces of the union.

But their spirits still laughed and frolicked on this spot and Judy watched them — Mark's eyes nervously scanning each horizon, searching for the security patrol. She, pushing him backward and leaning to take his hardened flesh into her mouth, mounting him and matching the sea with long, deep, wet strokes of her own, pleasuring him while silently shouting her victory to his watching mistress. *He's mine, now! Mine! You can't have him! He's mine! Mine!*

Judy remained a silent, motionless spectator. Behind her, a rising sea thundered. The wind flogged her. Her legs quivered with fatigue. Finally, she tried to reach beyond the grave, to touch her man for a last time, to remember the feel of his body, the sound of his voice, the scent of his flesh. Other newly made widows had attempted that reach by hugging their man's coat, or smelling his cologne, or sleeping in his sheets, or stroking his photo. Judy reached by intruding upon the spirits.

In two steps she was at the edge of the towel and instantly warm with the August heat and humidity. Her ghost smiled a welcome and stepped to undress her. Fingers unzipped her jacket. It was tossed aside. Judy did not see or feel her own fingers at the work. It was her spirit helping her. Her sweater was removed. The buttons of her blouse were undone, its hem pulled from the jeans, the garment dropped onto the sand. Then her shoes and socks were removed and the trousers unsnapped and pulled from her legs. She stood in her bra and panties, oblivious to the sting of gale-driven sand. She felt only a Florida August. The spirit's fingers unsnapped the bra and rolled the panties from her hips. Finally, she stood naked. She had become the spirit. She had reached back in time. She was alone with him — with Mark.

"Mark!" She fell on her knees to embrace the reclined vision, but her arms passed through it. "Oh, God, God, God, God! I want so badly to hold you again, to touch you. God, please let me. Just one more time, please, let me feel him." The request was not granted. Her hand tentatively reached to his face, but the coarse feel of male skin was only a memory. She brushed her fingers through his hair and across his lips — all memories.

A gust blew tresses across her face and she brushed them back. "I knew you would be here. When they told me even your body was gone, I cried so much. Oh Mark, I cried. Where would I ever go to feel close to you? Where? And then I knew. I knew you would be here. You would always want to stay close to this." She nodded her head in the direction of Pad 39A and the next winged giant being readied to fly from it — *Challenger*.

"I'll come back, Mark. Many, many times, I'll come back. I know you'll be here and I'll come back to be with you."

The first fingers of the rising tide swirled around her knees and sucked the sand from beneath her legs. But she made no effort to move. Mark was here. His naked spirit shimmered before her. The sensible world was gone, lost to memories. The healing process had begun, and the subtle details of their youthful courtship — the memories of the glances, the kisses, the touches, the embraces — came easily and vividly. And she captured them, gathering them in as a source of strength and life, a sustenance of memories to last her a lifetime. She cried and laughed as they swirled around her like the wind and water — the strange conspiracy of youth that had inexorably steered a boy and girl toward a fusion of body and soul under a star-fired New Mexican sky.

"Mark, I was warned, wasn't I? On that first trip into the desert with you, when you had your face to the sky. I was warned what loving you would cost." She raised her head and looked across the sand to *Challenger*. A sheen of tears came to blur the image. "But as lonely, as frightened as you've left me, I would do it all again. I loved you that much."

The great wave struck her back.

Friday, 25 November
Cheyenne Mountain

After the last ASAT engagement, Mason had renewed his request for updated tracking on the object he had seen moving away from the *KOSMOS* debris. Something did not just *explode* into a forty-two-degree plane change. It was powered there. What was it? A rail gun round, as Major Jacobson had suggested? Maybe. Then where was it now? His counterpart in the tracking-processing section was on the other end of the phone telling him it had disappeared.

"Are you sure?"

"Positive. We've gone over the data several times, Mike. There's nothing at forty-two degrees and twenty-two thousand miles."

"Okay, thanks." A bewildered genius hung up the phone.

Two hours later, Mason was not thinking about the mystery. A couple of margaritas had mellowed him enough to temporarily shelve the question. He had joined a contingent of young singles, all NORAD officers, at Haswell's house for a spontaneous celebration. Who were normally spectacled, pocket-penciled, calculator-carrying computer geeks were now lime-sucking, tequila-swilling, rock-dancing killers. As much as any of the pilots who had zoomed their Eagles and fired their ASAT's, *they* — the white collar moles of Cheyenne Mountain — were responsible for the untimely deaths of four Soviet spacecraft. And they celebrated like Top Guns. That a sunrise was just pinking the tops of the nearby Rockies was irrelevant. You never waited to celebrate *kills*.

"Some party, huh?" Haswell came to his side.

"Yea. My ears are bleeding. What'd you do, hook up the stereo to the margarita machine?"

"Hey, man, that tune's a classic. One of *The Cures*."

"Well, after it's done, you *should* hook up the margarita machine. I'll bet nobody could tell the difference." Mason teased him. His taste ran toward the real classics.

"Where's Jenny?" It dawned on Mason that Haswell's latest main squeeze was not on his arm.

"She's on her way. Had to stay to finish something for the colonel."

An attractive brunette lieutenant interrupted to claim Mason for a dance. The next round of *The Cure* was fired from the stereo, and the natives jumped in collective epilepsy at the explosions.

An hour and three more margaritas later, Mason was once again in Haswell's company. The brunette had proven to be a real thrill — with great tits, a nice ass, and a hip wave he suspected would be outlawed in most states and the District of Columbia. Long-neglected hormones were stirring in his body, and ahead loomed two infrequent destinations — Drunk City and Geek-sex.

"Hi, Jenny. Glad you made it." He greeted the recent arrival — Haswell's date.

"I see you've discovered girls." She teased him at his obvious infatuation with the brunette, who was currently retrieving another round of tequila snow cones.

"Yea. Linda's nice."

"Mike. Mike!" With the brace of margaritas in hand, the woman came to the trio. "You know the catalog count, don't you?"

"Hell, he knew *everything*... once. But now that he's fried his brain with a glacier of tequila, I'm surprised he knows his name." Haswell enjoyed tugging on his friend's alcohol-limped cape.

"Yea, I know the catalog count. I haven't fried that byte yet. Who wants it?"

"A couple of the guys have a bet going on what the count is now, after the four kills."

"Well, tell them the winning number is ten thousand, one hundred and fifty-one." As intoxicated as he was, Mason was absolutely confident in the figure — the number of objects being tracked by NORAD radar. The fragmentations from Red Sky's demise and the ASAT engagements had added one hundred and thirty-seven new pieces of junk. He had just seen the computer updates before leaving work.

"Two." Jennifer amended him.

"Two what?"

"The winning number is ten thousand, one hundred and fifty-*two*."

Mason started to object, but she cut him off. "That's why I was late, Mike. Turkey recorded a low-orbit *unknown* and the colonel wanted us to categorize it before we could leave."

"What is it?"

"Don't know yet. No electromagnetic signature. Probably just a spent booster we somehow missed." She scoffed at her own suggestion. "Though God only knows how we could have missed *anything* the way we've been watching the sky."

"Ten-thousand, one-hundred and fifty-*two!*" The brunette shouted the number to the gamblers while pulling Mason into a dance.

It didn't happen that dance. Or during the next. Or during the margarita break with Haswell and Jennifer that followed. The euphoria of victory, the alcohol, the female hip-wave were too neurotoxic for Mason to make the connection. But finally the words that Jennifer had spoken a half hour earlier roused a brain cell in his sodden skull.

An unknown… Turkey.

He laughed and danced and drank.

An unknown. Turkey recorded it. Unknown. Unknown. Unknown.

Mason stopped dead. The music still raged, but he did not hear. His smile disappeared. He was instantly sober.

"What?" The sudden change startled the brunette into a similar pose.

"An unknown! An unknown!"

"What are you talking about?"

"Jennifer said Turkey tracked an unknown! Where is she?" He shoved through the dancers. "Jennifer! Jennifer!"

"Hey, Mike. What gives?"

He broke into Haswell's dance, grabbing the woman's shoulders to stop her oscillations. "Jennifer, what were the orbit parameters of that Turkey unknown?"

The urgency of the question had the same confusing effect as it had had on the brunette. "What... the parameters?"

"Yes! What were they?"

"I don't remember exactly... an apogee around one ninety and a perigee of one thirty or forty. Why?"

"What was the inclination? It was forty-two degrees, wasn't it?"

"Yea. How did you know that? And what's the big deal? What's gotten into you?"

Mason did not answer. He could only stand there as the avalanche of realization roared over him. The object that had disappeared from geosync altitude was now in a low-earth orbit! He was absolutely certain they were one and the same.

"Something's coming back from the *KOSMOS!*"

"What?!" The cry was a chorus from Haswell, Jennifer, and the brunette.

"Remember after the *KOSMOS* breakup? Something moved into a forty-two-degree inclination. We lost it when we dropped radar coverage to support the ASAT attacks. After those were done and we looked again... nothing. It was gone!"

"Jesus!" Haswell spoke for all of them. "You're right, it's got to be the same thing! But why? Why would the Soviets return something to low-earth orbit from geosync? That doesn't make any sense."

The brunette added her wonder. "Yea. To bring something back from geosync sure isn't very cost effective. And why bring something back now? The *KOSMOS* is in a thousand pieces."

Mason listened to their arguments — arguments his brain had already raced through.

"So they would have to be bringing back something really important." It was Jennifer's observation.

"Yea. But what?" The ball had bounced full circle, back to the brunette. "It would have to be beyond *important*. It would have to be... I don't know... *irreplaceable*."

The woman's comment stalled the group. They were blind to the riddle's answer. Mason teased them with a cocky smile. "There's only one thing that's irreplaceable... man! The *KOSMOS* was manned! Her crew is coming back to the Soviet Union!"

❖

Friday, 25 November
Moscow

It was nearly noon when Yazov rushed into his flat. The embezzlement of sixty million dollars and its transfer through a maze of world banks had taken all of the night and morning. Without the experience of decades of similar, albeit much smaller thefts, he would never have been able to complete this one in such limited time. But it was done. Millions awaited them in banks in Argentina, Colombia, Hong Kong, Mexico City, Paris, Tokyo, and New York. It was the best type of money — electronic money — money a phone could magically wing across oceans and continents and deliver to steamy equatorial retreats and island hideouts. Kobozev had been wrong about everything else, he thought. But not this. They could disappear into lives of ease — and a life free of the she-demon that had ruled and ruined him.

But the work had delayed him. He had only three hours to pack and drive himself to the hunting lodge. That would barely be enough time, and if he was late, the others would never wait. They would suspect betrayal and flee, leaving him to face the firing squad by himself.

With single-minded purpose, he shoved past the blue silk mountain that was his wife and ran to the bedroom, where he pulled a suitcase from the closet and began to hurl clothes into it.

"Where have you been? What are you doing?"

"Leaving." He did not look up from the work.

"Leaving? Where are you going?!"

"*That*, my precious cow, is something you will never know." He turned to a bureau and began to strip its drawers.

Waddling through a litter of cast-off clothes, she grabbed his arm. "I asked, where are you going?"

"Let go of me!" The cow was not without muscle. The grip on his arm was a vice, and her twenty-kilo-weight advantage made his struggle to get free of it futile.

"I'm going to hold you until you tell me what you are doing! Now tell me!"

The noon hour chime from the mantel clock put him in a new panic. The pig would delay him enough that he would miss the rendezvous. He stopped the fight, glared into her bulldog face, and hissed an answer. "Kobozev's plot has failed. Our lives are in danger. We are fleeing the country. I have no idea of the destination. Now let me go!"

She did, the shock of the statement sapping the strength from her sausage fingers.

"What! Fleeing? You're leaving the country? What will happen to me?"

"Worried, my dear?" He raced to the bathroom and began to rifle through his toiletries.

"I won't be a minister's wife. The car! They will take my car and driver! The dacha! They will take it back! And the servants!"

"Don't forget this apartment, sweet." He relished the woman's panic. He wanted her to suffer as she had made him suffer. "I doubt the Party will endow it to you... or your trinkets. I suspect they will open the doors and let the other ministers' wives come in to shop. Wasn't it Valentina Shutov who so admired your emerald bracelet? It will look good on her wrist. Don't you agree? Of course, I doubt any of those ladies will want your gowns, seeing as how they are so nicely fitted to your exquisite figure."

The woman was a quaking mass. The opulent life she had lived for so long was ended — the shopping trips to Western capitals, the Black Sea vacations, the young, handsome gigolos that would do the things to her body her husband had long ago quit doing, the wonderful, limitless foods. It was all ended.

"I... I... take me with you, Andrey!" She was near tears with the plea.

"What?! You stupid bitch! You have brought this disaster on me! Your greed has put a gun to my head! I would sooner enter hell than live another day with you!"

"Please, Andrey!" She started for him. "I will change! I will..." Fearing she would try to hold him again, he attacked first, pushing her to the floor. One hundred kilos of formless blubber impacted with a resounding, if harmless, thump. Her limbs waved and kicked in the air like the legs of an upturned turtle. On her back, she was nearly as helpless.

With suitcase in hand, Yazov stood over her. "Oh yes, you *will* change, my precious. Lubianka prison has a way of changing all of its guests."

"Andrey! Andrey! Don't leave me! Don't! Please!"

He ignored the screams and hurried to his car.

Friday, 25 November
Volokolamsk Forest

"Hello!" The forest stillness swallowed the call. "Hello!" And the next. "Hello!" And the last.

Yazov's fingers slowly opened and his luggage fell to the ground.

They're gone! They're gone!

He had arrived fifteen minutes early, yet the lodge and its environs were deserted.

The afternoon was gray and the sky threatened snow. There should have been lights in the lodge, but it was dark. A ghost of wind stirred the door, and the creak of its rusting hinges emphasized the silence. His enormous eyes took in the other signatures of desertion. Five Zil automobiles were randomly parked. He recognized the ministerial license plates of Kobozev, Zhilin, Skripko, and Ryabinin. The fifth auto bore a rocket forces identification tag. He looked in each. All were empty.

In a deepening despair, he ran to the back of the building. There was no one. No waiting helicopter. Nothing. They had left him.

"Noooooooooooo!" The scream flushed a raven from the roof, and it took flight with a raucous squawk.

For a minute he was paralyzed with fear—a trembling rabbit fighting for breath, tightening his anus against the liquidation of his bowels. Finally, the hope of the damned rose to move him.

There must be some mistake! A change of plans. Yes! Yes! That's what it is! They have not left! The plans have changed! Of course! Kobozev has left a message in the lodge! They have walked to a site more suitable for a helicopter!

He ran to the front and was hurling through the open door when his foot slipped. He skidded into a painful collision with the log frame. The blow elicited a vicious curse, and his eyes dropped to see the source of the near fall. It was a dark pool of liquid. His right heel had gouged out a crescent smear of it, and the viscous wet was slowly refilling the depression. It was a sight that prompted an audible gasp. His brain knew instantly what it was, but that did not stop his hand from reaching for the fluid. An index finger touched it and drew a drop upward into the meager light. Blood. Warm blood.

His head snapped up and around, eyes darting in all directions, plumbing the dark, trying to understand the mystery. But there were no answers, just deep, silent shadows and the frozen snarls of Kobozev's trophies.

Trembling like a geriatric, he stepped further into the room, groping for the table and the kerosene lantern that had always been at its center. He needed light to find the message, the message that would explain all and lead him to salvation.

Fingers touched the lantern glass and were instantly drawn back in pain. The chimney was blistering hot. It had been used only minutes earlier.

What has happened?!

He felt the box of matches and fumbled with its contents, breaking one stick and then another in an attempt to strike a fire. Finally he succeeded and brought the flame to the mantel. It caught, and he adjusted the knurled throttle until the device yielded a dismal yellow glow. It seemed to multiply the shadows rather than fill them.

But it was enough light to see the hand — and the gun.

Fear straightened him and he stumbled two steps backward.

On the table opposite his position, a motionless hand rested on the trigger mechanism of a large-caliber rifle. The sitting man to which it was attached was a charcoal outline.

"What? Who?"

"Good afternoon, Comrade Yazov."

The greeting sucked the air from his lungs.

"Sergey, I... I... I thought you and the others had deserted me." Warm liquid poured down Yazov's legs. The smell of urine began to overtake the sulfur of the match.

"Oh *Andrey*." Kobozev traded the familiar, first name address that Yazov had started. The tone was anything but endearing. "You think I would desert you?"

"No. No, of course not. I mean, I thought... I thought there was a change of plans. I thought you had left a message in here."

"Oh. Yes, I see. A change of plans. Well, actually, there has been a change."

"The helicopter... it's waiting elsewhere? The others are there?"

A wicked chuckle came from the shadow. "I'm afraid there will be no helicopter."

"What?!" Yazov began a slow backward shuffle. The madman would do anything. He had to escape.

"You see, Andrey, it would never have worked. You were right about Ryabinin's hounds chasing us. The State… the Party… would never sleep until we were brought to justice. No matter the extent of our resources, they would always have more. If we used a million to buy a hiding place, they would use two million to find a Judas to betray us. No, it would never have worked."

"Then… then… we are doomed…" He made another step toward the door.

"Yes. Yes, I'm afraid so… doomed. Did you hear that Belidov died an hour ago?"

"What? No! No… I…"

"It was on the radio. Our beloved leader is gone."

"Then Sorokin has taken the chairmanship." He glanced backward. The exit was three meters distant.

"Yes. A pity. It will be the end of the motherland, you realize. He will return power to the people. In a year, Party members will be despised. In three, the Union will cease to exist. Our socialist brothers will be abandoned. I can see it clearly, Andrey. The glue has been power… absolute power. Without that, the Union of Soviet Socialists will unravel like a poorly made quilt. Such a pity. So much power and Sorokin will return it to the people."

"Where… where are the others?" Yazov was not interested in the future of the Socialist Union. It was his own future that concerned him.

"The others?" He toyed with the stuttering coward.

"Zhilin, Skripko, Ryabinin. Their cars are here."

"A pity about them, also. They were traitors, Andrey. And you know the penalty for treason."

"You? The blood?"

"They were traitors… just as you are, Andrey." The scrape of a chair signaled the rise of the ghost.

Yazov was a meter from the door. "No! Don't, Sergey! Please! What good will it do to… to…" He couldn't voice the words, *to kill me*. "It won't save you from Sorokin. Please." Under the immediacy of the death threat, his bowels could no longer be restrained. A loose, wet flatulence filled his pants, and the fetid odor of warm feces choked the room.

The loss of control disgusted Kobozev. "You are wrong, Andrey. Your death, Zhilin's, Skripko's, Ryabinin's, all of them, *will* save me."

"No! No, you are mad! But if we were together…"

"Mad?" He laughed long and full. "Think, Andrey. Who is there remaining who knows of our conspiracy?"

"Ah… General Chernavin! He would testify against you! See! You have forgotten! My death will not free you!"

"The cars, Andrey. Think! The fifth car… it had a PKO identification placard. I'm sure you noticed."

"Chernavin's?"

"Yes. He was the only one with spine. I called him and told him to meet me here at 1 P.M. on the pretense we were to discuss the destruction of the *KOSMOS* return vehicle. When I confronted him, Andrey, he did not defecate in his pants. He was a warrior and acted as one. He seized a weapon and tried to kill me. But I was quicker. He died like a warrior. The others died like groveling swine.

"So you see, there is no one, save yourself, to reveal me as a conspirator. And when you are gone, there will be no one."

"But the police, the KGB, they will investigate! They will know."

"Know what? That you were all involved in a conspiracy against Sorokin. That General Chernavin, a military hard-liner known to oppose Sorokin's liberal philosophies, assisted the conspiracy with Red Sky. That you personally embezzled millions of dollars to assist in an escape. That here, with your plot unraveling and with a growing panic that you would be apprehended, you turned into cornered, mad dogs. Arguments erupted. Some wanted to confess their crimes and seek leniency. Others wanted to run. Betrayal threatened all. Someone seized a weapon to save themself. Others did likewise. That in the fight, this lantern was upturned and a fire started. The fire consumed everything."

"But… this is *your* lodge! You will still be implicated!"

"Yes, it is my lodge. A remarkable good fortune, don't you think? It further insulates me from suspicion. Would I leave the evidence of a conspiracy at my own lodge if I was involved? Would I not take the bodies somewhere else… perhaps to *your* dacha? That a group of conspirators would use this place is hardly remarkable. It is isolated, quiet. I rarely come here. And don't forget, comrade, my ministry was the only one unneeded for the execution of the plot. Because of Red Sky's expense, your ministry's assistance was essential. And no plot would have been possible without the cooperation of the defense establishment. That explains Comrade Zhilin's presence. And how could the American president have been confronted without the Foreign Ministry's assistance... Skripko's assistance? And the Ministry of State Security would certainly have been needed... Ryabinin. But as for *my* ministry — the Ministry of Ideology, Propaganda, and Culture — where was it needed? Why should I have been involved? Which of my minions will report anything unusual in ministerial activities?"

"Sergey, you are mad! It will not work! There are others who know! Belidov's surgeon was here in this very room! He saw you!"

"Belidov's surgeon died last night in a tragic automobile accident."

Yazov's mouth flapped, but no words came.

"It was simple enough. I convinced Ryabinin the doctor was a risk to our escape. His agents took care of the matter. So you see... you, Andrey, are the only one left." The sentence ended with the tick of a hammer being pulled back.

"No! No! My wife... she knows! If I am killed, she will reveal you!"

"Andrey, do not insult my intelligence. Ryabinin had your house wired with so many listening devices even your wife's flatulence was recorded. She knows nothing."

"No! I talked with her in the bath... I..."

"Our talk is ended, Andrey. Your stink nauseates me."

He raised the weapon to his shoulder, an action that sent Yazov screaming for the door. But the attempted escape ended immediately. He tripped and fell onto the unmistakable bulk of a human body. A warm stickiness covered his face from forehead to chin and ear to ear. He shoved from it, and the essence of the gooey mask became evident. It was the remnant of Skripko's brain. Gray-pink offal stuck to Yazov's face, filled his nostrils, wetted his lips and tongue, hung in his eyes.

The horror ended his own brain function. All he could manage was a rise to his knees and a turn to his attacker. His hands clasped in a begging entreaty. An open mouth formed the shape of a scream, but nothing came out.

Kobozev moved the black blade of the rifle sight to fill that cavity, then eased his finger onto the trigger. It was a view he had anticipated for many, many weeks and one he would relish for years to come. Yazov deserved death. He was weak.

The explosion of the weapon rocked him backward, and when he next looked, it appeared nothing had changed. Yazov still gaped mutely. His eyes were still round and huge. His fingers were still interlaced in a plead for life. Then the body slowly collapsed face forward to reveal the effect of the bullet. The anterior half of the cranium was missing.

A minute later, Kobozev calmly stepped from the lodge and jerked back on the bolt action of the weapon. The spent brass tinkled against the rocks, and a curl of gunsmoke came from the breech to scent the air. He loved that smell — the smell of the hunt.

He tossed the rifle into the blossoming conflagration and walked to his car.

One hundred and seventy kilometers away — behind the Kremlin walls — Mrs. Yazov begged in a manner not too unlike her husband. Her hands were folded, her crying eyes beseeched.

"Please, Comrade Sorokin, promise me amnesty! I will tell you everything, just please spare me from the gulag! I wasn't part of the conspiracy! I didn't embezzle! It was Andrey! He is guilty… and Zhilin and Skripko and Ryabinin… they are guilty! And… Kobozev! *Kobozev* is the devil behind this treason!"

Friday, 25 November
Cheyenne Mountain

Killingsworth's helicopter rocked to a landing near the NORAD entrance. Mason's guess about the unknown — that it was a manned *Soyuz* capsule — had raced up the chain of command, and the president had immediately ordered the fat man to Colorado Springs to monitor the situation. So far, the Soviet retreat from Iranian waters had been total, and there was no evidence that would change. But the fact Soviet men had been aboard a machine Americans had attempted to destroy was a twist no one had anticipated. Whether it would color future Soviet actions was, in itself, an unknown, and President Corbin wanted his friend at the front lines.

General Griffing stooped under the whirling blades and rushed to greet the VIP envoy. The duo quick-stepped toward a waiting car, where an aide-de-camp held the door.

"Is the machine still in orbit?" Killingsworth screamed to be heard over the whine of jet turbines.

"We think it's landed, but it'll be awhile before we know for certain."

"Did you receive my request about Lieutenant Mason?"

"Yes, sir. He's waiting for you."

Killingsworth had insisted on an audience with Mason. He wanted no star-bedecked, spit-shined veneer between that genius and himself.

Ten minutes later, they were walking into the junior officer's work area. It was another of Killingsworth's requests — that the man remain at his duties. He dealt with enough prodigies in other fields to know they could be rendered ineffective if removed from their element and planted behind a podium.

"Lieutenant, it's good to see you again."

"Good morning, sir."

Killingsworth took a nearby chair. "General Griffing tells me the machine has deorbited?"

"That's our bet, sir." While speaking, the officer played the computer keyboard and the screen was refreshed with a world map. The sinusoidal weave of orbits was now familiar to the fat man. "This was the *Soyuz*'s last rev." Mason traced his pencil along the line that dipped through the South Pacific, came across South America, then uppercut into the bulge of Africa. "A deorbit burn about here" — he touched the mid-Atlantic — "would put them in the Soviet Union. This was their best deorbit opportunity and they'll take it. The *Soyuz* doesn't have the juice to stay up very long. Can you believe they still use chemical batteries? Like your car? Not a fuel cell or solar cell anywhere. Ha! What a joke!"

When it came to machines and their innards, Killingsworth could believe anything. His understanding of things mechanical stopped at the keys or buttons that started them. "How will you know if they've done such a maneuver?"

"Australia will be looking for them, sir. If they don't see the *Soyuz* in about five minutes... and I'd bet the farm they don't... then, they're on the ground."

Killingsworth had other questions to fill the time. "Lieutenant, on the plane ride out here, and in the light of your astounding discovery, I reconsidered the circumstances of the *KOSMOS* destruction. That examination has left me bewildered. If the *KOSMOS* was manned, then why couldn't the cosmonauts have intervened and saved the machine from a catastrophic malfunction? Why didn't they radio Moscow of problems so the demonstration could have been delayed?"

The questions erased the confidence from Mason's face. "Sir, I don't know. It makes no sense to me." The entire mountain was groping in the same fog.

"There is something else that doesn't make sense." General Griffing spoke. "The *Soyuz* orbit is inclined a fraction over forty-two degrees. Show him what that means, Mike."

Using a pencil, Mason roughly traced the forty-second parallel on the screen. "It means, sir, the machine will fly no higher in latitude than this. So it *has* to land south of this line."

It was immediately obvious to the fat man why the inclination was a question mark. The landing zone was limited to the extreme southern tip of the Soviet landmass — a sliver set between the Caspian Sea and China.

"Is it possible for the craft to land in that area?"

"Yes, sir, it is. Their recovery system is well proven, and I suspect they could put it down within a couple of miles of their intended target. But they certainly haven't given themselves much margin for error."

"Which is atypical for the Soviets." General Griffing added the comment. "In spite of what you may have read in magazines about their casual attitude toward human life, they're normally very conservative in their manned space missions. And that small target area isn't very conservative." He pointed at the screen. "Neither is a night landing, which is what they'll be making. They could have avoided that with a little planning."

"Could some type of malfunction have caused these discrepancies?" The question was directed at Mason.

"Well, sir, I have a hard time swallowing the malfunction theory. To get where they are required three major burns. Typically, spacecraft problems are discreet. They either stop you dead in your tracks, or they're an annoyance you work around. What we're seeing here doesn't fit that pattern. The machine was obviously healthy enough to get into a recoverable orbit. It's just not the *optimum* orbit. And what type of malfunction causes that? I have no idea."

Killingsworth's questions dried up. He was a babe in the high-tech woods and totally dependent upon these keepers of the computers — men and women younger than his own children — to lead him aright. Now they, too, were lost.

"Well, gentlemen, I guess it's good that if we had to be stumped, it was on something of academic interest only. The Soviets have met our demands. As long as they continue to do so, we can only observe. It is their spacecraft. They can do with it as they wish." He held to himself the primordial, unfamiliar stirring in his soul — a call for blood, a wish for a last ASAT missile. The *Soyuz* bore murderers. They should not be allowed to escape. But he knew even if the weapon was available, it would not be the American way to dispense such justice.

Mason returned the fat man's attention to the screen — specifically to the lower right-hand corner, where the letters, LOS — Loss Of Signal — flashed. "If it's still in orbit, sir, this will change to a steady AOS — Acquisition Of Signal — to indicate our Australian radar has picked it up." *Fat chance*, was an unspoken thought. "We've got about one minute."

The trio fell into a silent countdown vigil. It was interrupted by an adjacent operator. "General Griffing, sir, heat is being reported at Baikonur."

"Heat?" The fat man questioned his host.

"It's a call that one of our early-warning birds has detected the engine exhaust of a missile launch from Baikonur Cosmodrome. It's the Soviet equivalent of Cape Kennedy, near the Aral Sea. Looks like they're not wasting any time in replacing the satellites we destroyed yesterday."

Mason tuned out the discussion. A Soviet satellite launch was a boring routine. Confirming a *Soyuz* return was not. He continued with the countdown.

"Ten seconds."

"Five."

LOS... LOS... LOS... LOS... LOS...

AOS. The new abbreviation blinked on, and a page of data appeared. It took Mason only a second to determine there had been no change in the *Soyuz* orbit.

"What? I don't believe it! They're still there! They're still in orbit! What the hell is going on?"

"We've got a signature on the Baikonur bird coming up." Disregarding Mason's outburst, the other operator continued to report the status of

the Soviet launch. Computers had compared satellite-sensor data with a
library of past launch signatures and found a match.

"Mother of God! It's an ASAT!"

It was a call that brought an immediate end to the *Soyuz* watch. Men
reverted to their training as Armageddon watchdogs. Orders were
shouted. General Griffing ran to a phone. Mason pounded out new
queries to the computers. Killingsworth was abandoned in a daze.

"What is it, Lieutenant? What has happened?"

"The Soviets have launched one of their old-type ASAT's... an anti-
satellite missile!" He spoke without breaking stride on the keyboard.
"They're shooting down something! Probably retaliating for our attacks
of yesterday by nailing one of our birds! I've got the computer working
on the conjunction analysis! We'll know the target in a second. Maybe
we can maneuver it clear."

With the explanation, Killingsworth joined the organized panic. He
lunged for a phone. He didn't need a computer to tell him what the target
would be. It had to be *Atlantis*. The Soviets would yet kill her and her
crew. Mission Control had to be alerted. Pettigrew and Lieutenant Rowe
had to be ordered down regardless of the weather. But Mason's next
shout ended his dialing.

"It's the *Soyuz*! Jesus! They've targeted the *Soyuz*!"

Others had simultaneously seen the message, and the room echoed
with similar disbelieving exclamations.

"What?"

"They're shooting down their own spacecraft!"

"They're killing their own people!"

"Why?"

"Why?"

"Why?"

The whirlwind of confusion sucked all into its vortex. All except
Mason. He now saw it so clearly — the reason for the *KOSMOS*
explosion, the incomprehensible orbit of the *Soyuz*, the ASAT. Everything now fit.

"God! I don't believe it! It's Colonel O'Malley!"

"What?! O'Malley?! What do you mean?!" Killingsworth jumped on
the outburst.

"Colonel O'Malley!" Mason repeated the name in a louder shout.

"It's Colonel O'Malley!"

"I don't understand."

The officer sprang from his chair. "Of course! Of course! It's Colonel O'Malley, or Mr. Darling… or both! It's got to be! They weren't killed! Somehow they destroyed the *KOSMOS* and they're coming home in the *Soyuz*! The Soviets know, and they're trying to shoot them down with an ASAT!"

Killingsworth nearly fainted. It was not possible. O'Malley was dead! He had told his widow! "They're alive! Good God, man! You're telling me they're alive?!"

Mason calmed himself enough to paint the picture. "Yes! At least one of them is alive! It has to be! Whoever is in that *Soyuz* is coming back to the United States!" He typed the world map back to the screen. "See?" A finger moved across the western hemisphere's forty-second parallel. "Their inclination will take them over the southern two-thirds of the country! It's a shit inclination for going to the Soviet Union, but it's perfect for a U.S. return!"

❖

Friday, 25 November
Soyuz

Mark maintained his frustrated watch of the sea. The daylight portions of two revolutions had covered nothing but ocean, and he remained ignorant of his position. Only with a land sighting would he be able to navigate, to identify the best orbit for the final burn. He squinted into the horizon, but it remained an unchanging curved delineator between black and blue.

During one of the night passes, he had seen the lights of a very large city glowing through a heavy cloud cover, but a positive identification had been impossible. He had suspected it was a city of a democratic capitalist nation. The rich and free lighted their cities in megawatt bonfires, while the workers' paradises around the globe became lightless, black holes at sundown. But what capitalist city? Tokyo? Madrid? Rome? Atlanta? He could not be sure.

He had also seen vast stretches of dark that had been freckled with orange fire and knew with absolute certainty these were the equatorial lands of the colored poor — fires marking their subsistence consumption of the earth. But the fires, as the city before, were indeterminate. They could have been the blazes of the Amazon or Africa or Asia.

Ten minutes later the vigil finally bore results. An atoll, appearing as a pearl necklace cast upon royal velvet, scrolled into view. Others joined it. He was now certain he was watching the Pacific. On other flights he had see these same coral-encrusted reefs.

"Frank, I see some islands." Darling's center-seat position denied him a view. "This sure looks like the Pacific. And by the direction of the cloud shadows, I'd bet we're approaching an ascending node."

"Ascending node?"

"Yea. I think we're in the southern hemisphere, moving northeastward toward the equator."

"Can you tell anything about inclination?"

"No. These are just atolls… fly specks… nothing that's a recognizable landmark. But I don't remember them extending too far south of the equator… maybe twenty or thirty degrees. I sure hope we're inclined further than that or we won't be landing in the U.S." He turned from the window and faced the iceman, who was now sporting a Viking's blond beard. "But if this is the Pacific, we should be making a western-hemisphere landfall in another fifteen or twenty minutes. Tell Maksimov. We could be getting close to a deorbit burn."

Darling's translation refreshed the Soviet's fear. A western-hemisphere passage could mean they were as close as one or two revs to a deorbit attempt to the United States — another joust with suicide. Thus far, they had been incredibly lucky. But, next, the atmosphere awaited them, a reef of death to a hypersonic object. Only a ship of fools would blindly challenge it, and he was imprisoned in just such a ship.

"I wish to speak to the commander."

Darling translated, and Mark nodded he was ready to listen.

"I commend your skill, Comrade Commander. To have brought us this close to earth without proper burn targets was a feat of remarkable pilotage. But now we face the most dangerous aspect of the flight… entry. A mistake could easily destroy us. Please, I beg you, do not persist in this folly. Let me call Moscow and obtain the correct targets. There is still time. I can assure you will be well——"

"Nyet." Mark answered with the only Russian word he knew.

"Please, Comrade, I beg you to——"

"Nyet."

At the second rejection, Maksimov ended the plea. Rescue was his only hope. Moscow had to have heard him.

Mark returned his attention to the window and scanned the horizon. The prisoner's fears stood watch with him. Arriving safely in low-earth orbit from geosync did not guarantee the final deorbit burn would be similarly successful. Their bodies could yet be reduced to ash or crushed into a bloody pulp. But he was not without a plan.

During the deorbit burn, he would hold the same attitude he had held for the other braking maneuvers — tail into the velocity vector. But how much of a slowdown should he make? The only number he was familiar with was the delta-V for a shuttle reentry, a braking maneuver of about two hundred miles per hour. He would use that. But that left the question of *where* to perform the burn? How many miles from American soil? For the first time, that would be critically important. Shuttle deorbit burns were always done half a world away from the landing site — twelve thousand miles. But the shuttle became a glider in the atmosphere. The *Soyuz* would remain a cannonball. It was a difference that suggested he would have to wait until closer to the North American continent before slowing the *Soyuz* with the burn. But how much closer? Two thousand miles? Three? Five? If he erred on the short side, they would land in the water and probably die of exposure. An error on the long side would be more tolerable. Unlike the shuttle, he was not trying to land in California — *anywhere* in the United States would be acceptable. Still, a gross error on the long side could result in a complete U.S. overflight and an impact in the Atlantic.

In the end, all he could do was guess. He would use the western edge of Australia as a landmark for deorbit. That would put them several thousand miles closer to mainland America than the point of a shuttle burn.

Twenty-three minutes later land finally appeared. At first Mark saw it as nothing more than a color change, a faint growth of tan at the earth's edge, a *somewhere* on the western coast of North or South America.

"There's land ahead, Frank!"

"Do you recognize it?"

"It's still too far. But I don't see any snowcapped peaks. That rules out South America." As the Himalayas were to the East, the Andes were the roof of the Western world — a continent-long lighthouse serving as an early beacon for spaceship crews flying from the great Pacific Basin.

In an awkward stretch, Mark grabbed the RHC and slued the machine while maintaining his nose to the glass. The scan to the south was wasted — a serpentine tan disappeared under a blanket of clouds. He twisted the control in the opposite direction to look northward. The view brought a shout. "Baja! I see Baja! We're approaching the Mexican coast!" The six-hundred-mile-long finger of the peninsula was aimed directly at them.

Another touch of the RHC yawed his window forward, and he was rewarded with other confirming landmarks. The crescent of Tampico Bay embraced the Gulf of Mexico. The great wedge of the Yucatan stretched toward Cuba.

"It's perfect, Frank! We can burn on our next rev!" While their orbit was fixed in space, the earth's rotation under it had the apparent effect of moving their ground track to the west. In ninety minutes, their landfall would be California. In ninety minutes they would be home.

The Mexican badlands passed at three hundred miles per minute, and they crossed the U.S. border near the Big Bend of the Rio Grande.

"I see Houston!"

The runway pattern of Ellington Field appeared. It seemed to Mark it was a lifetime ago they had flown their T-38's from those same runways on the first leg of their journey to the *KOSMOS*.

The Gulf states set behind, and he searched forward to learn the answer to the question of the past many hours. What was their inclination? How high in latitude would they travel? It was a wonder that made him oblivious to everything but the view. Darling was similarly distracted.

Maksimov capitalized on the interruption. He had sighted Cuba receding in the starboard window and was busy tapping out several repeats of his name. *Hear me! Someone down there please hear me! Save me!*

The Mississippi River crawled across the land like a dark snake. A checkerboard pattern of farms spread from it. Lake Michigan rolled toward them, and their nadir touched Chicago before curving southward toward a descending node. The snow-dusted Appalachians heralded their approach to the sea. To the north was Long Island and the Hudson River. To the south, the multifingered estuary of Chesapeake Bay.

Four minutes after passing above Houston, the Virginia coast slipped underneath, and they glided feet-wet over the Atlantic.

Mark was joyous. Although he would have preferred their orbit carry them closer to the Canadian border, he would gleefully take what they had. Their next orbit would enter U.S. airspace somewhere in southern California and arc across the entire continent. It would be the perfect deorbit revolution! He felt bulletproof. God was on their side. Nothing would keep them from home.

Friday, 25 November
Cheyenne Mountain

Like the rest of the mountain moles, Killingsworth watched in impotent silence as the two computer traces slowly converged — a video game of creeping, electronic death. In minutes, the weapon would be within lethal range, and nothing in the nation's trillion-dollar arsenal could do anything to prevent that conjunction. The needed weapons — F-15 fighter-launched ASAT's — were gone. Warning calls had been — *were still being* — made on all known Soviet spacecraft radio frequencies, but there was no response. And no diplomatic protest was possible. How could the enemy be ordered to not fire on its own spacecraft?

"There is still some hope, Mr. Killingsworth." General Griffing sat at the envoy's side. "Whoever is in that capsule has to be very, very close to performing a deorbit burn." The radar image of the *Soyuz* inched toward the western edge of Australia.

It was a hope ended as a collective gasp swept the control room audience. Where there had been one dot to represent the weapon, now there were two. Then three. Four. A dozen. At each refresh of the Australian radar data, another spider trail of phosphor grew from a common apex until a wedge of brightness was smearing the computer screen.

"We have ASAT detonation." The console operator's tone was professionally calm.

"It's a focused charge." The comment was from another of the computer operators.

General Griffing explained. "The Soviet weapon has exploded, Mr. Killingsworth. They must have improved their design over the past years. The wedge indicates the weapon contained a shaped, high-explosive charge that focused the explosion."

Killingsworth watched the blade of the wedge scythe into the yellow dot that was the *Soyuz*.

CHAPTER 21

Friday, 25 November
Soyuz

"That's it, Frank... Australia." The western edge of the red-desert continent filled the horizon. "Tell Maksimov that I'm pitching around for the burn."

Mark's pulse was back to triathlon levels. In forty minutes, maybe less, they would be on earth. But that was the only certainty. Land, water, killer g-forces, incineration, life, death — where and how they would arrive on the planet were the unknowns. Adrenaline dried his mouth and he craved water, but they had failed to bring any from the *KOSMOS*.

A tap of the RHC shuddered the machine with thruster firings, and it began the lazy tumble that would aim the braking jets. The attitude ball signaled the correct position. Mark stopped the motion with another flick of the RHC, then watched for the coastline. That was nearing their nadir when Maksimov's joyful scream came.

"What the fuck?!" Mark jerked his head.

Darling demanded an explanation for the outburst , but the Soviet ignored him. During the maneuver, he had glimpsed his salvation from the starboard window. A huge, silvered craft was approaching from beneath. His plan had worked. Moscow had heard his code and had sent help.

He wasted no time on a close examination of the missile. Of paramount importance was to make the Americans his prisoners — to disable the commander's controls and transform their machine into a passive rendezvous target. It was easy work. All of the electrical system circuit breakers were on his side of the machine, and it took only seconds to pull those needed to deaden Mark's stick.

"I have disabled the *Soyuz!*"

"What the fuck is going on?!" Mark was still screaming.

Darling twisted in his harness in an attempt to get his hands on Maksimov's throat, but it was an impossible maneuver, like trying to wrestle in a phone booth.

"There! There! See! Moscow has sent a rescue vehicle!" Maksimov gestured to the window. "You are helpless! The *Soyuz* is disabled!"

The iceman managed a weak left hook to the Soviet's face. A marble of blood bubbled from his nose, was shaken loose, and disintegrated against the wall in a shower of red BB's.

"Goddamnit, Frank! Translate for me! What the fuck is going on?! We're going to miss the deorbit opportunity! Translate!"

"There is a rescue machine approaching! He has disabled the *Soyuz!* He says we are his prisoners!"

Mark grabbed the RHC and stirred. There was no response. The controls were definately off. He slipped from his harness and struggled past the screaming Darling-Maksimov tangle to look from the starboard window.

"Jesus!"

The approaching behemoth was close enough to see its CCCP tattoo. Sun-glinted cones of ice particles were erupting from its thruster firings, and it rolled and yawed like a coiling snake.

"Frank! Ask him what the hell this is!"

There were more screams — Russian and American — as Darling continued to try to brutalize the Soviet into reenabling the controls.

"He says it is another *Soyuz!* A rescue vehicle!"

"It's not a *Soyuz!* Tell him it's not a *Soyuz!* It doesn't even look like a manned vehicle!" Mark had seen no windows, no ball-shaped reentry capsule. "Let him go! Tell him to look!"

Darling ended his flail and translated. At first, the Soviet feared a trick and remained focused on his enemies.

"Look, you son of a bitch! It's not a *Soyuz!*"

He did, just a quick glimpse before returning wary eyes to the Americans. But the glimpse was enough to prompt another furtive look. Then another. And another. Then he stared. Then he screamed.

A new chaos filled the tiny volume as Maksimov hurried to reverse his switch actions.

"What?! What is it?!"

"It is an ASAT Mark! A weapon! He has reenabled your controls!"

At the word ASAT, Mark was back at the window. They couldn't have much time. The vehicle was hugely close. He smashed inward on the THC, not even delaying long enough to get into his seat. The braking thrusters roared, and the instantaneous onset of g-forces sprawled him across the other men. Gone was any concern of where they would land. Getting away from the killer was all that mattered.

He released the control. "Jettison the prop module! Maybe it'll cover us! Jesus, hurry!"

Maksimov's hands were a blur across several switches. A bang signaled they had shed the finished bulk of the propulsion module. Now, in every sense of the word, they were a cannonball.

"Are we clear of the ASAT?! Can Maksimov see anything?!"

It was a question unanswered. A cameralike flash illuminated the cockpit, followed immediately by the sounds of metal upon metal, of steel yielding under the kinetic hammer of other steel. The warning-light matrix blossomed in red and yellow Cyrillic glyphics. The hiss of escaping air deafened.

❖

Friday, 25 November
Cheyenne Mountain

"There are definitely pieces deorbiting."

"They escaped?! The capsule is coming back?!" Killingsworth moved to the edge of his seat, his spirit suddenly taking wing on the news.

But Mason felled him. "Sir, I can't believe they escaped damage from the ASAT. It was a perfect intercept. Detonation was at very close range."

"But you said they are coming back!"

"Yes, sir. One of these pieces is the capsule." He motioned at the phosphor star burst now on the screen. "But all that means is they were able to do a deorbit burn. No telling what type of damage they sustained or how it will affect their reentry."

"When will we know?"

"The Vandenberg radar should acquire them in the next couple of minutes. With that data we'll be able to make a prediction on impact."

Silence reclaimed the room.

Thoughts of Judy came to torment the fat man. From the moment Mason had concluded that Mark could be aboard the *Soyuz*, he had debated whether or not to tell the woman. He had not. The hope was too tenuous. If there was a greater agony of being told of her husband's death, it was being told of it *twice*. But he did resolve that if the machine proved nothing more than a celestial coffin, if Mark's body was aboard, he would immediately inform her. *There are no remains.* How vividly did he remember the despair that announcement had generated. He was certain even the knowledge his lifeless flesh had been returned home would help her recovery.

"The Vandenberg data is coming in. Bingo! They've got a good lock. One piece is way out in front. That's got to be the capsule. The rest of this mess is probably high drag debris from the propulsion module." Mason interpreted the new rush of data.

"Where, Lieutenant? Where is it landing?"

"That's a real shallow entry they're flying. They didn't burn much. But it's definitely suborbital."

"Where, Lieutenant? Can you tell me where they will land?"

"It's coming up now, sir." A ripple of new numbers filled the screen. "North latitude 41.2 degrees, west longitude 104.3 degrees, with a CEP of thirty miles."

Mason spun from his desk and led a crowd to a table map. Expectant eyes watched fingers race horizontally and vertically along the latitude/ longitude grid. They touched.

"Wyoming!"

Predicted impact was in extreme southeastern Wyoming.

"General Griffing! I want a rescue force converging on that area!" Killingsworth tossed the order over his shoulder while hurrying to the door. "And a driver to take me to my helicopter! I want to get to that area as quickly as possible."

❖

Friday, 25 November
Over Northern Colorado

A cold-front wind buffeted Killingsworth's helicopter on its sprint across the Colorado grasslands. In some places, the gale lifted plumes of dust from fallow farmland and muddied the air so thickly the pilot was forced to fly on instruments. Exceptionally strong gusts hammered the craft into sickening wallows.

Prayers distracted the fat man from the uncomfortable ride. Images distracted him. Hellish images of Judy opening the door to him in Mountain View. Joyful images of the woman being told it was all a mistake, that Mark was alive.

"Mr. Killingsworth, NORAD just called." The copilot leaned back, swiped the boom mike from his mouth, and screamed over the din of jet turbines and slapping rotors. "They say a farmer has notified Warren Air Force Base that some type of strange plane or UFO crashed into his field. The guy's place is located inside the radius of expected impact. They're certain it's the *Soyuz*."

"Crash?! Are you certain? Did he use the word *crash*?"

"Yes, sir. That's what they said. He reported a crash and explosion. But how he could see shit in this stuff, I don't know. Visibility is really going down. We've altered our course to the site. It's near the small town of Carpenter. We'll be there in ten minutes. Warren also has some medivac choppers headed there."

Killingsworth nodded and resumed his prayers, but now they were weak, faithless.

The dust grew thicker, the visibility poorer. The machine was enveloped in an opaque rust cloud. He stared into it, his mind's eye seeing Judy at the beach house — as he had left her. She had spurned him, the air force nurse, *everybody,* and walked north along the surf toward the spotlighted lair of monsters. It was the most heartrending of memories — a lonely widow searching for...? He could not imagine what.

The spell was broken by a change in the machine's vibrations. The pilot pulled into a hover and pointed at the ground with exaggerated strokes of his index finger. Killingsworth followed the signal and watched through swirls of dust. Other helicopters were landing, raising new curtains of the powdered earth. Men jumped from their sides and sprinted across the field. Toward what? A crater? A bloody capsule? He could not see. The air had become an ocher screen.

The pilot circled the machine lower. The dust thickened to make the images even more ethereal. Olive-drab figures crisscrossed in seeming panic. A military ambulance waddled across furrows. Military firemen in silvered suits waved and gestured and shouted.

Killingsworth was crazed by the delay. *Was Judy a widow?!*

The helicopter finally settled, and the crew chief helped him from his harness. At the side door exit he tried to mimic the jump of the others but ended on his face in the dirt. There was more maddening delay as he groped for his glasses and replaced them on his head. Then he plunged into the maelstrom. His street shoes filled with dirt. The grit blasted his skin and irritated his eyes. He did not care. *Was Judy a widow?!* The question had deadened his senses.

Out of one vaporous swirl, a charging medic loomed and very nearly ran him down. He tried to stop the apparition with a shouted question, but it was swallowed by the screech of a turbine.

A new sound came to his ears — the crack of windblown fabric — and he hurled toward it.

A parachute! At first, he took the billowing red and white nylon as a vote for life. But then he saw the damage. The snapping sound was coming from shredded panels. Huge sections had been torn out. A red piece flickered like a flame through the dust.

"No! God, No! Please no!" He gasped the supplications in a run along the shroud lines. His toe clanged against a shard of gray-green metal. Other metallic litter — some charred — appeared. The detritus of an explosion? His despairing soul said, yes. He was running to gore and death.

Curtains of dust parted, closed, and parted again. He heard voices. The back ranks of a crowd of firemen and medics appeared. In three more steps a spherical shadow rose above them. There was an open hatch! Men were lifting something from the hatch!

He came into the crowd as Professor Maksimov was lifted free.

Alive! They're alive! But who among the two Americans was alive? Killingsworth's soul exploded prayers.

The huge bulk of Darling was next to appear. Killingsworth was faint. *Please God!*

O'Malley!

"Colonel O'Malley! Colonel O'Malley!"

"Hobie!"

Medics helped him to the ground, and a doctor rushed to question him about possible injuries. Mark ignored him and stumbled to Killingsworth.

The men embraced.

"We did it, Hobie! We did it!"

"Yes! Yes! We did!" Tears were turning to mud on the fat man's cheeks.

"What about *Atlantis*? Bob and Anna? Are they back, Hobie? Are they safe?"

"They're fine, Colonel! They're still in orbit... delayed by the weather. But that door has been closed." He spoke while pulling Mark into a run toward the helicopter. "Now we must get to the radio! Mrs. O'Malley has to be told you are safe!"

Mark floundered on legs turned to rubber by the days of weightlessness. Twice he found himself on his knees in the furrows.

Through the dust, a helmeted crew chief appeared and frantically waved his arms toward the open door of one of the Hueys. They turned toward it.

"Mr. Killingsworth, the president is on the radio!" The sergeant offered a headset.

"Tell him to wait! Get this machine in the air immediately!"

The underling's eyes bugged at the command. "Wait? Sir, you can't tell the president..."

"Now! Get this machine up! Now!" He jumped inside and turned to help Mark. "Now, Sergeant!"

The added shout broke the NCO from his astonished freeze. He climbed aboard and relayed the command to his captain. The pilot snapped his head around with a *What the hell is going on?* look.

Killingsworth answered him with several vicious, upward jerks of his thumb. "Take off!"

The pilot shrugged his shoulders and complied. At least there were witnesses to the insubordination. He twisted the throttle grip and pulled on the collective. The machine shook itself from the ground.

Mark was as dumbfounded as the others at Killingsworth's urgency. He grabbed a headset and put it on, then thrust another into the fat man's hands. The screech of the turbine had turned them into mimes.

"What's going on, Hobie?"

"I'll tell you in a moment, Colonel. For now, I must give these gentlemen some orders." Over their talk, they could hear the pilot arguing with a bewildered command post. Nobody just told the president of the United States to wait!

The captain turned toward his passengers. "Okay, that's done, Mr. Killingsworth. And I'll probably be in Leavenworth tomorrow. Where are we going?"

"Wherever the air force can provide Colonel O'Malley and me with immediate jet transportation to Florida."

"That'll be Warren Air Force Base." He banked the machine to the right.

"Also, I want a radio hookup to the astronaut beach house at the Kennedy Space Center. I want to talk with Mrs. O'Malley immediately!"

"A hookup where?"

"The astronaut beach house at the Kennedy Space Center. Tell your people I am an emissary of the president! I want that radio call made immediately! They are to consider it flash priority! Nothing is to interfere! Do I make myself clear?!"

"Yes, sir." Orders from presidential emissaries were always clear.

"The beach house?" Mark could not believe it. "What the hell is Judy doing there? She told me she'd never go back."

"Colonel, there's been a terrible mistake. We thought you and Mr. Darling were dead. NORAD had seen *Freedom* tumbling away. There had been no possibility of survivors. Only after we saw a capsule returning from the *KOSMOS* did we understand it had been manned. And only after the Soviets attempted to destroy it did we suspect you or Frank or both had, in fact, survived."

Mark could imagine the confusion on the ground. Until moments ago, he thought they were as good as dead, too.

The fat man's face grew darker. "Colonel, I notified the next-of-kin... Mrs. O'Malley. She thinks you are dead."

Mark jerked at the bullet.

"You must understand, Colonel. The situation was grave, confused. The president was prepared to yield to a Soviet ultimatum. I was afraid of leaks, of the press uncovering our mission failure. I didn't want her to hear it from them. So I went to California and told her myself. And later, when there was a hint you might have survived, I could not bring myself to offer her such a tenuous thread of hope. I didn't want to have to crush her twice with news of your death."

"What about the kids?"

"No. Blessedly, your children have not been told. Mrs. O'Malley insisted she have some time to herself before going to them. She wanted to wait at the Space Center beach house. I took her there... and that's where I intend to take you."

The story immediately brought to Mark the same urgency that had overwhelmed the fat man. The mistake had to be corrected! Judy had to be told! The news would be killing her.

"She's not alone, is she?"

"No. An air force nurse is with her."

That revelation eased him slightly. Maybe she was under sedation.

The pilot interrupted. "Mr. Killingsworth, the air force has a jet waiting for you on the runway at Cheyenne. We'll be there in fifteen minutes."

"What about the radio call? I said flash priority!"

"Nothing yet, sir. A tropical storm is playing havoc with comm in that part of the world. The Warren Air Force Base command post is trying to patch something through Patrick's command post. They said that if they don't get to us before we land, they'll call you on the jet. Also, the president sends his congratulations to Colonel O'Malley for a job well done. He says he understands your urgency to contact Mrs. O'Malley and has authorized the use of every defense department asset to get you to Florida as fast as possible."

Nothing was faster than radio, and that was being blocked by nature. Killingsworth cursed the storm.

A few minutes later the cement aprons of Warren Air Force Base flashed under the Huey's nose, and the pilot flared the machine into a skidding landing. The crew chief was out the door before motion stopped. He, and everyone else, now understood the situation and was desperate to correct it.

"Go!" The NCO dragged Killingsworth from his seat and jerked on Mark's arm to speed his exit. A general officer with a radio in his hand was immediately at their side and ran them away from the helicopter.

"Mr. Killingsworth, Colonel O'Malley... the president himself ordered the fastest transport we could give you. This is it."

Both men very nearly stopped dead in their tracks. A Strategic Air Command B-1B supersonic bomber waited in takeoff position, engines idling. A stairway hatch hung open from its belly.

"Major Hagler will be your aircraft commander. He and his crew have been sitting strip alert here as part of our dispersal for the Persian Gulf crisis. One of you can take the IP jump seat and the other can sit at the defensive weapons systems officer's position. He's been pulled from the flight."

"Thank you, General. I'm expecting a call from Florida...from Colonel O'Malley's wife. It's absolutely imperative I speak with her. Please ensure the linkup is made immediately."

"Yes, sir." He glanced at Mark. "We understand your situation, Mark. We're doing everything we can. Unfortunately, that storm is complicating things."

"Thank you, sir. I appreciate it."

They had reached the bottom of the stairs and an NCO handed them each a SAC flight suit. Mark slipped into his. He had forgotten about the cosmonaut garb he was wearing. Killingsworth donned his and took on the appearance of an olive-drab pear.

They climbed the ladder and were helped into their seats by a baby-faced lieutenant. Mark took the instructor pilot jump seat — between the aircraft commander and copilot. Killingsworth was strapped into the defensive WSO's position. A twenty-first-century array of electronic wizardry wrapped around him. At any other time, he would have been terrified at the situation — squeezed into a windowless hole on a supersonic bomber, his head crushed into a helmet — but not now. To get to Florida, to end Judy's misery, to see her joy at embracing her husband, he would have flown a kite into hell to rescue her.

"We're rolling." Major Hagler advanced the four throttles to MIL power, checked his instruments, then continued the push to the hard stops — full AB power. He popped the brakes. The monster momentarily labored to move its bulk, then began a rapid acceleration.

Twenty minutes later, Hagler had the wings swept full aft and the Mach meter touching 2.0. An alerted air traffic control cleared the skies in front of them and handled the thousands of complaining phone calls generated by their sonic booms. *A mission directed by the president* was the pat answer.

"Colonel, Mr. Killingsworth... your call is coming in."

Mark listened through the command post chatter anticipating Judy's voice. Probably, he thought, she had already been told of his survival. At least he hoped so. If it would save her from even a second of the torture, then let someone else preempt him.

"Mr. Killingsworth, this is Colonel Kevin Osborne. I'm the Patrick Air Force Base commander. How do you read me?"

"I can hear you, Colonel. Please put Mrs. O'Malley on."

"Well, sir, we've got some problems on that."

"Damn you, man! I don't want to hear anymore about that storm! I want to speak with Mrs. O'Malley immediately! Do you hear me? Immediately! Do whatever is necessary to get her on this line!"

"Kevin… this is Mark O'Malley." Mark broke in. He knew Kevin Osborne. They had met at a mission briefing for one of his earlier space flights. "Listen, I can't tell you all the background on this, but there's been a mistake. My wife is at the KSC beach house. She's been mistakenly told I was a casualty on a classified operation. We need to correct that. She needs to know I'm okay. If phone comm can't be established because of the weather, then get someone to her to tell her that I'm okay, that I'm on my way there. Tell her you've talked with me. Just make absolutely certain she understands I'm alive."

A static hiss lengthened and Mark wondered if the link had been broken. Osborne finally answered. "Mark, there's no problem with the phone. I'm calling from the beach house right now. It's just that Judy… She's not here, Mark. We can't find her."

"What?!" Killingsworth bellowed. "She must be there! I made it clear she was not to be moved anywhere without my approval!"

"Sir, nobody moved her. The nurse who was staying with her said she went for a walk along the beach and never returned."

"A walk?! In the midst of a storm?!"

"It was before the storm broke, Mr. Killingsworth. The nurse said Mrs. O'Malley wanted to be alone and refused her company."

"She has to be out there, Kevin!" The leading edge of fear began to nibble at Mark's gut, the faintest of whispers something terrible had happened.

"Yes! She must be on the beach! Send a search party to find her!" Killingsworth added his demands.

"It's been done, Mr. Killingsworth."

"And you couldn't find her? That's insane! She has to be there!"

"Sir…" There was another lengthy silence. "Mark, I wish I didn't have to tell you this over a radio."

Mark's fear was now total.

"We found her clothes."

"Clothes? What clothes?"

"All of them... sweater, blouse, pants, shoes, underwear... scattered along a half-mile stretch of the beach."

"No! God in heaven, no!" Killingsworth's cry filled the airwaves.

"I'm sorry, Mark. God, I'm so sorry. We have boats looking for her. Maybe it was an accident. Maybe she went swimming and was pulled offshore. There's still a chance. There's still a chance they'll find her... that she's okay."

It was a ridiculous effort at disguise. Who went for solitary walks on a wind-buffeted beach, took off their clothes, then jumped in the frigid Atlantic during a storm? Certainly not someone interested in being found alive. *Suicide* was the unuttered word that shot at light speed between the plane and the beach house.

Mark could not reply, and Osborne finished the call. "Mark, I know what you must be thinking. But we could be reading this all wrong. Don't give up hope. We haven't. I'll call you immediately if we get any additional information. Otherwise, I'll meet you at landing. We're all praying for you. Patrick command post... Out."

❖

Friday, 25 November
Atlantis

Alive!

Mission Control passed the news of Mark's landing, and Anna and Pettigrew — ignorant of Judy's status — celebrated the resurrection of the dead. A friend, a pilot, a *brother*, was alive. They cheered. They cried. But never once did they touch each other. There were no victory embraces. That expression of human celebration was forbidden by each.

Anna found more of her tapes and soon had the cabin echoing with Beethoven. She hummed her way through the hours-long labor to prepare *Atlantis* for tomorrow's reentry, sometimes acrobatically tumbling across the mid-deck cabin in a spontaneous outburst of sheer joy. They had won! Red Sky was dead! Mark and Darling were alive!

Their appetites returned, and Pettigrew fixed their first hot meal of the mission — rehydrated shrimp cocktail, thermostabilized beef, iodine-tainted coffee, and vacuum-packed butter cookies. But if it had been the work of a five-star chef, they wouldn't have enjoyed it more.

Finally, the capcomm called that Mission Control was signing off for the sleep period. Anna deployed her sleep restraint in the mid-deck, while Pettigrew claimed the flight deck. *Atlantis* entered her fifty-sixth eclipse, and her passengers were swallowed by the quiet black. But it was a nighttime stillness unlike the others before. Now there were no distractions of grief or fear or exhaustion to overwhelm their feelings for each other. Decisions that had seemed so certain, so irrevocable only hours ago, now came creeping back as questions.

To leave NASA? To return to the marines? To run from her? Pettigrew stared into the white lace of the Milky Way and pondered his resolutions. They crumbled. Since Vietnam, he had lived half a life. In Anna, he had found the other half. How did one run from fulfillment, from joy… from life? At what distance did one escape the soul? Not even in the light-years of miles that filled his windows was such an escape possible.

To marry Richard? In the mid-deck, the question denied Anna sleep. She wrestled her restraint for a position that would bring sleep, forgetting that weightlessness made all positions the same. *Who was Karen? What was Bob afraid of? Does he love me? Can I ever love him?* The questions tormented her, and after two hours of struggle, she flew from the cocoon in search of the medical kit and its sleeping pills. But the music stopped her. It was coming from the flight deck. Pettigrew was awake and playing one of her tapes.

He's awake! Go to him! Talk to him! Ask him about Karen! Her feminine muse launched her attack, pummeling every argument Anna offered on why she should forget the man. The music enticed. She could see his shirtless back, the blue NASA shorts, his naked legs. He was watching the earth from the overhead windows. She tore at her nails. Richard was her salvation. Richard. Richard. Richard. She repeated his name over and over. But it was hopeless. With a final, ridiculous excuse that all she was doing was going to watch the earth, she pulled on a rung of the ladder and slowly floated upward.

"I couldn't sleep." Her voice was indifferently cool.

"I don't know a better place to be an insomniac." Pettigrew moved to allow her room while silently wishing she hadn't intruded. Already, her scent was in his nostrils. Her body heat warmed him. They floated inches from each other — a weightless bed with creation for the canopy.

But not a word more was said by either. Both were content to let the violins of the classics carry them across the Atlantic. Ocher sand dunes rose from the turquoise shallows of Africa's southwest coast. Thunderstorms with windswept headdresses towered over the interior forests and jungles. The Indian Ocean scrolled underneath — the bluest of seas. It appeared as firm as land, with absolutely no sense of motion or liquidity. Nearing Madagascar, the sun bowed from the sky and left its color-bow to steal their breath. It was this glory that finally moved Pettigrew to speak. "It's as beautiful as you said it would be."

Anna swallowed hard. She was thinking of the same moment — the restaurant dock, the sharing of souls as she had described an orbit sunset. But she did not reply. She could not. She knew if she opened her mouth, it would be to ask of Karen, to once again make herself vulnerable.

Pettigrew assumed her silence was the result of sleep. He watched the last colors shrink and blink out. Stars appeared, and he remembered the twilight on the dock — the rouge of sunset on her cheeks, the green of her eyes, the gold of her hair, her passion for the sky. It was a memory that made him wish for sleep, for an escape.

Minutes passed. Five. Ten. The moon set.

Anna prayed for courage — the courage to ask the question and to endure the answer. Could he say anything that would absolve him? Anything that would make her believe his professions of love? It didn't seem possible. He had used her. It was that plain and simple.

But the courage finally came. She took a last breath of resolve and pushed the words into the dark. "Bob, who was Karen? What were you trying to tell me when I was out there? I was confused… in shock or something… I can't remember."

Pettigrew squeezed his eyes closed and made his prayers.

"Karen was................you." He opened his soul, and Anna's spirit flew to embrace it.

❖

Friday, 25 November
Over the Gulf of Mexico

No reprieve — or death announcement — came from the beach house. The bomber sped eastward, the miles disappearing from the navigation system counter at a rate of twenty per minute. Behind them, the sun dropped and shadows from tropical storm Evelyn's tallest thunderheads lengthened at their front. The pilots turned up the instrument lighting until the cockpit was suffused in a blood-red glow.

Mark stared forward, watching the indigo blanket of the terminator rise before them. He saw it as the sea, immense and cold, and imagined Judy's naked body on it, floating like a little plastic doll, arms outstretched, hair flowing outward like sea grass, eyes open in death. He had done this to her. He had killed her. That he had taken the mission because the country needed him was an excuse as empty as the sky in front. He had taken the mission because flight was his first love — Judy a distant second.

Behind him, Killingsworth wallowed in his own misery. If only he had never told her. What proof had he had? He had *assumed*. Pettigrew had been right. The only measure of Mark's life had been *Freedom's* oxygen reserves. He had killed her.

One hour and thirty-eight minutes after leaving Wyoming, Major Hagler brought the plane through a blinding rain to a touchdown at the Kennedy Space Center shuttle runway. A grim-faced Colonel Osborne waited at the steps and escorted them to a car. Mark let Killingsworth ask the only question that mattered.

"Have you found anything?"

"No. Boats are still searching, but the dark and the rain…" He just shook his head. "The visibility is terrible. The last beach patrol just came in with negative results. There's a significant north wind and we're concentrating the search to the south. The storm should be out of here in the next two hours, and then we'll be able get some helicopters up."

They made the rest of the drive in silence. Several military vehicles, emergency lights flashing and sirens screaming, loomed from the rain and sped past. With each apparition, Mark's gloom deepened. Did one hold Judy's body? The radio chatter on Osborne's brick said no. The search was continuing.

The driveway leading to the beach house was crowded with air force and NASA vehicles. Several slickered figures manhandled a generator onto a jeep, a huge spotlight onto another. In the grimmest reminder of their mission, a medic fought to furl an olive-drab body bag that had been snagged by the wind.

Osborne parked the car, and the three men entered the house. It was the nerve center for the search effort, and an ordered confusion filled it. Men crowded around maps. Multiple radios hissed with reports. The TV was tuned to a weather channel, and droned lowly with maritime warnings. On the sofa was the nurse, herself now a patient. A doctor offered her hot chocolate. She appeared in shock with fixed, cried-out eyes — another person overwhelmed with guilt. On the table next to her were the neatly folded garments of a woman. Judy's bra and panties were on top.

"Mark, Mr. Killingsworth, this is Chief Krall. He's been directing the search." Colonel Osborne made the introductions.

The chief was blue-lipped, grim, obviously just in from the hunt. Water dripped from his hawkish nose. They exchanged handshakes.

"The nurse said your wife walked north, but we've about given up on that area." He pointed to a map. "That's not to say we couldn't have missed her up there. The visibility has been only yards. But the sea is running to the south at three knots, so we've moved the boats and most of the patrols in that direction."

"Footprints?" Killingsworth asked.

"Those were long gone by the time we got started. The tide is up to the dune line, and if she walked behind that, the wind erased the trail within minutes."

"Chief, do you assume it's.................suicide?" Mark strangled on the word. *Suicide*. The ultimate despair. When life is death and death is — what? Salvation? How could she have done it, he wondered. Even if he had died, there were still the kids to live for. Wouldn't Judy have lived for her offspring?

"Colonel, it's the clothes. Why would she have undressed? I think that points to some type of mental... well... unbalance. Whether that translates to suicide, I don't know. But regardless of why she entered the water, I have to be honest with you. It doesn't look good for survival. I'm very sorry to have to tell you that, but it would be wrong to say otherwise."

Mark understood. The chief was preparing him for the inevitable.

Like Judy had been, he was suddenly overwhelmed with a need for solitude, with a need to grieve in private. To remain in this gathering, in this house, to hear the radio squawks, to hear *the* radio call that would tell him his wife's body had been found, to see it arrive in a bag — he couldn't do it. He had to flee. He looked around the group. "Kevin, I want to be alone for a while. Could I have a rain poncho?"

"Colonel, please." Killingsworth immediately seized his arm. One suicide was enough.

Mark removed the hand. "Don't worry, Hobie. I'll be okay. I'm not suicidal. I just want to be alone."

Osborne handed him a slicker and a radio. "If we get any news, I'll page you."

Mark turned for the door, then stopped. There was something that could not wait. "Hobie, this isn't your fault. I would have come to the same conclusion. There was no way you could have known we were still alive. You did the right thing." The gnome's eyes were red rimmed from his earlier cry and hinted of another wave.

"Thank you, Colonel."

He passed by the nurse and offered the same absolution, then opened the door and stepped into the storm. As Osborne had predicted, it was slackening. The wind was still brisk, but the rain had lightened — enough to see the activity to the south. A jeep-mounted searchlight swept over the sand, and seaward, the running lights of several boats dipped and bobbed on heavy swells. On the largest, another searchlight probed the dark.

Mark walked from the patio onto the beach and turned north. He abandoned himself to grief, letting the wind rip away the first tears he had ever shed as an adult. They had never come before when death had surrounded him. Not as he had stood at attention and saluted the flag-bedecked coffins of his friends. Not as the mournful tune of taps had come to him. Not as the report of the honor guard's rifle firings had echoed. They had been the sounds and sights of death and loss, yet he had never cried, never felt the loss. Never. It was the natural law of the sky, and to embrace the sky was to accept the law — that it ultimately claimed its most ardent lovers. He fully expected that someday it would claim him, that he would meet a "natural" death in its infinity.

But Judy... a wife, a mother, a woman who had wanted only to love and be loved. Dead. Gone forever. An honor guard would fold the flag and hand it to *him*! It was not a natural ending for her! It wasn't supposed to be this way!

He had driven her to death. If only he had had the capacity to truly love her. If only he could have *known* her. He could see so clearly now, he had never really known Judy, had never come close to comprehending her love or her fears. A woman who had shared his life, who had occupied every moment of his adult existence, who had consumed his flesh in countless moments of intimacy, had remained as foreign to him as any stranger. He begged his Creator for a second chance. *Take me back to the windmill! Give me my life over! Endow me with the capacity to love her!* But the roar and hiss of the sea was the only answer.

Intermittent spatterings of rain swept across him — big, cold drops that thumped on the poncho. Unknowingly, he passed the area where Judy's clothes had been found and trod over the sand that had served as a bed for their August lovemaking.

An hour passed. Then two. He sat on a dune and hung his head and cried until his cheeks were raw from the salt. They were tears for all the missed love in his life. For his mother, his father, his children — even the warriors whom he had helped to bury. The sky would forever hold a piece of his soul, but he could see now, there had always been room for Judy, for the others. If only he had tried to admit them.

The weather broke, and he rose and resumed his northward walk. The first faint light of dawn began to color the sea gray. The xenon lights of pad 39A burned through a last rain shower and projected a shadow of *Challenger* on low, scudding clouds. It appeared as some winged, prehistoric creature, flying with the wind. The veil of rain dropped further, and pad 39B became visible. The oblivion of grief had carried him far, far to the north.

At first, he assumed the figure was one of the searchers. It was just a speck on the northern horizon — a fixed dot on top of the dune line. Its appearance stopped him, and he contemplated turning back. He wanted no company. But there was still a mile of sand between him and the intruder, and he decided to halve the distance before returning. He dropped his head and continued forward.

At the next glance, fifteen minutes later, he wondered if his worry about intrusion was unfounded. The figure had not moved. It was the piling of some demolished structure, he decided. He returned to his worry about the children. He would call them as soon as he was back at the house and have Killingsworth send a plane for them.

The appearance of the line of footprints leading northward was confirmation the figure ahead was human after all. He turned south without looking up.

He was minutes into that retreat when his brain suddenly comprehended the significance of the rapidly filling sand depressions that paralleled his own. They were small and closely spaced.

A paralysis stopped him. His heart thundered in his chest and throat and ears. The footprints were those of someone small! Someone small enough to be a woman! Someone small enough to be Judy! He whirled around and squinted his eyes against the wind, but the distance was still too extreme. The gray silhouette was impossible to identify.

His legs quivered. He wanted to run — to know — but a soul terrified of the other, logical explanations kept him rooted in place. It could be anybody, it argued. There had been women in the beach house. He had seen them. One of them could be searching. It could be her footprints. To give into a run would be to surrender to an impossible hope — the hope the search party had never considered to look to the extreme north. Why look farther north than where the clothes had been found? Judy obviously entered the sea at that point, and the sea ran to the south.

His legs moved — not a run but a spastic, long-legged stride. He passed the point where, moments ago, he had turned around. The footprints were fresher here, more petite, more like Judy's, and hope made greater inroads. He broke into a trot. His eyes bounced between the tracks and the figure. The prints became fresher yet, and the depressions at their front took on the shape of...? He wanted to believe it! He wanted so much to believe! He fell forward and looked at one. And then another. And another — lunging, crawling forward to see better, to get to one that was fresher yet. He cupped the depression from the wind, like a miser hoarding his gold, and pushed his face to it.

Toes! Yes! The feet were naked! Searchers would be wearing shoes! Judy's shoes were in the beach house!

Instantly he was up, his body focused on the figure. His legs churned the sand. The radio fell from his hand. His arms came to his side and pumped like the pistons of a steam engine.

"Judy!" He screeched into the gale. The figure remained distant, indistinct. He stumbled and fell and clawed forward on his hands and knees while scrambling back into a run.

❖

Judy stood on the dune fighting the mind-dulling effects of hypothermia and exhaustion. She should have reached the beach house long ago, but it was nowhere in sight. What happened?

Her clearest memory was of Mark's loss. She had fled to the beach to escape the nurse, to grieve in isolation. But the rest was a blur. What happened? Only with great effort could she recall.

The wave had surprised her — an attack from behind that had slammed her skull against the sand and split her lip. Her tongue probed that injury. It was warm and swollen. Yes, she remembered now.

She remembered — rolling, gagging, fighting for air. A vicious undertow had lashed her legs and dragged her seaward, but she had crawled hand over hand up the slope of the beach to escape it. Her arms were still leaden with the fatigue of that effort.

But her clothes? She had no recollection of removing them and wondered how they could have been lost.

She remembered collapsing on the sand, vomiting seawater, being enveloped by the rage of the storm. For what seemed like hours, she had lain in the sand, terrified to do anything else. Finally, she had bolted into flight — toward the beach house. When her lungs had been unable to sustain the run, she had walked. And when dehydration and hypothermia had weakened her further, she had crawled. But it had never appeared.

Now she understood why. The glow on the horizon was clearly sunrise. She had been traveling north. Panic had sent her in the wrong direction.

She squeezed her arms tighter around her body to help control her shivering. She would rest here until the sun was full up. It would warm her and give her the strength to reverse the miles she had come. Maybe the nurse would meet her.

She stared into the glow. It was the dawn of her second day as a widow. Would she count all the days, she wondered? Yes, she knew she would. For as long as she ever lived, she would count the days.

"Judy!" It came as a whisper. It was Mark's voice, urgent and pleading, and made her gasp. But she knew it was a trick of the mind, of her exhaustion. He was gone. Dead. The fat man had told her.

"Judy!" Louder, now, the call came, and she questioned her sanity. Maybe the hellish night was not done. Maybe the dawn was just a wish, like the voice. Perhaps she was imagining it all, a mirage.

"Judy!" It was louder yet and caused her to turn to the north. There was nothing. Then she looked south. Her legs crumpled as if she had been shot. Her fists came to her mouth. She bit the knuckles.

A figure was running toward her. A figure was calling her name. A figure. A man. An apparition — Mark!

It can't be! The fat man said he was dead!

She refused to embrace the possibility of salvation, of opening herself to the horror of a second death if her eyes and ears were betraying her. She momentarily seized the only explanation. It wasn't Mark. Although the voice was his, although the build was his, although the movements were his, although everything about the running figure was Mark, it was merely a cruel coincidence. Someone else had found her.

The cry grew louder, the image of the caller more distinct, and her soul struggled to seize the hope it had all been a hideous mistake. *Yes! Yes! A mistake! The fat man said there were no remains! No remains! Didn't that mean he could be alive? It could be Mark!*

She released herself to that joy.

"Mark!" She tried to stand, but her legs failed her. She fell forward and tried to crawl. Her screams turned hysterical — an incomprehensible babble.

Mark closed the final yard of separation in a lunging tackle and rolled her into his arms. "Judy! God! Judy!" He crushed her to his chest.

Judy screamed — loud, delirious, the screams of the insane.

"It's over Judy. It's over! God, it's over! We're safe! We're safe!"

Above them, a black, flickering shadow of *Challenger* hovered on the racing clouds.

GLOSSARY

AOS . . . . Acquisition of Signal — a shuttle is in contact with mission control.

Capcomm . . . . . Capsule Communicator — the astronaut who sits in Mission Control and talks with an orbiting crew. The term "capsule" is a throwback to pre-shuttle days when manned spacecraft were capsules.

CPU . . . . Central Processing Unit — the *brain* of a computer.

EMU . . . . EVA Mobility Unit — a space suit.

ET . . . . External Tank — the large, rust-colored tank attached to the belly of the space shuttle and which carries the liquid oxygen and liquid hydrogen burned in the shuttle's three main engines. After engine shutdown, the ET is jettisoned and is destroyed during reentry over a remote area of the Pacific or Indian Ocean.

EVA . . . . Extra-vehicular Activity — a space walk.

GNC . . . . Guidance, Navigation and Control — a position in Mission Control that is responsible for monitoring these shuttle systems.

GSE . . . . Ground Support Equipment — ground-based equipment that supports shuttle servicing before launch and after landing.

INCO . . . . Instrumentation and Communication — a position in Mission Control that is responsible for monitoring these shuttle systems.

JCS . . . . Joint Chiefs of Staff — the senior ranking officer from each of the armed services.

JSC . . . . Johnson Space Center, Houston, Texas — the heart of NASA's manned spaceflight operations. It is where astronauts train and where mission control is located.

KSC . . . . Kennedy Space Center, Florida.

LCC . . . . Launch Control Center. The LCC is located at KSC and controls the launch of a shuttle. After "tower clear", responsibility for the mission is handed over to mission control (MCC) in Houston. Actually, the word "control" is somewhat misleading in both the LCC and MCC titles. The space shuttle uses its on-board computers to fly itself into orbit. LCC, MCC and the crew merely observe how the machine is performing and will only intervene in the event of a malfunction.

LCVG . . . . Liquid Cooling and Vent Garment — spacewalk underwear. The LCVG is a one-piece, full-body garment having a weave of tiny tubes through which water is pumped to cool the astronaut. It also has air vents at the wrists and ankles to help circulate air around the body.

LED . . . . Light Emitting Diode — electronic, low power "light bulbs".

LIOH . . . . Lithium Hydroxide — a chemical used aboard the space shuttle and in space suits to scrub carbon-dioxide from the life-support atmosphere.

LOS . . . . Loss of Signal — a shuttle is out of contact with mission control.

MCC . . . . Mission Control Center. Located at Johnson Space Center, the MCC controls the mission from "tower clear" to "wheel stop", i.e., from a few seconds after lift-off until landing.

MDF . . . . Manipulator Development Facility — a building at JSC that has a full-scale simulation of the shuttle's remote arm. Astronauts train at the MDF by using the arm to maneuver huge helium balloons to and from a simulated shuttle payload bay.

MECO . . . . Main Engine Cutoff—when the shuttle's three liquid engines shutdown.

NASA . . . . National Aeronautics and Space Administration.

NORAD . . . . North American Air Defense Command — the organization responsible for the defense of Canada and the United States from air and space attack. The nerve center for NORAD is located in Cheyenne Mountain, near Colorado Springs, Colorado. As part of its mission, NORAD uses a world-wide network of radar and other sensors to track thousands of orbiting objects.

OMS . . . . Orbital Maneuvering System — two, six-thousand-pound-thrust engines at the rear of the space shuttle which are used for orbit adjustments. Unlike the main engine system, the fuel for the OMS engines is internal to the orbiter.

RCS . . . . Reaction Control System — a maneuvering system composed of forty-four, small rockets located in the orbiter nose and in pods on each side of the orbiter tail. The RCS jets are used primarily to control the shuttle attitude.

RHC . . . . Rotational Hand Controller — the "stick" that a shuttle pilot uses to fly the shuttle or a remote arm operator uses to "fly" the arm.

RMS . . . . Remote Manipulator System — the fifty-foot remote arm located on the sill of the shuttle payload bay and used to maneuver objects in and out of the bay.

RTLS . . . . Return to Launch-site Abort — a launch abort that will bring the shuttle to a safe landing at Kennedy Space Center. The RTLS abort "window" — the time in which a Florida return is an option — is open from lift-off to approximately four minutes. After that point, the shuttle is too far away to turn around and fly back. An RTLS would most likely occur due to the failure of a single main engine.

SDI . . . . Strategic Defense Initiative. Also known as "Star Wars", SDI is a program to investigate the feasibility of defending America from missile attack. Few people are aware the nation currently has *no* defense against such an attack.

SLF . . . . Shuttle Landing Facility — the fifteen-thousand-foot runway at Kennedy Space Center used by landing shuttles.

SRB . . . . Solid Rocket Booster — the white rockets attached to the sides of the external tank and which burn for the first two minutes of a shuttle ascent. The SRB's separate at twenty-five miles altitude and parachute into the ocean where they are retrieved for reuse.

STA . . . . Shuttle Training Aircraft — a Grumman Gulfstream business jet that has been highly modified to duplicate the handling characteristics of a landing space shuttle. Pilot astronauts will log nearly a thousand simulated landings in this aircraft before they do the real thing in a shuttle. If this seems excessive, remember — the shuttle is a glider, so the pilot gets only one chance to land. He/she better be good at it.

THC . . . . Translational Hand Controller — a control that the pilot uses to fire the shuttle's small maneuvering rockets. When the THC is pushed "in", it fires the rockets to move — to *translate* — the shuttle forward. When it is pulled "out", the shuttle is moved back. Up-and-down and side-to-side movements result in corresponding shuttle motions. There is also a THC associated with the remote arm. In this case, the manipulation of the control results in a corresponding motion at the end of the arm.

UCD . . . . Urine Collection Device. A male UCD is a waist-worn rubber bladder that connects to the penis through a "cuff" — a condom-like sleeve. A one-way valve traps urine inside the bladder. A female UCD is a brand-name, adult diaper modified with additional absorption material. UCD's are worn only when it is impossible to use the shuttle toilet, i.e., during launch, entry and spacewalks.

VAB . . . . Vertical Assembly Building — a fifty-story building originally designed as the assembly site for the Saturn-V moon rockets. Now it serves that purpose for the space shuttle.

VGO . . . . Velocity-to-go. VGO (pronounced "vee-go") is a parameter associated with orbit maneuver "burn targets". Every target will have a planned VGO — the planned change in the shuttle's velocity. This number — measured in feet- per-second — will "count down" as the burn progresses. At the end of the burn it should be zero.

WCS . . . . Waste Control System — the shuttle toilet.